The ambush began in earnest. I fell to my knees and tried to apply pressure to my partner's wound as gunfire erupted from every direction. I tried to ignore that and focused on keeping Chambers alive. Bullets buzzed and snapped overhead like so many angry hornets. I screamed for the medic again as blood poured out from under my hands. Chambers' eyes were wide as she writhed in agony. Muttley whined and licked her hand.

I let go of the wound long enough to fumble for my medical pouch. I had some hemostatic gauze in there that might stop the bleeding. The bullet missed the plate on her vest, blasting right through the soft armor of her vest and deep into her side.

"I got this!" A Cavalry medic materialized at my side. "Give me that." He took the gauze package out of my hand and went to work. "Hey!" he said, looking up from Chambers to stare me down. "I got this! Cover me!"

I nodded my head and tried to process the chaos around me. The Afghan National Army had been caught completely off guard. A low *BUUUUUURRRP* sound echoed through the village as the PMCs opened fire with the minigun mounted on their MATV.

The mosque. The shot had come from the mosque. Above the cacophony of battle a very loud rifle report resonated from the direction of the mosque. An ANA soldier's chest exploded, sending him tumbling to the ground in a cloud of dust.

BAEN BOOKS
by Larry Correia

BAEN BOOKS by Larry Correia

The Monster Hunter International Series
Monster Hunter International
Monster Hunter Vendetta
Monster Hunter Alpha
The Monster Hunters
Monster Hunter Legion

The Grimnoir Chronicles
Hard Magic: Book 1 of the Grimnoir Chronicles
Spellbound: Book 2 of the Grimnoir Chronicles
Warbound: Book 3 of the Grimnoir Chronicles

With Mike Kupari:
Dead Six
Swords of Exodus

To Purchase thse and all other Baen Book titles in
e-book format, please go to www.baen.com.

SWORDS OF EXODUS

LARRY CORREIA
MIKE KUPARI

SWORDS OF EXODUS

Copyright © 2013 by Larry Correia & Mike Kupari

A Baen Books Original

Baen Publishing Enterprises
P.O. Box 1403
Riverdale, NY 10471
www.baen.com

ISBN: 978-1-4767-3611-2

Cover art by Kurt Miller

First Baen paperback printing, October 2013

Distributed by Simon & Schuster
1230 Avenue of the Americas
New York, NY 10020

Printed in the United States of America

10 9 8 7 6 5 4 3 2 1

To Jess, for putting up with my crap,
to Emmee, for forgiving me for being gone so much,
to Wally, for making me an EOD Tech,
and to Glenn and Zog, for showing me the ropes.

Team Duchess: How is this happy fun time?

SWORDS OF EXODUS

*"The price of freedom is
the willingness to do sudden battle anywhere,
any time and with utter recklessness."*
—Robert A. Heinlein

Prologue: Set in Stone

SrA VALENTINE, M.
521st Expeditionary Security Forces Squadron
U.S. Air Force
Zargabad District, Western Afghanistan
Seven Years Ago

My shoulders ached. Dust filled my nose as the column came to a halt. I let my M4 hang on its sling as I pulled off my eye-pro and wiped my face with my shemagh.

Word came down the line that we were going to be here for a while. The cavalry soldiers we were embedded with fanned out and took up good defensive positions. Being a team of enablers, we were just expected to stay put unless they needed us. That was okay with me. My rucksack wasn't sitting right on top of my body armor and needed to be adjusted. After a quick check of my area, to make sure I wasn't near any pressure plates, I set my pack down and plopped down next to it.

"That's a good idea," said my partner. Senior Airman

Arlene Chambers was a dog handler. Her military working dog, Muttley, was tired from the oppressive heat and sat next to her, panting.

At least there was shade. The village of Murghab was so far from the nearest US FOB that our only support came via helicopter, and was uncomfortably close to the Iranian border, but it was picturesque in its own way. Our patrol had come down a narrow dirt path that ran alongside a small, babbling creek. On the other side of the trail was a six-foot mud wall. Behind the wall was a row of tall poplar trees that sighed in the hot breeze and kept us out of the sun.

A Cavalry NCO stopped to check on us as he made his way up the line. "How you doing, Air Force?" Sergeant Hanover wasn't really checking on *us* so much as he was checking on Chambers. She wasn't the only female out with us in Murghab. We had a two-woman Female Engagement Team up in front, interfacing with the Afghan women as part of our ongoing counterinsurgency efforts, but Chambers was easily the *best looking* female out with us, and she knew it.

My partner smiled at him. "Oh, I'm a little tired but good to go." She cracked open a bottle of water and tilted it forward. Muttley lapped at it eagerly, wagging his tail as he drank.

"How's the dog doing?" Hanover asked, kneeling down so he could pet Muttley.

"He's hot, but I'm watching him. He'll be good for the rest of the op I think. We're still flying out after sundown, aren't we?" There had been talk of extending our mission another day. It'd already been two days since a pair of Chinooks had dropped us off outside of the village.

"I'm okay too," I said with a sarcastic grin. "Thanks for asking."

Hanover laughed at me. "Patrol's been extended."

"What's going on?" Chambers asked. "Why are we stopping now?"

"We ran into some contractors up there. PMC guys in armored trucks. The ANA commander is flipping out because I guess nobody told him they were operating in 'his' AO. Our 'terp is trying to convince him that nobody told us, either, but he's pretty pissed." We'd only been operating with this Afghan National Army unit for a couple of days, but it had already become apparent that its commander enjoyed theatrical temper tantrums if it helped him get his way. I guess he thought it showed his men that he was willing to stand up to the Americans. All it really did was make Captain Drake, the Cavalry troop commander, want to punch him in the face. Hanover's radio squawked. "Alright," he said. "I gotta get up there. We'll call you if we need the dog to check anything." Muttley was pretty good at sniffing out explosives and drugs, both of which could easily be found in Afghanistan.

"Have fun!" I said encouragingly as Sargent Hanover jogged forward. I then stood up to stretch. So far, the mission to Murghab had been a bust. No contact with insurgents, no weapons caches, and thankfully no IEDs. It had been three days of just walking around, talking to the locals. It was still better than sitting back at the Expeditionary Air Base, stuck in a guard tower for twelve hours at a time. At least we got to get out into the war.

I scanned the village for threats, doing my best not to get complacent, as the leadership dickered with the ANA, the locals, and the PMC guys. Across the creek were more buildings made of mud, then a two-story mosque that was a lot nicer than anything else in the village. It wasn't made of mud, which was pretty remarkable for a village this remote, and was topped with a blue minaret. The generator behind it indicated that it even had electricity. *Fancy.*

Up the trail, I could see the PMC vehicles Hanover told us about. They were MATVs, like the ones US forces used, but painted white instead of tan. The dirt road they were parked on was one of few in the village wide enough for a big vehicle to use. The contractors were clad in Desert Tiger Stripe fatigues and mismatched head gear, and a couple of them were walking down the line with Captain Drake.

The ANA took the halt to mean that it was chow time. They were easy to spot in their mint chocolate chip digital camouflage fatigues, and were already stripping off their armor, laying down their weapons, and breaking out the rations. ANA units varied widely, from *pretty decent* to *dangerously incompetent*. This particular unit gravitated more toward the incompetent end. When we bedded down in strongpoints for the night, they busted out the hashish and started getting high. It was ridiculous.

"Great," I said to Chambers. "The ANA's hungry. We're going to be here for a while."

Chambers stood up, keeping one hand on her M4 and another on Muttley's leash. "They already had breakfast a few hours ago!" It was only about ten thirty in the morning, but we'd been on the move since first light.

"Second breakfast, I guess. Like hobbits."

Chambers laughed at me. "Nerd."

"I'm just saying. Afghanistan would be way nicer if hobbits lived here instead of Afghans." I paused for a second and looked around. "Hey . . . where'd the little dusties go?"

"Yeah, you're right," my partner agreed, looking around. A troop of Afghan children, aged five to probably thirteen, had been following us around all morning, begging us for treats and candy. "I haven't seen them in a while."

The air was suddenly filled with music as the nearby mosque began its call to prayer. Islamic music blared tinnily over a loudspeaker, making it difficult to be heard.

"That's weird too," I said, raising my voice. "Don't they usually do it after noon?"

A wry smile appeared on Chambers' face. "Do you think they have an atomic clock in there or something? This is Afghanistan. It's whatever time they say it is."

"You don't know that. Maybe they have a sundial or some—"

Chambers suddenly fell to the ground, landing in a puff of moon dust. She had a very surprised look on her face. I was about to ask her if she was okay when I saw the blood. I'd heard the shot. It just happened so fast it didn't register. My heart dropped into my stomach as I processed what was happening. "Medic!" I screamed. "Contact right!"

The ambush began in earnest. I fell to my knees and tried to apply pressure to Chamber's wound as gunfire erupted from every direction. I tried to ignore that and focused on keeping my partner alive. Bullets buzzed and snapped overhead like so many angry hornets, pock-marking the mud wall we'd been leaning on. I screamed for the medic again as blood poured out from under my hands. Chambers' eyes were wide as she writhed in agony. Muttley whined and licked her hand.

Oh God, oh God, oh God! I let go of the wound long enough to fumble for my medical pouch. I had some hemostatic gauze in there that might stop the bleeding. The bullet missed the plate on her vest, blasting right through the soft armor of her vest and deep into her side.

"I got this!" A Cavalry medic materialized at my side. "Give me that." He took the gauze package out of my hand and went to work. I didn't move. "Hey!" he said, looking up from Chambers to stare me down. "I got this! Cover me!"

I nodded my head, turned, and tried to process the chaos around me. The ANA had been caught completely off guard. They scrambled for the weapons they'd laid down, and most of them didn't have time to get their armor back on. A low *BUUUUUURRRP* sound echoed through the village as the PMCs opened fire with the minigun mounted on their MATV.

The mosque. The shot had come from the mosque. Above the cacophony of battle a very loud rifle report resonated from the direction of the mosque. An ANA soldier's chest exploded, sending him tumbling to the ground in a cloud of dust.

"Shooters in the mosque! Shooters in the mosque! They have a fifty-cal up there!" No one seemed to hear me. Orders were shouted over the radio. Complex ambush. Many insurgent personnel. Multiple wounded. KIA. Assault through. MEDEVAC delayed until attack helicopters could be spun up to escort.

Boom! Someone found an IED. *Christ.* All the while,

the medic struggled to stabilize Chambers. She was either unconscious or dead. I couldn't tell.

Something strange happened to me then. There was a coldness deep in my belly. It slowly made its way up, enveloping my heart and spine. My heart rate slowed, and my breathing slowed with it. The sounds of gunfire faded just a little, and everything seemed to slow down enough that I could process what was going on.

I was *Calm.* I hadn't felt like that since the day my mother died. My fear faded into the background. A plan rapidly formulated in my mind. The Cav guys were getting ready to counterattack, but this village was prepped for an ambush. There would be IEDs. The soldiers would have to move carefully, sweeping everywhere they went. They wouldn't get to the mosque before the shooters got away.

That wasn't going to happen. Before I realized it, I was moving. I left my partner with the medic and slid down into the ditch, splashed through the creek, and scrambled up the other side. Sprinting forward, I slid to a halt behind a mud wall, next to the two contractors who had been talking to Captain Drake. One had his head wrapped in a brown bandanna and carried an AA-12 automatic shotgun. The other was a grizzled-looking SOB with a trimmed, graying goatee, a body armor vest loaded with ammunition, and a brown South African-style bush hat. Around his waist was a leather gunbelt. A big revolver hung from one side, and a big knife hung from the other.

The old guy snapped off several shots from his stubby FAL carbine before covering back down behind the wall. The heavy rifle had a deep bark to it, being more powerful than the M4 I was carrying. "There are shooters in the mosque over yonder, son," he said to me, coolly. "You boys might want to do something about it."

A hole exploded in the mud wall we were using for cover as the enemy sniper put a round from his fifty through it. "They have a fifty-cal rifle up there," I said. "We need to take it out before the MEDEVAC chopper arrives. I can't do it by myself!"

"What about the rest of your troops?"

"I'm in the Air Force. My partner will die if that chopper is delayed. Will you guys help me or what?"

The old man with the FAL nodded. "Alright then, let's get it done. Lay down some fire, I'll move first." As he bounded off to the right, seeking the cover of another building, I started rapidly firing shots into the second level of the mosque. Civilians were running around in terror in front of it, and I hoped my rounds were going over their heads. The other contractor, the one with the shotgun, removed the drum from his weapon and replaced it with a box magazine that I guessed was loaded with slugs. He looked through the holographic sight bolted to the top of his boxy weapon and tore into the mosque.

These contractors didn't seem to be concerned with the rules of engagement. Neither was I. You couldn't tell who was who. The snipers in the mosque weren't the only enemy personnel shooting at us. The ones we could see were dressed the same as the Afghan villagers. Some of them may have *been* Afghan villagers. I didn't give a damn.

A man dressed in dirty white linens stepped around the corner of a mud hut. *Weapon!* He had an AK-47-type rifle with the stock folded. I put my red dot on his chest and cranked off probably half a dozen shots. He fell to the ground and I shifted my fire back to the mosque. The Cav soldiers behind me opened up on it as well. Several M4s and a SAW streamed rounds into the building.

"Now! Move!" the old contractor shouted. He leaned around the corner and fired. His friend with the AA-12 and I bounded over the wall and sprinted forward and to the left. The big rifle in the mosque roared again, kicking up a huge divot on the trail behind me. We took refuge behind a small building before the sniper could fire again.

From behind me, I could hear one of the Cav NCOs shouting at me. "Airman Valentine! Where the fuck are you going?" I ignored him. More shooters appeared in the doorway of the mosque, firing on us even as civilians ran into the building past them. We shot back. People fell to the ground. There wasn't any going back now.

Coughing from the smoke and dust, I removed the partial magazine from my M4 and replaced it with a full one. I stood above the bodies of two dead men. Unlike the Taliban insurgents we normally encountered, these two looked like they'd been pretty squared away. They both wore desert camouflage uniforms, and each had been wearing body armor. On the floor in front of them was a Steyr HS50 rifle, a monstrous bolt-action chambered for .50 BMG.

"Holy shit, son." It was the leader of the contractors. The old man shook his head. "I think these boys are Iranians, judging from the equipment."

"Huh," I said absentmindedly. I was going through adrenaline dump and was coming down off of the *Calm*. My hands were shaking. I could barely stand.

"You okay, kid?" he asked.

"Yeah . . . yeah. I just need a minute."

"That was some damn fine work . . . C'mon, let's get back downstairs. Your friends are here." We were on the second level of the mosque. The two contractors and I had cleared the place before the Cav had arrived. "What's your name, kid?"

"Valentine. Mike Valentine."

"John Hawkins," he said. "People just call me Hawk. I'm with Vanguard Strategic Solutions International." He handed me a business card. "When you get out of the Air Force, you give me a call. I'll put you to work making four times what they pay you for this."

I nodded jerkily and put his card in my pocket as we arrived on the lower level of the mosque. My heart dropped into my stomach when I took in the carnage.

The air was dirty and stunk of burnt powder. Several dead bodies were scattered on the floor in pools of blood. Several more Afghans were wounded. Only a couple of the Afghans had been armed, but they'd used the civilians seeking shelter in the mosque as human shields. I didn't know whose rounds had struck who, but it didn't make any difference to those that had been hit.

"Holy fucking shit." One of the Cavalry soldiers appeared in the doorway. He turned and yelled for a medic. The same medic that had been treating Chambers pushed past him and ran to a wounded Afghan man. I left Hawk where he stood and approached the medic, stepping over bodies as I went.

"What happened to Chambers?"

He took a deep breath and shook his head. "I'm sorry, man. She didn't make it."

I nodded at him as my chest tightened, but I couldn't choke out any words. I knew he'd done the best he could. I wasn't angry at him. I just needed air. The mosque felt as if it was suffocating me. The air stank of death. The wounded survivors stared at me with wide eyes. The dead seemed to be staring at me too.

Stepping back out into the sunlight, I leaned against the wall of the mosque and slid down to the ground. I unsnapped my helmet and set it on the ground next to me. I took off my safety glasses and buried my face in my hands. People came and went past me, but I paid them no mind.

After a few minutes, I was tapped on the shoulder. It was Captain Drake. I immediately came to my feet. "Relax, Valentine," he said calmly. "What the hell happened?"

He listened quietly as I explained, his face a mask.

When I was finished, he simply nodded. "We got a problem. You ran off with some civilian contractors without orders from any of my NCOs. There are a bunch of dead civilians in there. You've been briefed on the ROE. You know how this is going to play out, don't you?"

I felt like I was going to throw up. My partner was dead and I was probably going to be court-martialed. This day couldn't have gone any worse. At that moment, if I could've gone back in time and taken that bullet for Chambers, knowing full well that I was going to die, I would have done so.

But there is no going back, is there?

The Cavalry officer put his hand on my shoulder. "I'm sorry about Airman Chambers. And between you and me, that was some impressive shit you pulled off there. I can't believe some Air Force puke can shoot like that. I'll vouch for you when the time comes. I'll tell them the truth, but I'll vouch for you."

"Thank you, sir."

He left me alone.

In the distance could be heard the sound of a helicopter.

The room rattled slightly as an outbound C-130 took off. I stood at the position of attention in the office of Colonel Christopher Blair, the commander of the 521st Air Expeditionary Wing. I had on a clean uniform and was freshly shaved. I was in enough trouble without going in front of the Wing King looking like a bag of ass. The colonel told me to stand at ease after he sat down. I relaxed a little and moved my hands behind my back.

"Senior Airman Valentine," he began, folding his hands on his desk, "I'm afraid I'm in kind of a bad position here. On one hand, your actions in the village of Murghab were commendable. You advanced under fire and without support onto an enemy position, and cleared that position with almost no help. Senior Airman Chambers was killed by an enemy sniper team, and your actions resulted in that sniper team being neutralized. On the other hand," he gestured at the computer on his desk, "your actions, while not technically insubordination, did involve you disregarding your chain of command, standing general orders, and the rules of engagement. Furthermore, you were aided by employees of a PMC, which is to say, civilians. As a result, six Afghan noncombatants were killed and four more were wounded."

"Sir, the enemy personnel in the mosque were using

those people as human shields. They were also firing indiscriminately through the crowd."

"So the report says. That works in your favor. Not working in your favor is the fact that you and these two civilians entered and cleared a mosque without any Afghan personnel with you, which is a violation of the current ROE."

"Sir, we were under direct, immediate, and lethal fire from that position. Half our ANA had either been killed or run away. The ones that stayed were shooting up the entire village in a panic. They were useless."

"Also noted, Airman. Now listen to me. You stirred up a shit storm. An epic shit storm. The Afghan government is calling for you and the contractors from Vanguard to be put on trial by an Afghan court. There is no way that is going to happen, but they're incensed, to say the least. Worse, the Army wants to crucify you. A lot of people who weren't on the ground with you say that you're an undertrained Air Force kid with no business being in their battle space. They say you blatantly disregarded the ROE, killed a bunch of civilians, and they want you court-martialed. You committed the mortal sin of creating headaches for staff officers somewhere."

"Sir—"

"Now, before you get too upset, the Cavalry unit you were with spoke very highly of you and Airman Chambers. They said you two had been a valuable asset to them on other missions and that you made the best decision you could while under fire."

"What does the Air Force say, sir?"

"I'm going to be honest with you. Some people above my level are telling me to throw you under the bus, recommend you for a court martial, and wash my hands of you. If word of this gets out, they say, it'll reflect badly on the Air Force, and the last thing we need is more bad PR."

I took a deep breath and lowered my head slightly. I was going to Fort Leavenworth. I could already see it.

Colonel Blair ignored my moping and continued. "It's more complicated than that, however. You also uncovered the first concrete evidence we've had that Iranian special operations forces are in Afghanistan. The Afghan government has been denying this for years, even though we've suspected all along they've been dealing with the Iranians on the side. That causes nothing but headaches for the brass and their bosses on the civilian side. So as much as they want you crucified, they want this thing quashed so they can deal with it on the down-low. It hasn't gone public yet, but it will if you're put on trial. And believe it or not, there are a few people on the Air Force side who are willing to go to bat for you."

"So what's going to happen to me, sir?"

"Right now? Nothing. Your leadership put you in for the Combat Action Medal, which I intend to sign off on. You've earned that much. But you're not going out on any more missions with the Cav, or anyone else. You're not even going to stand watch. I told your squadron commander to put you in the armory or some other place out of sight. You're going to stay there, keep your head down, and finish out your deployment without any more incidents. You lost your partner out there. Take some time for yourself. Believe me when I say I don't want to see your name come across my desk again. Your term of enlistment is up in, what, a year?"

"About that long, sir."

"Right. You're going to just get out. As a matter of fact, you're not going to be allowed to reenlist, but in exchange for you quietly getting out of the Air Force and keeping your mouth shut about this whole thing, you're not going to be court-martialed. Your punishment will be handled administratively, and this verbal counseling session will suffice, as far as I'm concerned."

"Thank you, sir."

"Look," the colonel said, his demeanor softening. "I'm sorry about Airman Chambers. The official notifications have all been made, but I'm still working on the letter to her parents. We lost one of our own out there, and you were in a bad situation. I don't think what's happening to you is right. I think you should be getting the Bronze Star instead of punished. But there's not much else I can do for you. The best thing you can do is go along, get along, and just leave the military behind."

"I understand, sir," I said quietly. "Thank you."

Hours later, as the Sun sank slowly over the horizon, I found myself wandering the base alone, reflective belt around my waist.

I found a good spot where there wasn't too much background noise, and pulled one of my unit's satellite phones out of my pocket. I unfolded the antenna and, in the failing light, strained to read the card in my hand.

John Hawkins, Director of Special Tactics Training, Vanguard Strategic Solutions International.

I wasn't getting out for almost a year. I wondered, is it too soon to call? *What the hell,* I thought. *It's worth a shot.* That phone call changed my life.

LORENZO
Kuala Lumpur, Malaysia
Seven Years Ago

Hari Merdeka is Malaysian Independence day, and this particular one was one hell of a party. The place was packed with the rich, famous, and powerful, all struggling to hear each other over the extremely loud band. The crowd was Malay, Indonesian, Thai, Indian, Chinese, with a smattering of Westerners, all of them wealthy, many of them distracted by the huge fireworks over the city, and the remainder were schmoozing or cutting deals. For a supposedly Muslim country, there was a surprising amount of very expensive alcohol being consumed, and most of the beautiful women gyrating on the dance floor were thousand-dollar-an-hour prostitutes.

The restaurant was forty stories above the street, suspended at the intersection of two ultramodern buildings. It was a five-star luxury establishment, most of which was currently open to the night air, a veritable hanging garden over the busy street below. The massive Petronas Towers were visible through the rooftop tropical forest. Occasionally, a really bright firework would illuminate the catwalks above us, and you could just make out the shadows of the guard force stalking about, watching the crowd.

Security was tight, but fragmented. There were private guards for some of the more important people, and the perimeter staff made up of hotel employees. I had passed through two sets of metal detectors to get to this point. The food in the dinner cart I was pushing had been tasted by three separate people to check for poison. The guards had forced the chef, his assistant, and the waiter who would be delivering it, played by yours truly, to try some. The foie gras had been delicious.

I passed swiftly between the kitchen and the private dining area, with two black-suited men flanking me. They had patted me down before I had picked up the food, just to be certain, and they kept an eye on me the entire time. They were big for Malays, thick with muscle, shoulder holsters poking out from their unbuttoned coats. This particular private dinner party was a little on the paranoid side.

You would be too if you had stolen from Big Eddie.

Another guard was waiting, and he held open the heavy wooden double door for me and my goon escort. Away from the teeming crowd, the screeching pop band, and the Japanese businessmen eating sushi off of naked chicks, the private dining area was silent, almost peaceful. The roof on this section had not been retracted, and the restaurant had been decorated in the manner of a Zen garden, with lots of those funny little trees and sand with designs drawn in it.

It was a large room, normally capable of holding fifty diners, but tonight there was only one group allowed inside. The proprietors knew that these people needed privacy to discuss their business.

This latest guard held up his hand. I had been through this a few times tonight, to take their orders, to bring their drinks, I knew the drill. I left the cart, and raised my arms for yet another very thorough pat-down. The first two guards did one last check of the large dining cart, lifting up covers and steaming trays, looking under the fabric, probably checking to make sure no guest had managed to stick a bomb onto it in the minute it had taken to walk here from the kitchen.

Grimacing as the guard checked what would be a very uncomfortable place to carry a weapon anyway, I thought about the plan and tried to look as unthreatening as possible, which is actually pretty easy when you're as forgettable as I am. Tonight I was wearing a tuxedo like the other staff, but with the red sash of the chief waiter. My ID said that my name was Pard and I was a resident of the Salpeng Valley and its Tamil minority and I had worked here for five boring years. Being just another nobody was my specialty.

"Smells great," grunted one of the guards as he finished checking the food.

"Well, you're eating noodles when you're off shift, so don't dwell on it," said the other as he straightened my sash and patted me on the shoulder. "You're good. Make this quick and get out of here. The boss is talking business."

"Of course, sir." I rolled the cart toward the diners. Only one guard stayed at my side, the other two took up positions back outside to dissuade partygoers in search of privacy. The heavy door closed behind them.

The dinner party consisted of two men and a woman. The males were Indonesians in very expensive suits. The woman was a stunning blonde in a slinky black dress. They were seated on thick cushions around a short table. Another guard stood at attention a few feet behind his principle, the Browning Hi-Power in his shoulder holster plainly visible under his open coat. Only the guard noticed my approach. I slowed, but he nodded for me to continue. Ever subservient, I dipped my head, rolled the cart into position, and began removing steaming lids.

The woman was speaking. "Big Eddie will not tolerate you operating in the Strait of Malacca without his permission. That last freighter you hijacked belonged to him, and he is not pleased." Her voice had a slight European accent. "This is not a fight you want to pick." She really was a looker. Her hair had been pulled back into a tight bun, revealing a very perfect neck. She had movie-star looks, a body better than any of the professional girls at the party, and the eyes of a serial killer. I knew her *very* well.

The man laughed. "Katarina, please, I've had far too pleasant an evening to entertain idle threats. My people have controlled the Strait from Selenor to the sea for ten generations." His name was Datuk Keng and he was a pirate. He didn't look like a pirate in the traditional sense, lacking parrot, eye patch, or wooden leg, but believe me, he was the real deal. Keng had approximately three hundred men under his direct command, and they specialized in taking down merchant cargos, selling the boats, and holding the crews for ransom. "You can tell Big Eddie that if his ships are to pass through the Strait, then he must pay for protection like everyone else."

"Our records indicate that Big Eddie owes us twenty-five million in passage taxes." The other man at the table was Keng's assistant. Even pirates need accountants nowadays. "Ten thousand per shipment, plus interest and penalties for sixteen months of noncompliance."

"You really think you can extort money from someone like Eddie?"

"Ahh . . . dinner has arrived," Keng said merrily. "Ms. Katarina, I'm the king of this world. I can do whatever I want. Take that back to your employer, and tell him that twenty-five million is my final offer."

I placed the first dish of five-star goodness in front of Datuk Keng and made eye contact with Katarina.

"Smells wonderful," she said. Translation: Negotiations failed. Time for violence.

Two guards behind me, two more outside, but they were bored. This was just another meeting. They were pirates, tough guys, brutes. This standing around stuff dulled the senses, and I was just the submissive little waiter, whom they had dealt with all night long. *Complacency kills.*

"I must implore you one final time, don't force this issue with Big Eddie, or he will kill you."

Datuk Keng scowled, all pretenses of cordiality gone. Now I could see the man who plundered ships and murdered sailors. His face creased with rage. "You dare threaten me? I'll make this quick—"

I moved with lightning speed, reaching into the nearest guard's coat. The problem with shoulder holsters? The guy standing in front of you can draw your gun faster than you can. I popped the snap, yanked the Browning, and tossed it to Katarina.

She caught the Browning by the grip and leveled it at Keng.

"I'll make it quicker." *BLAM.*

Datuk Keng's head snapped back in a spray of red.

The guard tried to hit me, but I blocked it with my elbow, grabbed him by the tie, and fell, choking off his air and taking us both to the ground. That's why I won't wear a tie.

Katarina brought her hands together smoothly and pointed the gun at the second guard. He froze, hand on gun. She smiled. There was no question how that was going to play out. He raised his trembling hands slowly, aware that the only reason he wasn't dead was because we didn't want to make any more noise.

I rolled, sprang to my feet, grabbed a serving platter, and smashed the second guard in the head. He went right down. Then I kicked them both repeatedly in the face—tuxedo shoes are not the best for beating people senseless—until I was sure neither would be causing any trouble. One quick glance at the exit wound on the back of Keng's skull told me *mission accomplished*, now to get out of here in one piece.

I removed the other Browning from the second guard's belt and two spare magazines from his offside, stuffed those in my pocket, grabbed his radio, and headed toward the door. We had no idea if the room was insulated enough to dampen the sound of a gunshot.

Katarina placed the 9mm muzzle against the accountant's head. He began to whimper and plead for his life in Indonesian. "Listen to me very carefully." Her voice was utterly cold and distant. "Big Eddie wants his money. You will repay him triple the value of his stolen cargo. You will also pay him ten percent of all future takes. You will clear every attack with us from now on. Or we'll burn your little pirate kingdom to the ground. We can find you anywhere. We can reach you anywhere. You work for Big Eddie now. These negotiations are closed. Do you understand?"

He started to respond, she smashed him in the head with the butt of the gun. "In English!" This was the part of negotiation that Katarina excelled at.

"Yes, yes! Whatever you say, please don't kill me!"

Kat called over to me. "Status?"

I had taken up position behind a wooden column and had the gun trained on the door. There was no traffic on the radio. I was really glad that the party was so blaringly loud. "They probably thought it was fireworks."

"Good." Katarina turned her attention back toward Keng's assistant. "We'll be in touch." She hit him in the head with the pistol again, hard enough the sound of the blow made me cringe. The assistant flopped onto the floor unconscious.

"Let's go," I said as I changed the radio to a predetermined channel and hit *transmit*. "We're on the way down. Prepare for pickup."

"On the way," Carl, my partner in crime, responded over the airwaves. I knew that the car was already in motion and he would be waiting at the service entrance in exactly two minutes. Carl was reliable. I stuffed the Browning into my waistband and made sure my tuxedo covered it. The radio went into a pocket.

"Damn it!" Katarina hissed as she lifted the cloth of the cart. "The soup spilled. I can't ride in there. You know what this dress cost me?"

"Just go," I grunted. She had just murdered a pirate, but she was worried about her outfit. My girlfriend was psychotic. "You got a better way to walk out of here past twenty security guards?"

"You are handsome when you're stern, Lorenzo," she replied as she ducked under the cloth, slipped out of her high heels, and folded herself into an almost impossible position. "And you look like a Bollywood James Bond in that outfit. Very handsome."

"Shut up," I grumbled as I flipped the cloth down to conceal her, then pushed the cart to the door. It was heavier now. Katarina was taller than I was and extremely athletic, so she added a lot of weight to the cart. Not that I would ever guess her weight out loud, since she made her living killing people for an organized crime syndicate.

And I was what? Her *helper*?

It was a pretty shitty job when you thought about it that way.

We walked right out. I kept my head down, eyes averted. The guards at the door grunted at me as I passed. From observing them, I knew that they had approximately two to three minutes before another radio check, plenty of time to get out of here.

The crowd was thicker now, more people accumulating around the railing. The fireworks show was reaching its climax and the city was beautiful in the smoky light. Weaving the cart between socialites, I kept my head down and kept moving, not paying any attention to the sparkles or explosions. I risked one last glance back toward the private area as I reached the kitchen. One of the guards was pulling out his radio, checking in prematurely.

As soon as I was into the kitchen I was moving fast, the doors swinging wildly behind me. I nearly ran over one of the chefs, and collided with another waiter. The kitchen smelled of exotic meats and curry, lots of curry. Flames were leaping from a grill under a row of neatly carved chickens. We had to get out of here, now.

"Pard? What's going on? Is Mr. Keng not happy with his food?" the chef asked nervously.

"He's really not happy," I responded as I threw back the cover. "We've got to move."

"Which way?" Katarina asked, sliding out of the cart. I took off running. She carried her five-inch heels in her hand so she could keep up with me as she followed.

"Pard? What's going on?" the chef shouted after us, totally unaware that the man he thought he was speaking to was on a boat to India with a ten-thousand-dollar bribe in his pocket. I shoved past more kitchen staff, leaving them confused with what an Anglo woman in a party dress was doing running through their work space. I went right to the freight elevator and mashed the button furiously.

"What about the security check on the first level?" Katarina asked as the elevator started down.

I pulled out the stolen radio. "Carl, put the kid on."

"This is Reaper."

"Reaper . . ." Katarina hissed, rolling her eyes. "Such a terrible nickname."

"I need you to jam Keng's channel. Then I need to know what's going on at the first floor checkpoint. And tell Carl and Train we've been spotted. This might get hot."

"Okay," Reaper responded, sounding slightly distorted as the radio waves passed through layers of concrete and steel. *"Their channel is now filled with crap."*

"You know, if he's over sixteen I would be stunned." She bent over and put her shoes back on.

"He told me he's twenty-one, and he's a technical wizard. And since our last tech guy got blown up in Singapore . . ."

Reaper came back. *"I don't think they were able to contact security, but they may try the courtesy phones. I'll kill those."*

"Do it."

"On it," he responded enthusiastically. *"Reaper out."*

"What kind of name is that supposed to be?" Katarina snorted.

"I told him he couldn't go by his real name. Too dangerous." The floor numbers changed rapidly, but I didn't know if we would be fast enough.

"Yes, real names are dangerous in this business . . ." She put her hands on my shoulders and pushed me slowly back against the elevator wall. "Hector."

"Business, Katarina. Stick to business," I grunted as I pushed her away. She was the first person I had told my real name to in years. It was stupid, and weak, but infatuation does that to a man. She did that fake pout that I had found cute at first, though now it was just annoying.

"Whatever you say, Lorenzo, darling." She was beautiful, lethal, and I had been lonely. I had let her suck me into working for Big Eddie, and what a mistake that had been. Bad guy. Villain. Robber. Thief. Look up the definition and there was my picture. It was what I was good at. I was probably one of the best in the world. It was all that I knew, and all that I could do. And honestly, I loved it. I was a predator, through and through. But since everything had fallen apart back in back in Africa, I had tried to only prey on other bad guys. They had more to take, and I could always console myself that when I had to off one of them, I left the world a better place. According to my twisted moral code, they were fair game. Normal people were off limits, but working for Big Eddie, those lines often blurred. I had seen how real evil operated, and I was employee of the month.

I hate what I've become.

Concentrate on escaping. Be bitter later. I yanked the waiter's sash, opened my coat, undid my tie, and tried to look casual, sloppy. Just a guy wrapping up a night on the town and taking home a professional girl. I grabbed Katarina around the waist—her abdominal muscles were hard as rock—and held her close. "Look like we're guests leaving the party." She held out the other 9mm.

"Take this."

"Why?"

"Where am I supposed to conceal a full-size pistol in this thing?" she growled, gesturing at her dress.

True enough. She couldn't hide most of herself in it. I took the gun and shoved it into the front of my pants and made sure the cummerbund hid it. I didn't like carrying a cocked and locked handgun over my manhood, but didn't have time to think of a better spot.

First floor. The elevator clanked to a stop and the doors hissed open. Katarina giggled loudly and snuggled up; she was a superb actress. I did the half-drunk wobble out onto the linoleum. This was the service entrance, and guests shouldn't be coming down this way, but it was a heck of a party upstairs, and what happens in Kuala Lumpur, stays in Kuala Lumpur.

A few workers noticed us, but the place was swamped tonight. What was another drunk and his harlot? An older woman behind some sort of registration desk was wearing a traditional headscarf, and she shook her head sadly at the sight. She was old enough to have watched her traditional backwater country super-modernize, and all of the ancillary moral decay that came with it.

"Excuse me, sir. You should not be in this area," she said politely.

I waved my hand in her general direction. "We're leaving," I said dismissively, playing the lost rich guy. Katarina giggled again. The woman frowned, apparently deciding that she needed to notify somebody of lost guests, and lifted her phone. She jiggled the receiver a few times when she didn't get a dial tone. *Way to go, Reaper*. We continued down the hall.

The area terminated in some doors and a loading dock. Several workers were moving in cartons of food and booze from a truck. Carl would pick us up on the other side.

Katarina's nails sank into my arm. I froze. Several men were entering, squeezing around the delivery truck. They had the look of toughs, not dressed for a quality event. The guy in the lead was still wearing his sunglasses at close to midnight, was plainly hurried, and was talking into a cell phone. *Can't jam everything, damn it.*

He saw me as I saw him, across twenty feet of concrete and harsh fluorescent light, and he knew that these were the people who had just shot his boss in the face. His hand moved in a blur as he shouted to the other pirates.

Katarina had her arm around me, and her hand was only inches from the Hi-Power in the back of my waistband. I felt it leave as she dove to the side. I drew the second gun as I went the other way.

It was *on*.

The gun in my hand was a worn old military model. I punched the gun straight out, shifting focus from the pirate to the rudimentary front sight. I fired twice as I moved against the wall. Now I was crouching, moving forward into the loading area. I had to get out of that fatal funnel. Had to attack.

Katarina had the same idea. There were multiple gunshots from her side. The lead pirate stumbled, dropped his cell phone, started to turn toward her, black gun coming up in his hand. I nailed him again, and then he was down. The workers were screaming, scattering, hitting the floor, or running.

The other pirates were in a bad position, squeezing past the truck with no place to maneuver. It was like shooting fish in a barrel. I took the left. Katarina took the right. The wall behind me exploded into concrete fragments. The noise was deafening in the echoing space. A worker trapped in the crossfire spun, vegetables flying out of the cardboard box in his hands. A fine particulate mist seemed to hang in the space that he had filled. I fired down the narrow passage, dropping another pirate.

"Magazine! Magazine!" Katarina shouted. I reached into my pocket and tossed one to her. She was at slide lock, gun empty, and barely looked up to catch the mag. She slammed it home, dropped the slide, and kept shooting.

I dove behind a stack of boxes. Bullets zipped right

through. Glass bottles shattered, splashing me with wine older than I was. There was only one more pirate on my side of the truck, and he was firing wildly, trying to retreat, to get away from us. He disappeared around the rear of the truck . . . only to reappear a moment later, falling head-first onto the pavement. The crack of a .223 echoed through the alley.

The radio crackled. It was Carl. *"Got him! Now hurry up. There's more coming. It's like a fucking pirate convention out here."*

"Clear right!" Katarina shouted. I pulled the last mag and reloaded without thinking.

"Clear left. Let's go." The worker who had been shot was still moving, but he wouldn't be for long. Blood was welling from his chest in great violent gouts. He was lying on his back, hands twisted into claws, blood flowing from his mouth as he coughed. His dark eyes were open, staring at the buzzing fluorescents, seeing Allah, or Buddha, or Vishnu, or who knew what in this country.

Standing over him, gun dangling loose in my hand, I froze. I had seen this hundreds of times, and didn't know why this hit me. He looked right at me, and extended a hand, probably wondering why I wouldn't help him, wondering why he hurt so bad, why his heart was pumping blood out of his chest instead of to his brain . . .

"Lorenzo! Let's go!" Katarina shouted.

The old lady with the headscarf pushed past, oblivious to danger, oblivious to the stranger with the gun. She fell at the young man's side, cradled his head in her hands, and began to scream. He was already dead.

"Murderer!" she shrieked in Malay.

"But I didn't kill him," I said in English, but she wasn't paying attention. She was trying to stop the bleeding that had already stopped forever.

"Lorenzo!" Katarina shrieked. I snapped out of it and ran for the exit.

The next hour was a blur. There were more of Keng's men in the alley. And I killed them as I had killed so many before. The cops arrived, and Carl eluded them by driving like a madman through the streets of KL. Nobody could catch Carl, nobody.

All I could think of was that old woman with the headscarf. *Murderer . . .*

Dawn found us at a safe house in the Malaysian countryside. We pushed the van with bullet holes into the lake. Datuk Keng was dead. Big Eddie's work was done.

The new guy, Reaper, may have been young, but he'd done well. Carl had cracked open a beer and was sitting on the couch, surly as usual. Train was his usual jovial, goofball self. A nerdy computer kid, my best friend the angry mercenary, and a mountain of muscle with a teddy bear's heart. This was my crew, this was my family. They did this for me. They were watching the news coverage about what the local authorities were calling the Independence Day Massacre.

I left the room, wanting to be by myself. Carl studied me as I walked away. He knew me better than anybody, and I had no doubt he knew what I was about to do. I watched Katarina through the window as she paced back and forth on the lawn. She was on her cell phone, giving details to Big Eddie's representatives. She was dressed down now, just wearing normal clothing, not made up at all, and even then I had to admit that she was probably the most beautiful woman I had ever known, and fun, and amazingly smart, talented, pretty much everything I could ever want.

Too bad she was evil.

I overheard Reaper whisper to Train. "A massacre? Man, that was crazy. I've never seen anything like that before . . . How many people have you guys killed?"

"That's a stupid question, kid." Carl muttered. "Really stupid."

"Sorry."

"I can understand you asking," Train said. "Me, I've had to do it a few times. Carl here, if you had to get all of the people he's killed together, you would probably fill a bus. A big Greyhound bus. He and Lorenzo were mercenaries in Africa for a few years."

"Dude . . ."

"Shut it, Train," Carl growled.

"What about Lorenzo?" Reaper asked with a reverent tone.

"Lorenzo, well . . ." Train hesitated.

Carl responded. "If I need a bus, then Lorenzo needs a football stadium. Now both of you shut up."

I sighed, and banged my head against the window.

I intercepted Katarina on the lawn as she hung up her phone. She got right to business. "Big Eddie is not happy." Her accent was Swiss. She was half Spanish, half Swiss, and sometimes when she wasn't playing at being something else, her accent was very obvious. It sounded like "*Big Eddie eez not happy.*"

"And why's that?"

"Too much attention. Too much collateral damage. He says that next time—"

I cut her off. "There is no next time. You tell him I'm *done*."

"Lorenzo . . ." she spoke calmly. "Think this through. Nobody is ever *done* with Eddie."

"I am. Sorry, Kat, it's over."

"Are you talking about our employer, or are you talking about us too?" She looked sad, and even bit her lower lip, but I knew that was an act. A year ago I would have believed she was capable of sadness but now I knew that it was fake. Any normal human emotions Katarina had, had long since been expunged.

"Both."

"I thought you loved me . . ." she said, voice cracking, and this time, I almost could believe her. *Almost*. I turned my back on her and walked away.

Chapter 1: Paradise Lost

LORENZO
St. Carl Island
The Bahamas
February 6th

Seven years ago. Why was I dreaming about seven years ago? The clock by the bed told me that it was three in the morning. I was having a hard time sleeping again, just too restless.

Jill grunted in her sleep. Trying not to wake her, I got up carefully and went to the bathroom. The nondescript face in the mirror stared at me. *What's your problem, Lorenzo?* It was weird to think about Kuala Lumpur again. It had been a turning point for me. Of course, Eddie had come back to haunt me, dragging me into the mess in Zubara, but he was dead now and I was still alive. So what had I become? I was a free man. I was my *own* man. I was a retired thief. I was wealthy. I was in a relationship with a wonderful woman, even though I didn't deserve her.

But at what cost? *A football stadium.* The face in the mirror scowled. That's what Carl had described. So what was I now? For some reason, the words of my foster father were on my mind that morning. I could hear his deep voice, fading on his death bed. Warning me about good and evil . . .

I wouldn't be getting back to sleep tonight.

"Welcome to St. Carl!" the waitress said with extra cheer. Those simple words got my attention. St. Carl was a small enough island that anyone who wasn't a regular got that greeting, especially during the off season when tourists were few and the staff was hungry for tips. The room was kept dark, in sharp contrast to the bright Caribbean sunshine trying to force its way through the now-open entrance. The lunch patrons were sitting in a few tight clusters, mostly workers from the nearby docks, and a handful of others, all of whom I recognized, but I didn't know the three newcomers standing in the doorway.

The lead was a striking woman of Chinese descent, dressed casually, but not casually enough to pass for a St. Carl resident. Her black eyes were scanning across the room, looking for something, or someone. She was flanked by two men, one short Asian guy built like a cage fighter, and the other, a black man so tall he almost had to duck to get through the door, with a shaved head and more muscle than a side of beef.

Tourists, my ass. The door closed behind the three, plunging the room back into a nice, muted grey. I like grey. People like me just kind of fade away. I went back to my lunch, enjoying the spices and the ache in my muscles.

Unable to go back to sleep this morning, I had got in a workout. I wasn't close to my peak, but I'd still done thirty pull-ups, a hundred push-ups, and thirty minutes straight on an eighty-pound punching bag. Not bad for a *gentleman of leisure* on the wrong side of forty.

The woman said something, quietly enough that I couldn't hear, and the waitress waved them toward the bar. I noted that the woman kept scanning, always looking, dividing the room into quadrants, and giving every occupant a once-over. She made eye contact with me, but I just kept chewing my food like any other slack-jawed yokel, just an everyman, not worthy of any attention. I had developed this ability with a lifetime of practice. I was good at appearing unremarkable.

I was also a master of reading people. It was a gift. Two seconds of eye contact told me everything that I needed to know about her. This woman was a killer, and she was hard, but I didn't get the vibe that she was here to kill anyone in particular. She was here on business.

The woman broke away and headed for the bar. She stopped while the tall man pulled a wicker stool out and waited for her to sit. She crossed her legs gracefully, smiled at the bartender like a lion would smile at a gazelle, and placed several folded pieces of currency onto the bar. Beckoning him closer, conspiratorially, she started asking questions. The bartender, always a sucker for a pretty girl, took the money, scratched his head, looked around the room, shrugged, and pointed right at me.

And here we go. I sighed and took another bite.

The woman stood, delicately adjusted her blouse, and walked toward me. Her men took up positions at the bar, still close enough to shoot me if necessary. I waited for her to approach. The weight of the compact pistol on my belt, concealed under an untucked cotton shirt, was reassuring.

She stopped, hovering next to my table, while I nonchalantly finished my larb. Why Thai food for breakfast in a hole-in-the wall restaurant on a flyspeck island in the middle of nowhere? Because I *said so*.

Of course the bartender knew me. I own most of this damned island.

"Are you Lorenzo?" She asked politely in perfectly nuanced English. Such a mundane statement seemed vaguely threatening when she said it.

I made her wait while I took a long drink of water. Most everything I ate was seasoned to be lethally hot. "At times," I replied, pushing my dish away and wiping my mouth on a napkin. "Have a seat." She did. It had been a while since anyone other than my Jill had called me that name on St. Carl.

"My name is Song Ling." She got right down to business. "I have need of your services."

I raised an eyebrow. "You must not have gotten the memo, lady. I'm retired."

Nonplussed, she reached into a pocket and pulled out a business-size envelope. "You will want to see this." She held it out to me, her blood-red fingernails bright over the white paper. The nails were kept short, like those of most women more concerned about trigger control than fashion.

I was forced into my last job, too. It too had started with a messenger giving me an envelope, though Ling was far more attractive than the psychotic Fat Man who had served Big Eddie Montalban. That particular envelope had been filled with information on my extended family and threats against their lives. I had pulled off one of the most daring heists of my career, but the costs had been far too high. Too many people, friends and enemies both, had died because of the contents of that last envelope.

I didn't take it.

"Ling, was it? Look, I'm sorry that you came all this way for nothing, but I'm not interested." I pushed back my chair and stood. I could see both of Ling's goons tense up. "I hope you enjoy your stay on St. Carl. The rock shrimp really is good this time of year. You should try some. My treat. And then have a nice trip home."

"Your brother said you would react like this." She didn't even look at me. She placed the envelope on the table and spun it. "I didn't pick you out of the crowd. You look nothing at all like him. I was expecting a man of greater . . . stature."

I paused. That would explain how she found me. *Son of a bitch.*

I was a foster kid. I said as I sat back down. The envelope sat between us. Ling didn't speak. I had been correct in my earlier assessment, she was a hard one. "How do you know Bob?" I asked, because of course, of all my brothers, it had to have been him. For some reason she didn't strike me as the type of person that ran in the same social circles as my straitlaced, honorable, FBI Agent older brother.

She opened the envelope and pulled out a torn paper napkin. It had been scribbled on with black ink. She shoved it toward me. "He gave this to me, right before he was chased down, beaten unconscious, and taken away. That was . . . " she theatrically looked at her watch. ". . . seventy-two hours ago. I do not know if he is alive or dead."

"What?" I snatched the napkin from her. I recognized Bob's blocky handwriting.

HECTOR—NEED HELP. REMEMBER Q?
THEY KNOW.
DON'T WORRY ABOUT ME.
HE IS IN NORTH GAP.
HE IS THE KEY.
YOU MUST SAVE HIM.

The bottom half of the napkin was missing, torn off.

Q? Quagmire. Quagmire, Nevada. They know? Eddie's dead. His organization is destroyed. Gordon . . . The shadow government types. They must have found out about Bob helping us in Quagmire.

The Quagmire Incident had made national headlines the year before. Everybody knew about how a civilian jet, owned by billionaire philanthropist Eduard Montalban, had allegedly been shot down by a surface-to-air missile. That part was actually true. I knew because I was the one who had fired the missile. The rest of the story had never made it to the news, nothing about the gun battle with a bunch of secret government agents in an abandoned prison work camp ever made it beyond the usual conspiracy-theory sites. Except all of that was true as well. Bob had been there for every bit of it.

"Who's in North Gap? What does that mean?"

"North Gap is a decommissioned US Air Force radar station in the State of Montana. It is now used by a covert organization within the United States government. It serves as a secret prison and interrogation center for high-value, high-risk subjects. I'm here to offer you a trade, Mr. Lorenzo. You help me rescue someone from this facility, and I'll give you all of the information I can to help you find your brother. We will lend you our full assistance and allow you to use our intelligence network for this end."

"What happened to my brother? Where was he when he was taken? Why was he with you?"

Ling folded her hands neatly on the table. "Do we have a deal or not, Mr. Lorenzo? I do not have much time."

I could feel the anger bubbling to the surface, the same killing anger that I had used as a tool for so long, the same evil that I had thrown into the deepest, darkest well of my mind to be locked up safely for the last six months. "How about you tell me where my brother is right now or I cut your eyes out?" Her men sensed the change, and started to rise from the bar, hands moving under their shirts.

Ling didn't flinch. She casually raised her hand, and her goons grudgingly lowered themselves. The rest of the patrons kept eating, unaware that for a split second the room had teetered on the edge of a gunfight.

"Read your brother's words. That isn't what he wants. This is bigger than your brother. Greater than you, than me, than all of us." She spoke with the sincerity of a true believer, and those were the most dangerous kind. Ling produced a smartphone, tapped the screen a couple of times, then laid it on the table so I could see it.

"Do you know this man, Mr. Lorenzo?"

I looked at the picture on the screen. My eyes narrowed. "Yeah . . . I know him."

Ling leaned forward. "One life for another. Your brother is an honorable man, Mr. Lorenzo. I want no harm to come to him. Right now, my people are doing everything they can to locate him. But your brother insisted that finding this man was more important than his own safety. Please. We need your help."

I glanced down at the image again. A young man, with a young face, but hard eyes. His hair had been shaved off, and his face was crisscrossed with scars. As a matter of fact, I'd given him one of those scars.

Valentine.

VALENTINE
Location Unknown
Date/Time Unknown

You're a natural-born killer, boy.

Hawk had said that. I found myself thinking about his words and that day I first met him in Afghanistan. It had been a bad day but it changed me, set me on the path that I'd walked ever since . . . a long, winding, bloody path that ended with me in a small, windowless cell.

Sitting against the wall, I stared blankly into space. Footsteps would occasionally echo from the hallway outside my door. Every so often an ancient industrial heater would come on, filling the hall with a dull roar while it ran and kicking up small clouds of dust from the vents. Fluorescent lights buzzed unendingly; they never turned them off. I didn't know if it was night or day. I could sometimes hear voices from outside, but I was never directly spoken to while I was in this room. I wasn't allowed to speak. If I made noise, they came in and sedated me, or worse. So I sat quietly, back to the wall, and lost myself in thought.

I didn't know where I was, exactly. It was cold, and there were thick pine forests in every direction. I had been outside a few times. It may have been on a mountaintop somewhere, or up in Alaska. I had no real way of keeping track of time. This had to be intentional. I didn't know how many days, or weeks or months, I'd been in this place, but I grew increasingly certain that I would never leave. I knew that there was more snow on the ground the last time I'd been outside than there was the first time they'd let me out, so it was probably winter.

Of course, they hadn't let me out in a while, as part of my punishment for stabbing one of the guards in the knee with a pen.

Despite ending up in prison, I didn't regret knowing Hawk. The man was like a father to me, and I hadn't even known I'd been lost before I met him. I joined the military because I just didn't know what else to do with myself, volunteered for Afghanistan for the same reason.

My time with Vanguard Strategic Services International was something of a blur now, even though my career had lasted nearly five years. The deployments were all different, but they were all the same, too. We fought for the people who could afford to pay us in wars the rest of the world generally didn't care about. Others fought for duty, honor, and country. We fought because it was our job.

I was good at it. It's what I'm best at. A natural-born killer. Deep down, I'd always known. I killed my first man as a teenager. I grew up that day. I changed. And I knew I was different. I began to look at the people around me the way a wolf looks at a herd of deer.

Somehow I held on. My teammates kept me sane. We went through a lot of bad days and a lot of good ones. We fought together, partied together, and mourned our dead together. I traveled all over the world, and was paid a lot of money for what I did.

It all came crashing down in Mexico. Only three of us survived that mission, and our employer was forced out of business. My entire life was gone in the span of a couple of days.

I tried. I tried to return home, to the US, and get a regular job. I tried to live my life as a respectable citizen. I did that for almost a year, and I was completely miserable. Restless, disconnected from the people around me. When my former teammate Tailor showed up on my doorstep with a job offer, the deal was sealed.

Project Heartbreaker, they called it. We did good work, at first. I met the first woman I ever really loved. Her name was Sarah, and she made me a better man.

She died in a little country called Zubara. Most of us did, betrayed by the same shadowy organization that had brought us there. They were just cleaning up loose ends. Some of us managed to escape with our lives, and those who did went into hiding.

Not me. I was done running. I tracked down Gordon Willis, the man behind the entire operation, and shot him through the heart.

Then they caught me. So there I was, some time later, in a windowless cell, wondering when they were going to get around to killing me. I wondered if anyone had any idea what happened to me. *Did anyone even care?*

My eyes snapped into focus as the tromp of combat boots echoed down the hall. Three people, it sounded like. It didn't seem like it was mealtime, and they never sent three men just to slide my tray of slop through the door. I took a deep breath, and tried to steady myself as I stood up. I knew what was coming next.

A key hit the lock. The door swung inward. Three men in black uniforms strode in. I recognized all of them. I'd seen them all before. Reilly, Smoot, and Davis. They didn't speak as they shoved me against the wall and cuffed my hands together and shackled my feet. They jabbed me in the side to get me going, hard enough to leave a throbbing pain. I shuffled up the hallway, chains clinking like an inmate at the county jail.

There was a time when I'd tried to resist, tried to make myself a pain in the ass, hoping for rescue or escape. In my confinement, I'd worked out, doing push-ups and sit-ups in my cell to stay somewhat fit. As time went on, that hope faded. I gave up exercising. What as the point? I was going to die in this place. I was too much of a liability for them to ever let me go.

I hung my head slightly, but said nothing, as I clattered along in chains.

LORENZO

I studied the image for a time. "I don't know what

happened to him. Once he popped that guy in Virginia, he just dropped off the grid. I figured the secret government types murdered him." I slid the phone back to Ling.

"From what your brother has told me, you owe him a great deal." Ling's dark eyes almost bored holes into me. Of course she was right. Jill would be dead if it hadn't been for Valentine, but that wasn't the sort of thing Bob should be sharing. How much had my brother told this woman?

"No disagreement there, but the way I see it, the way *he* saw it, we're even. No offense, lady, and in normal circumstances, I'd love to go take on the entire US government to rescue somebody who shot me with a .44 magnum, but it sounds like my brother's in trouble. Family comes first."

"How noble of you," Ling said flatly. "My organization is searching for your brother as we speak, and as soon as we have information on his whereabouts, we will act. I understand your frustration. But until we are able to locate Bob, there is little that can be done."

"You might be surprised," I muttered.

"Perhaps not. I know exactly what you can do. You are one of most accomplished thieves in modern history. The Vladivostok gold train robbery, the Bahrain Museum of Antiquity heist, the South African Diamond Exchange, and rumors of many others. You are a master of disguise, stealth, and various intrigues." She smiled as she saw my reaction. Yep, the old poker face was out of practice. Island living makes a man soft.

"You missed a few of my greatest hits, but apparently you know me. So who the hell are you supposed to be?"

"I am a strike team commander for the organization called Exodus. I assume you are familiar with our work?"

I nodded slowly. Of course I knew about them. Anyone who worked in the circles I did had heard of Exodus. "You kill people. Slave traders mostly. Criminals, terrorists, drug lords . . ." Mostly I knew about them from their reputation, and it was a grisly one. They were a bunch of pseudo-holy-warrior kooks who never took prisoners and rarely left witnesses. "You pop anybody you decide is evil enough."

"There's a lot more to it than that, but you are fundamentally correct. This does not bother you, I trust."

I smiled. "I'm morally ambivalent."

"So your brother implied. Given your reputation, I'm surprised you haven't crossed paths with our organization before."

"I try not to take sides. And, no offense, I'm too good at what I do to be snared by a bunch of vigilante fanatics with automatic weapons. Please continue, Miss Ling."

Ignoring the slight, Ling glanced around the restaurant to make sure no one was listening before continuing. "My organization was working on a matter of some significance. We were planning a mission against a very high-profile target. Have you heard of Sala Jihan?"

"The Pale Man?" I snorted. Every professional criminal who had ever worked in the Eastern hemisphere had heard of him, but it was all legend and nonsense from the superstitious or crazy. He was central Asia's cross between the boogieman and Jack the Ripper. Villagers had been telling scary stories around campfires about him for hundreds of years. "I don't have time for fairy tales."

"He is *quite* real, I assure you." Her flash of anger was

very convincing. "Or at least some slave-trading warlord wants people to think he is real, and that he has returned. Someone calling himself Sala Jihan appeared a few years ago, and during that time, he's amassed an army and now controls the trade of slaves, illicit arms, and drugs across south and central Eurasia."

"That part of the world was Big Eddie's territory," I stated.

"Eduard Montalban was not in the same league as Sala Jihan."

"Then you didn't know much about Big Eddie."

"He was a bored rich man's son. A sociopath, of course, and dangerous, but in the end all of his power came from his family. His older brother is dead now, of course, and so is he. Thanks to you. That was well done, Mr. Lorenzo."

I happened to agree, but I was growing impatient. "What does any of this have to do with Bob?"

"Your brother was looking for someone with some extremely vital information. This individual he was searching for was also being pursued by a certain US government agency which I believe you have some experience with. The person Bob was after had fled to Sala Jihan's territory. It is easy to disappear there."

I had always thought of my brother as the law-abiding, rational one. That was why it had been kind of shocking to see him shoot some of his fellow federal agents, without hesitation, back in Quagmire. I could see Bob putting what he thought was *right* and *good* ahead of what was *practical*. I was the practical one of the family. "So where is he now, and how many people do I have to kill to get him back?"

"We're working on that. But first we need you to help

us rescue Valentine. Read your brother's words. It's what he wants."

"And why the hell is Valentine so important?"

She didn't get a chance to answer. One of her bodyguards, the tall black man, approached quickly and tapped her on the shoulder. "Ma'am, I received. We need to leave."

Ling brushed her hair back and stood. "We need your help, Mr. Lorenzo. Our plane will be leaving the airfield in ninety minutes. Gather your equipment and meet us there. If we do not see you, then we will attempt this rescue without you. The choice is yours."

I stayed seated and stewed for a moment. Technically, I owned the airfield on St. Carl, and this woman had landed on my runway without my permission. Of course, I leased it to the island, and tourist planes weren't uncommon, but I was already angry and that just made it worse. I repeated my question. "And why is he so important?"

She looked at me like I was stupid.

"We never leave a man behind, Mr. Lorenzo. Your brother understood that much."

"Reaper." The phone picked up as I charged up the stairs to my home. The beach stretched for a mile in each direction below me, and my boat was rocking softly at my nearby dock. Seagulls squawked overhead. Ling and her men were on their way back to the airstrip. I was supposed to grab my stuff and meet them there.

"Hey, Chief! What's up? Haven't heard from you in forever."

"Where are you at?"

"I'm kicking ass and taking names. Can I call you back?" I could hear clanking and something roaring in the background. Reaper played a lot of video games. "You like that, *bitch*? Huh? Witness my perfection! Go cry to momma, *noob*!"

"No. This is serious."

"Oh shit." Reaper was suddenly all business. "This line is secure. What do you need?"

"I've got some work for you to do." I looked at my watch. "Find out everything you can about a decommissioned air force base in Montana called North Gap. Then I want you to get my brother's file from the FBI database and forward it to me. I want to know where he was, and what he was working on."

"Wow. Jumping right back into the deep end." Reaper whistled. "That's gonna be a tough one. I'll get on it." For most people, a request to break into a secure government database would seem a bit odd. For Reaper, it was the kind of thing he did for kicks. "It might get really expensive."

"I'll cover it. And get me everything you can find on Valentine."

Reaper was quiet for a moment. "Like from Zubara? That Valentine?"

"Yes, that Valentine. Find me everything you can on him. Everything. I want to know where he came from, where he's been, and what happened to him after Quagmire."

"I'm on it!" Reaper paused for a second. "Are we back, Chief?"

He'd been bugging me about once a month for the last half a year about resuming our life of crime. Even though he was the only surviving member of my last team, and he was now independently wealthy from our looting of Big Eddie's treasury, he just couldn't leave it alone. I suppose some of us just aren't good at walking away.

"We're back."

"Sweet! I'm on this!"

I pocketed my phone as I stepped into the entryway. "Jill! I'm home. We've got to talk." My voice echoed through the vast space of vaulted ceilings, but no answer came. My home was huge. The average slum apartment I had lived in as a kid could fit in the living room. This had been the Montalban family vacation home on this island. The walls were white, the floor made of bright local wood, and an ocean breeze caused the curtains to flow softly over the very expensive furnishings. For a place that Big Eddie had hardly ever visited, he had spared no expense. "Jill!"

"I'm up here." Jill's voice came from upstairs. I ran, my sandals slapping on the marble stairs, then softly as I hit the thick carpet of the second floor landing. She was waiting in the bedroom, a large cardboard box open on the bed, packing peanuts strewn everywhere. She was wearing the little orange sundress that I loved on her, and didn't look up as I entered. "Those antique candelabras I won on eBay got here, and look! They're so pretty! I'm going to put these up in the dining room. So how was lunch, honey?"

I didn't respond. I stepped past her, opened the door to the closet, and examined the three black duffel bags sitting on the floor. The first bag was set up with US currency and clothing that would fit in most places in America. I grabbed it and dragged it out. I reached up a shelf and grabbed another black case, this one carrying my disguise kit and other tools of my former trade. I hadn't asked, but I assumed that Ling's plane would have spots to smuggle weapons past customs. It was kind of a given in these kinds of social circles. The last duffle was my go-bag, with weapons, ammunition, and gear kept ready.

After a moment, I turned around and faced Jill. She stood there, looking confused, with a silver thing in her hands. It was designed to hold candles, but had a lot of points and edges. Knowing her temper, I was concerned that I was going to have to dig it out of my forehead when I told her that I was about to jeopardize my retirement and take off with a bunch of nut jobs to attack a secret government base to rescue a mercenary.

"What's going on?" Jill asked. Her dark eyes narrowed dangerously. Her hair was pitch black, and tied casually in a ponytail. Her skin was bronzed. Island living had been good to her. She was just as beautiful as the day that I had rescued her from a band of Zubaran terrorists. Considering that the first time we had ever actually spoken, she'd attempted to shoot me, our relationship had come a long way. "That's your bug-out bag." She looked back up at me, an edge in her voice. "Lorenzo, what did you *do*?"

I grabbed Jill gently by the arms, partially to comfort her, and partially to prevent her from getting a good swing with the candle holder. The running joke was that Jill was half Filipina, so when she got angry, people got stabbed. I didn't know how she was going to take this. "Listen to me. Bob's in danger. He's been kidnapped," I said as calmly as I could manage. Jill gasped. She loved my brother. He'd helped save her from Gordon Willis, after all. "It's a long story. I'm going to get him back, but first I need to spring Valentine out of jail."

Jill looked confused for a moment. She hadn't heard that name in a while. "Valentine? Michael Valentine? He's still alive?" She'd known him a lot better than I had, since they'd spent some time together at Hawk's ranch. "I thought he was dead."

"I'll call you and explain everything. I don't have time now. There's a plane at the airfield leaving soon. I need to be on it."

She tossed the candlestick holder on the bed. "I understand. I'll grab my bug-out bag." Jill didn't have my background. She wasn't really a criminal, but she was tough. She adapted and overcame adversity no matter what, a trait which I really admired. Sometimes I worried that she had adapted to life with me a little too well. She hadn't even flinched at what I'd said. We were still technically newlyweds, but we had been through a lot together, so I knew how she was going to react to what I was going to say next.

"Jill . . . no."

She blinked rapidly, the way she always did when I said something stupid. "What do you mean, *no*? Bob's in trouble. We have work to do!"

"No, just me. It's too dangerous. These people I'm going with, I don't trust them. They're bad people." *Here comes the stabbing part.* "I need you to stay here."

"*What?*"

"I can't risk you, and I've got work for you to do, and I'll call and tell you, but I just don't have time now. I have to go."

"Lorenzo, you don't have a team anymore. Carl's dead. You never work alone."

"I called Reaper," I said defensively.

"Reaper hasn't done anything for the last six months but play video games and waste money on lap dances. He's not exactly in practice. If you don't know these people, then you need me to watch your back."

"Jill," I looked into her eyes, "do you trust me?"

She looked away. We'd been living an idyllic existence, my violent past left far behind. The evil that had plagued all my days had been locked away, seemingly forgotten, never to be brought out again. The horrible things that had befallen Jill were buried with them, and we'd begun a new life together.

That time ended now, and it was a lot to take in. Finally she turned back to me. "Yes."

I kissed her and held her tight. "I love you," I said softly, then let her go, her hands lingering on mine as I drew away. I slung the rifle case over my back, and grabbed my other bags. "I gotta go."

She followed me down the stairs and across the lawn. I stopped at my climate-controlled tool shed, unlocked the heavy padlock, and went straight to one of the wooden crates. This was the stuff I wasn't comfortable storing in the house. Jill fidgeted as she watched my preparations. She knew full well what I was doing.

"Be careful."

"Always."

Chapter 2: Head Games

VALENTINE
Location Unknown

My shackles clinked as I was led down to the last room on the right side of the corridor. A pit began to form in my stomach. This was the *information extraction* room. I had been in there several times before, but couldn't recall exactly how many times. Nor, for that matter, could I remember how long it had been. I just knew that this was where they took me when they wanted me to tell them something.

The room was a little bit colder than the corridor. Machines and equipment that I couldn't identify lined the walls. At the back of the room was a large tubular tank that resembled an MRI machine or something.

Near the center of the room was a chair like you'd find in a dentist's office, except this one had built-in restraints. My three escorts sat me down in the chair. Davis held me in place while Smoot stood watch, taser at the ready. Reilly then fastened both of my wrists and both of my ankles to the chair before doing up the waist and head straps. Once I was restrained, they raised the chair so that I was almost in a standing position. Several suction cups with wires leading to them were connected to my head. A band was put around my arm to monitor my heart rate and breathing. An oxygen tube was jammed up my nose. Machines in the room blinked to life as they were brought out of standby mode.

In front of the insane dentist's chair was a regular chair. That was where *she* always sat when we did this. The door to the room opened again. High heels clicked on a cold concrete floor as a pale, fortyish woman strode across the room. She sat stiffly in the chair in front of me, crossed her legs, and tapped on her iPad for a few moments.

"Good morning, Mr. Valentine." She didn't bother to look up.

My eyes narrowed. "To what do I owe the pleasure this time, Doc?"

Her name was Dr. Silvers. Olivia Silvers. She didn't look like much. Pale skin, thin build, flat hair, but she was in charge here, and she was an ice-cold bitch. I hated her with the utmost intensity, but in my present position, the most I could do would be to verbally abuse her. Her retaliations for that kind of behavior had convinced me that it wasn't worth the trouble.

It's not that they necessarily tortured me. They hadn't pulled out my fingernails, smashed my kneecaps, or anything like that. Hell, they didn't even waterboard me. Nothing that base. These people had other ways, sophisticated, monstrous ways of getting inside your head.

First would be the needles and then would be the questions. Sometimes the questions didn't make sense. Other times I didn't know the answers, but she'd keep asking. Sometimes they'd put something in the oxygen tube in my nose. Other times they'd put things in my food and I'd wake up in the chair. Or I'd have a nightmare about being in the chair and wake up back in my room. Sometimes I'd remember things that didn't actually happen. It was hard to tell what was real.

Whenever I resisted or fought back they'd just beat the shit out of me and throw me back in my room. Sometimes they'd withhold food or leave me strapped down for days on end. One time, they left me out in the snow for a few hours. They let a big guard dog attack me once for the time I'd stabbed Smoot with the pen.

Dr. Silvers looked up at me over her spectacles. She must have practiced that disinterested, condescending expression in the mirror, since she was very good at it. "The last time we talked, you told me about the death of your mother."

"I did?"

"You were quite talkative. You described the events of your mother's death in great detail to me, and I told you I'd look into the matter for you."

I'd been too drugged to remember. I sure as hell wouldn't have talked to Dr. Silvers about it. But deep down, I knew that I had told her everything.

"The men that murdered your mother were William and Jesse Skinner. The Skinner Brothers were, at the time, the subject of a multi-state manhunt. They'd been terrorizing small communities in the Upper Midwest for a year when you encountered them. The older of the two, Jessie, was suspected of multiple counts of armed robbery, rape, and murder. William was a high-functioning psychotic with extremely violent tendencies."

"I know all that. They killed my mom, for chrissakes. I went to court and was interviewed by the cops over and over. Why are you telling me this?"

"Oh," Dr. Silvers said, unperturbed. "Last time we spoke, you were having trouble remembering, so I looked into the matter for you. In any case this is what I want to talk about today."

"You want to talk about my mother?"

"Not specifically. I want to talk about what happened to you when you found her dead, when you realized that you were in danger. What did you call it?"

I looked down at the floor. "*Calm.* I was calm."

"Yes," she said, eyebrow raised. "I want to talk about this sense of calm with you."

Why is she asking me about that? It was hard to remember what we'd talked about before. I knew I'd been grilled about Gordon Willis a great deal. There had been a sense of desperation in the way she'd asked. He was one of theirs, but he'd gone off the reservation. He'd been working with Eduard Montalban, and I told them that too. I don't remember telling them about my involvement in Eduard Montalban's death, but for all I knew, I'd already betrayed Hawk, Bob Lorenzo, and . . . the other Lorenzo, too.

But why was she asking me about *the Calm*? Why was she asking me about my mom? I couldn't figure out what she wanted, and that scared me.

Dr. Silvers stood up, and stepped closer to me. "Michael," she said softly, her lips inches from my ear. "You are a unique individual. What we're doing now is figuring out the best course for you going forward. Do you understand?"

"No," I managed. I felt strange. Groggy, but my heart was racing. They were doing something to me again. I could feel it.

"That's alright," she said, not quite smiling. "I'll be with you on this journey, every step of the way."

I don't remember much after that.

LORENZO
Somewhere over the Caribbean
February 6th

The ocean flashed by below us. I leaned my forehead against the Plexiglas window as the plane, a loud, rattling, turboprop Cessna Grand Caravan, banked toward the west, giving me one final look at the white sand and green tropical forest that was St. Carl. I sighed, mentally shifted gears, and returned to business.

The plane had an unusual interior layout, with limited seating. A curtain hung between the pilots' seats and the rest of the cabin. The back half of the cabin had a gurney and some medical supplies, presumably for Valentine. The hulking black man sat directly across from me, a bemused expression on his face. He looked me in the eyes, but didn't say anything. It was pissing me off.

"So who are you supposed to be?"

"My name is Antoine," he replied over the noise and vibration of the engine. The accent suggested West African. A folding table was between us, and it concealed his hands. He either had them folded in his lap or was pointing a gun at me. He smiled, his gleaming white teeth contrasting with his dark skin. The plane vibrated as we gained altitude. My Gearslinger bag was in my lap, one compartment unzipped. I thought about my next move. I didn't trust these people, and they didn't trust me. They were *right* not to trust me.

"Thank you for coming with us, Mr. Lorenzo. Your help is greatly appreciated," Ling said calmly. She sat kitty-corner across from me. "Exodus is very—"

I cut her off. It was time for business. "I don't give a shit about you or Exodus, or how much you appreciate anything. I'm here for my brother. You're very lucky that I believed you when you said you don't know where he is. If I didn't, you'd be spilling your guts to me right now, literally, if necessary."

"You could attempt that," Ling said diplomatically. Antoine grunted, obviously protective of her. Shen sat across the narrow aisle from me. He looked relaxed, but I could tell it was a facade. He was ready to pounce if I made a wrong move.

"But that would take too long, and I'm sure you've got some sort of arrangement with your handlers. I know how this game is played, and I'm too old for it."

"Indeed."

"So that's why we're going to play a different game, I call it defining the working relationship." My hands moved with lightning speed. I reached into the unzipped compartment and found a round, metal object. Before Ling or either of her companions knew what was happening, I slammed the hand grenade down onto the plastic table. I raised my left hand, with the grenade's pin looped around my finger. The only thing preventing it from initiating was the death grip I had on the spoon.

Shen drew a pistol in a flash, and had it pointed at my left ear. Antoine's left hand had never come out from under the table, but my suspicion that he had a pistol in it was confirmed by the way he moved. Ling smiled slightly.

I stared her down. "If I let go, it goes off, with a lethal radius bigger than your airplane. Try anything, we all die. Am I making myself perfectly clear?"

Ling nodded slightly at Shen, so he refrained from blowing my brains out.

"I've found it's harder for people to lie when they're about to get blown up."

"I'm telling you the truth. I don't know where your brother is."

"Cut the bullshit. You think you can just come to my island, land this piece of junk on my airfield, and blackmail me into going along with this? Do you know who you're screwing with? You come into *my* house and threaten me? Really?"

Antoine's pistol came out from under the table. He raised the big FNP-45 up and pointed it between my eyes.

"Look at me, Lorenzo," Ling ordered. "I'm telling you the truth. My people are doing everything they can to find your brother."

I glared at her. She glared right back. She wasn't cracking.

Antoine was starting to look nervous, and I could see his finger tightening up on the trigger. The hammer started to creep imperceptibly back. He was going to shoot me, and try to grab my hand before I let the grenade go. I shifted my glare to him, daring him to try.

Reaching across the aisle, Ling placed her tiny hand on his massive arm. "No need, Antoine. He knows I'm telling the truth. What of your lady, Mr. Lorenzo? All she will know is that you got onto a plane with another woman and were never seen again."

I showed no emotion. I wasn't going to give them anything. I wasn't going to let up. I had to know the truth. "Ever see what happens to bodies in the ocean? Half of you will wash up on a St. Carl beach, bloated, green, crabs living inside. It's pretty gross . . . Where is my brother?"

She didn't blink. "My soul is prepared, Mr. Lorenzo. Is yours?"

A cold bead of sweat rolled down into my eye. I blinked it away. This woman was either as cold as ice or was giving me a performance worthy of an Oscar. *Damned true believers.* They were calling my bluff. *Shit.*

Ling folded her hands across her chest and stared at me, daring me to do it. I actually cracked a smile. Shaking my head, I very carefully slid the pin back into its hole, and folded it down on the other side. "I gotta hand it to you, lady. You've got some brass balls."

Antoine was up in a split second, moving amazingly fast for a big man. He grabbed the grenade and snatched it away from me. I let go without a fight. "The grenade has been safed," Antoine confirmed.

"Thank you," Ling said. She was calm, but seemed visibly relieved. "Shen?"

Shen skull-punched me so hard it was like getting cracked with a bat. Lights flashed before my eyes, and my face hit the table. *So she has a temper after all* . . .

Gideon Lorenzo, my foster father, was a big man. Physically intimidating, with one of those bald heads that managed to gleam in the sun. I always felt kind of dwarfed in his presence. "You want to look at the target, but the front sight is the important part. Focus on the front sight. The target is going to be blurry behind it." *He was standing slightly behind me and his deep voice boomed even through my ear plugs.*

The old Colt Series 70 bucked in my hands, and this time the can flew off the fence. I did what he had taught me, and focused, and pulled the trigger straight back to the rear. Seven shots, and I got five that time. I was getting the hang of this.

"Much better," *he said.*

"Way to go, bro," *Bob said. My brother was sixteen, and nearly as big as Dad. I was fourteen, and a shrimp in comparison, but I didn't have any of those Lorenzo family monster genes. According to the wall lines in my real father's mug shot—the only picture I had of him—he was only five foot five.* "You should stick with the 1911, you stink with the revolver."

"Bob . . . " *Dad said sternly.*

"I'm just saying. Hector can't shoot a round gun to save his life."

I was careful to keep the muzzle downrange like Dad had shown me as I reached over and slugged Bob in the arm. Realistically the muscles on his arm were so thick that he wouldn't have felt it anyway, but he made a great show of being injured.

"No horseplay," Dad ordered. "Bob, go pick up those targets. Hector will help me pick up brass. Remember, always leave the range cleaner than you found it. Your mother will have dinner ready soon."

I put the .45 back in its case, ditched my ear plugs, and started picking up brass. Dad grimaced as he sat down next to me. He had ruined one of his knees in Vietnam, and I knew it was bothering him lately. He watched Bob go downrange, and waited until he was out of earshot. I could tell he wanted to say something.

"Hector, I just wanted to let you know. Your real father's parole hearing was today."

I kept looking for brass. "I'm assuming they're keeping him in."

"Yes."

"Good. Hope he rots in there forever."

Dad cleared his throat. "You know, someday he may be fit to return to society. A man can be redeemed."

"Redemption?" I snorted. I was fourteen and knew everything. "How can somebody like him make up for what he's done?"

One giant hand clamped onto my forearm. I looked up from the brass pile. "Hector, listen to me. You might not believe me now, but no matter what somebody has done in their past, they can be forgiven. They can make up for what they've done. There still needs to be justice, and that person *has to pay for what they've done first, but anyone can be redeemed. Just remember that."*

I went back to picking up brass. "That's insane."

"He's insane."

"Obviously." Ling's voice. "Unfortunately we need him. We don't have the numbers for a frontal assault."

"They might kill Valentine as soon as we attacked anyway. No, you're right, Ma'am. If we're going to free him, then we need this man, even if he is unpredictable," Antoine responded. "Did you think he was bluffing?"

"A Godless, self-absorbed narcissist like him would never willingly sacrifice his life for the sake of others, much less in a childish attempt to prove a *point*. Frankly, I'm rather surprised that the fact his brother is in danger was enough to compel him to do this," Ling responded with some contempt. "However, he's very good at what he does. His reputation indicates that."

"Everything we have heard about this Lorenzo says that he's a ghost. He can go anywhere. The fact that we happened to encounter his brother, just when we needed a man like him, is I think, providence. Please let me speak to him."

I didn't recognize the latest voice, and it was close. I groaned as I cracked open my eyes. The side of my head throbbed and the light streaming through the plane's windows stabbed through my eyeballs and into my brain. The speaker was sitting across from me, a concerned look on his face. I was still in my chair.

Albert Einstein? I thought groggily. He was an older man, with wispy strands of white hair poking out from around his ears, and a mustache like a boot-brush. He studied me from behind his thick glasses. He was actually wearing a bow tie.

"Good afternoon," he said with a thick German accent. "I am Dr. Bundt." He was holding my STI 9mm casually in his bony fist, pointed toward my chest. "I'm afraid Shen hit you a little hard. I apologize for getting off on the wrong foot, but you were threatening to blow us up." His smile seemed genuine.

"Who're you?" The lump on my head hurt like a son of a bitch. Ling and Antoine were seated around me. Shen must have gone up front, behind the curtain. Brilliant Caribbean clouds scrolled past the windows.

"As I say, I am Dr. Bundt. I oversee the treatment and well-being of those unfortunate souls that we rescue. As you may expect, I have gained some experience in helping people."

"Ironic," I said, nodding toward my gun.

"Oh, this?" He turned it around and held it out to me. I glanced toward Ling and Antoine, waiting to see which one was going to shoot me first, but neither moved. "Go on, take it." He shook it slightly. I took the gun slowly, the textured grip was familiar and comforting. I didn't do anything stupid, figuring that they had probably unloaded it while I was out. I reholstered without looking. "No more of the threats, yes? We have a common goal. Both of us want to see your brother rescued. He is very well respected in our organization now. He was most insistent that rescuing Mr. Valentine should be our first priority."

"My brother, the *Fed*, is friends with a bunch of terrorists?" I snorted.

"I see there is much about your brother you do not

know," he said. "I think you will be very surprised when you see him next. In any case, if I were you, I'd be careful about using the word *terrorist*, Mr. Lorenzo. Is it not true that you were the right hand of Eduard Montalban?"

I rubbed the knot on my head, not wanting to argue. Hopefully Shen at least broke a finger or something. "Will you *please* tell me what is so important about that kid?"

"Mr. Valentine is one of us, though only in an honorary sense."

"One of you? When did that happen?"

"Mexico," Ling injected harshly. "A few years ago. He saved many lives, including mine."

Touched a nerve there. Ling had a personal stake in Valentine, and always looking for an angle, I filed that potentially useful information away for later.

Dr. Bundt continued. "In any case, that fact was irrelevant to your brother. For him, young Mr. Valentine was far more important than that. Bob believes Valentine was the key to something very important, something which could have grave repercussions for all mankind."

"And what would that be?"

"This I do not know. All he was able to convey to us was that there are powerful forces moving right now, and that something inside Mr. Valentine's head may be the crux of it all." Dr. Bundt shrugged his bony shoulders. "I do not know any more than that, I'm afraid. Once we rescue your brother you can ask him yourself. He was most adamant, though, that we need to get Mr. Valentine back alive."

"I wouldn't get too worked up either way." That stupid kid getting himself captured in Virginia could have compromised everyone that he'd been involved with, including me and Jill. If I found him alive I was going to choke the shit out of him.

"So what do you say, Mr. Lorenzo? We cannot complete this mission if we are at each other's throats."

"Fine. But understand this, Doc. You people fuck with me and I'll kill you all."

Ling smiled as if she'd just thought of something funny, then stood up. "This is going well," she said, and went forward.

VALENTINE

I'm having the strangest dream.

The images were confusing at first, but soon they formed a thread, a narrative, a story. *My* story. On some level I knew the thoughts were my own, but they felt unfamiliar and half-remembered. A memory of a memory.

I stood in a palatial bedroom, not sure of when I was there. An ornate, four-poster bed sits against one wall. Above it hangs a hideous painting of some tentacled monstrosity devouring a girl.

I'm not focused on the painting, though. A girl hangs from the ceiling by her bound hands. Her night-black hair is wet with blood. Her body has been ruined, mutilated, split open and dissected. She stares at me, judging me, damning me from empty sockets. The holes where her eyes should have been are black pits, so deep and dark that I fall right into them. I want to look away, but the darkness calls to me, invites me to give myself up to it.

I answer its call, and down I go, into the abyss.

You're a natural-born killer, boy. The words sound different this time, almost mocking me. Who had said that to me? What does it mean? I couldn't remember. I was lost in the darkness and couldn't find my way.

I found myself on a dusty trail in Afghanistan, next to a wall made of mud. The village around me is desolate and empty. I am utterly alone. My only companion is a dead body, laying in the dirt next to me, wrapped in a poncho.

I can't see her face, but I know it's Arlene Chambers.. We're waiting for a helicopter that wasn't coming. I look down at her unmoving form and place a hand on it. It's like touching a piece of driftwood, cold and dead.

It should have been me.

Why am I still alive?

Am I?

I cover my face with my hands, and the ancient, immutable dust and rocks of Afghanistan, witness to thousands of years of bloodshed, fade away. I am back in the abyss, and again, I welcome it.

Before I realize what's happening, I'm in a small village somewhere. I've been here before, but I can't remember when. This time I'm not alone. It's dark, but there are fires, enough of them that I can see. People are running for their lives. Men, women, children alike, fleeing in terror.

There's noise, gunfire. A large armored truck, an MRAP, slowly rolls through the village. A faceless machine gunner in the turret mows down anything that moves in front of him. Men in uniforms, carrying rifles, walk alongside it, shooting.

Why are they killing all these people?

I see a few more men, coming up behind the vehicle. These men are bulkier, stronger, and wear armor. One carries a FAL rifle in his hands, and shoots a terrified old man as he runs down the street.

Stop it! Why are they doing this? Who are these people?

The shooter with the FAL rifle is undeterred, unaware of my pleas. He reloads his rifle, quickly and smoothly, and fires again. A car pulls out into the street, desperately trying to get away, but it's no use. The machine gunner and the man with the FAL rifle tear into it. It rolls to a stop, crunching against a wall, its passengers' lives having been snuffed out.

I move closer to the man with the FAL, furious now. I don't know what's going on, but I desperately want to make him hear me. I'm like a ghost, silent, invisible. I have no mouth, and I must scream.

STOP IT!

The man with the rifle is aware of me now, somehow. He turns to face me, a cruel smile on his face. "Stop what?" he asks. His voice is familiar. It's mine. He's *me*.

No! I didn't do that!

"Didn't you?" he asks, still smiling. His voice sounds distant, like an echo. I look down, and now the rifle is in my hands. It's still hot to the touch. I can feel the heat of the fires, smell the exhaust of the truck, and hear the screams and gunfire clearly.

No! I protest. *It wasn't me! I didn't kill all those people!*

The ghastly mirror image grins at me malevolently. "You did kill a lot of people. You're a natural-born killer, remember? This is your natural environment."

The burning village is gone, and suddenly I'm in a helicopter. Dim red lights provide all the illumination I have. My .44 Magnum revolver is in my hand. Rafael Montalban is in front of me, on his knees, with a surprised look on his face. I fire, the gun bucking in my hand. Before he can scream, I kick him out of the aircraft. He falls away into the darkness and disappears.

The other one is next to me again, whispering in my ear. "It's what you do. It's *all* you do."

No . . . please stop. God, please, make it stop.

He laughs darkly. "God can't find you here. It's just you and me."

Leave me alone! I scream, in silence. The other is gone then, and I'm alone, floating in a void.

Is this hell?

I don't know how long I wondered that, but I wasn't afraid. After a while, I felt nothing at all. I drifted alone in darkness for ages, wondering about my state, but only barely. I was detached, wholly separate from myself, and I didn't have it in me to care. No one else did, why should I?

Suddenly I was aware of my body again. I'd returned to my corporeal form. My arms and legs began to feel heavy. My back was against warm metal. I was lying on something. Muffled sounds pierced the blackness. Metallic sounds, then voices. Then there was light, blinding white light. With the light, my skin felt cold, and I began to shake.

I didn't know what was happening. I still couldn't see anything. But one clear voice pierced the confusion, a cold, dispassionate woman's voice.

"Log that as eighteen hours, thirty-six minutes in the tank," Dr. Silvers said.

"That's amazing," a nasally man's voice replied. "I wasn't sure we'd be able to keep the program going for that long."

"Neither was I," Dr. Silvers said. "Mr. Valentine keeps exceeding our expectations."

The last image that crosses my mind, before mercifully losing unconsciousness, is of the sky, on fire.

LORENZO
Somewhere over Texas
February 8th

I looked up from the file in my hand, rubbed my eyes, and glanced out the window. Brown fields stretched for miles below. Somewhere down there was where I had been born. Somewhere to the east was where I had been taken in and raised by the Lorenzo family. Ling was sitting across from me, the folding plastic table in between us.

"So, what do you think?" she asked.

"Tough, but doable. This is pretty detailed information about the security at North Gap." We had floor plans, an incomplete list of personnel files, and even some intercepted e-mail traffic from somebody named Dr. Silvers. "How'd you get this?"

"Your brother gave it to me," she said simply. "Once he found out that we wanted to rescue Valentine, he provided everything. He has been looking into this secret organization, which he referred to as Majestic, for quite some time."

"And how exactly did you come into contact with Bob?" Ling was silent. She could tell I was fishing. "Fine. Be like that. What other resources do we have?"

"You're looking at them." She gestured at the others on the plane. "My sword is the only one which can be spared at this time."

"Sword?"

"An Exodus strike team. Most of our people are occupied with other operations." She didn't seem inclined to elaborate further.

"Flight plan?"

"We will be landing at a small airfield in Montana, approximately two hundred miles from the target. Dr. Bundt and Elvis will stay with the plane." Elvis was the pilot. I'd only seen him briefly, and he didn't seem to be the talkative sort. "We will need to secure secondary transportation from there."

"I've boosted a few cars in my day, won't be a problem."

"I imagine."

"Have you thought about our getaway? How you're going to get Valentine out of the country? These Majestic assholes may be illegitimate, but they have full access to all of the investigatory powers of one really big-ass government machine. If Valentine's important enough to get locked in a secret prison, they're going to be pissed off when they find out he's gone."

She shook her head. "This has all been rather . . . *hasty*. I'm still not sure how we're going to get Valentine out without them killing him."

"Don't worry. I'll come up with something. I always do."

Chapter 3: The Princess of Montana

LORENZO
Bozeman, Montana
February 10th

"You're serious. *This* is your plan?" Ling was incredulous.

I held up the spaghetti-strapped tank top and the denim miniskirt. "Come on. You need to look the part."

Ling glanced around the Walmart, embarrassed. She caught the skimpy top when I tossed it to her. "This is . . ." she looked at the tag, "a size too small."

"Changing room is right over there." I nodded my head.

"But . . ."

"Look. I know you don't trust me but you need to work with me here. We're going to an oil roughneck town in the middle-of-nowhere Montana, not the French Riviera. So unless you want to put Antoine in drag, this is the best I can come up with."

Antoine grunted.

Ling gave me a dirty look and went into the changing room.

"I hope your boss can lighten up for this," I told Antoine, "or at least fake it. She's a little intense."

Antoine folded his massive arms and glared at me. Over the last few days I had discovered that he was very protective of Ling. She was clearly his superior, but he seemed almost like a father figure. Shen, on the other hand, was a cipher. He hardly ever spoke. He stood a short way away from us, and seemed to be uncomfortable shopping at Walmart at two o' clock in the morning. Every freak, junkie, and crazy in Bozeman was wandering around the huge store, making a nuisance of themselves as the hapless employees tried to buff the floors and restock the shelves.

"You are from here?" Antoine asked me out of the blue.

"Not here, specifically. Born and raised in the US. Only been back briefly a handful of times over the last few years . . . And every time it seems a little bit worse, a little rougher."

"Indeed." Antoine looked around the gigantic store filled with more food and goods in one night than whatever West African village he hailed from had probably seen in its history. He chuckled, surely thinking *whatever you say, fat American. First world problems.* "Times are hard."

I may have detached myself from the world, didn't mean I didn't pay attention to current events, especially those that could present job opportunities. I was retired, not dead. "The economy is shit, but this country has bigger problems."

"I do not understand." Antoine looked to his partner. Shen as usual had nothing to say. "Compared to most of the world, this place is a paradise."

"Listen . . ." It was hard to explain. "I've lived in every shit hole on Earth, and they're all the same. It pisses me off to see the same thing creeping in here. There are always assholes who want to hurt the regular people, and then along come the control freaks who want to capitalize on fear of the scary assholes to control the regular people. The scary assholes just don't care, so repeat, repeat, repeat. Government's like a ratchet, and it just keeps on cranking down. This isn't the country I grew up in anymore. People got too scared of the assholes so now the ratchet's getting real tight. People think they're trading chaos for order, but they're just trading normal human evil for the really dangerous organized kind of evil, the kind that simply does not give a shit. Only bureaucrats can give you true evil."

"Exodus stands against any entity which would deprive man of his freedom."

I laughed. "Good luck with that. My brother and Valentine exposed a rogue federal agency killing folks and breaking every law you can think of. It was a big deal. They called it Zubaragate. It was all over the news for a couple of weeks, but what changed since?"

"Nothing." Antoine admitted.

"Nothing. Valentine's in prison and Bob's missing, and not a damn thing changed, because a majority of the people are stupid, willfully ignorant, naïve fools, who expect bureaucrats to save them and wipe their asses for them, and the ratchet just keeps on getting tighter."

"I am surprised this offends you."

I glanced over at him. Antoine was smarter than he looked. I had said too much. These people weren't my friends. They didn't deserve a look inside my head. "Yeah . . . Too much control. Too many people watching. I don't like people watching me." My phone vibrated in my pocket, interrupting my thoughts. It was Reaper. *Good.* This conversation was starting to piss me off. I tapped the Bluetooth headset in my ear.

"Go," I said.

"Go where?"

I sighed. "What do you want, Reaper?"

"I got Bob's file, and some other stuff. I'm sending it to you now." My phone buzzed in my hand as it downloaded the data packet. At least the cell service was better than it used to be.

"How much did you get?"

"Not as much as I wanted, Chief. I went in sideways, compromised another agency's system, gave myself the title of personnel manager, then requested some files. Tried to stay away from anything that would be classified, good thing too, 'cause once I did the whole system came crashing down. They were on me hard. I was lucky to get what I did. Bob's file was flagged."

"Of course it was. Did they track you?"

"Please. I'm The Reaper." He was always *The* Reaper when he was bragging. "Get this," he continued. "Bob was fired from the FBI. He went off the reservation, disobeyed a direct order, was working on a forbidden investigation, stuff like that."

This just kept getting better and better. "What the hell did Bob get himself into? Did they find out about his involvement with our incident last year?"

"I don't know. The reprimands and personal notes weren't classified. He was looking into something they told him not to look into. He tried to gain access to compartmentalized data. He pissed somebody off, that's for sure. It's no wonder he left the country. These people are scary."

Reaper was just telling me like it was, but it wasn't what I wanted to hear. So I changed the subject. "How's Jill doing?"

"She's a little freaked out. Worried about you, but she's okay. By the way, did I ever tell you there are some *seriously* hot girls on your island? Dude! I'm gonna have to get a vacation place out here. You want me to go wake up Jill?"

"No. I'll call her later."

"Hey, one more thing. Check this out." My phone vibrated again as Reaper sent me another file.

"What is it?"

"You wanted me to find everything I could on Valentine, right? Just look. You're going to love this."

What now? I retrieved my phone from my pocket and tapped the screen. I pulled up the image Reaper sent me. It was a picture of the cover of an issue of *Soldier of Fortune* magazine from several years ago. The screen was too small to read all of the print. The cover photo was a group of men in Tiger Stripe camouflage fatigues, carrying FAL rifles.

"What is this?"

"Just what it looks like. That's our buddy Valentine on the cover of *Soldier of Fortune*."

The cover headline read, "Switchblade Teams: Elite Special Purpose Units from Vanguard in Action!"

So that's why he'd been tight with Hawk . . . That tight-lipped old bastard had once been his boss. We'd worked for the same bunch, only I'd been there back before they'd gone all corporate and legitimate. "Unbelievable. Have you found anything else out?"

"Oh, tons. He's never been careful about information management. Between that and the Dead Six files that got dumped during Zubaragate, I found everything on him, easy. It's all there."

"Thanks. I'll go through it when I have time. I'll check in later." I dropped the phone back in my pocket as Ling came out of the dressing room. I cracked a mean grin and whistled. The outfit was just as sleazy as I hoped. And Ling certainly had the body for it.

"I look like a Bangkok whore," she said, awkwardly trying to pull the too-short skirt down a little farther. The revealing top she was wearing had *Princess* written across it in pink bubble letters.

"Yes, *Princess*, yes you do. It's perfect. Now if you could just try not to be so scary all the time, we might be able to pull this off."

Shen and Antoine were stonefaced. They looked at each other, at their superior, at me, and then back at each other. Ling glared at them.

"Not a word!" she snapped, spun around, and stomped back into the changing room. "So help me *God*, Mr. Lorenzo."

VALENTINE
North Gap, Montana

Seated in my usual spot on the floor, I stared into space and tried not to think. My head hurt. My mind was sluggish. I felt like I had just woken from a dream. Or maybe I was still dreaming. I couldn't always tell.

They had put me in the machine they called *the tank* multiple times now. I had only the dimmest recollection of it. It seemed to me that they drugged me before putting me inside it, but they had been drugging me so much the drugs didn't always work anymore. I remembered a mask being put over my entire face, covering my eyes, ears, nose, and mouth. Something else was wrapped around my waist. Other things were plugged into my body, and they'd put me in.

I wasn't sure what the machine did but I knew that somehow Dr. Silvers was drilling into my mind. I'd have vivid dreams, frighteningly real dreams, that seemed to come from someone else. I knew things that I hadn't known, and had forgotten other things altogether. I lowered my head and rubbed my temples. Trying to make sense of anything just made my head hurt worse. I didn't know why they just didn't kill me and be done with it.

Footsteps echoed down the corridor. It wasn't just combat boots on the cold concrete floor, though. I heard the click of pumps and the shuffling of sneakers. I didn't move as they unlocked my door. I didn't stand up. I merely looked up dispassionately, and wondered what they wanted with me now.

Smoot entered first, followed by Davis. They were dressed in black fatigues and black combat boots. Smoot drew a taser from a brown plastic thigh holster and leveled it at me. A red laser dot appeared on my chest. He fanned out to the side, keeping the laser on me, as Davis went the other way, armed with a baton. There was another guard waiting in the hall as backup.

Dr. Silvers entered the room next, rolling her eyes and shaking her head slightly at the overt display of force. It was plain to see that she held her security force in some contempt. As usual, she was dressed in slacks, a turtleneck sweater, and low pumps. A wrinkled white lab coat completed her look, as if she were beating us all over the head with the fact that she was a doctor of some sort.

Behind her was Neville, her assistant and toady. A thin, wiry man with unkempt hair, Neville had a nasal voice and seemed extremely awkward in all of his interactions with other people, especially the guards. When she didn't have him doing other things, he followed Dr. Silvers around like a beaten dog, espousing platitudes about her brilliance. I couldn't tell if she enjoyed his sycophancy or merely tolerated it.

She stood over me for a moment without saying anything. This whole thing was very unusual. I couldn't remember the last time I'd talked to her when I wasn't doped up or restrained.

"I'm not going to get up, if that's what you're waiting for."

She didn't respond. She just exchanged a glance with

Neville, then crouched down so she could be face to face with me. "How are you feeling today, Michael?"

I blinked rapidly. "How am I feeling?"

"It's a simple question."

"I feel like I went on a bender, ate a bunch of mushrooms, then got roofied. What the hell have you been doing to me?"

Dr. Silvers did something unusual then. She kicked her shoes off, then sat cross-legged on the floor, facing me, like she was addressing a frightened child. The two guards looked at each other with stupid expressions on their faces.

"When you first arrived," Dr. Silvers began, "my organization was in a state of panic. My superiors didn't know what to do with you. Project Heartbreaker had utterly failed. Then the worst breach of information security in our organization's history occurred. It quickly became apparent that your Dead Six superior, Curtis Hunter, was the man who compiled all of that damaging information. From that information, though, we learned that Gordon Willis had betrayed us and was secretly in league with Eduard Montalban. The team sent to bring in Willis found him dead by your hand. Tell me, Michael, what were we to think?"

I didn't say anything.

Dr. Silvers didn't let my lack of participation in the conversation faze her. "As I said, they were in a state of panic. Gordon Willis had proceeded on Project Blue without any authorization from our superiors."

"I don't know what Project Blue is," I managed weakly. I'd told them that a hundred times.

"I know you don't, Michael. Unfortunately, you killed

Gordon Willis, the last man we could locate that knew anything about Project Blue. My superiors were convinced you were in on his plot with the Montalbans."

"I'm not *in* on anything," I said. "I killed Gordon because he fucking deserved it."

Dr. Silvers put an icy hand on my forearm in an attempt to be comforting. I almost flinched at her touch. "I know that now. We've learned everything you know and it isn't anything more than we already know. The only other people alive who might know, like your friend Bob Lorenzo, have gone to ground."

My heart dropped into my stomach. I didn't remember ever telling her about Bob. I had been sure that despite everything they'd done to me, I hadn't given him up. I was wrong. I'd betrayed him. Who else had I given up? Hawk? Ling? Lorenzo? Well, screw Lorenzo, but Jill? I felt sick, and lowered my eyes. Dr. Silvers regarded me silently for a few moments, until I was able to speak.

"I don't understand," I managed. "Why am I still here? I told you I didn't know what you wanted to know. What do you want from me?"

"To be honest, we established that you'd been telling us the truth some time ago. We so desperately hoped you could tell us who Colonel Hunter's Evangeline was. Once it became apparent that you were of no value in that regard, my superiors wanted you liquidated. Just one more loose end tied up."

"Then why haven't you killed me yet?"

Dr. Silvers leaned in closer. She stared me in the eyes. "Because you have such potential, Michael. You are an exceptional individual, and you've already done great things for our organization. Your record from Project Heartbreaker is phenomenal. The fact that you survived Gordon Willis' attempt to sanitize the operation speaks volumes about your abilities, to say nothing of the fact that you managed to track him down and kill him all on your own. All of that natural talent, that drive, needn't go to waste."

My eyes grew wide. I was afraid. The clouded memories, the strange impulses, the vivid dreams and lucid nightmares. "What . . . what the hell are you doing to me?"

Dr. Silvers smiled at me for the first time. "Nothing you didn't agree to when you signed your contract, Michael. I'm just protecting our investment."

"I hate you."

"I know. That will pass in time. You'll see."

Anger pulsed through me. Every muscle in my body tightened. "Someday, I'm going to kill you."

She gently placed a cold hand on my cheek, like a mother comforting an upset child. "I very much doubt that."

I drifted in darkness, not sure if I was asleep or awake, or even if I was alive or dead. Images passed through my mind, fragments of memories, out of order, disconnected, adrift. They were but moments in time, seemingly unrelated to one another, but somehow I knew they were all mine.

I saw my father when I was young. He was giving me a tour of his airplane, the massive B-52 he flew for the Air Force. I was sitting in his seat, the navigator's seat, marveling at all of the dials and buttons and screens, an anachronistic mix of three decades of technological development. Then I was standing in a cemetery, looking down on my father's grave. It was raining, and the little American flag placed on it had fallen over. I was repairing a fence line with my mother, on the back twenty acres of our farm. A tree had fallen over and broken one of our fence posts, tearing down the electric fence with it. I was a teenager, and I carried off pieces of the tree as she cut them with a chainsaw. She put the saw down, wiped her brow, and smiled. There was something wrong with her face. There was blood. Her eyes were locked open, wide, her face a mask in death. I tried to close my eyes and look away, but the moment was lost and the sadness faded with it.

I was lost in the darkness for a long time. Moments of my life came and went, each time growing blurrier, more distant, until it felt like I was watching someone else's life.

I was sitting on a couch next to Sarah. She was playing video games against Tailor in Zubara. She was better at them than I was, and Tailor was getting increasingly, comically irritated, and kept insisting that girls weren't supposed to be good at video games. Hudson and Wheeler were there, laughing, making fun of Tailor just to get him riled up. I looked over at her as she concentrated on the screen, and my heart moved. She was gorgeous, and she didn't know it. She thought her nose was too big and was self-conscious about it. She worried about her appearance, but she was beautiful, and I loved her.

From the back of the van, I watched helplessly as Sarah shot a Zubaran soldier through the window. The soldier fired too. Wheeler was hit. The Zubaran solider died.

Wheeler died too. He was slumped over the steering wheel, unmoving. Sarah looked at me, as if asking me to do something, to fix it, but there was nothing to be done.

She was in my arms, warm and soft, I held her tightly, and I was afraid. I was afraid we'd never leave Zubara alive. I was afraid that I'd be the death of her, like I seemed to be for everyone else in my life. I wanted to push her away, tried to push her away, but my heart couldn't bear it.

She stayed with me. She stayed with me and it cost her life. It was raining. We were running. Gunfire was coming from every direction. I was hit in the leg and I fell. Sarah stopped and turned, coming back for me. I screamed at her to keep going, but she didn't listen. She was hit. I crawled to her, but she was already dead. There was blood. I wanted to die with her. I was ready to die. It was my time. In that moment I felt relief, as if a great weight had been lifted from my soul. It was over.

Somehow I could see myself, from above, like I was flying above my own body. My clothing was muddy and torn. Sarah's body was next to mine. My arm reached out for her, but she was too far away. There was someone else then, a dark figure moving quickly, pulling me away from Sarah.

Lorenzo. I met him again, but I couldn't remember when or where. We fought together later, I dimly recalled. We shared something, a bond that kept our fates lashed together. Death followed us everywhere we went. It took everyone around us, but kept passing us over. If anyone deserved to die more than me, it was Lorenzo. But somehow, we both managed to survive. It wasn't fair. It wasn't right. But even though I was ready to die, even though I promised Sarah I'd stay with her until the end, Lorenzo saved my life. I hated him for it.

My body moved slightly, and I became aware of it once again. I was still immersed in the darkness, but I retained my corporeal form. I felt warmth on my back as I slowly gained awareness. I realized I was laying on my back. It was like that fleeting, lucid moment between sleeping and awake, when you can still see your dreams but know they're not real.

A woman was singing quietly. I couldn't make out the words, but the voice was familiar. It was Ling. Ling was singing, not for me so much as for herself, but I remember clinging to the sound once. She was pulling me up by my vest, helping me out of a wrecked helicopter. She was standing in pale light in an empty construction site, her dark eyes impossible to read. She was standing over me when I awoke on a ship. The wind was in her hair as she sat on a rock, with the ocean crashing ashore behind her. *I wonder where she is?* The singing faded quickly. The images grew blurry. Her voice was gone, replaced with the hum of the machine and the sound of water going down a drain. A noise resonated somewhere in the distance, and suddenly I felt cold. I began to shiver.

The light was blinding. It appeared suddenly, white light so bright it hurt my eyes. My face and ears burned as the mask was pulled off my head. My eyes wouldn't focus, and I could barely move, but I could hear again.

"Dr. Silvers! D . . . Dr. Silvers!" Neville whined. I hated the sound of his voice. "Look at these numbers!"

"I can see them from here," Dr. Silvers sounded tired. "Wait . . . is he conscious?"

Neville sounded pensive. "He shouldn't be. I don't see . . . oh my. Yes, he's definitely awake."

I tried to sit up. Neville gasped. Dr. Silvers called for the guards, and I was pushed back into the tank. Exhausted, confused, blind, and in pain, I let myself slip from consciousness. I had nothing left in me.

A fleeting thought passed through my mind, a surge of anger so intense it startled me: *I'm going to kill you all.*

You're a natural born killer, boy.

Chapter 4: Golden Manatee Nights

LORENZO
Tickville, Montana
February 13th

The shadow government had a nickname: *Majestic*. They even used it for themselves like some sort of in-joke. I saw that name over and over as I pored through the information Reaper had sent me. Much of it came from the information Valentine had given to Bob the year before and it was borderline crazy town. If I hadn't been reading leaked classified documents, I'd have assumed it was all a bunch of bullshit.

Reaper was giddy with excitement. He still religiously listened to that late-night conspiracy theory radio show, *From Sea to Shining Sea,* and having me be forced to seriously entertain such things was simply awesome for him. I had to hang up on him so I could concentrate.

Picture the government, by the people, for the people, all that crap. Picture it as a body, made up of cells that were bureaucrats and elected officials. Each cell had a job. Sometimes the cells were replaced, but the body stayed about the same, except this one just kept getting bigger and fatter. Now picture Majestic as a cancer invading the body, slowly but steadily spreading. A black shadow on an X-ray, a secret conspiracy of very powerful people, steering that body to accomplish secret goals. Ever since the Zubaran coup there had been hearings, trials, special prosecutors. Thanks to Bob's data dump, people had been fired, and a few had even been sent to prison—and mostly pardoned—but the cancer was still there. Who were they really? Who did they work for? What were their goals?

Beats the hell out of me. Ling, with all of the intelligence assets of the Exodus organization at her disposal, didn't know any more than I did. I guess it didn't really matter. I had a job to do one way or another.

Lucky for us, my brother had managed to gather a lot of info about where Valentine was being held. It was obvious to me that Bob had help. You don't have that long a career in Army Special Forces and then the FBI without making some contacts. He'd managed to get us the location, a list of assigned personnel, almost everything except a prisoner list. I suspected there was no prisoner list. Even bureaucrats didn't like to make lists of people who weren't supposed to exist.

This particular corner of Majestic's invisible kingdom was a secret prison and interrogation center. North Gap was a desolate little radar base dating back to the early Cold War. Now it was staffed by about two dozen people, with a cover story about it being a weather research facility for the National Oceanic and Atmospheric Administration.

Bob's FBI file indicated that he had been reprimanded for demanding to speak to some of the people held here. Apparently they didn't like when people rocked their boat.

Back in Quagmire, Bob had warned me about the guys that made up this organization. Gordon Willis' men had been the dregs of law enforcement and military service. Men too violent, unstable, amoral, or crazy to work in a normal system, but still capable and having valuable skills. The staff at the North Gap facility seemed to be cut from the same cloth. Most of them were former employees of the Bureau of Prisons or different police agencies, kicked out for various reasons. Our target tonight was no different. Roger Smoot had been a prison guard, with allegations of multiple assaults, rapes, and possibly even murders of female inmates. Yet before the official inquires had concluded, Smoot had been whisked off the radar by Majestic and given a new job.

We had picked Smoot for two reasons. He was approximately my size and build, and in an afternoon of poking around Tickville, Montana, we had found out that he usually spent his evenings at a local dive of a bar called the Golden Manatee. What would possess anyone to name an establishment that, I can't say. There was a yellow neon blob above the entrance that I think was supposed to be a manatee.

Tickville was a pimple of a town which served one purpose. It gave the local oil roughnecks a place to get drunk, blow their money, and find some action. That was pretty much the basis of the economy and the Golden Manatee was the highlight of Tickville culture.

It was snowing as we pulled into the parking lot of the

Golden Manatee. Our stolen ten-year-old Ford Taurus station wagon fit in reasonably well with the beat-up pickup trucks and other crappy cars in the parking lot. Even with the heater on full blast, I was still painfully chilled to the bone. I had gotten used to a constant temperate weather for the last year, and Tickville in February isn't close to St. Carl at any time of the year.

We made our way inside. Ling drew the attention of every man in the place from the moment she walked in. I could tell she didn't like being the center of attention, and was already in a foul mood when we sat at the bar.

I tried to listen to the nearest conversations, trying to get a feel for the place. Some Department of the Interior administrator, who had probably never lived anyplace that wasn't completely paved, had recently put five thousand men out of work in this area with the stroke of a pen, killing drilling on federal lands in order to protect *pristine wilderness*, and you could feel the resulting surliness in the air. As somebody who lived his life off the grid and avoided authority, I wasn't exactly an expert on domestic policy, but anybody who thought it was a better idea to buy their oil and give tons of money to monsters like Adar, General-turned-President Al Sabah, and the Prince instead of the folks in Tickville was a fucking imbecile.

For the first hour we sat there, Ling kept her long coat on, and tried not to draw attention to herself. Even so, she'd been hit on or offered drinks by one knucklehead after another. Her patience was wearing thin, and I found it hilarious.

"He'll be here soon," I said calmly as I swirled the straw in my five-dollar, watered-down bar Coke.

"And if he doesn't come tonight?" she asked. I had to struggle to hear her over the distorted country music blasting from the jukebox. In one corner of the bar was a game where drunks could sock a punching bag to test their strength. It made a ridiculous amount of racket, even louder than the music.

"Then we come back *tomorrow.*" I didn't like Ling's attitude. She thought *she* was in a hurry? It was my brother who needed help. If Valentine rotted in a secret jail forever, it really wouldn't hurt my tender feelings. "Hey, look on the bright side," I said, trying to lighten the mood. "They've got punch cards. Ten dinners here, and you get a free basket of mozzarella sticks."

"As if you could make it ten times without contracting botulism . . . Look, Mr. Lorenzo, I can tell you don't like this any more than I do." She was trying to sound more diplomatic.

"True. I normally prefer more time to plan. A job like this? I would probably watch the target for weeks, get to know his mannerisms, the way he talks, the way he sounds. This is going to be a challenge."

There was a loud crash near the jukebox. Two men had gotten into a fight over the music. The guy voting for Lynyrd Skynyrd won by knocking the other guy over, toppling a small table and some stools in the process. The bar patrons cheered and laughed. Since nobody was squirting blood, the lady running the place didn't seem to care.

A few minutes later, a big man shuffled up and sat at the bar next to Ling. He wore a flannel shirt with the sleeves cut off. His face was covered in a short beard, but his head was shaved. His arms were covered in intricate tattoos, including a big one of Captain Morgan striking his famous, trademarked pose. *Classy.*

"Hey, pretty lady," the Captain said. "Buy you a beer?"

It was all I could do to not laugh at the look of revulsion on Ling's face, but she quickly hid it. She shook her head at him, sort of giggling, putting on the *shy Asian schoolgirl* bit. "No, thank you." *Giggle.*

Captain Morgan was undaunted, and it was plain to see he considered himself a smooth operator. "C'mon, baby. We don't get too many oriental women here. Where you from?"

"I am from China," she said, her accent suddenly thick. "Preeze, I have drink with my friend." She looked up at me while lacing her arm around mine, wearing a big fake grin.

"Fine, snooty bitch," El Capitan said, shooting me an evil look. "I'll see *you* later, cocksucker." He spat, pointing a crooked finger at me.

I rubbed my hands across my face. "Thanks a lot," I said to her, not looking up.

"I apologize for that. It would complicate things if I had that *zhu tou* pawing over me when the target walked in," Ling said over the sounds of "Sweet Home Alabama." She grabbed the glass in front of her and pounded it down in one gulp. "I'm really not such a prude, Mr. Lorenzo. It's just . . . I am often in a bad mood before a mission, because I worry about my team and have much on my mind. Now I'm worried about Valentine as well." She signaled the bartender, who came by and poured her another shot.

I watched the door. More people were piling in, but still no Smoot. Shen and Antoine were parked outside. For some reason I figured a 6'6" West African and Jet-freakin'-*Li* would stick out a bit. I was dressed like the other patrons, lots of flannel and denim, and could easily blend in with the crowd.

"Yeah, I've been meaning to ask you something."

Ling waited, staring at her reflection in the dirty bar mirror. She was wearing too much purple eyeliner and tacky lipstick. I had helped her with her makeup—don't laugh, I'm a professional.—It's not that she couldn't do it herself, it was just that when she did it, it was *tasteful*. "Yes?" she asked, looking not at me, but over my shoulder, studying the crowd.

"Level with me here. What's the story with you and the kid? This is personal for you, isn't it?"

Her gaze shifted so that she was looking me in the eyes. I could tell that my question had surprised her. "I . . . I owe him my life. I've helped him before. I helped him escape Zubara. He was very badly injured and nearly died. I was there when he woke up and remembered that the woman he loved had died."

Her name was Sarah and I'd watched her die. Around her neck had been an ancient key that I'd needed, and I'd risked my life to grab it. Instead of leaving Valentine to die there with her, I'd dragged him to safety. I didn't know if Ling knew that, but now wasn't the time for storytelling. Besides, there was more to her story than that. My gut told me Ling had feelings for the kid. There wasn't any point in asking about that. It didn't matter, for one thing, and she probably wouldn't admit it, for another.

"He's here," Ling said, looking at the door, eyes narrowing. Standing in the doorway was our target, one Roger Smoot.

Smoot had a shock of red hair. His face was also red from the cold, and he had the huge capillary-strewn nose of a man who drank too much. His beady eyes surveyed the crowd, looking for fun or trouble, or maybe both. A couple of regulars shouted at him from one of the pool tables, daring him to throw down some money on a game. Smoot waved back and headed their way.

"He's armed." Smoot had something bulky under his jacket. "Strong side hip. Give him a minute to settle in. Don't make this too sudden, or he'll get suspicious. Don't make it too easy for him." Ling pulled off her coat and handed it to me. She ran her fingers through her hair and adjusted her top, so she looked more . . . *perky*. Ling really was hot, and she apparently knew how to work what she had. "Err . . . never mind. You ready?"

"Of course. Honestly, Mr. Lorenzo, do you think this is the first time I've executed a honeypot? It doesn't mean I have to like it." Ling flashed me a warm, sultry smile that almost fooled me. She slammed down her third shot in one gulp, then slid off the bar stool with catlike grace. She stalked toward the pool tables to the sound of Steppenwolf's "Magic Carpet Ride"—I was really glad the classic rock guy had won that fight. Ling's transformation was amazing, and every set of eyes in the room locked onto her.

So much for blending in. I'm afraid Ling was a little too much for poor little Tickville. The only way we were going to pull this off was if Smoot was, in fact, as stupid as his file suggested he was. I watched as Ling threw down a twenty and joined the game of pool.

Ling was good. Within fifteen minutes she was acting

like she had had too much to drink, was bending over the pool table with a little too much enthusiasm, and was now Smoot's best friend. Smoot seemed to be enjoying himself, and I caught him giving one of his buddies a high five behind Ling's back. I had to admire her professionalism.

Smoot's file listed ten different accusations of extremely violent behavior against incarcerated women. I felt no guilt in unleashing Ling on him. After *impressing* Ling with his charm and mad pool skills, she returned to the bar and retrieved her coat. She was smiling, laughing, waving back at him.

"He is revolting. We're going to the motel," she muttered under her breath before going back to her new special friend.

Ling and Smoot left. A blast of winter air snaked across the bar before the door closed behind them. I waited a moment, then followed. Shen and Antoine would pick me up in front and then we'd tail Smoot back to Ling's place, which, in this case, was a cheap motel we had picked because it was mostly empty and had a poorly lit parking lot. I had no doubt Ling could handle herself, but her men didn't like the idea of leaving their commander alone with a rapist any longer than they had to.

The jukebox changed to Black Sabbath. *Good stuff.* I hadn't gone by the name of Ozzie during the time I worked with Switchblade for nothing.

Evil minds that plot destruction
Sorcerers of death's construction

I hummed along as I gently moved through the crowd. We had lots of work to do tonight so I was a little preoccupied. I froze when a hand landed on my shoulder.

"Where you think you're goin', shitface?" It was Captain Morgan, and he was drunker and braver than when Ling had insulted his manhood by refusing his offer of a beer. "You're friends with that oriental bitch.".

"Hey, man, she blew me off too. Let me buy you a beer," I turned around, all smiles. The Captain's hand curled around the collar of my flannel shirt. "Man, I love this song. Don't you love this song?"

Now in darkness, world stops turning
As the war machine keeps burning

"You think I'm stupid? I saw you talking. Thinking she's all too good for me? Then she leaves with that fuck head? Like he's better than me?" He was shouting now. A couple of other guys stood behind him, obviously his friends, grinning stupidly. "And you, you little prick. I never seen you 'round here before. Where the fuck do you get off comin' in here and stealin' all the pussy?"

And here we go. Years of experience told me how this was going to turn out.

"Didn't Patrick Swayze beat you up in *Road House*?"

The Captain's brow scrunched in drunk confusion. "Huh?" Then in drunk anger. "Oh, you wanna dance, boy? You think you're tough?"

It doesn't matter what country you're in. There are places like the Golden Manatee everywhere and the inhabitants are always the same. The adrenaline began to flow as Ozzie got to my favorite part of "War Pigs."

Day of judgment, God is calling
On their knees, the war pigs crawling
Begging mercy for their sins
Satan laughing spreads his wings

"All right now," I said, as I grabbed the hand on my shirt, dropped my elbow, and bowed my head. The Captain screamed as the pressure hit his wrist. He went right to his knees. "I don't want any trouble," I said calmly. He reached into his pocket with his other hand and pulled out a knife. *Idiot.*

I levered his arm and snapped his wrist before stepping back and kicking him in the face. I was wearing heavy work boots to fit in with the crowd, and the steel toe removed his front teeth.

"He hit Chet!" someone shouted. *This asshole looks like a Chet.* One of Captain Chet's friends charged me. I ducked the clumsy blow, and brought my knee into his stomach. The moose kept going, and went head first into the pool table.

"The Mexican broke my arm!" Chet screamed from the floor. I suppose all brown people look the same to guys like Chet. "Help me, Timbo!"

A giant of a man stood up from a nearby table, dumping the two girls sitting on his lap to the floor. "Who hit my little brother?" He bellowed. That had to be Timbo, and he was bigger than my old buddy Train, bigger than Bob, bigger than Antoine, like *holy shit, that's one big motherfucker* big.

"The Mexican!" the Captain cried, pointing his good arm at me. *So much for low profile.*

"Come on, boys, let's get him!" Timbo said. Half a dozen other brutes stood up from their tables. The number-one sport in Tickville was whooping ass, and it looked like I was playing for the visiting team.

The sound of a shotgun getting a shell pumped into the

chamber was loud enough to hear over the jukebox. All eyes fixated on the owner, a heavyset, surly-looking, middle-aged woman named Betty. "Take it outside, Timbo!" she ordered. "You wreck my place one more time and I swear to Christ I'll have the sheriff lock you up for a month!"

I'm a tough guy, but I'm a lot smarter than I am tough. While everyone was distracted by Betty's shotgun, I sprinted for the door, ducked an eight ball that somebody chucked at me from the pool table, knocked down a waitress, "Sorry!" and was out the door. A bottle shattered on the door frame next to me. *So long, suckers.*

Then I collided with two more big guys coming in from the snow. "Watch it, asshole." One grimy hand latched onto my left coat sleeve.

"Sorry," I replied, as I tried to shove past them.

"Grab him, Frank!" Timbo yelled from inside the Golden Manatee. "He beat up Chet!"

"He didn't beat me up!" the Captain protested, cradling his damaged arm. "He suckered me with some kung fu shit! Hold that son of a bitch!"

"You got it, bro," said Frank as he squeezed my arm.

How many brothers does this asshole have? I clamped onto Frank's hand with my right, levered my left elbow up and over, and broke his forearm. His head dipped down and intercepted with my knee at a remarkable velocity. I pulled away, dodged a wild swing from the other guy, started to run, and slipped in the snow. I hit the ground hard, scrambling to get away.

The crew from the Golden Manatee was piling out now, chanting, "Fight! Fight! *Fight!*" Except for Frank, who started screaming when he realized the floppy lump inside his forearm was a bone.

I felt a hand the size of a canned ham clamp onto my collar, lift me effortlessly, and toss me onto the hood of a nearby pickup. Timbo was strong.

"He broke two of our guys' arms! Who's gonna run the pumps on Monday?"

"Two arms? *This guy*'s got two arms. Eye for a tooth, asshole!" Timbo shouted. He was a biblical scholar too. I rolled to the side as he clubbed a dent into the hood of the truck. I landed on my hands and knees, kicked out, and connected my boot with his shin. "*Aaarrgh!*"

"He kicked Timbo!" There was a collective gasp from the crowd. They had fanned out, and now I was completely surrounded. Apparently, nobody was allowed to hit Timbo, because the circle was closing on me rapidly.

"There a problem here, gentlemen?" Antoine's voice boomed over the crowd, muted slightly in the drifting snow. Shen stood slightly to his side, arms loose and ready. Their breath formed steam halos around their heads.

"Me and Master Blaster here just had a little disagreement is all," I said.

"Why don't you all step away from my friend?" Antoine's tone made it clear that this wasn't a polite suggestion. He didn't look like a man to trifle with. He cracked his knuckles loudly.

Timbo was squatting, rubbing his ankle furiously. "Well, looks like we're about to have us a good old-fashioned rumble. We got a wetback, a nigger, and a . . . a . . ."

"Chink?" Shen supplied helpfully.

"Yeah. A *chink*! Get 'em, boys!" Timbo ordered.

A pair of burly-looking black men, more oil workers by the look of them, appeared behind Timbo. "What the fuck did you just say, cracker?" One of them socked one of Timbo's friends in the side of the head and pandemonium ensued.

"Don't kill any of them!" I shouted at Antoine. I had serious doubts that we were sticking with the low-profile plan at this point. I think Timbo thought I was pleading for my friend's lives. He couldn't have been more wrong. He grinned at me evilly, and charged.

Then it was on like a bad episode of *The A-Team*. There were eight of the locals against the three of us. Behind them, a dozen other locals brawled with each other, with more and more roughnecks running to join the fight, crew on crew, hitting people without even knowing what was going on. The parking lot of the Golden Manatee had turned into a rumble.

Shen got a running start, and slid through the snow, right into the leading pair of roughnecks. His hands were moving so fast it was hard to track. One of the men doubled over gagging and the next stumbled back, holding his nose, blood streaming between his fingers. Antoine was right behind. He caught one fist sailing toward Shen, spun the man off the ground, and tossed him a good ten feet into the tailgate of a truck. It rocked on impact.

I was on Timbo like white on rice. He was powerful, but he was sloppy and untrained. I moved between his arms and started hitting him. I hit him in the eyes, the nose, he kept moving back, trying to make room to swing. I kept on him, all knees and elbows, not wanting to break my hands. It was nonstop punishment. Timbo was a giant punching bag.

A worker took a swing at Antoine and hit him right in the face. Antoine swayed back slightly, and smiled, actually smiled, before he punched the man once. The blow made a sound like a bat hitting a watermelon and the man collapsed into the snow. Shen went after the next man, spin-kicked him in the sternum, and followed up with a flurry of blows to the face before he even had a chance to fall down. These guys were brawlers. Shen and Antoine killed slavers and warlords for a living. The last fighters took a look at the two of them beating the shit out their friends, then turned and ran. Apparently they were the smart ones.

Timbo was swooning now, blood rushing out of his nose, his mouth, and one ear. "Fall down already!" He finally got enough distance to launch one of those haymakers, but I was faster and kicked him on his inner thigh. He toppled over as his leg went numb, femoral artery temporarily stopped, making a noise like a felled tree.

The locals cheered and continued to brawl with each other. There were now probably twenty-five men beating the hell out of each other in the parking lot and it had spilled out into the street. I looked down at Timbo, backed up a step, and punt-kicked him in the ribs. He bellowed and flopped over, looking like some sort of injured walrus, or, well, I suppose *manatee* would be more appropriate. The others that attacked us were lying in the snow, moaning, whimpering, one man was vomiting from where Shen had punched him in the stomach, and another was actually, literally, crying for his mother.

All three of us grinned at each other. Nothing like a fist-fight for a team-building exercise. These Exodus guys were actually kind of fun to hang out with.

"Better go before the cops get here." I was surprised to discover that I was totally out of breath. It had been awhile since I had gotten my violence on.

"Are you okay?" Shen asked.

"It must be the altitude," I answered.

"Americans," Antoine lamented, shaking his head. "We must hurry!"

Antoine pulled our beat-up station wagon into a dark spot in the motel parking lot. We had rented three rooms on the far edge of the building. Ling's was the one on the end, and the other two were a buffer zone, just in case we needed to make a little noise. Smoot's car was parked in front of the last room and the lights were on inside. Luckily there were only a few other cars in the lot. The government plates told me which one was Smoot's ride.

"I'll go first."

"I'll come with you," Shen spoke from the backseat.

"Okay, Antoine, stay here."

"Very well," he said curtly. What could I say? I'd just watched this guy toss a full-grown man like a shot put. I assumed that being sneaky wasn't his specialty. I had disabled the interior lights, so it stayed dark when I opened the door. Shen nodded at his partner as we got out of the car and made our way toward the motel.

We had broken the bulbs in the overhang earlier that day so this end of the building was cloaked in darkness. We made no noise as we crept up to the window. I had to admit, Shen was pretty good. Not as quiet as me, but pretty damn sneaky. I risked a peek. Ling and our target were both sitting on the bed. Smoot stood up and walked into the bathroom. I signaled Shen to wait at the entrance. He squatted in the shadows.

I pulled my key card and unlocked the door. The door creaked slightly as I slipped through, carefully testing the carpeted floor before I let my boot touch down. We had planned for inadvertent noise, and Ling had turned up the radio. She was sitting on the bed, glancing at her watch. I could hear Smoot talking in the attached bathroom.

"Yeah, I can't really talk about what I do. You know how it is with government work."

"That is *so* exciting," Ling answered, playing up her accent, sounding again like the stereotypical naïve, passive, easily-impressed Asian schoolgirl. She saw me in the doorway. I gave her a thumbs up and started slowly into the bedroom. Ling mouthed the words *about time*. I heard the faucet shut off. *Damn it, he's coming back.* The closet door was slightly open, so I ducked inside, trying not to rattle the hangers.

The closet door was the slatted kind, and I could peer through it. Smoot came back into the room, now not wearing a shirt, and placed his gun on the night stand. Ling made a show of staring at the Glock 23 all wide-eyed.

"Don't let that thing intimidate you, baby. I take care of bad guys with that. See, that's the kind of thing I do. 'Sides, I got an even *bigger* gun to show you." He laughed and sat on the bed beside Ling, facing away from me. "So whaddaya say, baby?"

He put his bulbous nose against her neck. Ling looked

right at the closet door, and mouthed the word *now*. I had
to admit that I didn't attack because I was enjoying her
discomfort. It was payback for getting me into that bar
fight. I'm a bad man.

"The fact I'm a highly-trained badass scares people, but
don't worry, we're safe here. Just relax." Ling looked like
she was about to vomit. She mouthed the word *now* again.
Smoot sloppily kissed her neck, and pulled one of the
spaghetti straps down over her shoulder. She narrowed her
eyes, and said "Now," out loud.

"Okay, baby, don't worry," Smoot said happily. "You
want it now, we can do that." Ling's dark eyes flashed, and
she pushed him away. "*Rowr*," he said. "So you like it
rough? You are a dirty little . . . *HURRK*!" Smoot's voice
was cut off in a gurgle as Ling smashed him in the throat
with the knife ridge of her hand. He rose, hands clutching
his throat, gagging, as Ling spun, her tiny denim skirt riding
high, and kicked him in the side of the head.

"Oh shit!" I exclaimed from inside the closet at the
spectacular impact of her heel to Smoot's skull. Smoot hit
the bed, eyes rolled back, totally out. Shen leapt into the
room, having heard the noise, and ready to take down the
target. Ling pushed the spaghetti-strap back over her
shoulder.

"*Now* would be a good time, Mr. Lorenzo!" she
snapped, glaring at me through the slats on the closet door.

I fell out of the closet laughing. Ling cursed in Chinese,
turned on her heel, and stormed into the bathroom,
slamming the door behind her. Shen looked at me,
obviously confused, and he seemed unable to find anything
to say.

Chapter 5: My Funny Valentine

LORENZO
North Gap, Montana
February 14th
0400 Hours

I was exhausted. Preparations had taken all night, another downside of this sort of rush job. Normally I would have taken weeks to prepare my disguise, to converse with the target, learning their speech patterns, their mannerisms, the quirks that make them who they are. Usually by the time I'm ready to impersonate someone, I've become that person. Give me enough time and I could fool their own mother. Today, I'd be lucky to not get shot at the first checkpoint.

Smoot's uniform was just a touch too big, but there was no time to tailor it so that it would fit me exactly like it had fit him. The black BDUs had been in a duffle bag in the back seat of the government Chevy Tahoe.

The heater was running full blast, but I was still freezing. The road to the radar station was winding, and there was a sheer drop off one side of the mountain if you happened to hit a patch of unexpected ice. The wipers beat a steady cadence to keep off the steadily falling snow.

"Don't let that thing intimidate you. Don't let *that thing* intimidate you," I coughed, that didn't sound right. "Don't let that thing intimidate you." His accent had been Irish, Boston, but not thick. He hadn't lived there for a long time. *Don't lay it on. Clip the words faster.* "Don't let *that thing intimidate* you."

I checked my face in the rearview mirror. I wasn't happy. The molds had barely had time to cool for the latex nose and chin, the hair color wasn't quite the right shade of red, and even with makeup, my skin tone was a little too dark to match his pasty complexion. It takes experimentation to get things like that perfect, and I didn't have time to experiment.

This is never going to work.

I had spent half the night interrogating Smoot. He thought it was to gather intelligence about the security at the North Gap facility. That was only partly true. Mostly I was listening to how he talked, how he acted, to get a sense of him as a person. Of course, it was always better to observe a subject in their natural environment. Unfortunately, zip-tied to a chair with Shen occasionally hitting you is not a natural environment.

To say that Roger Smoot was a dirtbag was an insult to honest, decent bags of dirt. Getting inside his head had made me want to take a shower. His laptop had been in his car, filled with every weird, deviant, sicko thing you could think of. Unfortunately, there weren't very many job opportunities for me to pretend to be a decent human being.

The headlights cut a swath through the darkness. An old sign indicted that I was only three miles from the radar station.

This is it.

My phone buzzed. "Go."

"Hey, it's me."

"Jill?" I was surprised. I had been expecting Ling to check in to tell me they would be pulling off to await my signal. It was good to hear her voice, but right now I needed to get into character. "What's going on?"

"You didn't call me back last night. I just wanted to make sure you were okay." Her voice cut out as she spoke. I barely had any signal.

"Sorry. I'm fine. I had a lot of stuff to take care of last night." Like kidnapping, torture, etc. "I don't have much time. I've got to go. I'm about to go get the kid. I'll call you when I can."

"Okay, be careful. Please." She was tough, but I could hear the nervousness in her voice.

"I love you, Jill. I'll be fine."

"Okay, you better be, and happy Valentine's Day."

"Oh, I forgot. I'll do something nice for you when I get home."

"I love you, Lorenzo." The line went dead.

Valentine's Day. Hi-fucking-larious.

There was a guard shack at the end of the road. A hydraulic gate blocked the entrance. There was a chain link fence running around the entire property, but the real security was the host of motion detectors and thermal cameras. If Exodus had launched an attack, they would have been spotted miles away, and that probably would have ended with Valentine getting a preemptive bullet to the brain.

I stopped the Tahoe in front of the gate. The lights were on inside the shack, and a man dressed in black fatigues looked up from the flashing glare of a TV screen.

Plan A was to pass for Roger Smoot. Plan B was to pull my suppressed pistol from under the seat and shoot this man in the face. I was really rooting for Plan A. I rolled down the window. A jet of freezing air flooded the car as the intercom buzzed.

"Hey, man. How was leave?" he sounded bored. I didn't recognize the guard from any of the personnel files, but we had no idea how up to date those were.

"Dude . . ." I could tell Smoot was a braggart, a jerk, and in his mind, a ladies' man. "I totally scored with this hot chick. You should have seen her. Young, Asian, stacked like you wouldn't believe."

"In Tickville? Fuck you, you did not." He shook his head. The gate started to rise. I waved, and put the SUV back into drive. Suddenly, the gate stopped. The intercom buzzed again. "Hey, wait a second . . ." I placed my hand on the grip of my STI 9mm and mentally shifted to Plan B.

"Yeah?"

"You still owe me fifty bucks from poker night, asshole."

I let go of my gun, raised my hand, and flipped him the bird. "I'll pay you when I pay you! Now open the goddamn gate. I'm gonna be late." He laughed, and the gate rose. I stepped on it.

My headlights illuminated a few old dilapidated houses. Cookie-cutter, cheap base housing. A deer leapt across the road, and I had to admit that my nerves were wound tight enough, that it startled me.

I pulled my phone. "Ling. I'm in."

"Copy. We're at the bottom of the hill."

"There's one man in the guard shack. I couldn't see what kind of weapons. The glass wasn't thick enough to be bulletproof."

"Godspeed, Lorenzo." Ling's voice cut out.

Interrogating Smoot had showed me that there was no way I was going to get any weapons or electronic devices into the building. The Glock that Smoot had been carrying was personally-owned. I was going to leave it in the truck because everybody, even the guards, got checked at the entrance. Their duty weapons were stored in a locker inside.

The main building dated back to the early '50s. It was a three-story building, ugly and imposing, with very few windows. There were a couple of large radar dishes on the roof, and one giant revolving ball radar that had been rusted solid for decades. There was a second chain link fence around the building, only this fence was topped with razor wire. I parked next to the other cars took a deep breath, and stepped out into the cold.

Whatever is in Valentine's head better be worth it, Bob, because I'm freezing my ass off out here.

There was a single gate in the fence. There was another intercom, a keypad, and a camera that was looking right down at me. I pushed the intercom button.

"Identify," the bored voice said. The camera made a mechanical noise as it tracked on me.

"Roger Smoot."

"Enter your password." I typed in the four-digit number that Smoot had indicated. Since I had been rather persuasive, I was relatively sure that he had finally given me the right number. The light blinked green. *Good serial rapist*.

"Stand by for thumbprint scan."

Smoot had said that sometimes the electronics weren't very reliable when it was below freezing. "Hurry up, man. It's cold out here." I dramatically shoved my hands into the pockets of my black fatigues, and found the cold lump waiting for me. The box lit up, I pulled the thing out of my pocket and smashed it against the pad. The pad blinked twice as it scanned the print, and the gate unlocked.

I pushed the gate open and shuffled toward the main entrance. Somebody had shoveled and thrown down salt, causing a layer of cold slush to form. A heavy-set, jowly man in a black uniform and a coyote-brown gun belt opened the security door for me.

"You're late."

"I'm hung over too," I followed him in and nonchalantly tossed Smoot's severed thumb in the snow behind me. He wouldn't be missing it.

VALENTINE

There was a dull throb in the back of my head as the ceiling slowly came into focus. I didn't move. My muscles were cramped and I ached all over. I was dizzy and nauseated on top of it. My heart was racing, as if I'd woken from a bad dream. It's a hell of a thing, waking up and realizing you're still in the nightmare.

But I was still in my cell, so that's how it was. I had long since given up hope that this particular nightmare would ever end. I didn't move, didn't attempt to get up because I had no reason to. Why bother? What did I have to gain from getting up?

Whatever else Dr. Silvers' machines, methods, and drugs were doing to me, having to relive the nightmares of my past were the worst. So much death. So many dead faces, blankly staring at me, silently accusing me.

The ache wasn't as bad as it had been last time. I didn't know. I didn't care. A sense of ambivalence had overtaken me. It was more than ambivalence, it was apathy. I just didn't give a damn anymore. Whatever Dr. Silvers was doing to me, it was working. I couldn't even muster the will to sit up. My grasp was slipping. The painful memories were still painful, but more distant now. It was like being *Calm,* but all the time. As I lay there in the dark, I idly wondered what would happen to me if I let go entirely.

Just lay here and die, I thought. *No one would blame you. No one will ever know. You've already been forgotten.* I grew angry at the thought. So angry my body felt hot, like I was burning with a fever. My hands balled into fists, my jaw clenched. A singular, overwhelming impulse filled my consciousness: *kill them all.*

The fog in my mind cleared as I seethed, and I became more aware of my surroundings. *Wait a minute. The lights are off.* The surge of anger subsided somewhat, and my muscles relaxed. I didn't realize it before, but the lights were off in my cell. They never turned the lights off. The maddening buzz of the fluorescent tubes had ceased. The only light came from under the door to the hall. Had the tubes finally burned out? They'd been on, constantly, from the first moment I'd been tossed into that cell. The darkness was strange, but comforting. My cell felt different. It was like hiding under the blankets when you're a little kid. I'd given myself up to the abyss, and I felt at home in it.

I blinked hard as the room spun. I'd never done drugs in my life. Never so much as puffed a joint. Now? I could only imagine the chemical concoctions that they were pumping through my body. If I thought I had any future, I'd have been deeply concerned about the long-term side effects. I actually made myself laugh out loud at that thought. *Holy hell, I'm going insane.*

"And to think we always said *I* was the Queen of Crazy Town."

The voice had come from the darkness, only a few feet away. Someone was sitting on the edge of my bed. I stayed perfectly still, breathing loudly though my nose, jaw clenched, as I tried to stave off panic. My earlier sense of detachment was replaced entirely with fear.

"It's okay," she said. The voice was familiar. Friendly. It came from nearby, but was at the same time distant. Like an echo, or a memory. I clenched my eyes shut as I realized the room was now very cold, like they'd left a window open or something. "Please," she insisted. "You can open your eyes. It's okay."

If I'm insane I might as well embrace it. I willed myself to sit up. The room spun so badly that I thought I was going to fall out of bed. It settled down after a moment.

In the dim light, I couldn't see much of her. An outline,

a shadow, more of a presence. But there was no doubt about it. It was her.

It was Sarah.

I looked down at the bed. I couldn't face her. I couldn't bear it. I just shook my head and tried to focus. "I . . . I missed you," I managed. The words came out as little more than a throaty whisper.

"I know," Sarah said. There was a sadness in her voice that hadn't been there before.

"I'm sorry I left you."

"You didn't. You stayed until the end, just like you said you would."

"I . . . what . . . what are you doing here?"

"A better question is, what are *you* doing here, Michael?"

I looked up at her. It was easier to see now. Her face was as I remembered it. Auburn hair cascaded over her shoulders. Her eyes were a luminescent green. I blinked hard to make sure I wasn't imagining it. She was still there when I opened my eyes. "Even for a ghost, you're being awfully cryptic."

Sarah smiled as she leaned closer. "Let go. Please, just let it all go. Let me go. You'll need to if you want to survive," she whispered into my ear. Then she pulled away. It was like she was fading into the darkness. "You don't have much time left."

"Sarah, wait!" The words were hollow in my empty cell. I was alone. I was sweating, breathing heavily. I was dizzy, shaking.

Oh, God. I buried my face in my hands. *Oh God, oh God. What are they doing to me? Is any of this even real?*

"Mr. Valentine, can I be honest with you for a moment? I'm a little disappointed in you right now." The new voice came from my right, from the far side of the room. I could just barely see someone standing there, nothing more than a shape, out of the corner of my eye.

Gordon?

The dark figure hung there, but I couldn't bring myself to look directly at him. A bead of sweat rolled down the side of my head. The room was too cold. The air was heavy and stale, oppressive, even.

"You had a great deal of potential," Gordon Willis said. "You still do. My former colleagues here certainly seem to have picked up on it. A lot of people would kill for some of the opportunities you're being presented with. Heh, no irony intended, of course."

"This isn't happening," I said aloud. "This isn't real. This isn't real." I clenched my eyes shut and brought my hands up over them again. "Oh God. It's not real. It's the drugs. It's just the drugs."

"You didn't mind your dead girlfriend visiting," Gordon sounded disappointed. "Maybe it's the drugs, maybe not . . . Maybe in that messed-up head of yours I represent Majestic and all it stands for, so I'm just here to gloat . . . I must admit, this isn't what I was expecting. Of course, I wasn't expecting you to murder me in my own home, either, so I guess you're just full of surprises." He laughed.

"Go away!" I screamed. "You're not real!"

"I don't know what to tell you about that. I'm trying to be straight with you here."

Even in death he was full of shit. "What do you want from me?" I asked, finally looking over at him. Gordon was leaning against the wall. His shirt collar was unbuttoned, and a designer tie hung loosely around his neck. Behind it was the dark and bloody wound where I'd shot him.

"You're a survivor, Val. You mind if I call you Val? Anyway, you're definitely a survivor. More than you can say for me, right?" He laughed at his own joke again. "So putting yourself in my shoes, you can probably understand my surprise at finding you like this. Not at all what I was expecting. You never struck me as a quitter."

Gordon got closer to me. I looked away and shut my eyes again. "This isn't happening," I repeated to myself. "It's the drugs. This isn't real. This isn't real." I held myself in my arms, rocking back and forth. "God, please, make it stop. It's not real. It's not real."

"There are things in motion now that can't be stopped. You can be a part of it or not. But you're better than this. You have a unique opportunity here. Don't let it pass you by."

"Leave me alone!" I jerked upright in bed. My eyes were wide, and I was covered in sweat. My heart was beating so hard that I could almost hear it. Slowly, very slowly, I looked around my room. I was alone. The lights were still off. I hadn't dreamt that part at least.

Even as Dr. Silvers' techniques and contrivances had torn me down, even as I wanted to just give up and die, a part of me still resisted. The more times they fed me to the machine, breaking down my will, the angrier I became. Two halves of my mind were at odds with each other. Even as I contemplated trying to kill myself, I darkly desired to kill Dr. Silvers, to kill Neville, to kill Reilly and Smoot and Davis and the rest. *To kill them all.* Each time they worked their horrors on me, I came out more broken, more disconnected, but at the same time stronger, angrier. Hatred and apathy battled for control of my will.

My head suddenly hurt, as if merely thinking about it was giving me a headache. What was happening to me? Was I going crazy? I could've sworn I actually heard an audible click as my brain shifted gears. The misery, the anger, the rage, the fear, the regret, it all coalesced, condensed into a tight little ball of determination. A familiar cold wave washed over my body then. The jumbled thoughts rapidly fluttering through my mind slowed and focused.

For the first time in a long time, I was *Calm*.

I'm getting out of this hole.

LORENZO

The first floor of the building had an entry control point, a break room, and lockers. The second floor was offices, though Smoot said they weren't used much. The top floor was the control center, which was where I needed to go to disable communications and shut down the security cameras. The basement was where the prisoners were held, and where the uglier side of what they did here went on. Smoot had told me all about the mind games.

"You look terrible," the guard said as he ran the metal detecting wand over me. He looked like an out-of-shape bull. There hadn't been a file on this one.

"I was up all night, if you know what I mean."

"Yeah, whatever, Roger. Grab your gear and head up to the control room."

Luckily he gestured in the direction of the locker room while he was talking. I walked away, trying to look casual. The interior was old and run down, a relic from the Cold War. The modern computers and equipment inside looked entirely out of place. I made my way to the security lockers Smoot had told me about. I found his locker and, using his key, opened it and took stock of his equipment.

Inside were several sets of the black fatigues. Body armor, holsters, a helmet, and other gear were all in coyote tan, which must've looked really stupid with black uniforms. I put on Smoot's duty belt, only to find it was a little too big for me. I had to quickly cinch it down so it wouldn't look off. I buckled it around my waist and grabbed his issue weapon, another Glock 23. There was a knife too, a CRKT folder. I tested the edge, found it relatively sharp, then stuck it in my pocket.

Smoot told us quite a bit about the operations at North Gap. He had considered it a shit detail. Apparently Majestic had several out-of-the-way places like this. Prisoners came and went, but Smoot insisted that there weren't that many currently being held here. All of them had been picked up domestically, and he never knew the why. He knew who Valentine was, since the Zubaran info dump had made him something of a celebrity, though he had no idea why he was still being held, nor did he care, hated the guy though. Valentine had once stabbed him in the knee with a pen. Smoot didn't like it when I'd laughed in his face about that. I have room to talk. Valentine had done worse to me. I still can't hear right in one ear, the bastard.

Lucky for me, not all of the staff would be on duty at any given time. They worked in shifts like anyone else, and most of them would be in their residences in the refurbished base housing, asleep. If things got loud, that would probably change in a hurry. Smoot said that there were always at least two guards in the basement level at all times. As a rule, no guns were allowed down there except under extreme circumstances. Only a moron would let somebody like Valentine anywhere near a firearm. A couple more men would be in the control room on the third floor. I found the elevator and made my way up.

The radar station was tapered, so that the top floor was not nearly as large as the bottom. There were windows at this level, but it was dark outside. There were several desks with computer monitors, and three bored-looking men in black fatigues. Bundles of cables were strung across the room. Screens for controlling and monitoring the security systems were mounted on one wall.

One of the guards was using the Mr. Coffee. The second was screwing around on Facebook, and the last one was actually doing his job and watching the camera feeds. Thankfully, none of them bothered to do more than glance in my direction.

"Smoot, what's up, dawg?" the one at the coffee machine asked. He was tall, skinny, and dark. I remembered his picture from the files. Local law enforcement background, until he'd lost it and beaten a prisoner to death. Perfect Majestic material. He had a complicated Slavic last name. I'd just think of him as Mr. Coffee.

"Hey." When you're trying to impersonate somebody,

it's best not to talk much. You don't want to give them much to work with. "'Sup?"

"You hear what happened to Randy?" the one reading Facebook asked. I drew a blank on him. "Guess what happened while you were on leave?"

"Uh . . ." I was scanning back and forth. I needed to kill their alarms. I didn't know what kind of response would happen when a secret prison that wasn't supposed to exist was attacked, and I didn't care to find out. There wouldn't be much time before one of these assholes realized I wasn't who I was supposed to be, and I didn't want to start shooting until I could disable the comms.

"Randy got temped to Arizona, where it's warm. They're actually giving him something interesting to do. Lucky son of a bitch."

"Oh?" There was a fuse box on the wall, an ancient metal monstrosity with heavy cables running into it. I could just kill the power to the entire building. That could work. In the far corner was a big locker. That had to be where the long guns were stored.

"Uh-huh. Apparently higher authority asked Silvers if she could spare somebody for an op down there, and she picked Randy. Some FBI puke was poking around in organization business, and then he disappeared."

Bob? "Okay."

"Nobody knows where this FBI dude went. He just dropped off the map. They've been watching his house, but he hasn't come home. His wife and kids are there, so they're gonna raid the place, have a few words with the family. I bet the organization's going to try to apply some *leverage*, if you follow me."

Everything just changed.

"Man, wish I could've gone," Mr. Coffee said, taking a sip. "Anything to get out of this shithole."

The guard at the monitors finally spoke. "Screw that noise. This job is a cak walk. Steady pay, free housing, and we don't actually do any work. I don't know what you vaginas are whining about."

I casually made my way over to the bank of screens, to see what he could see. The facility didn't have a huge number of cameras, but it had enough that Ling and her people wouldn't make it to the building undetected unless I did something.

Facebook Guy disagreed. "Dude, this place blows! It snows half the year, there's nothing to do in town, and we don't get any action!"

"Action? To hell with that," the monitor-watcher rebutted. "I was in the operations division for a while, until I got shot . . ." I recognized him from the files. *Frost.* Former Army, drummed out for criminal misconduct, then recruited by Majestic.

I studied the screens. Several of them showed prisoners in their cells. Most of them were sitting on their beds or on the floor, not doing anything interesting. The fourth cell was different. Unlike the others, it was dark, and the camera was on IR mode. The prisoner was sitting up in bed. It looked like he was talking to someone that wasn't there.

"What're you doing?" Frost asked.

"Valentine?" I nodded toward the bank.

Frost looked at the monitor I suspected, confirming I had the right man. "Yep. Your buddy. How's the knee, by the way?" he laughed.

I smiled like that was hilarious. "What's he doing?"

"Talking to himself," Frost suggested. "I don't know. Silvers made your boy down there her pet project. I don't know what she's doing to him, but he's fucked *up.*"

"Who cares?" Mr. Coffee whined. "I'm sick of sitting up here, freezing my dick off, watching Silvers play head games with the prisoners. I want to get out there and get some action. Maybe get laid once in a while." I casually made my way over to him, as if I was going to get a cup of coffee.

"You say that like it's fun and all until command screws up and you get your asses shot off," Frost said.

Mr. Coffee rebutted. "Frosty, nobody wants to hear your war stories again." Frost gave him a dirty look and went back to watching the screens. Mr. Coffee then popped me in the shoulder. "Now this guy, he's got a way with the ladies." He laughed. "They should have sent you to Arizona, dawg. You'd probably get that FBI guy's old lady to talk." He guffawed at his own humor.

My pulse was racing. I struggled to stay in character. "Booyah! You know it, dawg!" Smoot habitually said 'booyah.' In general, he talked like a douchebag, and anybody who said *booyah* and *dawg,* I had no problem sawing their thumbs off. "When are they doing it?"

"What?" Facebook guy finally looked up from his monitor. "Geezus, Smoot, you look like shit. You got gonorrhea again?"

"When are they raiding the house in Arizona?"

"Randy said tomorrow night. Why, you wanna beg Silvers and try and get in on it?" He took another sip from his mug. "You really itching to get out of here that bad?"

I started to laugh, laugh like Mr. Coffee had said the funniest goddamn thing in the world. Then I hit him, palm-struck him in the face. I smashed his coffee mug into his teeth and up his nose. His head snapped back in a splash of coffee, blood, spittle, and broken porcelain. Before he could react, I grabbed the back of his head and smashed his face into the desk.

"What the fuck!" Frost shouted, jumping up from his row of monitors, stunned that one of his friends had just brutalized the other.

Facebook Guy was staring at me, wide-eyed, from his chair. He was in shock, stammering for words. I didn't give him a chance to speak. I grabbed the pot of hot coffee and lobbed it at him as hard as I could. The pot shattered on his face, sending scalding hot coffee and broken glass into his eyes. He let out a blood-curdling, high-pitched scream, fell out of his chair, and clawed at his eyes.

Frost fumbled for his gun.

I was faster.

BLAM

The .40 round entered just below Frost's left eye and took the back of his head off.

Mr. Coffee was still dazed, trying to get off the desk. No need to make extra noise, Smoot's knife came out in a flash. I plunged it into his throat and slashed my arm outward. Mr. Coffee's eyes were wide with shock as he gurgled and choked on his own blood. He slid down the desk in a red smear as his life poured out, but I'd already turned my attention to Facebook Guy. He couldn't see and had panicked, ineffectually slapping at my hands until I stabbed him in the throat. His screams turned into a sickening gurgle. Warm blood spilled out of the wound, and he went limp. I stepped back, trying not to get too much of it on me.

I stood up, surveying the carnage in the control room. These motherfuckers were going after Bob's family. *My* family. A radio on Frost's desk beeped. "Control room! Report in! We heard a gunshot! Report!"

I snatched it up. "This is Smoot. Frost had a negligent discharge."

"Frost did? You guys okay?"

I looked around at the bodies on the floor. "Uh, yeah. Scared the shit out of us. He was trying to teach us how to quick draw a pistol and he put a round into the floor." I paused for effect and moved the radio away from my mouth. "Yeah, Frost, I'm telling on you. You almost shot me."

"Put him on."

"Uh, he's kind of shaken up right now. He won't take the radio."

"For Christ's sake. I'll be there in a minute. Take his gun away."

I reholstered the Glock. The security camera feed showed a man on the first floor running for the stairs. I only had a moment. I flipped the radio to the channel I knew Ling would be listening to.

"I have control of video and comms. Execute, execute!"

VALENTINE

A gunshot echoed through the quiet building. It was

muffled, as if it had come from above, but there was no mistaking that sound. Something was happening. I didn't know what, but this might be the only chance I was going to get. With the onset of the *Calm*, my thoughts were clear and rational. The dark, bubbling anger from before was pushed to the background. *They might be distracted. I'm not going to get a better chance than this.* I swung my feet over the edge of the bed and stood up.

I nearly fell. My legs were weak and quivering. It took me a moment to steady myself. At last my head stopped spinning and I felt . . . not *good*, exactly, but better than I could recall. The *Calm*, with its clarity and sense of purpose, steadied me. I smiled in the darkness. I'd missed this feeling.

I was getting out, and I was going to kill as many of my captors as I could in the attempt. They might kill me, but the fear was pushed aside by the single-minded, determined focus the *Calm* brought with it.

I went for the door. *Locked*. No surprise there. There was also a camera. It was up in the corner, bolted to the ceiling so it could see the entire room. A red light glowed by the lens, as if to let me know I was being watched. I didn't know if the camera had a night vision mode, but I assumed it did.

There was a cable leading from the camera, across the ceiling, through a small hole drilled in the wall, and out into the hallway. The rooms of this building were made of cinder blocks and concrete. They'd made no effort to hide the camera's power and feed cable, just bolted it onto the textured ceiling. I could barely make out the black line in the darkness, but it was there, just too high for me to reach.

Stepping back across the room, I pulled my bed into

place beneath the camera. This was easy, because my bed was basically a gurney with wheels. Shakily, unsteadily, I climbed up and carefully stood. I smiled for the camera as I grabbed onto the coaxial cable and tugged.

Nothing happened. *Shit.* I tugged harder. Still nothing. It was on there really solidly. They could see me on camera. I didn't have time for this. I grabbed the cable with both hands and put my body weight into it. The cable ripped out of the camera. The fasteners holding it to the ceiling gave way. My bed rolled out from underneath me and toppled over with a crash. I landed hard on the floor.

Well. That probably got their attention. I didn't have a lot of time. They'd be coming for me. I needed a weapon. I looked down at the cable in my hands, and smiled. A pair of boots stomped down the hall. Gathering up the cable in my hands, I pressed myself against the wall behind where the door swung when it opened, and waited. The heater kicked on, filling the entire hallway with an obnoxious rumbling sound.

Keys jingled, then hit the lock. I could hear voices on his radio. The volume was up too high and the tinny noise echoed in the hallway, intermixed with static.

The door swung open.

It was now or never. Stepping around the door, I looped the heavy-gauge coaxial cable around the guard's neck and yanked it as hard as I could. I let myself fall. The thrashing guard went down with me. He was panicking, kicking, twisting, desperate for air. His hands clawed as his throat, but I held on for dear life. He tried to reach me, but I was underneath him. There was nothing he could do. His gurgles and gasps grew more desperate, his thrashing wilder. He kicked the door and the wall, tried to bash my face with the back of his head, but I didn't let go.

Then he went limp.

I held on for a few moments longer, making sure he was done, before pushing the heavy man off and sitting up. I was panting. My arms felt like lead and my hands were raw where the coaxial cable had dug into them. Luckily my grip had lasted longer than his air.

There had only been one of them. They usually sent two or more. Something was happening, maybe related to that gunshot. I didn't have time to sort it out. I had to move.

In the light coming from the hallway, I could see the dead man's face. It was Reilly. His eyes were grotesquely rolled up into his head and his crushed throat was purple. I smiled viciously at the corpse and began to strip the equipment off of his duty belt.

No gun. Of course Dr. Silvers didn't let them carry guns down here anymore. But he had other goodies for me: an aluminum side-handle baton, keys, handcuffs, and a radio. There was too much of it for me to carry in my hands. Unbuckling his duty belt, I rolled Reilly over and took it off of him. He was a fat man, and I'd lost quite a bit of weight during my stay. His belt was way too big for me. I looped it over my shoulder like a bandolier and stood up.

It was time to go.

LORENZO

Ling acknowledged she was on her way. I lunged across

the control room for the weapons locker. It had an electronic lock with a keypad. I had no idea what the combination was. This was why I hated rush jobs. Given time to think I would have remembered to beat that combo out of Smoot too. I swore and futilely slammed a fist into the metal door. More guards would be here in seconds and it would be nice to have something bigger than a pistol. At least I could take everyone else's ammo.

There was movement on one of the screens as I looted Frost's corpse. Valentine was standing on his bed, smiling at the camera. It was almost as if he was looking right at me. His face was green and white, his eyes shining creepily in the camera's night vision mode. He messed with the camera, and then the feed was cut.

What the hell was he doing? But I didn't have time to worry about it. The door opened and another man in black fatigues appeared in the stairwell. It was the guard that had checked me at the door. He strode in purposefully, loudly cursing as he moved. "Jesus tap-dancing Christ, Frost, I'll have your ass for this. Silvers is going to blow a gasket when she . . . when she . . ." He trailed off when he saw the puddle of blood and coffee coagulating around the desks.

I came from his periphery, so fast he couldn't react, and brutally smashed Frost's baton onto his shoulder. He bellowed in pain and stumbled back against the wall. Spinning the baton so that the short end was forward, I punched it into his sternum. He made a noise like a cat trying to cough up a hairball, and for a moment I was afraid he was going to puke on me. I whipped the baton around and cracked him in forehead. He fell to the floor after that, blood pouring down his face. I removed his pistol and shoved it into the back of my waistband, then I stood over him, with the baton pushed against his top lip. He was too dazed to do anything.

"S . . . Smoot!" he stammered. "What are you doing?"

"Smoot's dead." It had to be strange to hear an alien voice coming out of a coworker's face.

"Who are you? What's going on?"

I cracked him in the shoulder with the baton. He cried out.

"What's your name?"

"What?"

"Did I fucking stutter? Your name! What. Is. Your. Name." I jabbed the nightstick into his side.

"Greg!" he blurted out, wincing with pain. "Greg Spanner!"

Spanner . . . I seemed to remember bribery, stealing from evidence rooms, and witness intimidation, so no wonder he was a supervisor here. "Okay, Greg. Listen to me very carefully. How do you check in with your command?" The longer that Majestic didn't know that we had been here, the greater our chances of getting away.

"I can't tell you that." It looked like Greg was trying to find his backbone.

"That's what those assholes said." I gestured to the corpses. "See how that turned out? I'm not going to ask you again, Greg. You're either an asset or a liability."

"It's Silvers . . . Silvers!" I jabbed him again, just to keep him talking. It wasn't surprising that he was less than eager to lay down his life for a super-loyal organization like Majestic. "She sends in a status report every day!"

"How?"

"E-mail." He cringed as I raised the stick, tears streaming down his cheeks. "No, really, she sends an e-mail! Every morning, really early! She works all night most of the time, and sends the SITREP in before she goes home!"

"That's it?"

"Yeah!" He nodded rapidly. "It's on the secure network, though!"

"Lackadaisical motherfuckers!" I spat.

VALENTINE

The hallway was dimly lit.

I crept past the other locked doors, my footsteps covered by the constant rumbling of the industrial heater. White light filled a spot on the floor further down the hall.

I wasn't sure what to do. I wasn't sure what was driving me. I didn't have a plan. There was only the powerful impulse to get out and to kill anyone who got in my way. My thoughts were a whirlwind, too jumbled for me to even follow, but occasionally they'd slow down into a moment of pure clarity. I really wanted to see the sky again. The soles on my laceless shoes were soft and didn't make much noise.

The next section of hallway went right past Dr. Silvers' office. Her office had a window in it, to give her a nice view of the scenic hallway I guess. Venetian blinds were hung over the window, but they were open enough that I could see through. I darted across the hall so that I was next to the window. Through the slatted blinds, I could see Dr.

Silvers at her desk, idly typing away on the computer on her desk.

Ducking under the window, I crept down the hallway toward the open door. I had to move very slowly. I was far enough away from the heater that it would no longer cover any inadvertent sounds I made. Reilly's belt was still slung over my shoulder, and I had to be careful not to let any of his equipment scrape against the concrete floor. Past the window I stood up, back to the wall, and moved on as silently as I could to her office door. It was open.

A nasal voice came from inside. "Reilly's been gone for an awfully long time. We haven't heard anything else about the incident upstairs, either. Do you think everything is okay?"

Dr. Silvers let out a long sigh before responding. "I'm sure they're doing paperwork, Neville. One of those cretins almost shot his foot off. I swear I'm going to ban guns in this facility completely, take all of their toys away. I'm surrounded by idiots."

"But what about Reilly, Doctor? It shouldn't take that long to just check on a noise. And shouldn't Smoot be on shift by now?" *A noise? Didn't they see me disable the camera? Wasn't anyone monitoring the cameras?*

"Smoot is probably upstairs too, gawking with the other idiots. Now quit gibbering. Go check on him yourself if you want. I'm trying to work."

Very carefully, I peeked around the corner. The front part of her office had a countertop with a coffee machine on it. Neville was there, making a fresh pot. Seemingly unaware that Dr. Silvers didn't want to talk to him, kept flapping his mouth at her. "Have you sent in the daily

SITREP and report to higher, Doctor?"

Dr. Silvers muttered something to herself. "Yes, Neville, I have. Perhaps you'd also like to follow me to the restroom and remind me to wipe my ass?"

Neville laughed nervously again, even though it was pretty obvious Silvers wasn't joking around with him. It made me happy that she found him just as insufferable as I did, but he persisted. The fool never did know when to shut his pie-hole. "Doctor, perhaps if you just called Reilly on the radio . . ." He trailed off as Dr. Silvers let out another long sigh.

"I'm sure he's just dawdling, Neville, but if it will make you feel better. Soothing your paranoia is apparently the only way I'm going to be able to get any work done this morning."

My eyes went wide as I remembered that Reilly's radio was still in its pouch, on his belt, over my shoulder. Dr. Silvers hit the transmit button before I could turn his radio off. The radio squawked.

Oh shit.

I heard her stand up. "Reilly?" she asked, calling out into the hallway.

"I can't see anything, Doctor," Neville whined.

"Go look," Silvers ordered.

I moved while Neville hesitated. Drawing Reilly's baton from the belt, I lunged around the corner. Neville was so shocked he didn't even have time to react. I held the baton by the side handle, with the short end pointing forward. I was on top of Neville before he could even step back. My hand on his shoulder, I slammed the blunt aluminum baton into his gut, over and over again. I shoved him back, flipped the baton around, and whacked him upside the head. Neville's head snapped to the side and he flopped to the floor. I didn't let up. I raised the baton over my head, clutching it in both hands, and savagely beat the little bastard's skull in.

Spittle flew out of my clenched teeth as I clubbed him. I was on an adrenaline high like I'd never experienced. I didn't know what was happening to me, but killing Neville was the greatest feeling I'd ever known.

The Calm was gone. There was only rage.

Panting, sweat pouring down my face, I rose over Neville's lifeless form. Across the room, behind her desk, Dr. Silvers was pressed up against the wall. Her eyes were wide, a look of horror covered her face. I'd never seen her afraid before, and it made me so happy I laughed out loud. She'd mashed the alarm button and a loud warbling noise began to sound. It probably alerted the entire facility. I laughed at that, too. My hope of escape was extinguished, but I wasn't done just yet.

LORENZO

Greg Spanner, clad in black and covered in blood, blubbered on the floor of the control room after I'd beaten the hell out of him and threatened his life. Not too surprisingly, he felt talkative.

"Next question, Greg," I said. "That weapons locker over there. What's the combination?"

"One, twenty-five, thirteen!" he gasped, struggling to fight back tears. I had broken this guy, and he couldn't maintain his dignity. He was scared, he was confused, and all he knew was that he didn't want to die.

I'm good at this sort of thing. Once you push someone over the threshold, where they become more worried about living than anyone's opinion of them, they can be very useful. It doesn't work so well on the strong-willed, the true believers, fanatics, or people who've undergone intense training, but for low-level, wannabe jack-booted thugs like Spanner this technique was perfect.

"Now look at me, Greg. I'm going to go over there and see what's in that locker. You stay right there. If you get up, I'll shoot you. If you try to crawl away, I'll shoot you. Are we clear?"

"Who are you?"

That was the wrong answer. I kicked Greg in the stomach. He folded onto himself like wet origami. "Am I making myself clear?" I pulled his Glock.

"Yes!" Greg cried. "I swear!"

"Good. Stay put." I made my way across the control room and punched the numbers into the gun locker. Inside were several M4 carbines, a couple of shotguns, and ammunition for both. I took one of the carbines, turned on its EOTech sight, slammed a magazine into it, and worked the charging handle.

That's when the alarm went off. It was an obnoxiously loud klaxon, something originally intended to alert the residents of North Gap that Soviet missiles were inbound. My first thought was that the gun safe was alarmed somehow, but I didn't think Spanner was brave enough to try and trick me. "What's going on?"

"I don't know!"

Stepping over Frost's body, I checked the bank of monitors. The screen for Valentine's cell was still dead. There was movement on another screen. *Holy shit.* Valentine was out of his cell, viciously beating someone with a nightstick. Even in the gritty black and white I could tell he was painting the walls down there.

The son of a bitch picked a hell of a day to escape.

"Come in Ling," I said, keying the radio.

"I hear a siren. We just cleared the checkpoint," Ling replied. "Status?"

"We've got a problem. Our boy is out of his room."

"Say again?"

"He's out of his cell! He's escaping! He just beat the shit out of some skinny guy and somebody tripped the alarm." There was motion on many of the monitors now. They were coming out of the nearby housing and running through the snow and there was movement on the level below me. "Every guard in this place is on the move."

"You have to slow them. You have to get to Valentine before they do."

"Then you better go loud. Greg!" I snapped as I dropped the mic. "How do I kill the power in—" He was gone. *Son of a bitch.* The door to the stairwell was swinging closed. He'd run for it.

Chapter 6: Pushed Too Far

❦

VALENTINE
North Gap, Montana

Dr. Silvers stared at me, wide-eyed, as the alarm sounded. Guards would be here in seconds and this time they'd probably kill me. I didn't have much time, but I didn't *need* much time.

I lunged toward her. She gasped and made for her desk, yanking open a drawer. A gun was in her hand. I was on top of her before she could bring it to bear. I brought the baton down, smashing her wrist. The pistol clattered to the floor as the doctor shrieked in pain. I scrambled over the desk, powered by desperation and a euphoric surge of adrenaline, and came down on the other side. My free hand clamped around Dr. Silvers' throat, and I shoved her back against the wall. I dropped the baton, wrapped my other hand around her neck, and squeezed.

The normally ice-cold scientist writhed and squirmed as color flushed her pale face. She tried to scratch at me with her uninjured hand, but it did her no good. A puddle formed at her feet as her bladder let go. Her eyes began to roll back in her head. Darkness clouded my vision. A vicious grin split my face as I throttled this woman, a dark joy that I'd never felt. I was excited to watch her die.

I hesitated. My grip relaxed a little. Something was holding me back. I thought of Sarah, the last woman I'd seen die. Was that it? I tried to focus, to finish Silvers, but I just couldn't. The adrenaline rush receded. My hands hurt from choking her. The alarm was still screaming, but no one had come yet.

I let go of Dr. Silvers. Gasping and coughing, she slumped to the floor. I stepped back. My hands were shaking. My knees were weak. I felt dizzy and sick. I sat on her desk to avoid falling over.

Then the lights went out, shrouding us in complete darkness. Thankfully that silenced that annoying alarm. Dr. Silvers was too busy coughing to speak. The emergency lights kicked on a moment later, dimly illuminating the room with an eerie glow.

"M . . . Michael," the doctor managed. She always used my first name when she was trying to get into my head. It wasn't going to work this time. "Listen to me. You're not yourself. It's the drugs." She coughed again.

I cast a dark shadow across her face as I stood back up. "What did you do to me?"

"What did I do?" she wheezed. "My God, look at you! You escaped! You killed Neville without even blinking! I assume you killed Reilly as well?"

Why is she so excited about this? "I did."

She grasped her broken arm, obviously in pain, but she'd regained some composure. "Listen to me. You've been subjected to several experimental drugs as part of the procedure. They're still in your system. The rage, the aggression, the anger . . . you're having a reaction. You have to let me sedate you. I can help you, Michael. If you don't let me help you you'll die."

Shouts echoed throughout the building. Somebody started laughing. It took me a moment to realize it was me. They were coming and I didn't know why they hadn't gotten here already. Something else was going on. I had to make a decision before I ran out of time and squandered the only chance I was going to get.

Without taking my eyes off of Dr. Silvers, I reached down and found her pistol, a compact Glock. I racked the slide. No unfired cartridge was ejected, meaning she hadn't had a round chambered. If she'd gotten the gun on me before I broke her arm it wouldn't have done her any good. It figured, she didn't allow the guards to have guns down here but she had no problem violating her own rules. The little pistol had luminescent night sights, three green dots glowed above the slide. The dots made me think of fireflies, which told me I was still very high.

"Get up," I told her.

"Michael, please," she pleaded. "You can't—"

I cut her off. "Get up or I'll kill you where you sit." *The Calm* was returning. The rage subsided as my heart rate steadied. I was in control again.

Dr. Silvers still hesitated. I didn't. Reaching downward, I grabbed her by the collar of her white lab coat. She cried out as I yanked her to her feet. I pushed her ahead of me and wrapped my right arm around her neck. I leveled the Glock over her left shoulder and pushed her forward.

"Shut your mouth and *walk*."

LORENZO

The main fuse-box killed the power and that annoying siren, but then dim emergency lights had kicked in. I didn't have time to figure out how to shut those off so it would have to do. Most of the exterior lights were on another circuit and stayed on, but the relative darkness inside the building would help me. Last I'd seen on the monitors, several guards had come from the barracks and were standing outside the main building, pounding on the door. I had to get downstairs before Spanner or somebody else let them in.

Just then, the courtyard was illuminated with headlights as a beat-up station wagon came tearing up to the chain link fence. It did a tight one-eighty turn, skidding in the snow, and slid to a stop. Ling, Shen, and Antoine rolled out of the vehicle and immediately opened fire on the Majestic guards stuck outside. *Perfect timing.*

I made my way down the stairs, carbine shouldered, carefully checking the corners. *Nothing.* The stairwell was dark, illuminated only by one weak red light. I could hear shouts below me. I knew from the cameras there were more guards in the building. Carefully I leaned around the edge, trying to cover every possible angle, by myself. Stairwells are dangerous as hell to clear. A shadow moved below and I lunged back.

BLAM BLAM BLAM BLAM

I struck the wall hard, bullets whizzing through the space I'd been standing in. Puffs of dust and fragments kicked up as they struck the wall. I couldn't let him pin me down so I stuck the M4 over the side and fired several wild rounds at where the flashes had come from. The noise of the short-barreled carbine was brutal in the enclosed concrete space. *Great. More hearing damage.*

Then there was light below as someone opened the door to the second floor. I fired again as his shadow moved through and was rewarded with a startled cry. The door slammed shut behind, plunging me again into darkness.

I took the stairs two at a time, flying blind, and only hesitated a split second before jerking open the door to the second floor. Light flooded past, and there was blood splatter on the door. I ducked back as the holes appeared in the metal door, .40 caliber bullets flying through. He kept shooting, and I could hear the bullets impacting the wall behind my back. More beams of light shot into the darkness as they poked more holes in the door.

Then it was quiet, save for the muffled echoes of gunfire outside. It sounded like Ling was in a full-on gun battle with the rest of North Gap's personnel.

Doorways are fatal funnels. You don't ever want to get stuck in a doorway. There wasn't enough light in the stairwell for him to see my shadow, so I risked a peek through the crack, and caught a glimpse of a man running down the hall. I jerked the door open, and went through fast, crouched low, moving as swiftly as I could, but he was gone.

I was on the office level, lit only by emergency lights. *Where are they?* There was a trail of blood across the floor, leading into an open doorway. I approached silently. I could hear them speaking over the ringing in my ears and the blood thundering in my head.

"Oh man, oh man, oh man." He sounded like he was in a lot of pain, and it wasn't Spanner. "He shot me. What's going on?"

"I don't know! I don't know!" That *was* Spanner. "No one is answering on the radio. Who's shooting outside? We're under attack!"

WHUMP!

A concussion rang out from outside. Ling was using hand grenades. The lady wasn't messing around.

"Holy shit!" the injured guard said. "We're gonna die! Oh my God, we're gonna die!"

"Shut up and watch the door, you idiot!"

No hesitation. I came around the corner and put two rounds into the wounded guard's back, shifted my sight picture, and put two rounds into Greg's chest. They went right down. I turned back into the darkness. "Ling, what's your status?"

Back in the stairwell, the radio crackled to life. It was Ling. "There are a lot of them out here. We had to retreat to cover. They got the door open. At least five more personnel entered the building, all armed, and they have a dog. The rest are coming after us. We may not be able to assist you right away."

"On it," I acknowledged. My plan would've been working *perfectly* had that asshole not decided to escape.

VALENTINE

One floor above us was the ground level. I forced Dr.

Silvers up both flights of stairs, using her as a human shield. There was a landing here, a small room with two doors. One led to the rear courtyard. The other led to the main level, where everything else was. On a row of hooks on the wall hung several bulky winter coats. Next to the door was a well-used metal snow shovel. Gunfire had been echoing throughout the building and from outside. I was pretty sure I'd heard a detonation, too, like a grenade or something. I didn't know what the hell was going on and I didn't want to find out.

I peered out the small, square window into the courtyard. It was surrounded by a fence topped with razor wire. It was lit by overhead lights. A small whirlwind of powdery snow blew across the open area.

"You'll never make it, you know," Dr. Silvers said. Her voice was raspy. "Where the hell do you think you're going to go?"

I let go of her, stepped back, and leveled the Glock 27 at her face. She didn't flinch. She just clutched her broken arm and stared me down.

"I ought to kill you." My grip tightened on the little pistol. My finger made contact with the trigger.

"Then do it," she said calmly. "I'm in no position to stop you."

I really and truly did want to kill Dr. Silvers. I hated her. I didn't know what had stopped me from strangling her to death before, and I didn't know what was stopping me from shooting her in the face now. Whatever it was, I just didn't have it in me.

There was another loud noise nearby, like a door being kicked in. Now was not the time for a moral quandary.

Stepping forward, I raised the gun and cracked Dr. Silvers upside the head with it. She cried out in pain. Before she could fall I shoved her backward. She tumbled down the stairs and landed in a heap on the landing below.

Without pausing, I threw on one of the heavy coats, opened the door to the courtyard, and dashed into the cold night air. Being out of shape and exhausted, my dash was really more of a slow jog. The fence seemed farther away than I'd thought.

I didn't even come close to making it. Before I knew what was happening I was on the ground in the snow. Someone had tackled me from behind, slamming me down and knocking the wind out of me. I nearly lost my grip on the pistol.

Furious, I kicked and struggled. The man that had tackled me swore aloud and his grip loosened enough for me to roll over. He had a baton in his hand but couldn't bring it to bear. I twisted onto my side as he tried to reestablish his grip on me. It was Davis. His eyes went wide as he realized I had a gun. He blocked it and my first shot went into the air. He was right on top of me. The next shot was close and hot and loud, right above my face, but it hit him in the chest, which gave me time to lever the pistol up beneath his chin. I was splattered with blood and brains the instant I pulled the trigger. I kicked Davis' limp body off of me and staggered to my feet.

The door I had just come through popped open. There were black-clad men inside.

Sticking the pistol outward, I popped off several shots. The guards trying to funnel through the doorway were forced back. The slide locked back empty, so I dropped the

Glock in the snow, scooped up Davis' baton, and turned and ran for the fence again.

It was a strange feeling, like when you're still dreaming, but you're almost awake. It didn't seem real. I ran and ran, but the gate didn't get any closer. Darkness crept into my peripheral vision. My breathing was labored, and I could still feel my heart pounding in my ears. Then I smacked into the fence, shaking the thin layer of snow off of the top and causing it to fall on me. Confused, I dropped the baton and began to climb.

A terrible electric pain shot through me, and I lost my grip on the fence. I fell to the ground, and the pain stopped almost immediately. Looking behind me, I saw another man in black fatigues holding an air taser in his hand. One of the wires had fallen out of my back, probably because of the puffy coat I wore. I started climbing again.

Something clamped onto my right leg, and I screamed out loud as teeth broke the skin. A dog, *that fucking German Shepherd*, latched onto my calf. My grip gave out and I fell to the ground once again.

I found the baton. Twisting around, I struck the dog hard, smashing into the side of its neck. It yelped and let go. Everything slowed down once again, except my heart, which was beating so fast it felt like it was going to explode. Dr. Silvers had been right. The drugs were doing weird things to me. I felt my lips curl back in a snarl and my fingers grasped the baton so hard it hurt. Sweat was pouring down my face, stinging my eyes. My leg was bleeding, but the pain seemed distant somehow. A red haze clouded my vision as I focused on the snarling German Shepherd. *That dog. That goddamn fucking dog.*

It was named Gonzo.

I don't remember anything after that.

LORENZO

I ran for the stairs, leapt down most of them, and entered a darkened room on the first floor. Men in various states of dress, all armed, were moving through the building.

"Smoot! What's going on?"

Not knowing if my disguise had been damaged, I tried to keep my head down. "Valentine's escaping."

"We're under attack!"

No shit.

They ran through the break room, a small entry room, and out a back door and I followed. Gunshots echoed from outside. From the rear of the group, I couldn't see what was happening.

"I want him alive!" a woman shrieked. She had platinum blonde hair, a bloody lab coat, and was limping her way up a flight of stairs that led down into the basement. Blood was trickling down her face and she held her right arm as if she was injured. *Dr. Silvers, I presume?*

Before anyone else could make it outside, more shots rang out. Bullets zipped into the doorway. That had been close. One of the men in front of me, dressed in civilian clothes and carrying a pistol, snarled in pain as a round struck him in the wrist. Now Valentine had almost shot me too. Dude was on a roll.

The gunfire let up and the guards rushed forward. A

man lay dead on the ground, skull emptied. The guards and Silvers rushed forward. I hung back so I could keep everyone in sight. "Get him. Hurry." The doctor saw me. "Smoot, where the hell have you been? Valentine is escaping!" More gunfire resonated from the other side of the building. Exodus was still in the fight.

"He dropped his gun. Sic the dog on him!"

Valentine had reached the perimeter, but the guards had converged on him. Valentine hit the fence climbing like mad, only to be pulled down by a huge dog. It dragged him through the snow by the leg. It yelped and let go as he smacked it with a stick, but it circled around for another attack. The North Gap guards clustered around the scene, apparently confident Valentine was out of ammunition, and happy to give the dog a minute to work.

Valentine rose, screaming like a berserker. His face was covered in blood. His clothing was ripped, a baton in one fist, and every vein and muscle bulged on his face. The dog, snarling, leapt at him.

Valentine clenched the baton in both hands, holding it horizontally. The dog's slobbering jaws clamped onto the stick, and Valentine wrenched it brutally to the side. The German Shepherd's spine snapped audibly. Its limp form slammed into Valentine, pushing him back against the fence.

He tossed the dog aside and screamed for more. I had never seen a man so angry.

"Now!" One of the guards ordered. Pairs of taser barbs latched into Valentine's body. He twitched as electricity crackled through his muscles. They hit him long and hard, multiple guns sparking.

"Take him," Dr. Silvers said raggedly, walking through the snow with a limp. "Do not kill him! I'm not going to tell you idiots again!" The remaining guards swarmed forward, clubbing Valentine with their batons, sticks rising and falling rhythmically. Four men all tackled him at once, and even then they could barely contain his rage beneath their weight.

Enough of this shit. There were five of them left alive. They all had their backs to me. I was the only one armed with a rifle. I raised the stubby carbine and pulled the trigger. The gun roared in the cold air. I put a round into each of them, and 5.56 makes a horrible mess of people at such close range. I wheeled around and double-tapped the man who had been hit in the wrist. Then I went back and plugged each of the guards again, just to be sure.

It was suddenly very quiet. I stood there, hot carbine in my hands, bolt locked to the rear. Dr. Silvers was the only other person standing. She didn't move, she just stood there, staring at me, wide-eyed. She began to shiver, realizing that I was not who she thought I was. The shock of it hit her like a train.

A shape moved in the carnage. Valentine slowly rose, pushing limbs off of him. Now he stood, coated in a pink mush that was half snow and half blood. He saw me, surely not understanding why one of his tormentors had murdered the others, but it didn't seem to matter to him. He looked at Dr. Silvers intently, his bloodied form heaving as he gasped for air. Valentine got up, made it a few halting steps toward her, but then he began to shake, fell to his knees, and face-planted in the snow, like a puppet with its strings cut.

Chapter 7: The Sum of Our Parts

***

LORENZO
North Gap, Montana

The gray sky was slowly brightened as the Sun climbed over the horizon. It was still overcast and lightly snowing, but the darkness was receding to the west.

Near as I could tell, we had killed every last one of the North Gap facility's personnel, except for Dr. Silvers. There was a chance that there were some in hiding and they'd called for help. So we needed to get the hell out of Dodge.

But first, I found Dr. Silvers' office and ransacked it, taking everything I could get my hands on. Shen and I searched for intelligence on the Majestic organization while Ling and Antoine got Valentine secured for transport. I wasn't ever going to get a better opportunity to learn about the organization that was after my brother, and after everything I'd risked and everyone I'd killed, I wasn't about to let that opportunity go to waste.

Reaper would love this. The chance to explore an actual shadow-government secret interrogation facility? The kid would probably pee himself with conspiratorial glee. Looking around the basement, I began to wonder if maybe there wasn't a lot more to Reaper's conspiracy theories than I thought. The place was full of strange machines that I couldn't identify, like some kind of science-fiction torture dungeon. One of the computers in that room had a red sticker on it that said *Secret.* Which meant it could probably access the secure network Greg Spanner had told me about. I snagged every electronic storage device that wasn't nailed down.

Shen had broken open a metal container with a crowbar. He called me over to see something.

"What is it?" I looked into the storage bin he'd busted the lock off of. Inside were what looked like Valentine's personal belongings from when they'd nabbed him in Virginia. Clothing, wallet, watch, keys, that sort of thing, but right on top was a large, stainless steel .44 magnum revolver. I picked the Smith & Wesson up, opened the cylinder, and inspected it. "I hate this gun." For good reason. Valentine had basically shot me three times with the goddamn thing in Zubara, once right through an arms dealer. My tinnitus was a permanent reminder of how much I hated that gun, but Shen didn't know all that, and he looked puzzled. "Never mind. Grab it all."

Ling was waiting for us on the first floor. All three of the Exodus people were dressed in Mossy Oak camouflage we'd picked up in town. Dr. Silvers was with her, zip-tied to a chair. The good doctor was bitching at Ling about something when we came to the top of the stairs. Ling stared her down and said nothing until we entered the room.

"Did you find everything you were looking for?" she asked me.

"Yeah. We should go." We'd only been in here for a few minutes, but already that felt far too long.

Dr. Silvers saw her iPad in my hands, and her eyes went wide. She began to say something, but Ling jabbed her with the suppressor of her MP-9 subgun and told her to be quiet.

"It says I need a passcode to unlock this." I held up the iPad. "What is it?"

"Go to hell."

"Kneecap her," I said.

"Wait . . ." She hadn't even given the Exodus folks a chance to be threatening. "Seven, three, one, nine."

I tried the code and it worked. "Awesome."

"What of the other captives?" Antoine asked.

"Not our problem," I said. They might have been pure as the driven snow, but on the other hand, they might deserve to be in a place like this.

"Unlock their doors," Ling ordered. "We do not have time to sort out who they are. They are on their own."

I shrugged.

Dr. Silvers finally piped up. "You people have a lot of nerve, coming in here. Do you have any idea the hornet's nest you've just kicked? Do you have any idea at all what you're bringing down on yourselves?"

"Not entirely, but I'm sure we'll figure it out. Thanks for the hard drives."

The Majestic scientist shook her head in bewilderment.

"You. You're not Roger Smoot. Who are you? What the hell is going on? Why did you take Valentine?"

I smiled at her but offered no answers.

She grew frustrated. "It doesn't matter. You will never get away with this. We're too powerful. We're everywhere."

"You mean Majestic?"

She sneered at me. "They'll catch you, and then they'll bring you to someone like me. They'll drill out every last piece of information you know. There's nowhere you can run to, noplace you can hide, where they won't find you. Sooner or later, you'll end up in a place like this, and someone like me will be there to make you regret this decision. I promise you that . . ."

Ling stepped in front of Silvers. Her dark eyes were like daggers. Silvers trailed off as the Chinese Exodus operative stared her down. "You never imagined this day would come, did you?" Ling asked quietly. "I know your kind. You sit here in your little kingdom, removed from the world, committing your little atrocities because it's your job. You say you do these things because powerful men tell you to, but really, you do these things because you enjoy them. You never imagined that you'd have to account for your actions, did you?"

Dr. Silvers said nothing. Fear was on her face.

"Of course you didn't," Ling continued. "You never dreamed such a thing could happen, that one day it would all come crashing down, that your insulated world would fall apart. That day has come."

The doctor stumbled on her words as she tried to speak. "If . . . if you want information . . ." she trailed off as Ling seemed unimpressed with her attempt to negotiate. "What is this?"

"I would like nothing more than to shoot you and be done with it, however . . ." Ling's eyes narrowed. "My order has an old saying, when a criminal has been caught and justice must be satisfied, the wisest judges are his victims . . . Carry her downstairs. Leave her bound. Unlock the doors. We will let her prisoner's decide her fate."

"No! No!" Silvers began to scream as Shen and Antoine picked up her chair and carried her away.

"Harsh." Then I thought of the weird machines. "But fair."

"I am confident she will receive as much mercy as she has given . . . Come, Mr. Lorenzo, we've been here too long already."

I followed her outside. Valentine was wrapped in a blanket, passed out in the back of our car. He looked like shit. "Son of a bitch better live." I muttered. "I didn't just audition for public enemy number one for nothing."

Ling glared at me. "How can you—"

"Be so heartless?" She was obviously distressed by Valentine's condition, and she had to suppress anger at my callousness to his fate. I'd grown to like the Exodus operatives over the last few days, but that didn't make me their errand boy. "I just killed a whole mess of people to get your boyfriend back. I fulfilled my part of the bargain. So where the fuck is my brother?"

Ling sighed. "Altay Krai, in the Golden Mountains."

"The Crossroads?"

Ling nodded.

I couldn't believe it. I knew that area well. "Shit . . . Bob, you stupid idiot . . . And the rest of the note?" I demanded. Ling reached into a pocket on her black fatigue shirt and pulled out half a paper napkin and handed it over. It was the bottom half of the note that Bob had left me. "You had it the whole time?" I shouted. I was used to being lied to, but it didn't mean I had to like it.

"Yes. It wasn't my wish to be untruthful."

"Well, you did a bang-up job."

"It was your brother's idea."

Son of a bitch. I unfolded the torn napkin. "It's blank."

"Bob said you wouldn't trust us. He said you would not help unless you had an incentive."

I didn't answer. I was too mad. But Bob had been right. I stood there in the gently falling snow and the grey light of the Montana sunrise and cursed him to hell.

"Bob said you were the only man who would be able to free Valentine, and even at the last moment, when your brother knew he was going to be captured or killed, the very last thing he did was write that note and make us swear to free Valentine, no matter what . . ." Ling paused, uncomfortable. "He said you would react exactly as you did, and that you only had one weakness we could exploit."

"Loyalty," I spat the word.

"Yes, your brother knew that you would do anything to help those few people you've claimed as your family. But Bob said that Valentine was more important, or rather, something he knows, is so important that . . ." She trailed off.

"What?" I did not like where this was going, and the combination of fatigue and anger boiling through my system was threatening to blow.

"That if you tried to hinder us, or betray us, or anything

that would stop us from retrieving Valentine, we were to kill you," Ling stated calmly. "If necessary," she added, almost as an afterthought.

It was like being hit in the stomach with a hammer. I could taste sour bile in the back of my throat, and the idea of being betrayed by my own brother physically hurt. The napkin was still in my hand. I crumpled it into a tight ball and squeezed until my fingers ached.

What did Valentine know? What was so important that Bob would jeopardize his own life, ruin his career, endanger his family, and be willing to sacrifice his own brother? "Damn it, Bob . . ." That didn't matter now because tonight Majestic was going after Bob's wife and kids. His family. *My family.* I didn't know if I could do anything, but I wasn't about to do *nothing*.

"Ling, change in plans. We need to go to Arizona."

We drove down a lonely two-lane highway, heading into the sunrise, as we made our way back to the airport. The sooner we were in the air and the farther from North Gap we got, the better off we'd be. The longer it took them to discover our attack, the greater our chances of getting away. Every minute we traveled increased the diameter of the search they would have to undertake, and since we were talking about an outfit that probably had access to spy satellites and massive databases, I hoped to turn minutes into hours.

Valentine was in the back, on a litter, still unconscious. Shen had hooked him up to an IV. Our wagon had a poorly-done tint job on the windows that kept our patient out of the sight of prying eyes. That would be important when we stopped for gas. Antoine drove just below the speed limit. We wanted to avoid attention and law enforcement at all costs.

Ling and I went through Dr. Silvers' iPad. I was definitely curious about what they were doing to the kid, but I wasn't nearly as interested as Ling was. I was mostly looking for anything that would help me figure out what happened to my brother.

Some of the hard drives we grabbed were sure to be encrypted. I didn't know much about that kind of stuff. That's why I had Reaper. Silvers had used her iPad to keep notes on her work, and she'd been lousy with information security. I'm sure Majestic, being secret black-ops types, had rules against this sort of thing, but over the years I'd found that the know-it-all academic types considered themselves too smart to listen to mere operators. Silvers had been interrogating him about something called Project Blue, and specifically, something called the Alpha Point. Ling didn't know what that meant either.

"Big Eddie mentioned this back in Quagmire," I muttered. Ling looked at me curiously. "That's why Gordon Willis turned traitor. Those two were in on it together. It's something huge."

"Your brother was concerned about it as well, but he was unclear on what it entailed. It was this search that brought him to The Crossroads."

"Do you know who this Evangeline person is?"

Ling shrugged.

They'd sure worked him over good trying to find out. Whoever she was, Valentine had no clue one way or another. Dr. Silvers had become convinced of that early on.

So why did they keep him alive?

VALENTINE

The morning Sun was still below the horizon as I turned onto the long gravel driveway that led to our house. I'd been driving a long time and was happy to be home. Three of my friends and I had gone on a road trip to Detroit, and we'd driven all night on the way back. I'd dropped them off at their houses before heading home myself.

As I pulled to a stop in front of the house, I was making plans to sleep through the day. It was my last day of Spring Break, and I'd have to be back in school the next morning. I doubted that I'd get much sleep. Knowing my mom, in a few hours she'd drag me out of bed to help shovel the horses' stalls.

I parked next to my mom's pickup. There was a truck, one I didn't recognize, parked in the drive. I quietly made my way to the front door, wondering who could be over so early.

Holy crap, I thought. I wonder if Mom had some guy over while I was gone? *I was uncomfortable with that thought. Being honest, I couldn't blame her. It'd been eight years since my dad had died. My mom had been alone for a long time.* Maybe she has a boyfriend?

Those thoughts faded away as I walked into the house. I expected to find my mom sitting at the table, eating some toast and smoking a cigarette like she always did.

Whatever I may have expected, it wasn't what I found.

The kitchen was trashed. There was broken glass everywhere. The chairs around the table were dumped over. The refrigerator was wide open, and food was out on the counter.

My mom was on her back in a chair that was lying on the floor. She stared up at the ceiling and didn't say anything.

"Mom?" I asked, stepping closer. There were extension cords wrapped around her, like she was tied to the chair. Her shirt was stained with little red blotches; around her was a pool of dark red liquid.

"Mom?" I repeated. Why is she lying on the floor wrapped up in extension cords? Is this a joke or something? It clicked a second later. My mom is dead. She'd been tied to a chair and stabbed over and over again.

My breathing sped up. My heart began pounding so hard it felt like it was going to burst out of my chest. I became dizzy. My knees went weak. My stomach twisted, and pain shot through my groin. My mouth was dry. There was a loud buzzing in my ears. I stepped back, stumbled, and fell to the floor. My mouth was open. I was trying to scream, but no sound came out.

After a few seconds, I was able to tear my eyes away from my mother's brutalized body. A black and white lump lay in the next room. It was my dog, Buckwheat. He'd been killed too.

Something strange happened to me then. The dizziness stopped, my heart rate slowed, and the buzzing in my ears faded away. My head cleared. The shock and pain drifted into the background as the Calm overtook me for the very first time.

Focus, *I thought to myself*. Somebody did this. They might still be here. You have to get out of here and call the Sheriff. *I gritted my teeth and managed to get to my feet.*

It was in that moment that a man walked in from the next room. His image was forever burned into my mind: he had on cowboy boots and dirty, stained jeans. He wore a dirty white t-shirt and an old acid-washed jean jacket. His hair was long and uncombed, and his face was covered in stubble. His eyes were wide and his pupils were dilated. Hanging from his belt was a large hunting knife in a leather scabbard. Behind him was another man, taller and skinnier, with pale skin and no hair.

"Jesse, look!" the skinny guy said, pointing at me. "There's someone else here, Jesse!"

"It's just a fucking kid," Jesse said, wiping his nose with his hand. "How you doing, kid? Where's your mom keep the cash?"

"Let's cut him up, Jesse!" the skinny guy said excitedly, wringing his shirt in his hands. "Let's fucking cut him up!"

Jesse turned to his friend and shoved him. "Goddamn it, Billy, calm the fuck down! We been here too long already."

"But, Jesse, please!" Billy said, his voice getting even more high-pitched. "It'll just take a minute! Look how surprised he is! He came home and found his mommy all cut up! Surprise!"

Jesse slapped Billy, causing him to let out a squealing cry. "Get a hold of yourself, Billy! We don't—"

Billy interrupted Jesse. "He's getting away!" Jesse turned around to see me running up the stairs. The skinny one, Billy, took off after me, but I made it upstairs before he did. I rounded the corner, ran down the hall, and burst into my mom's bedroom. I slammed and locked the door behind me, just as Billy crashed into it.

"Come out, kid!" Billy said, almost giggling with excitement. "Come on out!"

My heart was pounding in my chest, but my head was clear. The shotgun! My mom had a pump shotgun in her closet. I hoped to God it was loaded, because I didn't know where she kept the box of shells.

Vaulting across the room, I pulled open the closet door and pushed my mom's clothes aside. In the back corner was a little-used Remington 870. I heard a crash as Billy began slamming his body against the flimsy door. I grabbed the shotgun and stepped out of the closet, opening the action as I did so. It was loaded. I slammed the pump forward, pushing the shell into the chamber, just as Billy cracked the door open. His arm reached in and began fumbling for the lock.

I was completely calm as I brought the stock of the shotgun to my left shoulder, pointed it at the door, and squeezed the trigger. The shotgun barked loudly in my mom's bedroom, and blew a hole through the door. Billy shrieked in pain and his arm disappeared back through the door.

Pumping another round into the chamber, I pulled the bedroom door open. Billy was lying on the floor trying to hug himself. Just below his left armpit was a gory wound. Blood was pouring onto the floor.

"Jesse, help me!" Billy cried, his screeching voice gurgling as blood filled his lungs.

I was on autopilot. It was like playing one of my

first-person-shooter video games. I wasn't afraid or upset. I felt nothing. I stepped over Billy and pointed the shotgun at his face. "Surprise," I said, and squeezed the trigger again. Billy's head exploded in a mass of brains and blood.

I looked up, pumping the shotgun again, just as Jesse appeared at the end of the hall.

"Billy!" he said excitedly, seeing me standing over the remains of his partner. "You killed my little brother!" I pointed the shotgun at him and fired again. I missed. The mirror at the end of the hall exploded in a shower of broken glass as Jesse disappeared back into the stairwell.

I ran down the hall after him, chambering another round in the shotgun. I rounded the corner and looked down the stairs. Jesse was pulling a pistol from his waistband. He looked up and saw me point the shotgun at him. He turned to run, stumbled, and fell down the last few steps. His gun clattered across the floor and out of sight. I fired again, but missed again, blowing a hole in the wall of the stairwell. The intruder rounded the corner at the base of the stairs as he bolted for the door.

I went after him, running down the stairs as fast as I could. I went through the kitchen just as Jesse burst through the front door. I fired yet again. The buckshot ripped through the screen door and shattered one of the potted plants hanging on the porch, but I missed my target again.

Jesse jumped off the porch and ran for his truck. I stumbled on the steps and fell to the ground, skinning the heel of my hand in the gravel and dropping the shotgun. I didn't even feel it. I pushed myself up, grabbed the 12-gauge, and pumped the last round into the chamber. On my feet again, I took off in a run.

I caught up with Jesse just as he pulled open the door of his truck. He hurriedly tried to climb in, but I was right behind him. I aimed for the back of his head and fired. Jesse's head exploded, spattering the interior of his pickup with the contents of his skull. His lifeless body slumped forward onto the seat, slid off, and crumpled to the ground by the running boards. It left a stream of blood as it went.

I stood there, frozen, pointing the now-empty shotgun into Jesse's blood-spattered truck for what seemed like a long time. I heard a faint ringing in my ears, and my hands began to shake. The Calm was wearing off, and I was rapidly going into shock. I slowly lowered the shotgun and turned away.

In a daze, I made my way back to the house, stopping only to throw up once. I sat on the porch, resting the shotgun next to me, and stared off into the distance. I didn't feel anything inside. I'd always imagined that when you killed someone for the first time, it'd be dramatic, or emotional, like in the movies. Now that I'd done it, I didn't see what the big deal was. I just sat there, not feeling a damned thing, as the Sun climbed into the sky.

LORENZO
Connley Field, Montana
February 15th

The tiny airport was uncontrolled. There was no tower, and only the most rudimentary of hangar facilities. Our Cessna was almost ready to roll, and Antoine and Shen were gently loading Valentine in. It had taken us hours to get here, stopping only for gas. We could have used a closer airport, but the nearer we were to the target, the more attention we would be sure to draw. This one had a great combination of obscurity and lack of witnesses.

"I understand what you feel you must do, Lorenzo." Ling said as she handed my bag to me from the back of the station wagon. "But I see one possible problem. If you encounter any Majestic agents—"

"And this plane was nearby both times? They'll focus on us like a laser beam. It won't matter where we go, they'll track us down. I know." We both knew how our foes would react, and the radar coverage over North America was just too good for them not to pick out the pattern. The government, when properly motivated, could process a whole lot of data very quickly.

But I had to go. I couldn't just call Bob's wife, Gwen, and tell her to run, because surely the phone would be tapped. I had nobody in that area who I could rely on, and we were short on time, with the clock ticking toward the scheduled raid. "I can't just leave them. If these were normal government types, I wouldn't worry. But these people . . ."

"Yes, I know." Ling had just got done reading a whole lot of disturbing notes and emails about Silvers' interrogation techniques.

I barely knew my sister-in-law. In fact, I had only met her twice, but I wasn't about to let her be taken away by the kind of people who thought it was fun to give Valentine enough drugs to pickle an elephant and employed people like Smoot. "Then you know I've got to do this."

"It endangers my men and jeopardizes our mission."

"My mission is to get my brother back, and I'll be damned if I bring him home and his wife and kids are rotting in some secret prison shit hole . . . Look, you drop me off in Flagstaff, then take right back off. Even as powerful as Majestic is, it'll still take them time to put it together. There's an airfield in Santa Vasquez, Mexico. I know a guy there, and you can get a new plane, nice and clean. I'll cross the border and meet you there, and if I'm . . . held up, you just bail without me."

Ling folded her arms and studied me. "Bob was right about one thing."

"What?" The Cessna engine turned over with a cough and a belch of oil smoke.

"You love very few people, but to those, you are extremely loyal."

It was a stupid weakness. "Don't rub it in."

"I meant it as a compliment," she said sincerely. Ling folded her arms and studied me. "You helped us. We will take this risk."

"Thanks." Then I noticed something about the airfield. I stopped, tilted my head, and thought about it for a moment. It was stupid, but it could work. "Maybe we don't need to land. That way if I screw up and attract any attention, you guys are still in the clear." I pointed at a large green sign on a nearby hangar. "I've got an idea."

The hangar had a padlocked chain on the door, and was clearly closed for the winter. Ling followed my finger and read the sign.

SKYDIVING LESSONS AND RENTALS

"You can't be serious."

"Ms. Ling, serious is my middle name," I said with a smile.

I woke up looking at Albert Einstein again.

"Good evening, Mr. Lorenzo," Dr. Bundt said over the noise of the Cessna. The good doctor had come to the rear of the plane and sat next to me. "We'll be passing over Flagstaff in thirty minutes."

"Groovy." I yawned and stretched. At least I had managed to get a couple of hours of sleep. The view out the window showed that it was nearly dark. Perfect. "I'll get ready. We'll need to pick a good spot. We've got to avoid witnesses, but someplace close enough that I can catch a ride into town."

"Understandable. You have done this before, I assume?"

"Jumped out of an airplane? Yeah, a few times." When Big Eddie had commissioned me to rob the Cape Town Diamond Exchange, my team had inserted with a HALO jump. We had practiced a multitude of times, jumping five or six times a day in the week leading up to the actual heist. Of course, one of Eddie's men had landed on a wrought-iron fence and disemboweled himself, so I couldn't exactly say that it had been *flawlessly* executed. I changed the subject. "How's your patient?"

Ling was forward of us, sitting on the floor, leaning on the fuselage, next to the unconscious form of Valentine. The table had been removed, and Valentine was stretched out. He still looked like shit.

Dr. Bundt shook his head. "At this point, I do not know. He'll live, but I do not know what shape he will be in. The boy has seen some serious trauma, and has been heavily medicated for quite some time. He still hasn't woken up."

"Well, when he wakes up, the kid and I need to talk." It was not a request.

"It may not be that simple, I'm afraid. Not everyone comes back fully from that kind of trauma."

"He's tough," I said simply.

"If only that were all there was to it. You see, when someone faces something so horrible, when something breaks inside their—"

I cut him off. "Whatever, Doc. I know how horrible works. Some people wimp out, let the hurt, the evil, *own* them. Others lock it up and hide it, and some people are really smart, and they keep it, and learn to use it as a weapon."

He paused, studying me. "And I assume that you are the latter?"

I had already said too much. "Don't bother to psychoanalyze me, Doc. You're wasting your time."

"It is what I do," he said simply. "But if I were to make an educated guess, in a professional capacity, I would say that you had a very horrible childhood, violent, poor, probably a criminal background, most likely abusive. I can tell that by your reputation and behavior. You trust no one. Your natural instinct is to dislike everyone you meet. Your first reaction is to view them either as a threat or something you can use to your own advantage. Basically, you are what I believe you Americans would refer to as an *asshole*."

"I'm the nicest asshole you'll ever meet. You know I'm not paying for this session, right?" I moved over to check my stolen parachute.

He followed me. "But that's not all you are. I can only assume that you had some respite, some brief time where you actually learned to love. Where you actually learned about family and loyalty, and that not everyone in the world existed just to prey upon one another. I can tell this by the way you speak about those that you consider your own. For them, you are very protective. Perhaps those good times were somehow taken from you, rendering you bitter and full of hate for so long—"

"I'm not one of your freed slaves in need of fixing. Now if you'll excuse me . . ." I hoisted the parachute and headed forward.

His bony hand clamped down on my wrist. "Mr. Lorenzo, if I can ever be of assistance . . ."

I sighed, crouched uncomfortably in the cramped compartment. He meant well. "Dr. Bundt, just so you know. When I was a kid, I watched my old man beat my mother to death. I stabbed one of his eyes out with a fork when he came for me next. The judge that put my dad in prison took me in and gave me a home. He was a good man. A few years later, some scumbags killed him for his watch. So I hunted them down and murdered every last one of them. I've spent the time since hurting people and taking their stuff. So there really isn't much you can tell me that's going to fill me with warm fuzzies, if you know what I mean."

"See? I was actually pretty close," he said happily.

I gently removed his hand from my arm. "Score one for psychiatry." I moved toward the cockpit. Ling was asleep, still holding Valentine's hand. I'd suspected there were some feelings there, at least on her side of the equation. Antoine and Shen watched me carefully step over them as I made my way to the cockpit.

"We're getting close," the pilot said without turning around. "This area's actually really forested. Where do you want to get out?"

"That's the highway below us. I just need to be close enough to run to it. Pick me a good, open field where I won't break my neck, and I'll try for that. I'll get ready, you just give me the signal."

The pilot nodded. As I turned back around, Shen spoke.

"Was Doctor Bundt trying to analyze you?"

It took me a moment to respond. I could count the number of times that Shen had initiated conversation in the last week on one hand. "Yeah, apparently my psychological profile says I'm an asshole."

"I could have told you that," he said, and actually grinned. Shen extended his hand. I shook it. He had a grip that could bend rebar. "It was a pleasure working with you."

"Yes, I thought I was going to have to kill you at first, but I would work with you anytime," Antoine said simply. "It was an honor."

Well, I'll be damned.

"Thanks, guys, but this is only a detour. I'm not dead yet." I passed forward a note that I had written some instructions on. "When you get to Santa Vasquez, the man you need to speak with at the airport is Guillermo Reyes. He runs all of the smuggling through that area. Tell him I sent you, and he'll arrange for new tail numbers and transponder. Don't let him give you any shit. Shen, would you help me at the door?"

Shen moved to assist as I struggled into the chute. I had checked it on the ground in Montana, and it had appeared to be relatively new, in good condition and packed correctly, rigging seemed nice and tight, and if it wasn't, at least I wouldn't have to worry about it for very long. My Suunto watch had an illuminated altimeter, and had always been very accurate in the past. The light was fading, and I was planning to open low enough that hopefully I would minimize any witnesses.

I was dressed in jeans, a baggy grey long-sleeve shirt, and the same boots I had been wearing in Tickville. The holster for my STI 9mm was a standard concealment rig, nothing really jump capable, so I fixed that by zip-tying the STI's grip to my belt. I had a pouch for the suppressor, and I hoped that it would hold, same with my two spare magazines. You may think something is securely attached to your person, but hitting the ground after a jump has a tendency to separate a lot of gear from their owners.

"There's a good pasture ahead. Looks fairly flat. The highway is one mile to the west," the pilot shouted. "Get ready."

I noticed Ling watching me. We had woken her. Her black eyes were difficult to read.

"If you don't hear from me in six hours, assume I'm dead," I said as I pulled the stolen goggles over my eyes. "I'm sorry about what I said earlier."

"No, you're not. But thank you for saying so. Good luck, Lorenzo," she said, smiling, still holding Valentine's hand. "See you in Mexico."

Shen opened the door behind me. The roar of the

passing airstream was deafening. The pilot pumped his fist in the air. It was time to go. I gave the Exodus operatives a wave, and stepped backward into the hundred mile-an-hour sky.

It had been awhile. The feeling was terrifying and exhilarating at the same time. The wind tore at my clothing, battered my face, and sucked the moisture right off my grinning teeth. I could only vaguely see the color and texture of the ground. The Sun was setting, and I knew that the odds of someone seeing the grey, terminal-velocity blur that was my silhouette was slim. I held my arms at my sides, clenched tight, legs extended, head down as I tore through the air at absurd speed.

There was the highway. The headlights were beacons. I could see the field that the pilot had picked out, a giant strip a slightly different shade of brown than the rest of the countryside. The numbers on my altimeter were changing rapidly. I'd changed the ground level on it before jumping, which was good because Arizona was a lot closer to the sky than Saint Carl.

Jill would really love this. She's never jumped before. I can only imagine how fun she would think this is.

Strange, the thoughts that wander through your head when you're streaking toward the ground at a speed sufficient to turn you into a red paste. Here I was, taking a stupid risk with a very high potential for death, and I was thinking about Jill. Well, that was understandable, since she was the best thing that had ever happened to me. Someone like me certainly didn't deserve someone like her. Hell, someone like me didn't deserve to be alive at all, let alone happy. It was probably best not to think such bad karmic thoughts while whistling through the air, flipping gravity the bird.

Pay attention. The ground was closer now, and every fiber of my being told me to deploy the chute. I'd disabled the automatic deployment preset. I checked my altitude again. Still a little too high on the horizon. A single police report that might show up in a government database would defeat the purpose of this idiotic stunt. I waited.

I flared my arms and legs out, feeling the current change over my body, turning myself into a giant air brake. The ground was close, screaming toward me. *Ground! Ground!* I told the panicky part of my brain to shut up. *NOW!*

I pulled the hacky-sack-looking ball from the base of my pack. The pilot chute shot out, but the big ram chute seemed to take forever to unfurl. The slider kept it from opening so fast that the straps would smash into me. That was always the sucky part. The parachute cracked and snapped above me. I glanced up. Nice and open, and I was shedding velocity.

It was only open for a few seconds, then there was the earth, scrolling beneath me at too high of a speed. This part was always really difficult in low light. Flare too soon, stall and free fall the last little bit, flare too late and you hit the ground too hard. I was out of practice, but landing felt pretty clean. My boots hit the ground running. I made it about ten huge steps before I stepped into a soft depression and pitched sideways, twisting my ankle before landing on my hand, elbow, shoulder, and then I was rolling in a mass of dirt clods, parachute fabric, and cord.

Yep. It's been awhile.

I lay in the dust, spitting dirt and catching my breath under a pile of blue fabric. My right ankle throbbed. Not my best landing by any means, but it would do. I untangled myself and stood. The field was dark and quiet in every direction. All clear. I checked my gear. One spare magazine was somewhere in the dirt, but I didn't have time to look for it.

Unbuckling the chute, I crumpled it into a ball in my arms and began to limp in the direction of the highway. That had been fun, but now it was time to catch a ride.

I had thrown the chute in a drainage ditch. I had no doubt it would be found shortly. Everything I knew about agriculture could be written on a 3x5 card, with plenty of space left over, so I had no idea how often people checked those kinds of things, but all I needed was a day or two.

My ankle was good and swollen by the time I reached the highway. I stepped out in front of the first set of headlights, waving my arms above my head. It was a pickup truck. The driver hit the brakes, and I had to step back onto the shoulder to keep from getting run over. The Dodge stopped twenty meters past me. I trotted up to the window as the driver rolled it down.

"What the hell's the emergency?" He was an older man, with a puffy trucker hat and a scruffy grey beard. Both the driver and the passenger, a younger clone of the driver, eyed me suspiciously. "You look like hell," he drawled.

"I've had a rough night. I need a ride into town."

"Where's your car?" he asked. The old man kept his

right hand down at his side, probably on his gun. This was Arizona, after all. "I don't pick up hitchhikers." Smart people in Arizona.

"Long story." I knew that I looked suspicious. Especially since I still had Smoot-colored hair, was dusty, and I was walking along a highway in the middle of nowhere. "It's embarrassing, okay?"

He put the truck back in drive and started to roll.

"Okay! Okay!" I said. The old man braked. "I had a fight with my girlfriend. I called her fat, 'cause she's totally let herself go. We pulled over so I could take a leak. She was mad, and drove off without me. My cell phone's in the car. I fell in a ditch running after her. Just give me a lift to the next place with a phone, and I'll call one of my friends in Flagstaff to pick me up. Come on, man, please?" I'm a very convincing liar. Might as well cut to the chase. I held up one hand with several twenties. "I can pay you for gas!"

He looked at me disdainfully and spit a mighty stream of chew out the window. "Get in back," he said with a jerk of his head.

Chapter 8: Shadows

𖤍

Lorenzo
Flagstaff, Arizona
February 15th

It was a school night, so hopefully Bob's kids would all be home and not out screwing around. All I needed to do was break in without being seen by the government agents who were surely staked out around the place, convince my sister-in-law—whom I barely knew—to trust me, and get them out of there without being spotted. Then somehow I needed to get them across the border, and to someplace safe. *This sucks.*

I made one pass through Bob's nice suburban neighborhood in the Jeep Cherokee that I had boosted from the truckstop on the outskirts of town. I knew where Bob lived because I'd broken in the last time I'd been here. *He really should just give me a key.* I spotted the watchers on the end of the street in an unmarked surveillance van. There was no one in the cab, heavily tinted windows all around, the standard stuff, it was really obvious. I tried to look nonchalant as I cruised past them, by the front of Bob's house, and around the corner.

I parked on the cul-de-sac that backed up to the Lorenzo family's backyard and checked my watch. It was pretty late and there was no one outside. It was drastically warmer than Montana, and happy insects swarmed the street lights. Some neighborhood dog started barking in the distance. It took me a few moments to pick the yard to cut through, no sign of pets, no motion-detecting lights, and it didn't look like anyone was home. It was a straight shot through the yard and over the back fence.

Two minutes later I was using my bump keys to break into Bob's back door. He still had the same high-tech alarm system. This time it took me almost a minute and a half to bypass it. All that soft island living had made me sloppy.

The lights were on inside the Lorenzo house. The TV was playing in the family room, something obnoxious with a laugh track. A radio was on upstairs. I crept through the kitchen, trying to formulate a plan. This woman had married my brother, so I had no doubt that I was a split-second from getting a load of double-aught buckshot to the face if I startled her.

There were children's toys scattered across the living-room floor. The wall was covered in family pictures. They were all happy and smiling. I listened to the sounds of the house. Something was wrong. There were supposed to be several people home, but it didn't feel right. I had broken into a lot of homes, and I knew how an occupied house felt. Nobody was here.

The bedroom closets were open. Clothes were spread on the beds. It felt like they had bailed out of here in a hurry. There was a pink Post-It note stuck to the mirror just inside the front entryway. The message had been written in neat, cursive handwriting. The pen was still lying on the hardwood floor directly below the mirror.

> *Dear Government Assholes,*
>
> *I've been married to an FBI agent for fifteen years. Did you honestly think I would be stupid enough not to notice your van full of idiots watching my house and following me around?*
>
> *I don't know what you've done with my husband, but we have made contingency plans. You will not find us. You will never find us. But my husband will find you. You picked the wrong family to fuck with. Bob is ten times the cop you pussies are.*
>
> *Hugs and kisses*
Gwen Lorenzo
>
> *p.s. Kiss my ass and die, you filthy, crooked sons of bitches.*

It shouldn't have surprised me that the Lorenzos had a bugout plan. I was rapidly discovering that there was a lot I didn't know about my relatives. It looked like my mission had already been accomplished. I was willing to bet that Gwen and the kids had gone out the same way that I had come in, probably had somebody waiting to pick them up in the cul-de-sac. Hell, I might have passed them on the way into the neighborhood.

It appeared that Bob had married up.

"Well, since I'm here . . ." I muttered to myself. I might

as well see if he'd left any clues as to what he had been working on that was so damned important.

His office was the only locked room in the basement. It took me ten seconds to pick. Judging from the looks of the place, he took after Dad. The desk was a mess of papers, a type of organized chaos that the Lorenzo men seemed to cultivate. Every wall had pictures, newspaper clippings, maps, timelines, and hundreds of Post-It notes stuck up. Under the notes were awards, commendations, citations for bravery, framed and then forgotten, things that most people would have thought to be very important, but Bob was too personally humble to worry about things like that. There were five guns hung on the wall behind the desk, muzzles pointed down in a half circle, the main rifles of WW2, an M1 Garand, a Russian Mosin Nagant, a British Enfield, a German Mauser, and a Japanese Arisaka, and that was the only space without notes taped to it. That's because those had belonged to our father.

I scanned the notes. Names, dates, some circled, some with question marks after them. A lot of it was from the data that Valentine had dumped on the internet before he wasted Gordon Willis. There were a few familiar words that popped up a lot, like *Blue* and *Alpha Point*. The most common word was *Majestic*. It appeared over and over again. It was everywhere, oftentimes with an exclamation point behind it, like an angry afterthought.

Majestic is the shadow government. Majestic is the cancer.

There was a handwritten note on the top of the desk.

To whom it may concern,

If you're reading this, I can only assume that I am dead. I hope you're not one of them. If you are, congratulations, you bastards win again. I've made arrangements for my family. If I disappear they know to go someplace where you'll never find them. They know nothing, so leave them out of it. I've kept them in the dark to protect them.

If somebody else finds this, I hope this information proves of more use to you than it has to me. I have spent the last few years of my life learning about a secret government organization usually known as Majestic.

They are the end result of secrets and decades of lies. At one time they existed for a good reason, to defend our country, to do the dirty jobs that others could not do, but they've become corrupt, perverted. They exist only to grow in power. They are in every facet of the government. The Bureau is infested with them. They're watching my every move.

I first found out about them as a young agent, after they arranged the murder of several witnesses to their crimes. These were innocent people. Since then I've been watching them, learning, and what I've found out is terrifying. They're always in the shadows, pulling the strings. They are above the law.

They are not evil. Just like a disease isn't evil. It just is. Majestic is a disease. May the truth be the cure.

Robert T. Lorenzo

I began flipping through Bob's ramblings. If I hadn't had first-hand experience with this sort of thing I would've thought it was the rantings of a crazy man. He'd been working on this for a *long* time, way before he'd gotten Valentine's information from Zubara.

Just like Silvers, Bob had been preoccupied with this Project Blue. There was a printout with a few photos on it. *Four Majestic operatives were involved with the creation and implementation of Project Blue.*

I didn't recognize the first man, he looked like a politician type. Under his name had been written *Former Senator Barrington, head of operations, killed under mysterious circumstances.* The second man I had seen briefly in Quagmire, Nevada last year. He was a popular guy in my house, since he'd tried to have Jill murdered. *Gordon Willis, murdered/possible suicide in Virginia. Head of Majestic black ops.* The third picture was somebody else I'd met in less than perfect circumstances, mostly because his men had just captured me and he had my fingers broken during an interrogation. *Colonel Curtis Hunter, Dead Six field commander. Killed in Zubara.*

The last spot was blank except for where Bob had drawn a giant question mark. Apparently he didn't know who the fourth man was.

Blue was the doomsday option against Ill.

I paused. I hadn't seen a note that explained who or what "Ill" stood for. I doubted Majestic needed a doomsday option against Illinois.

Four operatives knew about Blue. Barrington came up with the plan. He enlisted the other three to implement it. Willis took command when Barrington was killed. Hunter and unknown subject set the Alpha Point. Hunter got cold feet. He must have realized that Majestic was up to no good. Gave up Majestic to Valentine when Willis betrayed Dead Six in Zubara. Two down. Before Willis can bring more operatives into the plan for Blue, he dies.

Four men knew about Blue. Three are dead. Majestic scraps Blue. But the final operative has gone rogue. Why? Maybe he thinks Majestic killed his compatriots?

Majestic is panicking. I've watched these bastards for years, and I've never seen this before. Majestic doesn't know what Blue entails and they're scared of it. Zubaragate hurt them. If information on Blue leaks, it will kill them.

My phone rang. "Damn it." I didn't have time for this. I had to know what was going on. "What?" I snapped.

"It's me," Reaper said quickly. "I've intercepted some traffic. They're keeping the details hushed up, but there's been an alert out of Montana. Dude, they know."

I can't get Valentine out of North Gap. The only other person alive who knows about Blue is the final operative. Majestic was looking for him in a place called The Crossroads, he's tied to some sort of mythical figure known as Sala Jihan, the Pale Man. I've got to find the final operative. It is the only way to destroy Majestic once and for all.

"Boss, are you listening? The government knows!" Reaper insisted.

"Okay. I've got to go." I put my phone away. I had to get this stuff out of here, fast. The goons outside would probably move as soon as they got the word. I looked for something to shove paper into, and spotted a small garbage can. It would have to do. I dumped the can's contents on the floor. At the very top was a crumpled letter from the FBI telling Bob that he was fired from the bureau for gross misconduct.

CRASH! I cringed at the sound of the front door splintering open.

Discretion is the better part of valor. I comforted myself with that platitude as I ran away like a coward. I've done my fair share of fighting, but I always try to fight on my terms. I always have a plan. I always ambush. And when I don't have the element of surprise, I retreat. I'm a thief first and foremost, and thieves who pick fights tend to die young.

The Majestic goons got the call and moved right in. At least two hit the front door, and the third circled through the backyard. I hid behind the fridge, my 9mm in one hand, garbage can full of paper in the other, and waited for the Majestic goon to kick in the back door, stomp through the kitchen, and run right past me.

They were expecting a woman and some frightened kids, an easy target, probably lots of screaming and crying, real obvious stuff. I waited for the man in the suit to leave the kitchen, and he headed down the stairs to the basement. I slipped across the floor without a sound, paused briefly at the back door to scan in both directions, figuring correctly that they'd rushed in rather than form a perimeter, and then took off in a full sprint for the fence. It was wood, five feet tall, and I vaulted it without slowing.

I landed with a grunt on the neighbor's lawn, having forgotten about my swollen ankle. The yard was dark, a couple of big bushes, a swing set moved slightly in the breeze, but it appeared to be clear. I hadn't been spotted. Seventy feet and I would be back to my stolen Jeep and out of here.

"Move and I'll shoot you down where you stand," a man said from behind me, utterly calm. I hesitated, my pistol at my side. I could spin and dive, factor in his reaction time. *Ca-click*. The sound of a hammer being cocked was piercingly loud. "You're fittin' to get tumped. Drop your piece."

The voice had a slow drawl to it. My trained ear told me probably Arkansas, and somebody who meant business. The gunman was ten feet behind me, and was just another shadow in the bushes. He had me dead to rights. I tossed my STI on the grass. "I'm guessing you aren't the guy that owns this house."

"Nope. Turn around real slow-like." I did as I was told.

The man moved forward, the glint of a revolver coming out of the darkness. He was keeping his voice down. "Well, if it ain't Bob's kin, his brother, the thief."

"I know you?"

"Nope. And you never will. I asked around about your rep after Bob met you last, so I don't think we'd make good friends. I only recognize you because of the old family pictures on his wall. Bob's a sentimental type . . . I watched you go in his house, all sneaky. Real smooth."

I had been pretty sure that nobody had been watching. This guy was good. "And I'm assuming that you're not with them," I said calmly, nodding back toward the house. "Who're you?"

"Let's say I'm a friend of the family." He moved closer. He was probably in his early fifties, tall and lean, his face weatherbeaten and creased, long hair tied back in a ponytail, and eyes that scanned me like a wolf. His revolver was classic blued steel and polished walnut, and the front sight never wavered from my heart. "I owe Bob a favor. Me and him share some mentors, if you know what I mean . . ."

"You're an agent? Some sort of operator?"

He snorted. "I'm no G man."

"You're the one that helped Gwen and the kids get away?" Our voices were barely whispers. On the other side of the fence I could hear the angry shouting of the Majestic men as they found the note left for them.

"That's what I do. Where you take things, I hide them. Where you hunt things, I protect them. The family's safe. I aim to keep them that way. That's all you need to know, brother."

"Tell Gwen I'll bring him back," I stated.

"I reckon you will." He lowered the hammer, tucked the gun back under his nondescript denim shirt, and faded back into the shadows. "My gut tells me Bob underestimates you about as much as you underestimate him. Nice to meet you, *Uncle Hector*. You won't see me again." He was gone as suddenly as he came.

I retrieved my gun and files, made it to the Jeep in record time, and drove out of the neighborhood as fast as I could without drawing undue attention to myself. Even then, I almost managed to run over a fat guy out power walking. A yellow Mustang left the cul-de-sac a moment after I did, headed in the opposite direction.

The man in the shadows . . . I had only spoken to him for a moment, but from what he said, and the steel in his eyes, I knew exactly what he was. I had dealt with his kind before. They were my antithesis.

A black Suburban with red and blue wig-wag lights flashing inside its windshield passed me as I left the subdivision. I turned onto the main road and headed for the highway. I left no trace that I had been in my brother's home, so the road south should be clear. I had only slept a couple of hours in the last two days, and I was a long way from Mexico.

My thoughts returned to the man in the dark. I'd spent most of my career in countries that didn't have much in the way of professional law enforcement, and men like that always appeared eventually. They were the ones who took care of problems society couldn't, protecting innocents and their valuables from men like me, and usually disregarding the laws to do it. They weren't organized, but the sorts that drifted into that line of work inevitably knew each other, and shared information about my kind. That fellow with no name had probably dealt with a lot of people like me, and more than likely left them in shallow graves.

Majestic would never find that family. Bob had chosen well.

LORENZO
Santa Vasquez, Mexico
February 16th

The Sun was approaching its high point as I rolled into the Santa Vasquez airport. At this point I was running on nothing but energy drinks, and my brain was twitchy from fatigue and caffeine. The trip across the border had been uneventful, and the only people that had seen me take a cow trail across were a couple dozen illegals. The last time I had been through those hills, I had ended up running into some Chechens. Heading south was a lot easier than heading north.

Airport was a generous term for an asphalt strip surrounded by corrugated tin shacks. It didn't look like much, but I knew there were probably a good thirty to fifty flights landing here every day, and I was willing to bet that almost all of them were somehow drug related. Mexico had calmed down a bit since the revolution, but it had been business as usual here the whole time.

My nose was assaulted with the burning chemical stench of Santa Vasquez as soon as I stepped out of the Jeep. It was winter, so it was only in the nineties. Good old Mexico.

I spotted the Exodus Cessna parked in one of the sheds, and started toward it, still holding the garbage can under one arm. I saw the hulking form of Antoine first. A broad smile split his face when he saw me.

"Glad to see you, my friend," he shouted.

"Let's go home," I said simply.

Chapter 9: House Guests

VALENTINE
Location Unknown
Date/Time Unknown

When my eyes opened next, I was staring at an unfamiliar ceiling. I was lying in a clean, soft four-poster bed. A ceiling fan lazily rotated above me. It was a much more pleasant setting than the last place I'd woken up in. My head began to spin as soon as I sat up. As I waited for the dizzy spell to pass, the sounds of water running, or rain, resonated in the background.

The last thing I remembered was being in the snow. I'd been in pain. I remembered fear, then rage, then violence. I'd been trying to escape from . . . where had I been? I rubbed my face and tried to think. My head throbbed. My body ached. I had gaps in my memory and thinking hurt. It was like the worst hangover ever.

Had I really escaped? Gone were the cold cinder block walls and concrete floors. There was no hint of chill in the air. Instead I found myself in a cozy wooden bungalow with nice furniture. The windows were open, but covered by screens, and shaded from the sun by low hanging eaves. There was a screen door at one end of the room. Beyond it was a wooden deck and a cluster of tree trunks.

Where the hell am I? Is this another one of Dr. Silvers' tricks? Pain shot through my leg as I stood up. It had been bandaged, and my clothes had been changed. Instead of my blue sweats, white T-shirt, and shoes with no laces, I was wearing only a t-shirt and a pair of gaudy swim trunks. I had no idea where my shoes were. My body protested with each movement as I hobbled toward the door. The pain in my right leg calmed to a dull throb after the initial shock, nothing I couldn't deal with. Barefoot and confused, I quietly pulled the door open and stepped onto the deck. What lay beyond took my breath away.

White sand stretched out in front of me until it met clear blue water. The sound of gently rolling waves filled the air, and I could hear the cries of seagulls. I stepped off the deck and onto the sand; where the deck had been rough and cool, the sand was warm and soft. I kept limping forward, out from under the shade of a clump of palm trees, toward the water.

I felt the sun on my neck for the first time that I could recall. I looked up into the deep blue sky, squinting in the light as puffy white clouds drifted overhead. I looked back at the bungalow, and then again toward the water.

This isn't real, my mind protested. Scattered memories came back to me; I'd been deceived before, by Dr. Silvers' machines, her mind games, her tricks. But the sand was warm between my toes and the wind was gentle on my face. I could smell the salt in the air. It certainly *seemed* real.

I wandered across the beach, not at all sure where I was going. No one else was around. I hadn't gotten very far before exhaustion caught up with me. I had no idea how long I'd been in that bed, and it was obvious that I was in bad shape. I focused on a clump of palm trees ahead of me and made my way toward them. My head still ached and I wanted to get out of the sun.

In the shade, the sand was much cooler. I sat down, facing the water, and just stared into the distance. I'm not sure just how long I stayed there, listening to the waves, trying to clear my head.

"Michael!" someone cried. The woman had a clear soprano voice. I rolled my head and saw a woman standing on the beach, holding something in her hand. I couldn't tell who she was, but she turned in my direction and began to run toward me. "Michael!" she repeated as she got closer. I rubbed my eyes. When I looked up again, the woman was kneeling next to me.

"Ling?" I croaked. It couldn't be real. I refused to accept it. Yet I was looking into the dark almond eyes of someone I never imagined I'd see again. She threw her arms around me and pulled me against her. The last time I'd seen her, we were on a different beach, and she certainly hadn't given me a hug. "Is it really you?" My voice was a hoarse whisper. Her neck was smooth and soft against my cheek; her hair was wet and smelled nice. She squeezed me tighter and rubbed her hand up and down on my back.

"It's really me," she said. "I'm sorry I wasn't there when you woke up. I was in the shower."

"Can I have some water? I'm . . . I'm really thirsty."

"Here, drink," she said, handing me a plastic bottle. I lifted it to my lips and reveled in its icy coldness. I downed the whole thing, coughing when it was empty.

"Jesus," I said, my voice clearer now. "That's good. What happened? How . . . where are we?"

"Someplace safe. Our host would prefer I not tell you the name of this place."

"You helped me escape from . . . from . . ."

"North Gap. The place you were held is called North Gap. It's in America, in Montana. We got you out." The concern was apparent on her face. Ling gently placed a hand on the left side of my face. I recoiled slightly as she touched me, but fought the urge to pull away. "Are you all right?"

I tried to speak, tried to answer her, but I didn't have the words. "Thank you," I said. It was all I could manage. I was suddenly too emotional to say much more.

"You are safe now. It is a long story, and you need to rest."

Ling and I sat there, looking out over the water, for a long time. The waves rolled in and out. A sailboat slowly moved across the horizon. Part of me was still expecting to wake up any time, to find myself attached to one of Dr. Silvers' infernal machines. I'd been so far gone that I'd been talking to the dead. The rational part of my mind never expected to actually escape. I was just trying to give them a reason to kill me, to end it all.

A seagull landed nearby and studied us greedily with its beady little eyes. I was free. I was alive. Ling, like a guardian angel, had come to my rescue. The gull was soon joined by one of his friends, then another, then another.

"Are you ready to go?" Ling asked.

I was free. Tears welled up in my eyes.

"No."

LORENZO
St. Carl Island
February 17th

"Looks like sleeping beauty's awake." I put my bare feet up on the banister and leaned back in the wicker chair. The ocean breeze was cool, and the palm trees around the front of my house swayed gently.

"Really? Oh good," Jill said as she came out of the house, drying her hands on a towel. "He's even walking? Good for him."

I gestured with my drink toward the beach. "Yeah, I think he's lost, but Ling found him." Valentine and Ling were sitting under one of the trees, facing away from us, and looking out over the gentle waves. The ocean was a brilliant blue beyond them, and they appeared to be deep in conversation. Some seagulls had surrounded them, preparing to attack. St. Carl had some aggressive seagulls.

"Oh, they make a cute couple. I like Ling, she seems really nice. A little intense, but nice." Jill said as she sat down next to me. She had pulled her hair up into a bun while she had been cleaning and organizing gear. I couldn't help but smile when I saw the grease smudge on her cheek.

"He's a schizo mercenary, riddled with PTSD, and she's a terrorist with ice water for blood. *Cute* isn't the first word that comes to mind. I'm sure they'll have a bunch of beautiful little sociopathic killing machines someday."

"Like you have any room to talk," Jill said curtly. "How many countries are you wanted in again?"

"Fifteen. Well, sixteen, but I don't think Somalia is technically a country right now." She had me there. Jill was the most normal person currently residing at Casa De Lorenzo, but that wasn't saying a whole lot. She'd been dragged into my world against her will, just a witness who'd been in the wrong place at the wrong time. Jill was a survivor, and she'd taken to it well enough. Though it pained me to admit it, if it hadn't been for that kid lying down there on my beach right now, Jill would certainly be in a shallow grave in Quagmire, Nevada.

"You know, you don't need to be so pissy about this. I really like Val. You did a good thing getting him out of that horrible place."

"I didn't do it for him," I said sullenly. "He better be worth it."

Jill laughed at me. Her dark eyes twinkled when she laughed. "You know, you can actually admit to doing a good deed once in a while. It won't ruin your image."

I didn't respond to that. Jill was an honest-to-goodness decent person. She saw the best in everyone, even me. Of course, she was wrong about me. I wasn't a good person. I certainly wasn't worthy of her, but she seemed to disagree. I made a show of finishing my drink, sat the glass down, and stood. "Well, I'm going to have a few words with Mr. Valentine."

Jill's hand clamped down on my wrist. She was not a very big person, but she had the iron grip of someone who had grown up in a martial arts studio. When most little girls were playing with dolls, Jill's dad had her punching speed bags. "No," her voice was firm.

"Jill. I just killed like a dozen people. He owes me, and the son of a bitch is gonna talk."

She didn't let go. "Sit . . ."

"Honey . . ."

". . . *down*."

She wasn't going to budge on this one. I could tell. I flopped back into the chair with a pensive grunt. "Let's not fight in front of the terrorists."

Jill didn't take the bait. "First off, if those men in Montana were anything like the ones that had me in Nevada, they don't count as people. Second, you're going to leave him alone. Val's been through a lot of trauma. They need some time, and the last thing they need is you going in there and being your usual pushy self. You're not exactly in touch with your emotions."

"I've got plenty of emotions." I started to count on my fingers. "Anger, hate, revenge—"

"Revenge is not an emotion."

"You've been watching those relationship shows on cable again, haven't you?" From the look on her face, my attempt at evasion was going down in flames.

"I'm serious, Lorenzo. Leave them alone. You can harass him later, and when you do, you'd better be nice."

I sighed. "I'm not good at *nice*."

"You're nice to me. Besides, we have a few days before Reaper completes our covers anyway."

I bit my lip and watched a seagull land on the porch railing. It looked at me with its evil little rat eyes, contemplating where to poop. "On our covers . . . The Crossroads is one of the most dangerous places in the world."

"We've been over this," Jill said sharply. Meaning that we'd already had a fight once. "I'm going with you. You need somebody you can trust. And besides, I do okay at this stuff, remember?" She stood, kissed me gently on the forehead, and headed back into the house. "End of discussion."

This domestication thing certainly had its ups and downs. With few exceptions, I had spent most of my life only looking after myself. It was hard to deal with having to protect somebody else who was just as bullheaded as I was. Half of me was proud of her, wanting to help save my brother, to watch my back, and though she wouldn't admit it, I knew she wanted revenge on Majestic for shattering her life. The other half of me was kind of pissed that she wouldn't just agree to stay home where it was safe.

In the distance, Ling snuggled closer against Valentine. I wanted nothing more than to go down there and get an answer as to just what in the hell made him so damned special. The seagull cocked its head at me.

"Little fucker," I said as I pulled my STI with my right hand and my Silencerco Osprey suppressor with my left. I started to screw them together while the seagull stared stupidly at its coming demise.

"No killing gulls on the porch!" Jill shouted from inside.

Shit. "Yes, dear," I answered as I stuck my gun back in its holster. "It's your lucky day, punk." The gull emptied its bowels all over my porch, squawked at me, and flew off. It's a sad day when a man gets no respect in his own house.

VALENTINE
St. Carl Island
February 18th

It was all a lot to take in. The thing that really boggled my mind was the fact that it was February. Between not having any way to keep track of time and Dr. Silvers' mind games, I had no idea I'd been in North Gap for so long. And now I was on Lorenzo's island. According to Ling, he owned most of it. That was just weird.

The first time I'd actually *met* Lorenzo was in Zubara. I put a bullet through an arms dealer named Jalal Hosani, and that same slug hit Lorenzo . . . who unfortunately had been wearing a vest. The night that Fort Saradia fell to the Zubarans, Lorenzo had broken into my room, trying to steal an old Arabian puzzle box that I'd taken on one of my operations with Dead Six. I closed my eyes as that memory came back to me. That was the night Sarah died. I would've died with her if he hadn't dragged me out. We'd met one last time, this time as reluctant allies to get Jill back from Gordon. We parted ways when I'd gone after Gordon. I'd never known much about him, hadn't wanted to, and figured I'd never see him again.

The snarky thief had done quite well for himself. Somehow he now basically owned an island and lived a life of leisure and luxury. Meanwhile I was getting mind-fucked by a mad scientist working for a shadow government organization. It hardly seemed fair, all things considered.

Returning my attention to what I was doing, I clicked through the files on Ling's laptop. I was alone in the bungalow, but before Ling left she showed me all of the information that they'd recovered from North Gap. Much of it was about me. It was unsettling, to say the least. Dr. Olivia Silvers had taken me on as a pet project. Originally, they were interested in me because of Project Blue. Once they realized I'd told them everything I knew, Silvers opted to keep me there for her own purposes, stringing her superiors along that I might still be useful. I suspected that her doing so was the only reason they hadn't just taken me out back and shot me. I basically owed her my life.

I wasn't going to send her a thank-you card.

I had barely been able to sleep the night before. I'd been drugged, sedated, restrained, exhausted, and unconscious for so long that I just didn't want to lie in bed anymore. Then there were the dreams. They weren't *nightmares,* exactly. These dreams were different. There were numbers that didn't mean anything to me, places I wasn't familiar with, and people I mostly didn't recognize, voices, overlapping and contradictory, some familiar, some not. They had to be subconscious leftovers from my time in Silvers' tank.

One person I did recognize from the bizarre dreams was Lorenzo's brother, the *other* Lorenzo, Bob. Probably because I had given him up. He was the one I'd given Colonel Hunter's flash drive to, and he'd dumped that information onto the internet. From what I'd heard from Ling, Project Heartbreaker was now a well-known government scandal. From what I'd heard today, it turned out that Bob had been trying to expose them for years. I regretted not trusting him more when we'd last spoken. I wanted to find him. We needed to compare notes.

Ling's rescue had retrieved a box with all the things that had been in my possession when I had been captured. My custom Smith & Wesson 629 Performance Center Classic .44 Magnum revolver was returned to me, complete with holster, the couple boxes of ammo I had in the car when they took me, and speed loaders. I'd meticulously cleaned and function-checked the heavy stainless-steel firearm. It felt good in my hand. My arm felt more whole when I held it. Having it on my hip again was a welcome comfort. It wasn't just my gun, though. My clothes were in there, loose-fitting now, since I'd lost weight in captivity, as well as my shoes. I found my Benchmade *Infidel* automatic knife, too, which I was happy to have back. More important than that was my father's harmonica. I'd been carrying it everywhere since Afghanistan and was happy I didn't lose it.

Staying focused was difficult. I looked at the screen again. I had just watched a security-camera video of one of my interrogation sessions. It was a surreal experience. You'd think it'd be hard to watch, but I found myself oddly detached from it all. My concentration was interrupted by a knock on the door. "It's open."

Lorenzo stepped into the little beach house. "Hey," he said awkwardly.

"Yo," I said. Lorenzo was an unassuming-looking man. He might be Mexican, sort of, maybe Middle Eastern, or even Indian. He had tanned skin, dark hair, and no really remarkable features. His face was accented only by unshaven stubble, like a permanent five o'clock shadow.

He was shorter than me, but muscular. His eyes always seemed to be watching you and he moved like he was wound pretty tight. It was really hard to tell how old he was, probably somewhere between thirty and forty-five. It was probably closer to the higher end just because of his apparent level of experience.

"You were in Switchblade, huh?" he asked.

I looked up at him. "Yeah . . . yeah I was. Switchblade Four, to be specific, for a few years. How'd you know?"

"Reaper did some digging on you. You guys made the cover of *Soldier of Fortune.*"

I smiled. "Yeah, I remember that. We all had to pay up, a case of beer each."

"Who was your team leader?"

"Huh? Ramirez. Jesus Ramirez," I said, pronouncing his name *"hey-sous."* "But we all called him . . ."

"You all called him Jesus," Lorenzo interrupted, pronouncing it like Jesus from the Bible. "And everyone would make bad puns about when Jesus is coming back, or Jesus is watching you, or Jesus saves."

I looked around nervously, not sure what to say. "Uh . . . Yeah, we did. Did you know him?" Lorenzo knew Hawk somehow, but neither man ever told me what their history was.

"A long time ago, back when he was the FNG. So Ramirez was a lifer?"

"I guess so. He was older than most of the team leaders. He'd been in that spot for a while, but was getting ready to move over to training, with Hawk, or maybe Corporate, when . . ."

"How'd he go out?"

"Helicopter crash. Mexico."

Lorenzo's face was a mask. If he was bothered by Ramirez' death he didn't show it. "Was Decker still in command?" he asked, the tone of his voice changing slightly. It sounded like there was some bad blood there.

"Not really. Decker was the CEO and head of Operations for all of Vanguard, but I only met him a few times. I heard he still did training and stuff, but I never saw him on any of our ops unless he was showcasing us for potential clients. He was the corporate front of Vanguard. He wore a suit instead of fatigues and surrounded himself with lawyers and accountants."

An unfriendly smile appeared on his face. "That's Decker for you."

"How do you know Decker? Or Ramirez? Or Hawk, for that matter."

"That's none of your business, kid," he said levelly. He was quiet for a moment, took a deep breath, then looked me in the eye like he was trying to bore a hole through my face. "I worked with Decker, and Hawk, and Ramirez a long time ago. Before there was a Vanguard corporation, before Decker became Mister *Legitimate Businessman*. It was just Switchblade back then. It was a different world. It was before PMCs got big, went mainstream. We did the dirty work."

"So did we," I suggested. "We just had PR firms to put a pretty face on it all. So what happened between you?"

"Things got complicated," Lorenzo said. He pulled out a chair, flipped it around, and sat across from me, leaning on the chair-back. Between us was a small wicker table with Ling's laptop on it. "I need to ask you some questions."

My eye twitched involuntarily. "What is it?"

"I'm not going to pretend that I busted you out of there because I like you. No offense."

"None taken."

"My brother came into contact with your girlfriend in Asia."

"He did?"

"Did she tell you?"

"Obviously not."

"My brother told Ling that there was something in your head important enough to die for. Now, I risked my life getting you out of there, I brought you into my home, and I want to know what it is."

I shook my head and chuckled to myself.

"What the hell are you laughing at?" Lorenzo growled. He was agitated.

"I don't know," I said simply.

"You don't know what?"

"Whatever it is your brother thinks I know, I don't know."

"*What?* He talked on and on about Project Blue. What the hell is Project Blue?"

My eyes narrowed. "I don't *know.*"

Lorenzo came up out of his chair. I stood up too, trying to back away. He grabbed me and pushed me against the wall, spilling my chair over as he did so. I was still shaky enough that I couldn't put up much resistance.

"What the fuck do you mean *you don't know?* My brother was willing to get me *killed* over this! He's probably dead now because of it, and you're telling me you don't know? You're fucking *lying*! Tell me what—" Lorenzo abruptly fell silent as I pushed the muzzle of my revolver into his chin.

"I don't know," I said quietly. "They asked me the same thing. I told them I didn't know. They kept me in solitary confinement, I told them I didn't know. They moved me to some secret prison, and I told them I didn't know. They used drugs on me, and I told them I didn't know. They shocked me with tasers, attacked me with a dog, beat me with sticks, left me out in the snow, fucked with my mind, and I kept telling them I don't know. I don't fucking know what . . ." I began to cough. I'd been screaming in Lorenzo's face. His eyes were wide, but hard. "I don't know," I repeated, trying to catch my breath.

"I saved your life, *twice*," he spat, still not moving. "I risked my life to go get you, because my brother thought you were worth it. And you mean to tell me that it was all a *mistake*?" His voice was cold and level, and he was so mad he was nearly shaking. "Then you come into *my house* and stick a gun in my face?"

I met his glare. I was *Calm*. Lorenzo's life was in danger, even if he was too stubborn to realize it. "Get your goddamn hands off me before Jill has to come down here and clean your brains off the ceiling fan." Lorenzo stared me down defiantly, but his grip on my shirt loosened. I pushed him away and backed up until I was leaning against the wall. I kept the gun trained on him. The thief was livid. He stood there, glaring at me, looking like he wanted nothing more than to break my neck. My gun didn't waver. He was pretty fast with a pistol but I wasn't going to give him a chance.

"I'm sorry, Lorenzo. I'm sorry you all went through this

for me. You think it's what I wanted? You think I wanted Ling to risk her life for my sorry ass? All I wanted was to die, this time and the last time. Twice in a row you got involved, didn't let me die when I was supposed to, and both times you got pissed at *me* because of it. I'm sorry, okay? I don't know what Project Blue is, and I don't know why it's so important to Bob or Majestic. The last thing Colonel Hunter told me before he died was 'Evangeline,' and he didn't say who that is or why she's important. He didn't say anything about Project Blue. I'm sorry, but I just don't know."

Lorenzo didn't say anything else. He just turned and walked out of the beach house. After he left, I set the revolver down and buried my face in my shaking hands. I hoped that Ling would get back soon.

LORENZO

"What's wrong, chief?" Reaper asked, looking up from the multiple computer screens that now filled one of my spare bedrooms. His stringy black hair was draped over half of his pale face. Even a few days of glorious St. Carl sun couldn't darken Reaper. The boy had no pigment. "You look pissed."

"Son of bitch pointed a gun at me, in my own fucking house. My own house!" I punched the door frame hard enough to hurt my hand. "I should have taken that .44 and shoved it up his ass. And this is after I saved his miserable life, the lousy, screwed-in-the-head, ingrate mother—"

"Say what?" Reaper cut me off as he pulled his iPod earbuds out. I could hear the blaring death metal from ten feet away.

I bit my lip. Yelling at Reaper, however tempting, wouldn't help anything. "Nothing. Never mind. How are you doing on the cover identities?"

Contrary to what you see in movies, you can't just create a whole new identity on a whim. It takes preparation and resources. Some countries were easier than others. In the third world, it was a piece of cake, wave around some money and tell people whatever you wanted. In nations that had computerized recordkeeping, professional police that actually investigated things, photo ID, taxes, and other horrible things like that, it took a lot more work. The key was always some sort of number. A number let you create history. In the US, it was a social security number, and most of the developed world had some sort of equivalent. There were people who made huge sums of money farming these things. For cheap, you end up with an ID that is being shared by hundreds of illegal aliens. For guys like me, you end up with a social security number that belongs to somebody who actually existed, but never developed any of their own history. Invalids, for example.

In the modern world, people don't just pop into existence anymore. Those golden days were long gone. Now when you created an identity, you had to groom it. I had a dozen names ready to go from six different countries. Each of those imaginary people had jobs working for corporations that were wholly owned by other international corporations, and so forth, in a maze of shells actually owned by me. These imaginary people got paid a salary, which of course flowed back into other accounts that I controlled, which then went back to the corporations, to pay them again later. They all traveled for a living, with addresses consisting of PO boxes. And once a year, they even automatically filed taxes in their respective nations, just like my shell corporations did. I kept quite a few clueless accountants very happy. Keeping these things up cost me a lot of money, but they were oh so worth it.

Reaper spun his chair back around and pointed at the screen. "Me and you, no problem, I've got like twenty to choose from. For the others, I'm using some of the IDs I created back when we were in Malaysia. They were the escape set I developed that we never ended up using . . . I was thinking, the Exodus guys have their own, but if they needed one for Valentine, I could use one of Carl's old ones and shop the picture. Carl was too short, but we could always say he had a growth spurt."

I didn't know what Exodus' next move was. Shen, Antoine, and Dr. Bundt had been hanging around a lot before, but I hadn't seen any of them in the last couple of days. They had gotten rooms at the little tourist hotel in town, probably to give Ling time alone with the kid. Dr. Bundt had been mildly annoying, but I had actually enjoyed working with Shen and Antoine. Neither one talked a lot, and both liked to hit people. You can't ask for much more than that. Ling could sit around and mope with her boyfriend for all I cared, as long as they did it someplace far away from my people.

"You'll have to ask them. Valentine might not live that long, but whatever gets him off my island faster, awesome. . . . " Having the most wanted man in the world staying in my guest house didn't really fit with that whole *low profile* vibe. "And when we find Bob?" We would need ID for my brother to get out. Of course, that was assuming this was still a rescue mission, and not just to identify his remains.

Reaper handed me a Russian passport. I opened it, and there was the picture that Reaper had lifted from Bob's FBI file. "You said your brother spoke Russian."

"FBI started him in organized crime, Russian mafia stuff in New York, or at least that's what Mom said on a Christmas card one year." She had always been so proud of him. I had no idea what the cards she had sent to the other kids had said about me. Probably some variant of "Crazy Hector is still screwing around, wasting his life." "I'm assuming this ID was groomed for Train?"

"Yep, they're both fuckin' monsters, so the stats work. And the peace day resistance . . ."

"Piéce de résistance," I corrected.

"Whatever, the best part," he grinned when he handed me the next ID. I knew he had millions of dollars in the bank, but he had never found the time to get his crooked front teeth fixed. "Jill will have to pretend she's ten years older, but she does speak Spanish fluently. She's a businesswoman with a mining company based in Madrid."

"That was fast."

"Well, I originally developed this one for Ilsa, She-Bitch of the SS."

"Katarina wasn't *that* bad."

"To *you*," he snorted. "She hated me. Dumping that psycho was the best thing you ever did."

"What do you have left?"

"I'm fleshing out our Spanish mining corporation.

We've even got a bitchin' webpage. Jihan's slave mines are turning out a lot of metal. It will take a couple of days for the money to transfer over. Jill's going to be the negotiator. You're the interpreter. I'm a technician. I've contacted Uri in Volgostadorsk—"

"Little Federov? The gun runner?"

"Obviously. Our mining company is going to bribe him not to molest our *survey gear* on the rail line to The Crossroads. You know how those greedy Russian bastards are, and I don't want my good shit stolen."

"How much?"

"A hundred grand."

"Our gear damn well better be left alone. You do remember I stabbed Uri's brother in the kidney, right?"

"No, a mysterious super-thief who worked for Big Eddie stabbed his brother. You're just a lowly interpreter. And it was in the spleen, not the kidney. You're thinking of the other guy. Train shot Federov's cousin in the kidney."

"Oh yeah, that was awesome." I chuckled. "Good times . . . Speaking of which, I'm a little rusty. I'm going to go shooting."

"Actual targets, or seagulls? 'Cause I don't think Jill likes it when you shoot the seagulls."

"A seagull *is* an actual target. I think of them as my own interactive pop-up range." I needed the practice, and besides, it helped me blow off steam.

My performance in Montana hadn't been good enough. I'd been slow. I'd let some wounded jackass escape. I'd missed a few shots and my reactions weren't what they used to be. That was simply unacceptable. The paper targets had been shredded, replaced, and shredded again. I'd lost count of how many hundred rounds I'd fired today, but there was a pile of spent brass in the sand underfoot, and my thumbs hurt from loading magazines.

The island wasn't that big, but I was using suppressed weapons, and the Montalbans had fenced off this secluded area. There wasn't a damn thing else I could do until Reaper was done with his prep work. It gave me time to train and time to think.

Bob had been taken in The Crossroads. He'd been poking around in a warlord's business, so that wasn't a surprise. My one supposed lead was a basket case who apparently knew jack and shit about what this was all about. The timer beeped. I shouldered my new Remington ACR and put a controlled pair into each of the target's center of mass. I checked the timer's recording of the last shot. *Not good enough.* I reset the timer and went again.

I didn't know if I could trust Exodus, but what choice did I have? They were up to something in The Crossroads, but wouldn't divulge what it was. That meant that the only resources I could really rely on were me, Reaper, and Jill, who I wasn't comfortable with taking at all. Not that she hadn't proven herself capable at this sort of work, but taking her to The Crossroads filled me with dread.

I heard the four-wheeler coming a long way off. It made a lot more noise than a 5.56 with a can on it. I emptied the carbine's magazine into the last target's head, put it on the table to cool, and waited for Jill to arrive.

She parked behind me and killed the Honda's engine. "What're you doing?"

I shrugged. "Practicing."

"You're sweating."

That's because I'd been doing a set of push-ups or sprints between the strings of fire. Shooting was more challenging when your arms burned and you were short of breath. "It's a warm day."

Jill got off the four-wheeler and came over. "What's wrong, Lorenzo?"

"Valentine pulled a gun on me."

"Shocking. I warned you not to be pushy . . . And you didn't kill him."

"Thought about it," I muttered.

"I'm impressed. What else is bugging you?"

She knew me too well. I'd thought long and hard about this. "The idea of you going to The Crossroads. I really don't think you realize what that place is like or what the kind of people who work there are like."

"I understand the risks." She folded her arms. "I know what I'm doing. We play it low key. We're just investigating. We're not looking for a fight. Come on, you've taught me all sorts of stuff. You admitted yourself that I'm talented at your sort of business."

"You're a talented *beginner*."

"I can take care of myself." Jill went to the table, picked up my STI 9mm, lifted it and quickly shot the furthest target twice in the chest, and after the briefest instant, square in the face. She'd become an excellent shot.

"The men that took Bob aren't made out of cardboard."

"Neither was the Fat Man or the other jerks I shot that night."

That was true. She'd never choked under pressure yet. "I don't want you to get hurt . . ."

"Well, duh. And?"

I sighed. "I need help, but I don't have to like it, and I sure as hell don't like putting you in danger."

"You're cool putting Reaper in danger. I'm tougher than Reaper."

"Sure, but I'm not . . ." I hesitated. "I'm not in love with Reaper."

"Wow." Jill looked at me for a long time, but luckily she didn't get all weird on me. "That's remarkably sentimental by your standards. And good about Reaper, because *ewww* . . . that would be awkward for everybody." Jill grinned.

"Here's the thing. The Crossroads is a city of bad guys. You're not a bad guy, Jill."

"Nope. I'm not. You know I've got no interest in the things you've done in the past, and if this was just some heist then I'd tell you to go to hell, you're on your own. Because I'm not a bad guy, but this time, *neither are you*. You rescued Val from evil men. You're going to The Crossroads on a *rescue mission*. For once, relatively speaking, you're not the bad guy here."

"I . . . Well . . ." *Holy shit. She was right.*

"Listen, I know you're scared." She held up a hand before I could protest. "Yeah, yeah, you're not afraid of anything, whatever. Spare me. I have to do this. Bob didn't hesitate to help when I was the one in danger. He's off on a mission to bring down the bunch of corrupt assholes that ruined my life. So what kind of hypocrite would I be if I stayed here safe in my island mansion while you go off on a dangerous rescue mission and get killed because I wasn't there to help?"

We'd already had this fight, and I'd already had to admit she was right. I needed help, but I certainly didn't have to like it. "Fine." I tossed her another mag of 9mm. She caught it. "Get to work then."

VALENTINE

The deep rhythm of the rolling waves helped clear my head.

It had been an emotionally overwhelming few days. Dr. Bundt had sat me down in the beach house to look me over. It was strange to see this man again. The last time we'd met, I'd just woken up in another unfamiliar place, on board an Exodus ship, after having a traumatic brain injury where he'd had to drill a hole in my skull to drain a subdural hematoma.

Sitting there, getting quizzed, while he'd shined lights into my eyes, had just been too much. I'd been poked and prodded and questioned enough. I found myself having an anxiety attack, almost a panic attack. I stood up so fast I startled the old man, and took off out the door. I had gone back to my shady palm tree, sat down on the sand, and stared out over the water, trying to regain my composure.

Hours passed with nobody showing up, leaving me alone with my thoughts. The sky was on fire as the Sun slowly sank below the horizon. The clouds burst with shades of red and purple, and the sky itself was almost golden. A few days before, my only goal in life, as I dimly recalled it, had been to live long enough to see the sky again. Now I was in paradise, watching the most beautiful sunset I'd ever seen. For the last couple of days I hadn't known hunger, fear, nor cold. I'd had plenty of rest, good food, all the sunshine I wanted.

It was too much. It was just too much. Completely overwhelmed, I sat under that palm tree and stared helplessly into the sunset until the sky darkened. The stars began to shine overhead when the Sun finally sank below the sea. There are few things more routine and constant than the rising and setting of the Sun, but at that moment, you would have thought I'd never seen it before.

Ling came to me as the horizon darkened. I was so lost in thought I didn't notice her approach. "Hello," she said, pulling me back to reality. "Dr. Bundt told me what happened. He said it was best to give you some time to adjust. I hope I'm not disturbing you."

"It's fine," I said simply.

Ling seemed unconvinced. She sat next to me in the sand. "I know what it's like, you know." I looked a question at her. She brushed a few errant strands of hair out of her face before explaining, "When Exodus rescued me, I was still very young. Yet in those years I'd lost my family, fought in a war, been injured, and barely avoided being killed in the destruction of Shanghai. Yet after surviving all of that, I was made a slave. They kept me chained to a bed in a shack, letting me outside only to relieve myself. I wanted to die. I gave up hope completely.

"When Exodus saved me, it took a long time for me to accept it. I didn't speak for almost a month. I was afraid to. I was afraid it wasn't real, as if . . . well, it seems silly now, but I had this idea in my head that if I spoke, it would break the spell, end the dream, and I'd wake up under my tattered blanket, still chained to that wretched bed."

I said nothing, but I was consumed with a feeling of guilt. Well, not guilt exactly, but rather shame. I looked over at Ling and wondered. This woman was about the same age as me, maybe a couple years older. She had easily seen as much, if not more, horror in her life than I had. From what little I knew of her captivity, it had been far worse than mine. I feared many things during my short time in North Gap, but I'd never once been concerned that I was going to be gang-raped. Feeling pathetic, and not sure what to say, I wrapped my arms around my legs and stared at the sand.

Ling startled me by placing her hand on my shoulder. "I'm not telling you this to make you feel bad, Michael. I'm not trying to . . . how would you say, *one-up* you with my own story. It's important that you understand you're not alone. I know what you've been through. Many of us do. People like you make up the heart and soul of Exodus."

Her face was illuminated by the same milky moonlight that shimmered off of the calm Caribbean Sea. "Are you trying to recruit me?" I asked flatly.

She smiled at me and squeezed my shoulder. "No. Though I think you'd make a fine addition to our order. I tried to recruit you for some time after seeing what you were capable of in Mexico. But after all you've been through, after all that's happened, and knowing you as well as I do now . . . no. You're not ready, Michael. Exodus isn't a job. It's a lifelong commitment. It's an oath. You don't just join, you become part of it, and it becomes part of you. Much devotion is required. You . . . your heart belongs elsewhere, I think. Your loyalties lie elsewhere. You just do not know where that is now that you have been betrayed by your country. Am I incorrect?"

I had to think about that for a moment. Normally I didn't like it when people analyzed me, especially after months at the mercy of a mad scientist drilling into my subconscious with drugs and machines, but coming from Ling, it didn't feel invasive. I wasn't being prodded or interrogated. Her simple honesty put me at ease.

"No. Maybe. But it wasn't my country that betrayed me. The *government* did. There's a big difference. Our system was never perfect, but I think it's falling apart now. I mean, that's no surprise, things had been getting worse for a long time. I lived out of the country for almost five years straight when I worked for Vanguard. Every time I came home things seemed a little bit worse somehow. Even the government isn't just some big faceless entity. It's people. People did this to me. They chose to do this to me. They made their decisions, and I made mine. They're probably used to there not being any consequences for those decisions, but I made sure at least one of them paid a price."

Ling smiled. "Now you sound like an Exodus operative. Powerful men deserve their day of reckoning as much as anyone else. They too are answerable for their actions, even if they don't think they are. It makes no difference if they're warlords, criminals, or excuse their actions with the supposed legitimacy of government. They're just men, as you say, and men must be held to account."

"You're going somewhere with this, aren't you?"

"I am." She hesitated for a moment, looking out over the shimmering ocean. "It took a lot of doing to arrange for your retrieval. Many in our organization did not want to risk it. We're already considered a terrorist group by the United Nations. We almost never operate inside the United States in any capacity. The last thing Exodus wishes is to risk the attention of the US government. I had to pull many strings. It was made clear to me that under no circumstances was I, or anyone on my team, to be captured alive."

"So why did you do it?" I'd been wanting to ask her that since I woke up. "What on earth compelled you to risk so much on my account?"

"Because Robert Lorenzo said you might know something about this Project Blue, and that that knowledge could be used as a weapon against this shadow government organization, Majestic." She hushed me before I could once again protest that I knew nothing about Project Blue. "They are an example of everything we stand against. Agent Lorenzo was wrong about Project Blue, but he was not completely wrong. You still have knowledge that can hurt them. You know things, have seen things, even done things on their behalf. That kind of information is power."

"Bob already used everything I knew. It caused a huge scandal that was almost completely forgotten, what, six months later? It just got passed over and the media went onto the next story. God forbid they risk making some politician they like look bad."

"It is as you say." Ling nodded. "The corruption runs deep. But you did hurt them, whether you realize it or not. You have the power to hurt them again, should you choose to. As does Agent Lorenzo, if we can find him."

If only I had the answers everyone thought I did. Majestic was terrified of Project Blue. They were so compartmentalized, so secretive, that even they didn't even seem to know exactly what it was Gordon had unleashed. Colonel Hunter's notes had mentioned Dead Two and Dead Three being involved in a *Project Red* in China. The Second Chinese Civil War had broken out when I was in grade school, and continued off and on again for the better part of a decade before the final cease-fire. Nukes had been used and millions died.

Millions died. A pit formed in my stomach. My own Dead Six had been involved in an intervention in a foreign country. Had D2 and D3 been doing the same thing? Had Project Red started the Chinese civil war?

Ling didn't seem to notice my racing thoughts. "I met Bob Lorenzo by chance," she explained. "He told me there were four men who knew about Project Blue. Three of them are dead. One was a United States Senator, the other two were your former superiors, Curtis Hunter and Gordon Willis."

I clamped my eyes shut. "Jesus."

"I think you can see why Agent Lorenzo was so interested in you."

"So who was the fourth guy?"

"I do not know. Neither did Bob. He didn't know the man's identity, but his investigation indicated that he had fled to The Crossroads." Ling said that last part like she expected it to mean something to me.

"Don't know it."

"It's a lawless region, the intersection of North China, Russia, Kazakhstan, and Mongolia, kept lawless by the inability of those nations to control the remote parts of their territories."

"Okay. This is where you met Bob? What were you doing there?"

The Exodus operative looked at me for a moment, but said nothing. She was hesitant again. "We are planning a very large operation there. The Crossroads is controlled by a powerful warlord known as Sala Jihan. The profits come from his mines, mines that hundreds, maybe thousands, of slave workers die in every year. It's not a secret, simply another blight on the world that Western media ignores."

"You didn't answer my question."

Ling's expression hardened. "Exodus intends to eradicate Sala Jihan and remove his vile stain from the earth." Ling was a very well-spoken, calm, almost dispassionate woman. Half the time she seemed very cold. Seeing that fire in her, the true believer, still surprised me, even though I already knew it was there. *But holy crap, there was the crazy.* Ling continued, "In Agent Lorenzo . . . Bob, we found a kindred spirit. Before he was captured he asked me to find you. He said you would be able to help."

"What the hell do all these people expect me to know?"

"Michael . . . I have no right to ask this of you. You've been through enough, but in order to secure my organization's blessing on the rescue attempt, I told them that you would be an asset to us."

And there it is. "I thought you said I wasn't cut out for Exodus?"

"That's not what I said. It's not like we're above taking in outside help, as you're well aware." She waved her hand, indicating Lorenzo's island. "Lorenzo is going to The Crossroads to search for his brother. I promised him that we would do everything we could to help him in this endeavor if he helped us save you, and Exodus always fulfills its covenants. But for you, Michael, there is no obligation. You do not have to come with us, but I'm asking for your help."

I blinked hard. This was insane. "What is it do you think I'm going to be able to do?"

"I *know* what you can do. You're a warrior," Ling said. "I also know what you've been through. I do not wish to place such a burden on you. Let me ask you this: if not with me, where will you go? Majestic will not stop hunting you. They may have the entire intelligence apparatus of the United States at their disposal. Anyone you associate with, anyone who shelters you, will be in danger. Exodus is uniquely prepared to deal with people in your position. Let me help you one more time, Michael. I'm not forcing you to join. I'm not forcing you to fight our battles. I swear to you, you can walk away if you wish."

"I'm not sure what to do, Ling."

Standing up unexpectedly, she brushed the sand off of her pants. "All I ask is that you weigh your options carefully. Whatever you decide, a plane will be here tomorrow, and I will be leaving on it. Sleep well, Michael." Ling walked away without looking back.

LORENZO
St. Carl Island
February 18th

We'd had one final meeting with Ling to discuss travel

arrangements and contacts in The Crossroads. I was far more comfortable seeing to my own than tagging along with Exodus. She'd told me that their little turboprop Cessna would be leaving and a larger, longer-range jet had just landed to take them to Europe in the morning. Of course, it had also landed on my airfield without my permission. At this point I think Ling was doing that just to piss me off.

Antoine passed on several contacts and specific intros to use with Exodus operatives in the region. Shen updated Reaper on some of the radio frequencies and code phrases we could use to communicate, though I was positive he didn't give us any of the important ones. Ling hit it off with Jill by complimenting her decorating of the living room. It was a real chick bonding moment. Everything was now set for our meet in The Crossroads.

That left only one thing in question.

"What the hell do you mean, *you're not sure if Valentine is going with you?*"

"Easy, Lorenzo," Jill put her hand on my arm.

"I always mean exactly what I say," Ling stated. "Michael is not my prisoner. He is free to do as he pleases. If he does not wish to accompany us on this mission, then that is his choice."

"Holy shit, Ling. After all we went through to get him . . . And you want to just leave him . . . And on my island? Oh fuck that. Get him *off* my island."

"What would you have me do?"

"Have Shen choke his ass out or Antoine can throw a bag over his head and carry him, I don't care!" Considering how wanted Valentine was, he'd been here too damned long already. "I don't give a shit what you do, as long as he's on your fucking airplane in the morning, because otherwise I'll—"

"He's no trouble," Jill interjected. "We've got space."

"Oh, hell no!" I shouted.

"I know you don't like him, but we're not going to be here anyway! He's been through a lot of trauma, Lorenzo!"

"Trauma is when Majestic finds out he's here and then *kills us*, Jill." Shen, Antoine, and Ling exchanged glances and then politely backed away from the table like they totally weren't paying attention to the erupting argument. "Stop right there. You Exodus bastards aren't sneaking out of this one. Get Valentine out of here or I will."

"And what do you intend to do with him?" Jill demanded.

"He can learn to *swim*. Or hell, I'll be generous. I'll give him an inflatable raft. Haiti's that-a-way."

"Mike helped save my life, Lorenzo," Jill shouted. "Maybe you should go inflate that raft for yourself."

"Oh, snap," Reaper said. "Somebody's sleeping on the couch tonight!" I glared at him. "Never mind."

Ling shifted. I looked to see what had gotten her attention. Valentine was standing in the doorway, looking pale and tired.

"Oh good, our house guest has arrived. Feel like apologizing to me?"

Valentine didn't say anything in response.

"Apologizing for what?" Ling asked.

"Sticking a gun in my face under my own roof."

"Sorry," he said, totally not meaning it. Valentine nodded at Jill. "Good to see you, Peaches." She smiled at the use of her alias from Quagmire, because of course this asshole would be charming to my girlfriend. Then Valentine looked at Reaper. "Good to see you too, Skyler."

Reaper frowned at the use of his hated real name. "I'm with Lorenzo. This fucker's got to go."

"Yeah, about that, we were just discussing your leaving on a jet plane tomorrow."

"Or we were discussing about how you were welcome to stay here until you felt better," Jill added.

I turned back to her. "No. We weren't."

"He's been through a lot, Lorenzo. He's a *good* man." Jill was starting to get her *stabbing face*. "If it wasn't for him, I'd be dead."

"You still might get the chance if he gets spotted and they track his escape back to us! Do you feel like becoming a fugitive again? Because that's what we'll have to do if they connect us."

"Mike can stay here as long as he needs to. That's what Hawk did for me!"

Of course, she'd bring somebody doing a good deed into it. I smashed my hand into the table. "Damn it! He's—"

"Gone," Ling pointed out.

I looked back at the doorway. Sure enough, Valentine had left.

Apparently he'd made his decision.

LORENZO
St. Carl Island
February 19th

I'd gone to the airport to see them off. Ling hadn't seen

Valentine, and she seemed a little sad about that. I was sad too, because now I was contemplating how to get rid of him, up to and including murder, without my girlfriend finding out of course.

However, it turned out that Valentine had decided to leave after all. He showed up as Exodus' Gulfstream jet was being loaded, with all of his earthly possessions shoved into one of my laundry bags.

"Hey," he said when he saw me hanging out by the hangar. "Jill gave me a lift. She's back by the gate."

"She's nice like that. So, what are you going to do?"

Valentine stopped and looked over the St. Carl airfield, at the brilliant green trees surrounding it, and then across the vast ocean. "I don't know. All I want is to be left alone. I don't want anybody else dying because of me."

"I know that feeling well." I didn't *hate* Valentine exactly, but he had a way of screwing up my orderly existence that was borderline supernatural. "Maybe I'll see you in The Crossroads, but if not, good luck."

The plane was warming up behind us. "If I think of anything else, anything that can help you find your brother, I'll call." What remained unspoken was how unlikely that really was.

There was still one thing that was bugging me, though. Mostly because it had come up during my argument with Jill, and I actually didn't know the answer. "The news said that Gordon Willis offed himself. I bet Jill five bucks that was a crock and you murdered him."

"Yeah, I killed him. Shot him in cold blood, right in the heart, right in his own house . . . Do you think that'll make Jill think less of me?"

I shrugged. "Hard to tell. It wasn't like she was his biggest fan."

"I heard her stick up for me last night. She called me a good man. I don't even know why that matters to me. Do me a favor . . . Don't tell her the truth. Make something up."

I could respect that. "You know Majestic will never rest." The assumption was that I would probably never see Valentine again, so I might as well say it. "They'll find you eventually. Me springing you will just make them think you're even more valuable than they thought before. They'll hunt you to the ends of the earth until they find out what they want to know about this Project Blue."

"I'm beginning to get curious myself," he replied with a wry smirk. "When you find your brother, tell him I'm sorry that I didn't know what he thought I knew. I . . ." Valentine trailed off, looked away for a second, and sighed. Finally he held out his hand. "Thanks for getting me out of there."

I hesitated, then took his hand and shook it firmly. He gave me one last nod, and then left to face his destiny, a man living on borrowed time. I watched the plane leave St. Carl, and bank sluggishly toward the west.

Jill was waiting for me at the airfield's gate. "So was I right?"

"You were right. Gordon committed suicide."

"Told you so. I win."

I handed her a $5 bill.

Chapter 10: Blue Eyed Girl

VALENTINE
Location Unknown
February 21st

The flight from the Caribbean was long, punctuated by a refueling stop, but I spent much of it sleeping. Dr. Bundt told me that I needed rest, and offered me a sedative. I refused. I'd spent more than enough time pumped full of drugs. I wanted my mind to be clear, even if clarity hurt.

I was still in shock. My entire world changed in an instant when I woke up on Lorenzo's island, and already it was changing again.

We touched down at a bustling airport in a picturesque coastal city. I didn't know where we were, and didn't bother to ask. The Exodus jet taxied to a private hangar, where three large BMWs with tinted windows were waiting for us. I was hurried into the back of one of the cars and we sped across the city, eventually leaving the urban landscape and the sea behind.

We drove for over an hour, far into arid, mountainous countryside. Our destination was a sprawling estate surrounded by rugged, rocky terrain. At its center was an ancient, partially-crumbling castle tower. It was accompanied by many newer-looking buildings, including a mansion that overlooked a cliff.

A short while later I was left standing alone in a large, ornately-decorated office. The far wall was one large bay window that stretched from floor to ceiling. Through it rugged mountains, brown under a clear blue sky, stretched out as far as the eye could see. I moved closer to the window and looked down. The mansion was built on the precipice of a cliff. Beyond the glass was a vertical drop that had to be several hundred feet.

"Impressive, isn't it?" someone asked, in an Oxford English accent. "Forgive me, Mr. Valentine, I didn't mean to startle you." An older, well-groomed gentleman in an expensive-looking grey suit walked confidently across the room and stuck out his hand. At his side was a much younger, prim-looking woman in a pencil skirt and high heels. Her hair was done up in a tight bun and thick-rimmed glasses adorned her face. She held a tablet computer in her hands. The man looked me in the eye as I shook his hand.

"Who are you?" I asked.

"Mr. Valentine," the woman said, in a Mary Poppins English accent, "allow me to introduce Sir Matthew Cartwright, High Councilor of Exodus."

"Thank you, Penelope," he said, sounding just a bit embarrassed. "Of course, with your current popularity, that is an alias. I do not intend offense."

"Understandable, *Sir* Matthew."

He smiled. "The Sir part is correct, but the Crown hands out titles like candy these days, so pay it no mind."

"High Councilor? So you're the Exodus commander?"

"One of thirteen, actually. It's mostly a formality. Exodus is an organization which takes pride in its traditions. In any case, welcome to Azerbaijan."

Azerbaijan. A little country on the Caspian Sea, I recalled, used to be part of the Soviet Union. "So, does this *Council of Thirteen* run Exodus then?"

"Run it?" He seemed taken aback by the question. "It would seem that Ling hasn't told you much about our organization, has she?"

"She's told me practically nothing."

"Yes. Quite the stickler for operational security, that one. Well, it's all for the best. But since you're here, I think it's only fair that we pull back the veil just a bit, as it were, wouldn't you agree?"

"Uh, sure," I said. He seemed excited to tell me all about Exodus. Despite everything I had to admit I was curious. For all that I'd done with Exodus, the Mexico op, fleeing Zubara, staying at their secret base in Southeast Asia, and being rescued by Ling, I still knew very little about the organization. They were well-funded, with a global reach, and had access to state-of-the-art equipment. I also knew that if Ling was typical of their membership, they pursued their goals with a passionate tenacity bordering on fanaticism. That tenacity had saved my life multiple times, however, so I could hardly complain.

"Our lineage can be traced back a very long time, to the Crusades, in fact. Our founders were wise men, knights, scholars, men of the cloth, originally brought together on a quest to free the Holy Land. They were no strangers to war, but the corruption they found disgusted them, craven acts of barbarism from both sides, fueled by greed and lust, burdensome truths, even by the harsh standards of the day. The needless suffering they witnessed had disgusted them. *Verily I say unto you, inasmuch as ye have done it unto the least of these my brethren, ye have done it unto me.* A secret meeting was held in Constantinople, and a pact was made."

"I see." I hadn't been expecting an in-depth history and philosophy lesson.

"These men decided to pursue a higher calling, of protecting the common man, the poor and the downtrodden from the injustices of the mighty. It was a noble goal, quixotic even, and like many such things, it failed for a very long time. Sadly, it still does, occasionally."

"Ling told me Exodus goes back six hundred years."

"Correct. Our organization, as it exists today was based upon that earlier pact, but was founded in the fifteenth century, during the waning days of the Byzantine Empire. This time we had a few more persuasive leaders, and Exodus was born. In a world filled with evil, we would be a sword of righteousness."

"They call you people terrorists." I didn't have to specify who *they* were. The United Nations, INTERPOL, and numerous national governments were all on the list.

Sir Matthew chuckled. "Indeed they do. Supposedly, our world is made up of orderly nation-states and codified international law. You and I both know that there is an entire world that exists in the cracks between those borders, beneath that thin veneer of societal order, Mr. Valentine. Civilization only ever dangles by a thread. We bring justice to the truly evil. Many of our warriors are former victims themselves, willing to save others from the depravities they themselves have experienced. Exodus does not bow to diplomatic or economic pressure. We are not beholden to the weak wills of politicians. We don't negotiate with evil. We do not care what is popular, we simply care that things are *right*."

I raised an eyebrow. "Who picks what is right?"

"A fine question," Sir Matthew agreed. "A question which would surely be debated by our membership, which is why Exodus does not waste time delving into the grey areas. Why muddle things when there is so much pure, unquestionable evil to go around? I speak of real evil, Mr. Valentine: the massacres, the brutality, and the slavery that goes on, ignored by the civilized world, every single day. I've read your dossier, about your career as a mercenary. You've seen these things for yourself, have you not?"

Before I could answer that, the heavy wooden double doors that led to the office flew open. In rushed a slender young woman with hair that was such a light shade of platinum blonde that it almost looked white. I hadn't seen her in a couple of years, and she'd definitely grown, but there was no mistaking this girl.

"Michael!" she said, hurrying across the room and throwing her arms around me. I felt myself blush a little as she hugged me enthusiastically. "I'm so happy to see you!"

I composed myself and stepped back a bit. "You've grown," I managed. In the time since I'd last seen her, the gangly teenager had matured into a lovely young woman with striking features. She was still short, the top of her head not quite making it to my shoulder, but her hair was longer, almost reaching to her waist.

"Yes. I understand that the two of you have already met," Sir Matthew said. He seemed uneasy for some reason. I didn't think it'd be possible, but Penelope looked even more uptight. *Did I just commit some kind of faux pas?*

"Michael saved my life," the girl said.

"Mexico," I agreed. "It's been a long time, kiddo. And I don't even know your name."

"I'm sorry about that." Her intense blue eyes looked deeply into mine. It was almost unsettling. She had the most unnatural eyes I'd ever seen, and that's coming from somebody with heterochromia. It felt like she could see through you. "My name is Ariel."

"Like in *The Little Mermaid*?"

"I loved that movie when I was little. That's where I picked my name from."

"Wait, what? You picked your name?"

She ignored my question. "Come with me! Let's go for a walk. I want to show you around. You've been through a lot."

Sir Matthew protested. "Ah, My Lady, Mr. Valentine and I have much to discuss . . ."

"Later!" she said, interrupting him. "There'll be plenty of time to talk about the work later. He needs to relax! You have no idea what he's been through!" She tugged on my arm and began to lead me out of the room. I looked an apology to my host.

He shrugged. "As you wish, My Lady. Mr. Valentine, we'll talk later."

Ariel was visibly fighting off tears as we casually strolled down a long hallway. Brilliant sunlight spilled into the corridor from a row of floor-to-ceiling windows on one wall. Paintings and tapestries lined the other wall. It was a really nice place, even with a teenage girl trying not to cry.

"I'm sorry, Michael," she said, rubbing her eyes. "I get overwhelmed sometimes. Seeing all the scars on you was just too much."

Most of my scars were covered by my clothing, so I wasn't entirely sure what she was talking about. The girl was strange, there was no doubt about it. I can't say I've spent a lot of time around teenaged girls, but this one was a lot more emotional than I was prepared for. "It's okay."

"No, it's not!" she insisted. "Every time the work comes into your life, you suffer. You lost so many friends to save me. And Sarah . . . Michael, I never knew her, but I'm so sorry."

"How do you know about Sarah?"

She hesitated for the briefest instant. "Ling told me."

I closed my eyes for a moment and took a deep breath, remembering the vivid dream about Sarah I had when I was still in captivity. It seemed so real that it still shook me to my core. "It's okay," I repeated. "It is what it is. I made choices, and I have to live with the consequences of those choices." I didn't want to talk about it anymore. That didn't seem like the sort of thing you should dump on a teenage girl.

"Things will get better for you." Ariel sounded remarkably confident in her statement. "They will. I know it's been a hard road for you, and I don't think it's over yet, but someday things will be better for you. You'll see. You are supposed to be here."

"Why? Why did Exodus get me out of that hole? Why risk so much on my account? Ling saved us in Zubara. As far as I'm concerned, any debt owed to me from Mexico was squared."

"Ling proposed the operation." Ariel's demeanor visibly changed. She sounded less the emotional teenager and more like a veteran commander. The transition was almost unreal. "The organization wasn't very receptive to it. The operation at The Crossroads is our priority. There aren't a lot of people to be spared, much less aircraft and intelligence and everything else that would be needed. Sir Matthew didn't think it was worth the risk to save you. We're always hesitant to do anything in the US. He lobbied the Council against Ling's proposal. But you are too important."

"I don't know anything about Project Blue, if that's what you mean."

"I know. I don't know anything about it either, and that troubles me. But you're still important."

"Okay, hang on a sec. What is it you do for Exodus anyway?"

"Things . . . I don't know."

"Things?"

"I'm like an advisor."

"Kiddo, please don't be offended by this, because you're obviously a very smart girl, but how are you at all qualified to advise an international, clandestine, completely-illegal paramilitary organization?"

Ariel covered her mouth with one hand and giggled like I'd just said something funny. "I have a . . . unique way of seeing things. Patterns, connections, causalities that other people don't see. That's how I help with the work, and that's how I know you're important, Michael. I just know it. I wanted to find you ever since you disappeared. I just didn't know where you were, until Ling met Agent Lorenzo."

"That was a crazy coincidence."

"I don't believe in coincidence," Ariel said firmly. "Fates intertwine. It's all connected, even if we can't see the end yet."

I said nothing. I didn't believe in fate, and I certainly didn't want to get into some kind of philosophical argument with the strange girl, but when she put it that way, with such determined conviction, I began to wonder.

Ariel continued after taking a deep breath. "After Ling found out where you were, I knew we had to get you back. When I was being held by those men in Mexico, I gave up. I know what it's like to be left in a dark place without hope, and so does Ling. We were the ones that lobbied the Council. But we couldn't spare a lot of people."

"So Lorenzo was brought in."

"Yes. I hated to do it. He was trying so hard, living on the edge of peace, and we pushed him back over. I hate myself for it but it needed to be done. His own brother knew it needed to be done." Ariel sniffled a little. "Do you know how hard it is for someone like that to change his destiny? It scares me to think what we might have unleashed."

"Don't get all metaphysical on me, Ariel. Lorenzo's a dangerous, angry little man, but he's just a man. If he hadn't been smart enough to wear a vest one day in Zubara, I would've shot him dead, and that would've been the end of him."

My young companion looked thoughtful for a moment. "And then you, yourself, would have died in Zubara too, am I wrong? Fates intertwine, Michael. Remember that. We needed him because it wasn't your time, so it must have been the right thing to do," She sounded more upbeat and very confident. I didn't bother asking her how she knew about Lorenzo saving my life. Exodus knew a lot more about me than I was comfortable with.

"I thought I was a dead man," I said. "But then there was Ling, waiting for me when I woke up. Just like before. My guardian angel."

Ariel smiled at that. "She loves you, you know."

Huh? "Whoa, whoa, whoa. Love is a pretty strong word, don't you think?"

"I don't think, I *know*," Ariel insisted. "She loves you. Duh. You can't be that surprised."

I thought about it for a moment. "We've hardly spent any time together. She never, you know, flirted with me or anything. She was always all about business."

"You don't know anything about girls, do you? Do you remember, back in Mexico, when we found our way back to the group? You appeared unexpectedly, carrying me in your arms? You were a mighty white knight, dressed in green, but you know. That's when she fell for you, in that moment."

Just like a Disney movie, except for all the guns. "Heh . . . I guess it was pretty dramatic." I didn't think of it that way at the time, but I had been busy trying to stay alive.

"I saw it on her face in that moment, even though she couldn't admit it to herself. It really came together for her while she was taking care of you after you got hurt. The first time, I mean."

I'd been unconscious on that Exodus ship for a long time with Ling watching over me. "Florence Nightingale syndrome?"

"Something like that. I don't think she's admitted it to herself. She's been hurt before. She's not ready yet."

"What should I do?" *Why am I asking this girl for advice?*

"I don't think you're ready either, Michael," said Ariel, looking up into me with that eerie gaze of hers.

I hadn't had nightmares about Sarah's death for a week. That was progress, I suppose.

Still unsure of what to say, and more than a little uncomfortable at how insightful she was, I changed the subject. "Listen, about this thing in Central Asia, I don't know much—"

"Exodus buries the work in layers of deceit. I hate it. I hate all the secrets and lies. But it's necessary. Sala Jihan has ways of finding things out."

"Sala Jihan. The warlord?"

Ariel looked up at me like I'd said something strange. "Yes," she agreed. "He must be stopped. Besides, you're a wanted man. Majestic is almost everywhere, but they're not allowed in The Crossroads. Jihan's shadow may be the safest place for you. There are some places that even Majestic can't go."

"So where do I come in? I'm not in any kind of shape to do much right now."

"Every little bit helps, Michael," Ariel said with a smile. "The right man in the wrong place can make all the difference in the world. You're supposed to go, because remember, fates intertwine."

"I have a confession to make, Michael," Ling said, breaking the silence as we boarded an ornate elevator. She pushed the 'basement' button.

After some of the weird things I'd heard from Ariel, this should be good. "Okay."

"The reason I've brought you here is in the hope that you would be persuaded to help Exodus in The Crossroads."

That was her confession? After what Ariel had said part of me had been wondering if Ling would come out and say she had feelings for me, but right now she was all business. "Ariel seems to think I should go." Ling had insisted that my going with her off of Lorenzo's island in no way obligated me to go to war with her. This was the first time she'd brought it up since we got on the plane.

"The young lady is full of surprises . . . and is surprisingly perceptive. So?"

"I . . . I don't know."

"I have an ulterior motive for asking you to come on this operation with us. It's not just that we need every possible body. I told the Council you'd be an asset to us. Exodus doesn't like bringing in outsiders, but we're going to have to rely on them a great deal in this case." The elevator came to a stop. The mirrored doors opened, revealing a very spartan underground level. "Saving Ariel in Mexico made you a hero in the eyes of many. Having you on board would be excellent for morale."

I exhaled heavily, suddenly feeling very silly. "Really?"

Ling always had one hell of a poker face. There was nothing to be gained from trying to read this woman when she was being professional. She left the elevator and started down along concrete hallway. "Really," she confirmed. "It's a rare thing for someone who is not a member of the order to risk so much, and sacrifice so much on our behalf."

Following along, I wondered if my reputation had been somewhat inflated. The thing in Mexico was more luck than anything else, and I'd hardly done it singlehandedly. We passed strangers in the hall. All of them were watching me. "I hope I live up to everyone's expectations," I managed.

Ling flashed me a brief smile. "I reported events precisely how they occurred, but I must warn you. People who weren't there may have heard, and then embellished it in the retelling. I have heard some interesting versions of what happened in Cancun. The fact you singlehandedly held off a battalion of UN peacekeepers and the cartel is remarkable."

"Great." I sighed.

Ling paused, and turned to face me. The expression on her face softened. "I'm . . . I'm sorry," she said, looking down briefly. "I'm putting you under a great deal of pressure, aren't I? Please forgive my presumptuousness."

"There's nothing to forgive. I owe you my life. Asking me to help out after all you went through to get me isn't unreasonable. I just . . ." I trailed off. I was having a hard time putting it into words. "I don't know what it is you think I can do. I don't want to let you down."

"I *know* what you can do," she insisted. "I've seen it with my own eyes."

"Mexico was a long time ago."

"Not that long. And you have only grown in experience since then, am I wrong?" She didn't wait for me to answer. "Michael, I . . . like you. Even so, I would not ask you to come with me if I did not think you would truly be an asset to the operation. I believe in you, even if you do not, and I believe we need your help. Many of our members are inexperienced in combat. For quite a few of them, this will be their first time going into battle. They're well-trained and enthusiastic, but inexperienced and outnumbered. Having a seasoned veteran with us, even if only in an advisory role, will be beneficial."

I chewed on that for a second. Somehow, I had gotten the idea that Ling was asking me to come along out of pity or something. I know it sounds dumb, but after everything I'd been through I wasn't necessarily thinking straight. Her little pep talk was good to hear, and it wasn't like I didn't have experience in training other forces. In my time at Vanguard, I helped train multiple armed forces, from Africa to South China. Corporate called it "partnership."

That sounded right. *Partnership*. With Exodus. Just an advisory role. *I can handle that.* I looked back up at Ling. "By the way, why are we in this basement? Where are we going?"

"We need to outfit you with equipment for the operation. You'll need weapons, body armor, clothes to wear, cold-weather gear, and so forth."

"I haven't said I'm going yet."

"You haven't said you are not. Come on, we have everything you may need."

"What are my needs, exactly?"

"If you decide to join us you'll be with me. What I'm

going to be doing remains to be seen, I'm afraid."

"It's not like you to not have a plan."

Ling smiled again. "No, it's not. My mission was to rescue you. There was no guarantee that operation would succeed or that I would return alive. They planned the operation at The Crossroads with the assumption that I would be unavailable."

"Assume the worst-case scenario until proven otherwise." That attitude had kept me alive, even if it brings frequent accusations of pessimism and cynicism.

"You and I will be among the last to arrive at The Crossroads," she said. "Shen and Antoine are already on their way there."

We reached a large supply room, where paramilitary clothing and gear of all sorts was stored on racks and in bins. The room smelled like a surplus store. Two attendants spoke briefly to Ling in French. One of them pulled out a measuring tape.

"Hold on," I protested.

Ling tilted her head to the side. "Humor me, Michael. You need new clothes one way or the other." It was true; I'd been wearing the same set of clothes I'd had on when I was captured the year before.

They took my measurements, then went to work supplying me with new clothes. I was skinnier than the last time I'd done something like this. "So Shen and Antoine are already gone? They're breaking up your team?"

"My team has been broken up for quite some time. Shen and Antoine are all who remain. They'll be put to better use elsewhere." There was sadness behind Ling's professional mask. "But I still need soldiers I can count on."

Sometime, when we were alone, I resolved to ask her about what happened to her team. Right now I felt like I was being swept along by a very strong current. "So, if I was to say yes, how would we get there?"

"There are only two practical ways into The Crossroads," Ling replied. "Rail and road. There is an unpaved airfield, but in the winter it is snowed over and requires a short-field-capable aircraft fitted with skis. Arriving there by air would likely attract more scrutiny than we want. We'll be flying into Kazakhstan and traveling the rest of the way by road."

"You just drive there? Even in the winter?"

"The Kazakh government expends a lot of effort to keep the mountain roads accessible year round, to help the mountain villagers, of course. Obviously this has nothing to do with the wealth generated by the illicit flow of drugs, arms, and slaves."

The quartermaster brought me several sets of fatigues in the British Pencott camouflage. I held up the overwhites. "Like I haven't had enough snow lately." One attendant fitted me for body armor while the other attempted to find a pair of boots that would fit me. He said something to Ling in French. "What did he say?"

"He said that Americans have very big feet."

I was given a backpack, hats, gloves, goggles, a face mask, knives, a radio, rope, even an ice axe. It was a ridiculous amount of gear, so much that I had to borrow a hand cart to transport it down the hall with. "Jesus," I said, looking at my cart full of swag. "You guys don't screw around with gear issue, do you?"

"It wouldn't do for a person of your reputation to show

up poorly prepared. We will go by communications and get
the encryption loaded into your radio before we depart.
Communications are going to be difficult, at best, during
this operation."

"I can imagine." *The more dudes you have running
around with encrypted radios the less likely it is that
anybody will be able to hear anybody else.*

"And here we are," Ling said. "The armory." A set of
heavy vault doors had been opened, but a locked gate was
installed behind them. Two men were present in the vault.
One was armed with a pistol on his hip. The other had
some kind of large revolver in a shoulder holster. *A man
after my own heart!*

I pushed my little cart off to the side of the hallway as
Ling spoke to one of the armorers. She showed him some
kind of identification badge. He studied it closely before
letting us in. Exodus ran a very tight ship.

My mouth fell open. I have been through a lot of
combat in my life. War has been my profession for years.
But behind that paper-thin veil of stoic professionalism,
I'm a gun nut at heart, and the racks of weapons left me
salivating. "Which one do I get?"

"Whichever one you want, Michael," Ling replied. The
pistol-packing armorer didn't say anything but gave me the
stink eye. *Fair enough. I wouldn't want some jackass
poking around in my gun safe either.* The one with the big
wheelgun, a short, dark-skinned man of ambiguous
ethnicity, grinned widely at me with extremely white teeth.
He could recognize a fellow enthusiast.

I returned my attention to the racks, only giving a
cursory glance at the heavier weapons. I wasn't interested

in carrying an M240 through the mountains in waist-deep snow. No, I was looking for a rifle. Something that suited me. There were plenty to choose from. One rack had nothing but SIG 551 carbines fitted with all of the latest accoutrements. Another contained similarly-updated Steyr AUG bullpups. Against one wall was a rack of M4-style rifles; against another were HK G36s.

"Maintaining this many different systems has to be a strain on your resources."

Near each rack were bins full of magazines and boxes of tools and parts. In a way, it made sense, though. Exodus is a clandestine organization that operates outside of the law. I wasn't sure how they acquired weapons, but I was certain it wasn't the legal way. It's probably easier to keep your weapons purchases on the down low if you buy small lots from a variety of sources, rather than trying to standardize across the board.

"Exodus purchases what we can, where we can, with few questions asked."

In addition to the racks of rifles, there were more specialized weapons, like bolt-action sniper rifles and shotguns, but that wasn't my thing. I was getting discouraged. I could see nothing but rows of 5.56mm assault rifles.

As if reading the disappointment on my face, the revolver-toting armorer approached me, still smiling. "You no find what you like?" he asked in heavily-accented English.

"These are all five-five-six. Got anything bigger?"

The armorer's beady eyes lit up. He crossed the room, rummaged around for a few seconds before returning with a rifle in his hands. "SIG Seven-Sixteen," he said eagerly, handing me the rifle. I retracted the bolt slightly, checking the chamber, before shouldering it. "Seven-point-six-two. Gun for *real* man."

The rifle had a barrel about sixteen inches long and an adjustable stock. It was semiautomatic only, and was topped with a Valdada 1.5-8x variable scope. *This will do.* I felt the corner of my mouth curl up in a grin. "Okay. I only need one more thing. Do you have any forty-four magnum ammunition?"

The armorer's eyes lit up. "Forty-four!" He stepped back and reached for the big revolver slung under his left arm. I tensed up as he drew it, but relaxed once I realized he just wanted to show it off. It was a stainless steel Taurus .44 Magnum with a six-inch barrel. "Like Dirty Harry!" he insisted. He reholstered his gun and disappeared into the back again. The other armorer silently sat in his chair and glared at me. The six-gunner returned with half a dozen boxes of Czech and Serbian .44 Magnum ammunition, all jacketed hollow points.

"Will that suffice?" Ling asked, eyebrows raised.

I set the rifle in the padded case I was given, and zipped it up. "Oh yes. I think I'm all set here."

Ling looked me over. "So I assume this means you're *in,* as they say?"

The rifle felt good in my hands. I had nothing else to live for. I was the most wanted man in the world. A knight had just given me a talk about fighting evil and a strange girl had gone off about fate.

"Looks like it."

"We're going into harm's way, Michael," Ling said. "You don't have to go with us."

"So you keep insisting."

I'd spent most of my life fighting other people's battles. My body was weak and my mind traumatized. I wasn't in any shape to fight, and I wasn't really sure what I was fighting for. But what was I supposed to do? Turn back now, after all Ling had done for me, and let Exodus down? They thought me a hero. Would they think me a coward if I walked away? Why did I care?

Ling awaited my answer.

"Would I have to give the rifle back?"

"I'm afraid so," Ling replied.

"I get to keep it when we're done, though."

Assuming I'm still alive . . .

The Exodus mansion had an impressive library.

After a couple of long meetings with Sir Matthew and some of his functionaries, where we discussed the terms of my agreement with Exodus, including modest compensation, I was allowed to roam much of the mansion at will. We would be departing for Kazakhstan soon, and things were going to kind of suck after that, so I was enjoying the luxury while it lasted. I had a huge, soft bed to sleep in, hot baths whenever I wanted, and all the food I could eat. It was amazing.

The other residents of the mansion, or the staff, or whoever they were, generally kept their distance. Everyone was exceedingly polite, but I was still an outsider and they were generally leery of me. The only ones that ever really talked to me were Ling and Ariel.

Sir Matthew was proud of the mansion's library, and I could see why. There were thousands of books there, ranging from ancient volumes to an entire shelf of paperback pulp novels. A bookish person could keep himself busy in there for a long time. There were many comfy places to sit, with cozy reading lights, and a cheery fireplace crackled and popped in the corner.

I wasn't there to read, though. The library had a computer, and for the first time in a long time I was able to get onto the Internet. I had been out of the loop since my capture the previous summer. I had no idea what all was going on in the world. I had heard bits and pieces about the fallout of Bob Lorenzo dumping, to the press, Colonel Hunter's flash drive, but I wanted to see for myself.

I spent several hours in front of that computer, clicking away at news sites, and catching up on blogs I used to follow. I downloaded a .PDF of *The Project Heartbreaker Commission Report*, which resulted from the Congressional Committee appointed to investigate. It was a long read, hundreds of pages, so I mostly skimmed.

I was startled when the quiet room was suddenly filled with the clicking of high heels. Penelope, Sir Matthew's assistant, quickly walked into the room, carrying a couple of books. There was surprise on her face when she noticed me sitting in front of the computer.

"Ah, Mr. Valentine," she said. "I didn't know you were given free run of the premises. I trust you've been making yourself comfortable?"

She said disdainfully. Cripes. "Yeah, everyone's been super nice. I appreciate that."

"Well, feel free to use our facilities. I might remind you that while you're using the computer, please don't access any social media or personal e-mail. I'm sure an individual of your experience is familiar with operational security, so I shan't lecture you."

That sounded like a lecture to me. "See, I'm glad you said something. Hell, I was going to whip out my cell phone, hold it up over my head, make duck lips at it and snap a pic of myself, slap it up on Facebook, and tag myself in it so all my friends would see."

Penelope's brow furled into an unattractive glower.

"Actually, turns out I can't do that," I continued. "I don't have a cell phone. Or Facebook. Or . . . " I paused, thinking about it for a second. ". . . *friends*, for that matter. So no worries, hey?"

The uptight Englishwoman composed herself. "Please forgive me, Mr. Valentine, I did not mean to offend you. Please excuse me." She hurried out of the room, heels clicking as she went. She took the books she'd brought in back out with her.

I had no idea why Penelope disliked me so much. I simply shook my head and returned my attention to the screen, scrolling through the file.

"She is *such* a bitch sometimes," Ariel said.

"Gah!" I jumped up in my chair.

The strange platinum-haired girl was standing right in front of the desk, looking through me with her eerie gaze. Her eyes reflected the flickering light of the fire and shimmered. She grinned at me. "Did I scare you?"

I laughed. "Holy hell, kiddo, you're like a damn ninja. I didn't hear you come in."

"I learned to be sneaky when I want to be," she said mischievously, leaning on the desk. Dressed in blue jeans and a T-shirt, she looked like a perfectly normal American teenager, except for her weird eyes. "And you do so have friends. *I'm* your friend, stupid. Whatcha doin'?"

"Just reading up on everything I missed, while I was . . . you know, *in captivity*. What is that woman's problem with me?"

"Penelope? Oh, she's nice most of the time. She just doesn't like you."

"Yeah, I can see that. What the hell did I do?"

"Don't worry, you didn't do anything. She's mistrustful of outsiders, like a lot of people in the organization are. I think you also remind her of her ex-husband. He was handsome, like you, a tough military guy."

When I looked at myself in the mirror, I saw an emaciated shell of the very average-looking person I used to be. I felt neither handsome nor particularly tough, but I found myself blushing at the compliment all the same.

Ariel giggled, and leaned over to see the screen. "So what are you reading . . . oh." Her demeanor darkened, and some of the light left her eyes.

"It's the *Project Heartbreaker Commission Report*," I said quietly. On the screen was picture of a man with a hard face and an eye patch. *Hunter, Curtis Alan. Lieutenant Colonel (Ret.), US Army. KIA in Zubara.* "I knew these people," I said absentmindedly, as I scrolled through the faces of the dead. "Worked with them, fought with them, mourned our dead with them. We destroyed a nation together. We . . . " I trailed off.

McAllister, Sarah Marie. Fmr. US Air Force. KIA in Zubara. Sarah looked a bit younger in the picture than she had the day she died. It probably came from her old military ID.

Ariel gently placed a hand on my shoulder. Tears were trickling down her cheeks. "She was beautiful," she sniffled, sitting down next to me.

I took a deep breath. "Yeah, she was. She didn't know how beautiful she was, either."

"I'm so sorry." She squeezed my shoulder more tightly.

"For a long time, I felt like I was supposed to have died there. I told her I'd stay with her until the end. I promised her. I couldn't keep her safe, I couldn't protect her, but I promised her that much. I was supposed to die in the mud at Fort Saradia, next to her."

There was a fierce light in my young companion's eyes, reflected firelight. "No, you *weren't!* I already told you. It wasn't your time. You need to listen better, damn it!" She punched me in the shoulder.

"Ow! Okay, okay, I'm sorry. I was just saying. For a long time that's how I felt. I resented Lorenzo for saving me. I resented him because I owed him a favor and he's a giant asshole, and I resented him because I felt like I broke my promise to Sarah."

"But you didn't, did you?"

"No . . . no, I guess I didn't." I thought back, again, to the frighteningly real dream I had. In that dream, Sarah's eyes shined like Ariel's sometimes seemed to. It was so vivid, so intense, that I wanted it to be real, even though I knew it was just a drug-induced hallucination. I shook my head. "It's still hard. I miss her every day."

"Things will get better for you," Ariel said quietly. "I just *know* it. Please be strong, Michael. Please don't give up. You saved me. You're my knight too." She hugged me tightly, tears in her eyes. I awkwardly patted her on the shoulder, worried that someone was going to walk in and get the wrong idea.

I grabbed the mouse and kept scrolling. "Don't worry, kiddo," I said, trying to sound comforting. "I'm stubborn. I'll be okay."

"I wish you didn't have to go to The Crossroads," Ariel whispered. "I'm scared. I have a bad feeling."

I smiled. "I thought you said things were going to get better for me?"

"I've been wrong before," she said ominously.

I stopped scrolling when a very familiar face appeared on the screen. It, too, was an old picture. From my last DOD ID card, if I remembered right. *Valentine, Constantine Michael. Fmr. US Air Force. KIA in Zubara.*

Before handing over Colonel Hunter's flash drive to Bob Lorenzo, I changed my own status from "MIA" to "confirmed KIA." I figured if they thought I was already dead, it'd give me a better chance of staying off the radar. A good theory, and one that might've worked if I hadn't gotten my stupid ass captured.

I nodded at the picture. "Ever feel like someone just walked over your grave?"

Ariel sat up and wiped her eyes, but didn't say anything. I closed out the report and asked her if she was okay.

"I actually came down here to tell you something, Michael," she said. The tone of her voice was subtlety different. "Majestic doesn't know where you are right now, and they're panicking. You're dangerous to them, because of what you know, because of the scars they left on you, and because you escaped. You're safe for now, I think, but they will never stop hunting you. You have to find Mr. Lorenzo's brother. The two of you might be able to end this. Maybe."

"Don't you worry. If Bob Lorenzo's at The Crossroads, I'll find him and we'll find a way clear of all this." *Another good theory.*

"There is one more thing. Promise me you'll watch over Ling."

"Ling can take care of herself, I think."

"Promise me! She's the closest thing to family I have. Please."

"Okay, honey. I'll do everything I can to bring her home safe. I'll stick with her through the whole thing."

"You promise?"

"I promise."

Ariel seemed content with that answer, and smiled.

Chapter 11: Tourists

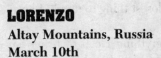

LORENZO
Altay Mountains, Russia
March 10th

The train wheels beat rhythmically on the steel tracks. Our private passenger compartment was old-school comfortable, with thick couches, real wood paneling, and an actual bearskin rug on the floor. The bar was stocked with expensive vodka and caviar. As wealthy western businessmen, we rode first class. I had scouted the other passenger cars, and they were typical Russian, the middle cars were run-down utilitarian things housing ethnic Russians and some replacement soldiers for their outpost, and the cars at the end of the train were pure third world, unheated splintery wood, almost cattle cars that were packed with Kyrgyz and Uzbek workers.

The massive diesel engine labored to get us through the mountain pass. Jill tugged on the bottom of the black window curtain. It rolled up with a snap, revealing a glorious view. We were 6,000 feet above sea level and climbing. The peaks of the Golden Mountains towered far higher around us, and my lungs ached from the lack of air. North Gap, Montana had been pleasant in comparison. I knew I had better get used to it though. The Crossroads itself was at 8,000 feet.

"It's so pretty," Jill said. "All that snow . . ."

I looked past her. Huge white drifts covered miles of black rock. Giant angled sheets of ice reflected the sunlight so clean and white and brilliant that it made my eyes hurt. Behind those black rock walls were mile after mile of glaciers, one of the greatest reserves of fresh water on Earth. Miles of pristine evergreens were interspaced with sluggish glacial springs.

"Looks cold." I was feeling disagreeable. We were behind schedule. A late snowstorm had held us up in Volgostadorsk. We were supposed to have flown in, but reports said that it was going to take some time to clear the runways with that typical Russian enthusiasm and efficiency. In other words, the one plow was broken down, and the guy that could fix it had to sober up first. The delay had put me in a foul mood. Well, fouler than normal.

"I think it's the most beautiful place I've ever seen," Jill said. Reaper looked up from his laptop, squinted at the bright light, grunted, and returned to his files. Reaper didn't appreciate any beauty that wasn't pixilated. Well, unless you count strippers. Jill shook her head sadly. "You guys have no appreciation for nature."

"Nature's an evil whore who'll kill you in a heartbeat," I replied. Even though I didn't like people, I liked being surrounded by them. The wilderness made me uncomfortable. In a crowd, I can fade away. In the woods, I was pretty much clueless.

"It's supposed to be spring, but when the Sun goes down tonight, it'll be ten degrees below zero. A blizzard here can kill you in a manner of minutes. There are packs of wolves in that forest where the males weigh a hundred and fifty fucking pounds and eat their body weight in meat every few days," Reaper said. He looked up from his computer. I raised an eyebrow. "Wikipedia," he explained.

This territory held the intersection of Russia, China, Kazakhstan, and Mongolia. Only Russia and China officially touched, with the Kazakhs and Mongols being separated by about twenty miles. Historically this area had been a crossroads of the ancient world, and the birthplace of the Turkic people. For most of the last couple centuries it had been a kind of no man's land, populated by small villages and ethnic minorities. Over the last fifty years there had been a few border skirmishes, and one really unlucky Russian military disaster, but mostly this area had been ignored. It was steep, cold, hard to get to, and generally considered the ass end of the universe by everyone involved.

That had all changed about twenty years ago, beginning with a natural gas pipeline from southern Siberia into North China, and that had led to the construction of the rail line through the mountains. Then an oil pipeline had crossed it from Kazakhstan through Mongolia which had brought its own railroad. These lines had intersected in a mountain valley that at the time had held nothing but an abandoned Soviet military base and the ancient ruins of some people that had long since been forgotten, and a small town had sprung up at this new intersection.

Then an enterprising businessman known as Big Eddie had decided that this little crossroads was a superb hub for trafficking in all sorts of illicit goods. Afghan and Kazakh opium heading east, north, and south, the Russian Army selling off everything that wasn't nailed down, and Chinese military hardware heading every which way. The Crossroads became a kind of international super-flea market of illicit goods. Soon every criminal, terrorist, and wannabe warlord converged on it, looking to buy and sell. People like that needed neutral places to meet and conduct business, and Big Eddie kept the peace. That mountain village had turned into a boomtown of the criminal underworld, and the boom had brought the deals and the money. Every faction on Earth wanted a piece of the action.

But The Crossroads wasn't all fun and profit. Criminal factions tend to solve their problems with violence, and old grudges die hard. The factions needed muscle, and this attracted the mercenaries, Muslims run out of Chechnya, Mongols hungry for work, Uyghur, Kazakhs, Kyrgyz, Han, and every other group you could think of. If a rough man needed work, there was no better place to find it than The Crossroads.

Once it was found that the surrounding mountains held huge stores of gold, silver, copper, and zinc, all in a place where there was no government interference or regulations on how to get at that wealth, legitimate business had flocked to The Crossroads, and the area exploded. After a few years the town had swelled to almost twenty thousand people. And it was a *tough* town. All four of the legitimate governments that bordered The Crossroads were happy to look away from the bad things that happened there, as long as they got paid.

It had been the crown jewel in Big Eddie's empire. Of course, none of the residents and visitors to The Crossroads knew who he really was, only that he ran the show with an iron fist, and he always got a cut of the action. Apparently that had changed rather drastically when I had shot that poodle-petting freak out of the sky, but nature abhors a vacuum, so now there was someone new at the top of the food-chain.

That's where we came in.

"We'll be in The Crossroads in a matter of hours. From here on out, we're in character. Get used to it. I don't want any—" There was a knock at the cabin door. "Hang on. I got it."

A waiter was in the hall, pushing a steam cart. The terrain flashed by behind him through the opposite bank of windows. We were entering a valley. He was a young ethnic Uzbek, and spoke in poorly accented Russian. "Good afternoon, sir. Lunch is served," he lifted the cover and displayed his wares. "Today, fresh salmon from Katun River, with potatoes in lamb bone marrow pudding." It actually looked really good, but I had eclectic tastes.

First class so totally rocks. "Wonderful," I reached into my pocket for a tip. The train lurched as the brakes were forcefully applied. I stumbled and caught myself on the doorframe. The screech of metal on metal echoed up through the carpeted floor. The waiter braced himself and kept his cart from spilling. "What's going on?"

"I not know," he answered, looking bewildered. "No stop here."

"Giant wolf on the track," Reaper suggested from behind me.

"No." I saw the pillars of black smoke out the window. There was, or had been, a small village here. The homes had been tiny wooden things with thatch roofs, and there had only been five or six of them at the most. All of them were burning now. There were bodies strewn around in the bloody snow, none of them were moving. The train finally came to a full stop, with our car looking right at the remains.

"What the hell?" Reaper said as he looked over my shoulder. "Whoa." Jill pushed past me and into the hall and stared out the window. Other first-class passengers left their cabins and joined us, staring at the scene. There was muttering and gasping.

A blast of freezing cold and the smell of smoke flowed through the hall when the rear door opened. "Make way! Move aside!" The soldiers from the next car were pushing their way forward, in their greatcoats with AK74s in their hands.

"What is this?" asked a large man with a Ukrainian accent, gesturing at the carnage. "What happened?"

"Sala Jihan happened," muttered a wizened old Uyghur man who was now standing next to Jill. She was frozen in shock. I don't think she had seen anything like this before. I had warned her about this part of the world. It was no place for the good. "The Pale Man sends a message to these people."

The lead soldier grabbed the waiter by the shoulders

and shook him. "Go forward and tell the engineer to get this thing moving. He should not have stopped. Go! *Now!*" The waiter ran from the car in the direction of the engine.

"Aren't you going to help those people?" the Ukrainian businessman asked.

The old Russian soldier had a master sergeant's insignia on his great coat, and he looked like he had been around this rodeo a few times. "They are beyond help, Comrade . . ." *Yep, he was old guard . . .* "This is not our affair. There's no use in getting involved."

"But we are still in Altay! This is your jurisdiction!" The Ukrainian demanded. The train lurched forward with a *chug chug* noise as we restarted our journey.

"We may still be in Russia, according to the map," the soldier said with some resignation. "But it is not our *jurisdiction* anymore." The Ukrainian began to bluster. Some of the other passengers began to shout. The younger soldiers looked jumpy with their Kalashnikovs as the train car rolled forward. I grabbed Jill by the arm and tugged her back toward me. She was still transfixed on the village.

Then it was suddenly silent. Every one of us was looking out the window, without the words, as our train slowly moved past the things only a few feet outside the window. Some villagers had been left as an example. They had been impaled on stakes along the tracks. Even after all of the horrible things that I had seen in Chechnya, Bosnia, and Africa, I couldn't accurately describe what had been done to these people, flayed, burned, tortured, exposed muscle and dangling skin, white teeth and open eye sockets, and things I couldn't really understand.

I pulled Jill closer, and forced her eyes down. I

shouldn't have let her come. The crowd tracked on the examples, heads moving as one as if in slow motion, as the train built up momentum and left them behind. Finally, the Ukrainian spoke, his voice quivering and higher pitched, like a child that had just woken up from a nightmare. "What manner of man could do something like that?"

The old Uyghur spoke again. "Is not man." He spat on the floor. "Is demon."

We all went back into our cabins and closed the doors, lunch forgotten.

LORENZO
Crossroads City
March 10th

"Welcome to the wild-wild-middle," Reaper said as he stepped from the raised platform of the train station and into the slush-and mud-covered street. The air smelled like cooking smoke, diesel fumes, and unwashed people. It was remarkably cold, but the street was crowded with busy people from every culture you could think of. The music of twenty languages bombarded my ears.

The surrounding mountains around us had been stripped of all their trees, and the amount of growth that had occurred here since my last visit was positively shocking. I grunted as I lifted my bags, marveling at the sprawling development that had seemingly sprung up overnight. The Crossroads had exploded.

The three of us were dressed in Mountain Yuppiflage, brightly colored, Gore-Tex parkas and snow pants. We looked like typical Europeans or Americans at a ski resort. I hated wearing anything colorful, but we had a cover to keep up. My coat was puffy, green with big black stripes. I was wearing a black neoprene skull cap and Bolle sunglasses. I hadn't shaved for the last few weeks and had a pretty decent beard going. Then again, I was one of those guys with a Homer Simpson face who could grow a goatee in forty-eight hours. The last time I'd been in The Crossroads I had been clean shaven with long hair, and that had been seven years ago, so hopefully I wouldn't run into anyone who would recognize me.

Jill's coat was yellow and Reaper's was red. With his hair pulled back in a ponytail and the facial piercings gone, Reaper actually could be pretty convincing as a professional techie type. He carried a briefcase filled with information about our make-believe mining concern. Jill was going to play the part of our young go-getter junior executive in search of cheap ore.

"Which way to our hotel?" Jill asked in Spanish. Her breath formed a steam halo around her face. We would be in character from here on out. "You, find out where the hotel is, and then get my luggage."

"Yes, ma'am," I answered humbly. For somebody with no criminal past, Jill had no problem playing pretend, either that or she just really liked ordering me around. I examined the crowd, looking for a potential guide that wouldn't just rip us off or lead us down some alley to get robbed and murdered. The throng of people was pushing and shoving, unloading cargo from the train, yelling in a dozen different language, and just taking care of random bits of business. They were dressed in everything from expensive Western clothing, like us, to Russian-style long coats and fur hats, to traditional robes and fur coats. Almost everyone appeared to be armed. The people who weren't, were either too poor to afford a gun or too rich to bother, and those guys were obviously flanked by armed henchmen.

I picked out a kid, probably eight years old, who was begging by the entrance to the first-class car. He held out his hands as I approached. I wasn't quite sure what he was, so I started with Russian. "Do you know where the Glorious Cloud is?" He cocked his head, so I asked him the same thing in Chinese. My Chinese wasn't as good as my Russian, but apparently he understood and replied with some rapid-fire chatter in a dialect that I barely understood. I held up some cash. We had a guide.

The boy led us through the streets of Crossroad City. The main road from the train station was asphalt and I think the side streets were gravel. There was so much snow and mud slush that it was hard to tell. I saw a few motor vehicles, usually bigger trucks, Russian 4x4s, a few horses and yaks, and surprisingly enough, bicycles. I wasn't sure how the riders managed to stay upright riding through ice, but they did. There were a few waiting rickshaw drivers who shouted for our business, but Ling had told me the Exodus meetingplace was near the train station. Being on foot gives you a better feel for a place anyway.

The buildings were of every sort imaginable, from concrete bunkers, to mud-walled compounds, to wood-frame buildings that would look normal in suburban

America. The streets didn't even vaguely resemble straight lines. There was no rhyme or reason to how Crossroads City was laid out. There was no zoning here. Hell, there was no law whatsoever. People built whatever they felt like.

I watched the people. Business was being conducted on every corner. There was no central marketplace because the entire town was the marketplace. You could go to any street here, buy three machine guns, a sack of opium, and a chicken, and have change left over. One man handed over a small stack of currency to a street vendor, and the vendor passed back an RPG rocket.

"Gift wrap that for you, sir?" Jill giggled.

"Quiet." I could feel eyes on us. Everyone was watched here. Every worker, every peasant, and every hired tough was a potential spy.

The nicer buildings had sign posts in front of them. There usually wasn't anything actually written, just carved symbols, but I recognized a lot of them, Red Dragon Triad, Luminous Path, Chechen Brotherhood, Russian mob, Al Qaeda, Yakuza, heck, even the Sicilians had a rather nice brick rambler. Since I had left, The Crossroads had grown into a super criminal United Nations. If a mob boss six thousand miles away might need to get some particular bit of rare merchandise, or place an order for a huge amount of product, or even just have his emissaries sit down across the table from their rivals, this was the place.

Each faction had some toughs hanging out by their front entrance. Normally I would expect all sorts of posturing between the groups, but they seemed to ignore each other. All of them glared at us *legitimate* businessmen. As we passed in front of the sprawling Russian compound, one of the drunker Russians shouted something profane at my girlfriend while simulating something really nasty with his AK. *Classy bunch*.

We had to step aside to keep from being run over by a giant septic-pumper truck. "Well, at least they don't just throw it in the street, like most of the places we've worked," Reaper muttered. "Though they're probably gonna go dump it in the water supply."

This was Reaper's first time here. He'd probably be surprised that even criminal scumbags didn't want nasty water. "You had your shots."

"Stop, thief!" one of the street vendors shouted in Chinese. Ironically, three quarters of the people on the street looked up to see if they were the one being talked about. A young man in a fur robe crashed past me, pushing his way through the crowd and past the Russian compound, a bag of grain thrown over one shoulder. The various factions' toughs laughed and pointed.

The thief didn't make it far. A black shape materialized from around the corner ahead of the runner, and moved to intercept at an astonishing rate of speed. There was a sound like a watermelon hitting a bat, and the thief's head snapped back. He did most of a flip before landing in the snow.

The crowd froze. The noise in the immediate area died down to muted whispers. The man in black stood over the twitching thief. The new arrival was short and broad, cloaked from head to toe in some thick, shapeless furs with a large hood. Under the hood was a black mask and round, tinted goggles. The goggles surveyed the crowd, and I swear that even the Yakuza and the Chechens shrank back under that gaze. Canvas bandoleers of rifle ammo crossed his chest in an X, on top of that was a leather necklace strung with wolf teeth. He had an ancient M44 Mosin-Nagant bolt-action rifle in his hands, and a single drop of blood fell from the stock from where he had brutally clubbed the runner.

"One of the Brothers!" a nearby street vendor hissed. The black-clad man's head snapped in the direction of the voice, and the vendor fearfully averted his gaze.

The thief moaned, spat out a mouthful of blood, and started to rise, sack of grain spilled open beside him. He rolled over, realized who had taken him down, and immediately began to cry. I didn't know what language it was, but begging for mercy sounds pretty much the same everywhere. Without a word, the man in black flipped out the M44's bayonet and stabbed forward once. The scream turned into gurgling as the spike was twisted. Then the street was quiet again. The man jerked the spike out in a red splash. The tinted goggles surveyed the street once more before he wiped the blood off his bayonet on the thief's pants. He turned and walked away, never having said a word.

A moment later the street came back to life, as if nothing had ever happened.

The crowd was ignoring the dead body, except for a couple of street urchins who were already stealing his shoes and coat. Our guide looked wistful at the missed opportunity. "Who was that?" I asked the kid, putting my forefingers and thumbs in a circle over my eyes like I was wearing goggles. The boy said something I couldn't understand.

"The Brothers are the Pale Man's personal bodyguard.

They keep the peace in town," said one of the more sober Russian mafia who had sauntered up behind us. He took a drag on his cigarette and blew it out in a cloud. "They don't ever talk, and they never show their faces. Nobody smart fucks with them."

"I don't think they're so tough," said the drunker Russian that had been offering his sensitive undying love to Jill just a moment before.

"Like I said, nobody smart fucks with them," said the first. "Shut the fuck up, Gregor. War between houses and stealing in general is bad for business. The Brothers kill anybody that messes with that, unless they take a liking to you—then they drag you off to the slave mines." I was supposed to be the interpreter, so I quickly translated all this into Spanish for Jill, and the lead Russian took that as an indicator as to who was supposedly the boss. "Welcome to The Crossroads, lady. Should you businessfolk need any assistance, some of my men are always looking for freelance *security* work. And most of them are smarter than Gregor here. We're much more reliable than those slant-eyed homosexuals." He nodded down the street toward the other factions' houses.

"We'll keep that in mind, thank you," Jill responded politely, glancing nervously toward the dead thief, who was now missing most of his clothing. Even the grain was gone. "Are they just going to leave him there?"

The Russian shrugged. "It serves as a warning. If he's got family, they'll collect him eventually. Or not. The wolves creep into town at night when nobody's around, take care of it." He laughed, but I didn't think he was making a joke. "Enjoy your stay here."

I said goodbye to the Russian killers and we continued on.

A minute later our guide pointed at a wooden, three-story building, with a giant porch that circled the entire thing. Surprisingly, it looked rather nice. Nobody ever said anarchy had to be uncomfortable. There was a sign over the double door written in a few languages. I was able to read the third one down: *Glorious Cloud Hotel*. A roughly-carved wooden dragon was wrapped around the sign pole, breathing wooden fire. I gave the boy about $20 worth of rubles, and the way his face lit up, I could tell that was a big deal, easily worth passing up on looting the dead guy's shoes.

The interior of the Glorious Cloud was immaculately clean, and once the door was closed to the chaos of the street, the hotel lobby was peaceful and smelled like incense. The lady behind the desk was elderly Han, and extremely polite. She took our money, handed us a key, explained the meal schedule, and pointed us up the stairs to our rooms.

I handed her one final coin. "A tip." She took the coin, and rubbed her thumb around the outside edge without thinking. She looked at me curiously when she found that one edge of the coin had been smashed flat.

"Will you be staying until the thaw?" she asked.

"I'm told the forest is beautiful in spring." I completed the Exodus code phrase.

"Thank you, kind sir. Please enjoy your stay at The Crossroads."

The view out our window was spectacular. We were on

the top floor, and the town stretched out below us in a confused mass before sprawling out into the edges of the mountains. The Crossroads were situated in an X-shaped valley. Each leg was about nine miles long, with the bottom two descending into China. Lake Tansai and the big dam built by the Russians was barely visible in the distance. Against the mountains a few miles away was the abandoned military base which had been taken over by Sala Jihan and turned into a fortress. If my brother was still alive he would be in there. The entire mountain around the base was torn open by a gash that could probably be seen from space. Those were Jihan's mines.

The Glorious Cloud's rooms were small, but clean. Reaper was off taking care of our *survey* gear that porters had delivered to the hotel.

I felt Jill's arms encircle me from behind. She squeezed me tight and tucked her face against the back of my neck. I could feel her warm breath. "You okay, honey?" I asked quietly. I had to remember, this was my world. Not hers.

"Yeah, I'm fine. I've just never seen anything like that before."

I didn't know if she meant the thief getting executed in the street, or the villagers' bodies left up as warning signs. Either way, it wasn't a pleasant welcome. "I know. I warned you about this place. I shouldn't have let you come."

"I didn't give you a choice. Don't worry about me. I'll be fine. I'm not going mushy on you. I have to do this. Bob's my family now too, and not only that, I owe those Majestic assholes."

"They did ruin your life."

"I can't say they ruined it anymore now, can I?" She

squeezed me tight, as if afraid to let go. "But they did change it pretty drastically. I have to help you do this, you know that."

I gently disentangled myself, turned to face her, and took her into my arms. I well and truly loved this woman. "You really did beat me down over you coming on this job."

"Yeah, that was like our first real couple fight." She grinned. "Unless you count when we first met and you punched me in the stomach."

"Well, you tried to shoot me first."

"Fair enough." She snuggled in closer. "You know what else? We've been laying low on St. Carl for so long, we've never actually taken a trip before. This is our first vacation together."

"Hmm . . . Hadn't really thought about that," I said. "We should make the best of it." Then she bit the bottom of my ear. I checked my watch. Exodus could wait.

"Thank you for meeting with me, Mr. Lorenzo."

"Nice place you've got here. Wasn't this in *Raiders of the Lost Ark*?"

"I haven't seen that film." Ibrahim was an Iraqi Kurd. He was about my age, and appeared to be in extremely good shape. His greying hair was kept short, and his dark eyes studied me carefully as I sat across from him. The Exodus operative and I were sitting at a table in the rear of a bar near the hotel. The room was dark, smoky, loud, filled with boisterous drunken Mongolians, and reminded me of a third-world version of the Golden Manatee. "So, you're the man that freed Michael Valentine?"

"Yeah. That was loads of fun."

"His reputation is great amongst the men, and having a hero figure along for this sort of operation is good for morale."

"So Valentine's a hero figure now."

"You are not familiar with his exploits on our behalf in Mexico?"

"No, and it would be impossible for me to care less."

"Nonetheless, you have our sincere thanks." Ibrahim chuckled. "Shen told me that you were not friends with Valentine; however, Shen spoke very highly of your bravery and skills."

"Shen's here?" I glanced around the bar. I had no doubt there were some other Exodus types hidden among the patrons, but I hadn't seen him, but he was one of the only people I'd ever met who might be as unnoticeable as I was.

"He and Antoine are in The Crossroads. They will be assigned to one of the swords in anticipation of our assault, an assault which will have better odds of success now, thanks to your actions."

"Save the flattery, Ibrahim. I know the deal. So, has Ling kissed and made up with your superiors?" I asked with a smirk. "Invading Montana had to piss them off."

"How did you know that?" Ibrahim was suspicious.

"Ling was motivated. Even if your bosses had told her no, she would've still gone for it. Antoine and Shen would follow her no matter what . . . Chill out. You don't have a leak. I'm good at reading people. It's what I do. Whatever permission Ling had to pull off that stunt wasn't given *too* freely. Exodus is a low-profile bunch, and that certainly wasn't low profile. You might be happy to have your motivational poster on heroism, but that's a happy bonus is all."

"You are perceptive," Ibrahim was nodding. "Shen also warned me about that."

"Good. So we won't waste any time blowing smoke up each other's asses. Has there been any sign of my brother?" Behind me there was a crash as two Mongolians got into a fight. The topless dancing girl was knocked off her table.

Ibrahim shook his head. "Sadly, no. I can show you where he was attacked after speaking with Ling, the market overlooking the arena, but there has been no sign since. My people have been listening, but no one has spoken. Ling was the last person he was with, before he was captured near the fighting pits. I'm sorry." He must have seen my face darken, and attempted to change the subject. "After what Shen told me about you, I am glad that you and your people are here to join us."

"Listen, I think you and your folks are doing a good thing. Killing slavers is like killing cockroaches, but just so we're on the same page, I'm here for my brother. Nothing personal, I'm not the joining type. I'm going to meet with this Jihan asshole, see what we can find out, and go from there. If my brother's dead, I'm going home, but I'll pass on any intelligence I can gather just on the general principle that I don't like asshole warlords."

"I understand. The path that God has chosen for me is not for every man, but nonetheless, I appreciate your offer. And if your brother is still alive and being held in the fortress or in the mines . . ."

"Then, I'll gladly help you stack the bodies so deep they'll call it Great Wall of China, the Sequel."

Ibrahim laughed and struck the table. "Excellent, my brother!" He raised his cup of tea, I raised my drink. "To killing assholes!" It was good to see that not every team commander in Exodus was as intense as Ling.

"So what can you tell me about the situation? A lot of things have changed since I was here last."

"When Big Eddie died, there was a battle for control of The Crossroads. Whoever controls this place runs Central Asia. The Russian Mafia and the Triads lost a lot of men, as did the other factions that joined in. It was chaos. A situation which Exodus loved. While The Crossroads was unavailable, the evil which feeds upon this place was stymied. It was a glorious, but for all too short time. By the way, thank you for killing such a terrible man."

"Yeah, I'm all about making the world a better place."

Ibrahim swirled his tea and studied it. "Then after a few months of fighting, a new group arrived here. A man had taken the name of Sala Jihan, the Pale Man. Are you familiar with the old tales?"

"A little. Mostly campfire stories to scare little kids. Eat your vegetables or the Pale Man will come and get you, that kind of crap."

"Yes, the Pale Man supposedly terrorized this land a thousand years ago. Born of human mother and sired by the devil, he reigned with blood and fire. His slave armies crushed everything in their path." Ibrahim paused to take a drink. "He was a force of incredible evil. Finally, he was defeated by a great Mongol prince and imprisoned deep beneath the earth, but the local tribes maintain a tradition. There is a prophecy that someday he will return and reclaim his throne of blood."

I laughed. "Don't tell me you think this is the same guy?"

Ibrahim smirked. "No, of course not, but I think we are dealing with a very talented and evil man, who took the name of someone the locals are already terrified of and used that to his own advantage. In the many years I've been in the Order, I've never seen a man such as this. His people came into this valley, and within three days he had utterly defeated the Mafia and the Triads. He impaled many of them on stakes in front of their houses, declared peace, and moved into the old base on the mountain. He's gotten the money flowing again, so the other factions are happy . . . for now."

"Think we could use that for our advantage?"

Ibrahim shrugged. "With as many spies as there are in this place, I'm hesitant to approach anyone. Certainly one faction would love to take Jihan's place, but as they say, it is the nail that sticks up that gets hammered down. Big Eddie's old faction, now called the Montalban Exchange after his real identity became known, seems like the most likely candidate to attempt a coup. It is led by one of Eddie's former lieutenants. They have a reputation for ruthlessness. Frankly, I don't care who takes over afterward, but Jihan must die. In the last year, he has systematically enslaved tens of thousands."

"You're exaggerating."

"Some things I do not joke about, my friend." Ibrahim reached into his shirt and pulled out a folded sheet of paper. It was a map of Asia. There were hundreds of red dots scattered around the map. "Each of those dots is, or was, a village. Jihan contacts the local governments, finds out who the troublemakers are, and then makes them go away. The Chinese hate the northern Uyghur minority, for example, so should one of their villages be raided, they do not care."

"That's a lot of dots."

"The youngest men are taken into his army and brainwashed as child soldiers. You will see them around town. Their faces are disfigured with a branding iron. He keeps a garrison at his base and uses them as guards over the mines. Do not let the fact they are slaves cause you to underestimate them."

"I've dealt with child soldiers in Africa. I know the deal."

"Not like this, you do not. His indoctrination techniques are very effective. The young women are sold internationally, through the various factions, for uses which I'm sure you understand. Everyone else works in the mines."

"I saw the mines from my hotel window," I said patiently. "You can't tell me there's ten thousand people housed there."

"Obviously not. There's a fifty percent fatality rate in the first month. The bodies are thrown into a very large hole . . ." He must have seen the look of disgust cross my face. "He works them to death, weeds out the *unsuitable*, and replaces them with more. Are you certain you still want to go home if your brother is dead?"

"I'm not a good guy, Ibrahim. That's a job for guys like you and Valentine. My concern is me and mine. That's it. People like me don't adopt causes."

"Not the most honorable philosophy."

"It's kept me alive." I shrugged. "And your assets?"

"I have a few swords here. The others are staged in Mongolia, waiting for me to summon them." He smiled, knowing that I knew he was being purposefully vague as to their strength. I didn't even know how many men made up a sword.

"So what are you waiting for?"

"There are others available. They're wrapping up their tasks and then coming here. In the meantime, we're trying to gather as much intelligence as possible. We will need every man possible. We believe there are several hundred slave soldiers guarding Jihan's fortress."

"ETA?"

Ibrahim smiled again. "And I tell you this, and you find in your meeting with Jihan, that perhaps he would be willing to trade your brother for information about a gang of assassins plotting against him? Please, Mr. Lorenzo. The only way you will know our plans is if you volunteer to accompany us. No offense."

"None taken." This was business after all. "One other question. Who are the Brothers?"

"You saw one?" he asked. I nodded. "They are the Pale Man's elite personal guards. Since they never show their faces, never speak in public, and always dress the same, we don't know how many there are, but they enforce his rule in town. Everyone is scared of them. They are brutal."

"How many would you estimate there really are?"

"There are at least three."

I snorted. "Three goofy little bastards have managed to terrorize a town full of psychos, murderers, and hired thugs?"

He smiled at me. "You saw one, so I'm assuming you saw him murder someone."

"How'd you know that?"

"Because that's the only time you see them. If they reveal themselves, then somebody is about to die. Trust me, Mr. Lorenzo, the Brothers are very good at what they do. They and a small garrison of perhaps twenty slave soldiers have kept the factions from warring more effectively than hundreds of Big Eddie's mercenaries ever did. You must understand, this is a superstitious place, and Jihan has used that as a weapon. Do not underestimate his forces. These are not the back-country thugs you might be expecting. So, what is your plan?"

"We have a business a meeting scheduled for tomorrow at the fortress. I'm going to—" There was a sudden loud crash at the front of the bar, followed by a lot of shouting in Mongolian. Two people seated near the entrance stood and headed directly back toward us. I placed my hand on my pistol, but Ibrahim signaled for me to wait.

"They're friends. What is it?"

The first spoke. "Montalban Exchange is starting some trouble out front. They're looking for somebody and want to come in." He was a handsome young man, and surprisingly enough had a bland American accent. "They're led by that big Viking-looking dude."

The second was a female, with the hood of her coat up, and a scarf covering the lower half of her face. She had really pretty blue eyes. "The Mongols disagree." She sounded Russian. "I think they're going to fight." She discreetly took a Makarov from inside her coat and placed it in an outside pocket, so it would be easier to shoot some unsuspecting sap.

"We'd best be going then." Ibrahim stood. "Mr. Lorenzo, this is Svetlana and Roland, two of my sword. You can reach us through the Glorious Cloud should you have any further information you wish to share. We'll be in touch. May Allah grant you good fortune on your mission."

Chapter 12: The Greatest Trick the Devil Ever Pulled

LORENZO
Sala Jihan's Fortress
March 13th

A weather-beaten statue of Stalin looked out over the valley. The concrete features had been mostly obliterated by wind and rain, but even then the blank eyes of the Man of Steel seemed to follow us as we drove past.

A Land Cruiser had picked us up in front of the Glorious Cloud, exactly on time. The driver was a young man with a large brand scar on each cheek. He had not said a single word the entire thirty-minute trip. None of us spoke either. Jill was nervous. I wanted to reach over and squeeze her hand, but that would have been out of character for a translator and his boss, so I refrained.

The road skirted the edge of the river and passed through the old dry lake bed before climbing into the mountains. The terrain at this altitude consisted of rock and scrub brush. There was no way to approach without being seen. The maps showed a possible path through the mountains to the back of the fortress, but it was impassable for vehicles and would be a difficult trek on foot.

The walls were tall, thick concrete. Guards paced atop, watching our approach through binoculars. The walls were too smooth to scale, and too tall to hit with ladders. Our driver steered the Land Cruiser between concrete barricades designed to keep a truck bomb from getting a good run at the entrance. The steel gate was already open, waiting for us. I noted the thickness of the gates as we passed through. Short of a tank or a whole lot of explosives, I didn't see Exodus getting through that quickly either.

Through the tinted glass of the Land Cruiser, I could see that the inside of the fortress was made up featureless concrete bunkers, each with its own heavy steel doors and narrow, metal-shuttered windows that served as firing ports. There was a raised concrete landing pad, sufficient for a few helicopters, though nothing was parked there now. The snow suggested that nothing had landed there all winter.

Reaper was gawking at something out his window. Behind the landing pad was a small hill with a tank parked on top of it. *Shit. That's no tank.* Instead of a single large barrel poking out of the turret, it had four smaller barrels and a rotating radar dish on top. It was a ZSU-23, a nasty antiaircraft machine, and unlike most of the military equipment rotting in this part of the world, it appeared well maintained. Four 23mm autocannons would rip the hell out of anything Exodus tried to land here.

The Land Cruiser stopped, and our doors were immediately opened for us by waiting staff. None of them

would make eye contact. Behind them were more
emotionless child soldiers. The oldest was maybe sixteen.
They were of various ethnicities, but all were dressed in
snow camouflage, wearing some sort of load-bearing vest,
and carrying an AK or SKS. Each one had savage burn
scars on their cheeks or forehead.

"Greetings and welcome." A muscular man in a
business suit approached. His face was unscarred. He was
here voluntarily. "I am Talak Aziz. I will be your escort
during your visit here. After so many e-mails it is a pleasure
to meet you in person, Ms. Garcia and Mr. Cook." He
nodded at Jill and Reaper. I smoothly translated everything
that he said into Spanish. Jill smiled and nodded as Talak
gestured us toward the entrance of the largest bunker.
"You will need to go through our security check, for your
own protection, of course."

"Of course," Jill responded.

The soldiers gave us a thorough pat-down and even had
a metal detecting wand. A woman checked Jill. We had left
everything dangerous, sharp, pointy, or flammable at the
hotel. This meeting was just to gather intelligence on our
foe, nothing more.

Satisfied that we weren't assassins, Aziz took us inside.
The entryway for this bunker had been decorated with
expensive Persian rugs and Japanese landscape paintings.
It was surprisingly nice compared to the stark exterior. A
slave girl took our coats and disappeared. We were led
through the bunker to a meeting room set up in much the
same manner as the entrance, and we were seated on
cushions. Talak remained standing as he introduced us to
the men in European business suits who were already

waiting. I struggled to keep up and to correctly pronounce everyone's name. They were all older, professional, and had that stink of dirty money on them.

I was disappointed. These were Jihan's functionaries, the guys that actually handled the business end of things, the money changers, the accountants. They were here to discuss the exchange of slave-mined ore for cash, and the shipment thereof to our subsidiaries for processing. They were talking dollars a ton and how much different countries' customs officials cost to bribe. I wanted to meet *The Man*.

Jill did a superb job. Reaper had coached her well. She played the part of a junior executive whiz-kid rather well. Her nervousness was actually perfect, because to Jihan's functionaries it read as her being scared about brokering a big-money deal. She was the only woman in the room. They probably thought she was the negotiator because she was pretty. Jill knew nothing about the technical end of things, wire transfers, transportation, amounts required, and the methods of exchange, which was obvious to the functionaries, but she wasn't supposed to. That's where Reaper came in. He didn't look like much, but if he hadn't damaged it with all the death metal and Red Bull he'd probably have an IQ up around Stephen Hawking's. He'd memorized every mineral-business-related factoid known to man in the last few weeks.

Meanwhile I looked unimportant, translated, and soaked up everything I possibly could about these people and their operation. Aziz was doing the same thing as me. You could hang a fancy suit on a killer gorilla, but it was always going to be a killer gorilla at heart.

Jill and Reaper wasted an hour butting heads with the hirelings, but it was a waste of time. I had only gotten a look at the security arrangements for a few seconds. This was not helping our mission at all. We hadn't fabricated an entire corporation, wired millions of my own money into it, and come all this way to look at spreadsheets.

Jill must have been feeling the same way. "My superiors were hoping that I could meet this Sala Jihan." As I translated that last bit, the hirelings stiffened up. Talak shifted nervously. "He's a very mysterious figure."

"Ms. Garcia, I'm afraid that will not be possible," stammered one of the functionaries. "Sala Jihan does not participate in these sorts of activities. He is a very busy man, and has engaged us to represent him."

"Yes, it wouldn't be proper," said an older Chinese man with a bad hairpiece. "We can assure you that we are fully vested with authority—"

Jill held up her hand. "And I can assure you, gentlemen, I am here to arrange the purchase of millions of dollars of precious metals a year from your operation. My superiors insisted that I not agree to anything until I have met the head of your organization in person."

"As you are aware, Sala Jihan's methods are different than what you are used to in the west." I tried not to chuckle as I translated that. *No shit.*

"Meaning that he uses slave labor?" Jill replied. The men shifted awkwardly. "We're fully aware of that, but we're expecting an emerging demand for copper that is unprecedented from the Indian market this year, and my company intends to fill that need. We don't care about the slaves. We care about building a long-term relationship so we can make a lot of money before one of our competitors grows the balls to come here themselves. You are sitting on billions, but you're limited to what you can sell through greedy mobsters. My company is offering a legitimate distribution channel. We feel the profit opportunity outweighs the possible negative press, but my superiors don't even know that Sala Jihan is *real*. I meet him, or there will be no deal."

The hirelings looked at each other, fearful of losing this deal, but more scared of contacting their boss. Talak actually choked when I translated *cojones*. He spoke up. "I will inquire if the Master is available. In the meantime, please continue with your negotiations." The big man left the room.

The meeting continued, only now that they knew Jill was playing hardball, it was a lot more heated. Ironically, since our entire operation was imaginary, Jill was having quite a bit of fun sticking it to them and playing up the heartless corporation angle. Twenty minutes later the door slid open and Talak entered, looking rather grim.

"The Master will see you now."

The trip across the compound alone was worth it. I was able to see more of the security, where the interior choke points were, where the vehicles were parked, and and where the guards slept. All of that would be good stuff to pass on to Ibrahim. Most importantly, I was able to spot which building had been the Russian brig. A handful of prisoners watched us from the other side of the bars with eyes pleading for mercy. It was very possible that—if he was still alive—Bob was inside that prison building. I scanned every window, but unfortunately didn't see a single giant, bald Caucasian.

Talak took us to a concrete slab with an elevator shed on top of it. Behind the shed was a giant circular depression in the snow. A Brother stood to the side of the door, studying us with goggled eyes, arms folded, and weapons slung over his back.

"He seriously lives in a missile silo?" Reaper asked. Talak didn't bother to respond, he only nodded at the guard, who continued to watch us soundlessly. The faceless black mask was strangely intimidating, but he stepped out of our path.

The elevator car was basically a steel frame with a mesh wire floor to stand on and handrails to hold on to, and a giant exposed pulley above us. It swayed dangerously as we stepped into it. Talak picked up a wired control box and punched the down button. With a lurch, the car began to descend. It was dark and strangely humid inside the shaft.

"I cannot promise a long visit," Talak explained, only his eyes and teeth really showed up in the dark. There wasn't a single light installed on the car. "He is a very busy man and agrees to speak with very few. You are rather fortunate."

"That will be quite all right," Jill responded after I translated, obviously agitated. I had forgotten that she was a little bit claustrophobic.

Talak turned to me, and the look he gave me indicted that this message was for me alone. "Listen, translator, if your employer says anything insulting, I would caution you not to relay it, or you will not make it out of this hole, because he *will* kill the messenger. Understand?"

I nodded slowly.

"Excellent."

After what seemed like forever, the car clanked to a halt, and Talak opened a scissor gate. We stepped into some sort of control room. The ancient computers were covered in cobwebs and dust. Punch cards were slowly eroding into the floor. He pointed at the far door. "Through there is the Master's living quarters. I will wait here for your return. Are you certain you wish to do this?"

If they wanted to kill us, they would have just done it on the surface and saved themselves the work. This was just more of that superstitious weirdo crap that Jihan was using to control The Crossroads. I glanced at Reaper. He looked even whiter than usual. Jill was sweating, surely thinking about the tons of rock crushing down above us. This Jihan really was a master of the mind fuck. "Ma'am," I gestured forward.

Jill swallowed hard. "Of course." She screwed up her courage and went through the far door. There was a long hallway, interspersed with submarine-style blast doors. They were currently open, but I made note that if Ibrahim needed to get down here, he was going to need to need explosives, cutting torches, and time.

We emerged into the flickering light at the bottom of the silo. It was a big area, the giant missile long since removed or launched. The open space spiraled up toward the surface, finally disappearing into shadow. I had been expecting some sort of palatial thing, with gold and diamonds, and the gaudy things that warlords liked to adorn themselves with to impress the fearful, greedy, and stupid. This was nothing like that.

The space was mostly open. The outer ring was just a walkway that circled the entire room. A catwalk extended to the center, where there was a circular concrete pad about twenty meters across. The base of the concrete disappeared into a pool of dark water that had settled in the bottom of the silo. The center pad had no decoration, just some nice, but very basic furniture; a bed, and some wardrobes, mirrors, and cabinets. On the far side of the pad was what appeared to be an altar, illuminated by candles and two large, metallic pans that were burning wood and incense. The crackling fire was the only source of light, and the smoke drifted toward the top of the silo.

"Weird," I muttered.

"I am Sala Jihan," a voice boomed from the island. "Come closer."

Jill started down the catwalk, with me right behind her. Reaper lagged a little bit behind. The metal echoed under our boots, and through the steel mesh, you could see down into the water. I couldn't see the bottom.

Sala Jihan was waiting for us, reclined on a plush red couch, facing the catwalk. He was wearing what looked like a red silk bathrobe tied with a black sash, was barefoot, and his hair was wet, like he had just gotten done swimming. The legendary Sala Jihan lived up to his title, the Pale Man. His skin was white, not like Reaper, but like a cave fish, almost translucent. I thought he was an albino until I saw his pitch black eyes.

Two more Brothers flanked Jihan. Even here in the near-dark they were still wearing their goggles. I didn't see any weapons, but I had no doubt the squat little men were fully ready to destroy us.

"Hello, I am Maria Consuela Garcia, and these are my associates—"

Jihan silenced her with a wave of his hand. "I know who you are," he answered in perfect Spanish. "Your translator will not be necessary," then he switched to accentless English. "Or would you prefer this?"

"Either will do," Jill responded slowly.

Jihan stroked his face thoughtfully. He had a thin mustache, pointy goatee, and long black hair. He was kind of like me, difficult to guess an age, but he appeared relatively young and fit. "I do not normally agree to meet outsiders. What would you ask of me?"

"My company just wanted to know what manner of man we were dealing with."

Jihan smiled. Perhaps it was a trick of the light, but his teeth looked like they had been sharpened, then his lips closed and I could no longer tell. He gestured at his surroundings. "I am but a humble man who likes to dig in the Earth. I find precious things as I dig, and sell them to people like you. It funds my . . . hobbies."

He exuded evil. It was hard to explain. A man like me needed to be an expert judge of character. I had known truly evil men before, but not like this. They say the eyes are the window to the soul, and in some of those men, I had seen broken souls, or in the case of Eddie Montalban, an emptiness. But in these black orbs, I saw something . . . *else.*

"Thank you," Jill said, her voice quavering slightly. She felt it as well. "I, uh . . . well . . ."

I noted the altar behind him. I had just assumed that Jihan would have been another Muslim warlord, but that altar was from something different, something *older*. "And what is it that you're digging for?" I asked, not knowing why I spoke, but regretting it immediately.

The warlord turned his head slightly, as if noticing me for the first time. The two Brothers visibly tensed beneath their robes. Jihan paused for what seemed like an eternity, studying me. It was as if somebody had turned on a million candle power spotlight, and I wanted nothing but to slink away and hide.

Finally he broke the awkward silence. "You are no mere translator, little man." He let that hang. I didn't respond, rather I tried to look as pathetic and bewildered as possible, but his black eyes were on me like a CAT scan. He continued to stroke his goatee. "You are a killer of men . . . a son of murder. So tell me, Maria, why did you bring an assassin into my home?"

My stomach rolled over in an acidic lurch. Nobody ever saw anything in me that I didn't want them to see. I was grey, unreadable. *What kind of man is this?*

"He's also my bodyguard," Jill spoke quickly. "The Crossroads have a reputation for being dangerous, and my company felt that security wo—"

He raised his hand to silence her. I felt the adrenaline begin to flow, fully expecting him to give the order to have the Brothers gun us down. Jihan smiled again, those strange eyes never breaking away from my own. "Yes, this country is quite dangerous." Something large splashed in the water under the catwalk. Reaper jumped. "It is wise to have one such as this to do your bidding." He gestured at me. His fingernails ended in points. "You may return to your organization and tell them that you have spoken with

Sala Jihan, and that I am real. The precious things I take from the earth are yours to purchase. You may go now."

"But I was hoping to—" Jill began.

"That will be all." Jihan said in a manner that left no doubt that we would be feeding whatever the hell was in the pool if we didn't go away right now. The Brothers stepped forward and escorted us to the edge of the catwalk. I couldn't wait to get out of there. We walked—entirely too fast—across the catwalk back to the outer concrete ring. The Brothers stopped at the edge and folded their arms, a definite barrier to reentry.

"One last thing, oh, son of murder." Jihan's voice boomed behind us. I froze, a feeling of dread tingling up the base of my spine. Then I pushed Jill after Reaper out the blast-door exit before turning around.

"Yes?"

Jihan rose, the flames and smoke dancing behind him. "Where you have gone, death has followed like a loyal servant, but do not think to return to this place . . . For here, death answers only to me."

I nodded once, turned, and left the room.

We'll see about that.

"Shit! What the fuck was that?" Jill shouted once we were back in the relative safety of the Glorious Cloud and away from spying ears. "Weird-ass bizarro shit! Did you feel that?"

Of course I had. Sala Jihan gave off a vibe similar to a bag of serial killers and electric eels, but I played the stoic. "Feel what?" I muttered.

"It was like all of the good in the universe got squished

at the door to that place. Just, kind of . . . hell, I don't know . . . wrong." Jill threw up her hands in frustration, lacking the words to explain it.

"He's a slave-trading warlord. I warned you before we ever came. You wanted to play this game? Well, that's the opposing team. What did you expect? A nice house in the suburbs with a white picket fence, maybe some garden gnomes?"

"Not that, that's for sure," she answered. "There's something wrong with that man."

"He's messing with your head. It's his MO. That's how he runs this place so well. Yeah, he's one evil son of a bitch, but he's only human."

"I don't know, Chief." Reaper spoke for the first time. He was even paler than usual.

"Oh, not you too!" I said in exasperation. "Reaper, we've been through so much craziness, and you're gonna let this guy scare you?"

He bit his lip and looked down, embarrassed. "Well, yeah."

"Damn it! Don't be such a pussy," I spat. It wasn't fair. Jihan's act had shaken me as well, but I couldn't let it show. I had a mission to accomplish, and if my brother was alive, he was probably in that fortress. "Can I count on you or not?"

"Lorenzo!" Jill exclaimed. She wasn't used to me being mean to Reaper. "That's unnecessary."

I ignored her and glared at my subordinate. Jill gave me her Death Frown. I had known Reaper since he was a kid. He looked up to me like some sort of father figure. I knew he'd be brave if I required it of him. "I've never let you down," Reaper stated, clenching his hands into fists. "I ain't gonna start now. Screw this guy, he's goin' down."

"That's the spirit. Fuck Jihan. Now here's the plan. Make notes of everything, and I mean *everything*, that you saw in the compound, and we take it to Ibrahim and Exodus."

"So you've decided you trust them?" Jill asked.

"No, not really. Every human being I actually trust is in this room," I said. Reaper looked relieved when I said that. "In fact, before I set up another meet with Ibrahim, I want to poke around town some. We only have their word that it was Jihan's people that took Bob. I feel like Ling was telling the truth and Bob's notes point in that direction. Exodus has similar goals. Enemy of my enemy is a friend, and all that. If they're going in and if I'm along for the ride, then I can get a look inside that prison building, but trust them? Hell no." I tossed Reaper a notepad. "Start writing while it's still fresh."

"What I wonder is, how did the Pale Man see right through you?" Reaper wondered aloud. "It isn't like you look dangerous or anything. You've done gigs way harder than that. Hell, you convinced the President of Sumatra you were his cousin that one time."

"Beats me," I shrugged. The locals would probably have some supernatural mumbo-jumbo explanation, but we were both men who knew how to sell a roll. Except I hadn't been able to see through his act at all. "He knows me now. So getting a covert look inside that prison isn't likely." I ditched my western style coat, and began rummaging through my bag for some more native clothing. My holster went on, disappearing under a bulky Turkic overcoat. "While I'm gone, don't let anybody in. Don't trust anyone. Not even the Exodus people. Don't answer the door, and if somebody tries to push their way in, shoot them a lot. Keep the fire stoked and toss your notes in there if anything feels off. If I'm not back by midnight, go right to the escape plans. Don't come looking for me, because you'll get eaten alive out there. I'm going down to the fighting pits. That's the last place Bob was seen."

"Sounds safe," Jill said. She was far too smart to even suggest going with me.

"Honey, this is The Crossroads." I chamber checked my 9mm before holstering it. "Nothing is safe here."

VALENTINE
Eastern Kazakhstan
March 13th

Our small caravan of trucks made its way along a mountain highway. Five trucks in all, loaded for bear with Exodus personnel and supplies, had departed the airport in the city of Semey, hundreds of miles to the west. We'd been driving for over fourteen hours. Kazakhstan was a huge country that had nothing equivalent to an American interstate highway. It had been slow going along poorly maintained two-lane highways the entire trip.

We switched out drivers as necessary, stopping only to refuel and for piss breaks. The residents of the little villages along the road to The Crossroads were used to comparatively rich foreigners buying gas from them, so we didn't draw any particular notice. The highway was cleared of snow, just as Ling said it would be.

Along our route there had been very little in the way of local law enforcement. I'm not sure if it was due to such things being bad for business at The Crossroads, or if the Kazakh government simply didn't bother to police the remote areas of the country. Either way, the lack of cops made me feel better. I hadn't had any good experiences with government authorities lately.

We did encounter one army checkpoint, as Ling had warned me we might. It was pretty far from the border. Their sole purpose seemed to be keeping track of, or possibly shaking down, the suspicious types who looked like they were on their way to The Crossroads. You know, people like us.

My heart rate doubled as we approached the checkpoint. There was an entire squad of soldiers, all armed, and we were all trapped in vehicles. I kept my head down and stared at the seat in front of me as a bored-looking Kazakh soldier looked in the window at me. Ling assured me that it was going to be okay. And so it was. A wad of currency was handed over, along with a carton of cigarettes and a couple bottles of booze, and the Kazakh soldiers lost all interest in us. We were left to go on our way without being searched.

We were in the home stretch after that. We slowly rumbled along Highway P-163. All around us were stunning mountain vistas and breathtaking, unspoiled wilderness, and damn, was it cold. The driver of the rattling diesel truck noticed that I was struggling to stay warm and turned up the heat. I didn't feel good.

Ling seemed to notice my discomfort. "It's the altitude. It will take some getting used to."

I shook my head. "Are we almost there?"

"Yes. We are just crossing the border into Russia now."

"No more checkpoints?"

Ling smiled. "Not so close to The Crossroads. It's bad for business."

The Russian side of the border didn't look any different than the Kazakh side. We continued to follow the river down a long, winding valley, until the highway began to veer off to the south. It was then that I saw, in the distance, the river pooled into a huge reservoir. Beyond it sat an imposing, ancient-looking dam.

"That hydroelectric plant was built in the Fifties," Ling informed me. "It powers The Crossroads and most of the small Russian villages in the area. The Kazakh government buys electricity from the Russians as well."

"Why did they build a dam so close to the border?" We were only a few miles from North China.

"1950 was the year the Soviet Union and China signed the Sino-Soviet Treaty of Friendship and Alliance. Stalin wanted to bolster relations with the People's Republic of China. The dam supplied electricity not only to Soviet villages, but to Chinese villages on the other side of the border. The town that became The Crossroads was once called the City of International Friendship. It was intended to be a symbolic beacon of international Communism."

"From what you've told me about the place, it doesn't sound very friendly."

"It was all lies, of course. Hardly anyone ever lived in their city of friendship, even at the best of times. When the

Sino-Soviet Split happened in the late 1950s, The Crossroads was all but abandoned. Now the former communist city has turned into probably the most capitalist place on earth. The Crossroads is home to every international crime syndicate and black market imaginable. Anything goes, so long as you have the means to pay for it."

"You will never find a more wretched hive of scum and villainy," I mused.

Ling looked a question at me. She didn't get the reference.

"Seriously? Uh, never mind. What else?"

"The Soviets built a military base here after the Second World War. Joint military drills with the People's Liberation Army were conducted after the Friendship Treaty was signed, but like the town itself, it was all symbolic. During the Sino-Soviet Split the garrison was reinforced. Anti-aircraft batteries and surface-to-air missiles were emplaced. In the sixties, R-5 intermediate-range ballistic missiles were stationed here, and silos were built to house them."

Holy crap. "The Russians put *nukes* this close to the border?"

"Oh yes. They were quite displeased after the Communist Party of China formally denounced the USSR."

"Do the Russians still use the base?"

"Michael, didn't you read the briefing material I gave you?"

"I, uh, skimmed it." I'd slept on the plane from Azerbaijan and spent most of the road trip across Kazakhstan sleeping as well. I had only glanced over the information, and mostly read up on what little there was about this Sala Jihan.

Ling shook her head. My physical condition wasn't much of an excuse for pity in her crowd. "There was an incident in '63. Most of it is rumor in any case. Madness high in the mountains, a Soviet drug experiment gone wrong, who really knows? The soldiers at the base mutinied. They turned on their officers and killed them in a ritualistic fashion."

"Ritualistic?"

"There aren't many details. According to the stories, the soldiers went insane. They didn't just kill their officers, they were sacrificed on a crude altar, their organs cut out, eaten, and their blood drunk as some form of sacrament."

"Jesus!"

"I doubt that is true. What is known is that a base, close to the Chinese border, housing nuclear missiles of the Strategic Rocket Forces, mutinied. The government was in a state of near panic."

"They bomb it?" That was the Russian response to most things.

"Yes. The Soviets lost several bombers in the effort, but they managed to destroy the air-defense sites. Elite KGB troops were parachuted in. After two days of fighting they retook the base. None of the mutineers survived. Shortly after that, the missiles were withdrawn from the area and the base was abandoned."

I whistled. "Wow. And I thought I had personal problems in the Air Force."

"They kept it secret, and the secret grew into a legend. The Soviets were afraid of this valley after that, leaving only a small number of troops to guard the dam. That garrison was removed when the Soviet Union collapsed and has never been replaced."

"So who runs the dam now?"

"The Pale Man runs the dam, Michael," Ling said, with a slight change in her tone of voice. "He runs everything through his intermediaries. Crossroads City sits right on the border between Russia and North China. Roads to it run in from Mongolia and Kazakhstan. The rail line from Russia to China is up and running again. The governments of all four of these nations abide the atrocities that go on here so long as they get a share of the profits."

As we passed the dam, I could see Crossroads City in the hazy distance, miles beyond the reservoir. It sprawled out haphazardly in every direction. A brown haze hung low in the air above the town, obscuring the view. I had heard of this place, of course. It was hardly a secret. It had its own Wikipedia page. To the world, it was just another lawless wasteland that occasionally rated a news blurb. It wasn't considered any different than the Horn of Africa, the Balkans, or countless other places where law and order had broken down. But The Crossroads *was* different. It wasn't lawless. It had Sala Jihan's law.

I looked at Ling as she gazed out the windows, and tried very hard to quash the terrible feeling that was eating at me. It wasn't just pre-operation jitters. Something was wrong with this place, and I very badly wanted to go home.

I'd promised these people that I'd help them, though, and I intended to see it done.

Chapter 13: The Arena

The Arena was right where I remembered it. The ramshackle buildings that had sprung up around the ancient ruins were situated high on the banks of the river that bled from the nearby Lake Tansai. If I was to follow the river for about thirty miles, it would eventually lead to Lake Hanas and the village of Kola Su in Xinjiiang. That was one of our possible escape routes if this went horribly wrong.

I had been to Kola Su once before, a very long time ago. It was a beautiful little place, rustic, but with beautiful old buildings and long, graceful, white bridges. Katarina and I had shared a small cottage there for a few weeks while laying low after one of Eddie's jobs. I still remembered one particular moment, waking up on a sleeping mat, and glancing over at Katarina, wearing

291

nothing but my shirt, framed in the glorious sunrise, the crystal clear lake behind her, and her throwing rice balls at some weird looking Chinese ducks. That image had stuck with me for a lot of years. It had actually been a relatively peaceful stretch in an otherwise turbulent time of my life.

I shook my head, forgetting those useless memories, and refocused on the present. The arena was one of the larger structures in town, made of stacked bricks by the long forgotten people that had originally settled this place. It was sloped, with multiple tiers providing seating, so the residents of The Crossroads could watch their favorite sport: *violence.*

It didn't really matter what kind of violence either. The malcontents here were ready for anything that involved blood. The space inside the arena was set up for anything. There were smaller circular pits for cock fighting, dog fights, snakes and mongooses, and wider circles for wild horses to kick and bite each other to death. The losers ended up quartered and hanging from stalls in the marketplace. Eddie had even had the idea of posting these events live on the internet, and taking bets from a worldwide audience. I knew that he had made a particularly large amount of cash on a fight that had involved a Russian bear versus a pack of wild dogs.

The highlight of this casual brutality was the human fights. Nothing brought out the bets like a slugfest between random crazy people, and judging by the size of the crowd gathered around the main fighting pit and cheering from the arena steps, that was exactly what was going on right now. There were about two hundred people, and before I even saw the contestants, I could tell who was involved by the spectators. A group of Russians were the loudest, shouting, and chanting for their guy, while on the other side, a smaller group of Mongolians had some sort of song going on. I merged with the middle group, made up of everybody else who didn't have a dog in this fight, and jostled my way to the front of the pit.

If the fights had any rules, they were usually agreed to by the factions beforehand. If the rules were broken, then the two groups would usually settle the difference by shooting each other. At least that was how it had worked in the past when Eddie was in charge. With the Brothers running the show, I wasn't sure how disagreements would play out. An old Chinese man was walking back and forth around the lip of the pit, big wads of colorful money in each fist, shouting and pointing, taking bets from the mob.

Ah, a knife fight. So much for rules.

Both men were shirtless, even though as the Sun dipped behind the mountains it wasn't even twenty degrees out. The Russian was older, with short, graying hair, and muscles like twisted rope. The Mongol was bigger, younger, looked stronger, with his hair tied back, and was wearing, believe it or not, what looked like pink hot pants. Both of them had a lot of laceration scars, and were armed with very short knives. Of course, long knives make for a shorter fight.

The Chinese bookie was done taking bets. He shouted something unintelligible, both sides began to scream, and the fighters started to circle.

Having no need to watch this, I scanned the crowd. I was looking for information, and watching two psychopaths cut themselves to ribbons for entertainment, pride, and a little bit of money was not my idea of a good time. The market area that Bob had last been seen in was only a little bit further to the north.

One face caught my eye. The easiest way to spot a tail was to wait for some event that naturally draws everyone's attention, like for example, a knife fight. Then all of the normal people tend to look at the action. Somebody up to no good will be looking at you. The man was walking toward me, moving smoothly through the bustling crowd. He was really tall, broad shouldered, blond, with a bristling beard. His eyes were a cold Nordic blue, and he looked away as soon as he saw me turn. Now he was watching the fight like everybody else.

Got you, asshole.

I pushed to the side past a few random peasants, hunching down into my coat, and pulling my fur hat lower on my head. I didn't know who the tall guy was, and I didn't know if he'd brought friends. Best to fade away, then take stock of the situation. I made it all of fifteen feet before somebody bumped into me and tried to pick my pocket, which wasn't really a shock in this bunch. *Amateur.* I blocked the grab, caught the thumb and twisted it in a direction that nature had never intended. The pickpocket cried out, but I was already gone.

I circled toward the other side of the arena, but couldn't spot the tall man. *Damn it.* He had to be moving too, and a split second of being distracted by a random thief had given him enough time to fade. He was good. You would think somebody that tall would be easy to pick out in central Asia, but both the Russians and the Mongols had some big boys.

The crowd went nuts at first blood. One of the fighters had just gotten lit up.

The stone wall at the side of the ruins was in the shade. I scanned both ways, didn't see the tail, and ducked into the dark. There was a tunnel there that ran beneath the seats for about twenty feet before coming out the other side. As soon as I was alone, I tossed my fur hat, took out my black skull cap and pulled it on. Every little bit could help, and if my tail had programmed himself to scan for that hat, it might give me an edge. My sunglasses went on, and if it wouldn't have looked suspicious walking around without one, I would have ditched my Turkic coat.

Who was following me and why? Could it be one of Jihan's men? But that didn't make sense. He ran this place. If he wanted to take me out, he would have just done it back in the silo. Maybe somebody was just looking to kidnap and ransom a wealthy westerner, and I was supposedly Jill's translator. It was doubtful anybody would recognize me from the last time I'd been to The Crossroads.

I stepped over a passed-out drunken Kazakh, thought better of it, went back, and relieved him of his stinking coat. I draped mine over him, and pulled the filthy thing over my shoulders. He really got the better deal out of that trade. Then I was into the light on the other side of the seats, head down, hands in my pocket, walking briskly in the direction of the market.

"Hello, Lorenzo."

I stopped. The noise had come from above me, from the arena seats. Turning slowly, I nodded at the tail. He was good. He must have seen me enter the tunnel, and he had hurried right across the top and waited for me on the other side. He was sitting on the third row of stones, studying me emotionlessly, not breathing hard from what had to have been a good run to catch up. Everyone around us was watching the fight, so nobody noticed the HK .45 dangling from one hand.

His voice was dead calm. I'd seen the gun, so he moved it under the edge of his coat and kept it there, hidden, but still ready. He had spotted me even when I was trying to be grey. He had tailed me without my noticing for an unknown amount of time. Once I'd made him, he'd caught up and revealed himself rather than shoot me in the back. That meant he wanted to talk business. It was rare that I let somebody get the drop on me. This was a professional.

"Do I know you?"

He ignored the question. "You met with Sala Jihan. That makes you an important man around here." He could tell I was doing the math. "I've been told that you're extremely fast, but I *am* faster, so don't do anything stupid. You're coming with me."

An American? "Where are we going?" I saw no opening. My body was relaxed, hands loose and ready, but my brain was flipping cartwheels at a million miles an hour. I would only have a split second to move and get to my gun. We were only a few feet apart. There would not be any room for error.

"Montalban Exchange."

Oh fucking shit.

"No thanks."

"Have a seat." He patted the spot next to him with his left hand. The tall man waited only a moment before adding, "Not a request." He nodded his head toward the far side of the market.

I followed his gaze. Several men were getting out of a 4x4 with tinted windows. "I don't really feel like having a gunfight right now," I said simply as I walked up the steps and sat next to him.

"It wouldn't be much of a fight."

What the hell was he doing? Montalbans? Did they know I'm the one that blasted Eddie? Would they care? The stone was cold and uncomfortable. We were now at bad breath distance. Around us the crowd continued to scream and chant, apparently the knife fight was one hell of a show.

We were both silent for a moment. He was big, and it was obvious even while wearing a heavy coat that he was thick with muscle. He didn't have a neck. Instead, muscles like pot roasts came out of his shoulders and met up under his ears. An anvil-like head sat on top. I sat just to his left, his right hand was crossed over his body, under his coat, pointed at my midsection now.

"No." He shook his head slightly. "I know what you're thinking, because I'd be thinking the same thing in this situation, but if I was supposed to kill you, you'd already be dead. And even if you got lucky, you wouldn't get back to the Glorious Cloud before we got your people."

Shit.

"I don't get menaced by Vikings that often. So who're you?"

"My name's Anders." I waited, but he didn't elaborate further. He seemed content to sit, half watching the fight, and half waiting for me to try something stupid. Finally after a moment, he spoke again. "So, who do you think will win?"

"Huh?"

"Russian or Mongol?" His voice was emotionless, as if watching a fight to the death was like watching the Weather Channel.

Both of the combatants were bloody now, spinning, and circling, lashing out at each other, then dancing away. Inwardly I was dying, trying to think of something, anything, that I could do. So I decided to answer his question. I wouldn't say I was a master of the blade or any macho horseshit like that, but I had been stabbed, cut, and slashed, and even killed quite a few people with various sharp or pointy things myself over the years.

The fighters were hurting, both were breathing hard, slick with sweat and blood. The Russian had the more serious injury, a cut to the muscles of the abdominal wall that was bleeding profusely.

"The Russian," I said.

"Wanna bet?"

"Twenty bucks says the Russian kills him in the next two minutes."

"You're on," Anders responded. "The Mongolian's bigger, younger, stronger."

"See how the Russian has those faded blue tats? Russian prison tats. They're always blue like that. Means he's done hard time." The Russian twisted and dodged as the Mongol swept in, a flurry of back and forth swipes. "The crucifix means he's the highest possible rank. The crown on top makes him *Pakhan,* a leader."

"So? He's old." Anders looked to be about my age, but it was hard to tell with the beard.

"The skulls mean he's a murderer, and the number means he's done a bunch," I pointed. "The stars on his back are one for each year he was in, and the knives pointing up in the stars . . ."

The old Russian had waited long enough and his boys had placed enough bets at bad odds. The young Mongol thought he was winning, so he pushed in, hard and fast. The Mafioso took a small cut to the chest, but climbed right up the Mongol's arm, driving the short blade in, running it up the limb, opening it like cleaning a fish. The younger fighter screamed.

"Shit," Anders muttered.

"The knives are pointing up, which means his murders were straight-up prison fights. If they were down, then it would have been by stealth. So counting from here, it looks like he's won twenty-six knife fights."

The Mongolian stumbled back, blood flowing everywhere. A knife wound is all about running the clock. As soon as you cut somebody, a clock starts. The body can compensate for a lot, but the more you hurt it, the less it can compensate for, the faster the clock runs down. When the clock hits zero, you're done.

The Mongolian was getting wobbly now. The Russian probably could have just hung back and let him bleed out, but that wouldn't have been sporting. He went low, caught the Mongol's wide swing, and ran the blade from the kid's belly button around to his kidney. The Russian jumped back before there was a response, and then a shower of blood doused the side of the Mongol's pink hot pants. The

Russian pumped his fist in the air and bellowed as the Mongolian went to his knees in the black dirt of the arena. The Russian side of the arena went nuts, chanting his name. A rope ladder was rolled down for their champion.

"Make that twenty-seven. Now pay me my twenty bucks, asshole."

"I'll pay you when we get back to my place," he said. "Now . . ."

Pain burned through my arm as Anders jabbed a long, spring-loaded needle into my neck.

"Gah!" I stood up and yanked the needle out. "What the fuck?" A thick burning sensation worked its way down my shoulder, into my arm and my chest. It was like hot wax was being pushed through my veins.

Anders was nonplussed. He watched me carefully, ready to pull his .45, but didn't move. "Calm down, Lorenzo. Trust me, you're going want to keep your heart rate down."

I cursed and swore at the pistol-packing viking, but the words didn't come out right. I was mumbling, babbling, not sure of what I was saying. My mind raced but I couldn't focus. Darkness edged into my vision. I tried to back away, but his men had already come up to keep me from falling and making a scene.

As I faded out, I realized Anders was standing next to me. "Shit works fast, don't it?"

Black.

Chapter 14: Hunting Season

✠

VALENTINE
Crossroads City
March 15th

I was roused out of bed early in the morning, long before the Sun came up. Exodus had established a number of safe houses in Crossroads City, spreading themselves out to try to reduce their apparent signature and keep a low profile. Ling and I had been dropped off at one of them with all of our clothing and equipment. Not everyone was in place yet, so Ling was very busy.

The building was one of the structures erected by the Soviets in 1950. Bland and featureless, it was on the far north end of town, crumbling from decades of disuse and tagged with graffiti in four different languages. It had electricity, sort of, but no functioning toilets or showers. Field-expedient means of hygiene were necessary and unpleasant.

We were posing as a group of mercenaries for hire.

There were several such groups in town, and while we were sure to draw the ire of our supposed competitors, we were less likely to gain the notice of Sala Jihan. Enterprises of all sorts and varying levels of legitimacy came and went through The Crossroads all the time. With Sala Jihan's own forces keeping the peace, we weren't especially concerned with being attacked outright.

After a brief, frigid scrub in an improvised shower, I dressed myself in some civilian attire I'd been given and found Ling in the main room. Two men, other Exodus personnel I guessed, were with her.

"Good morning, Michael," she said, as I walked in. "Allow me to introduce my comrades." Ling indicated a fit-looking Middle Eastern man with a thin mustache. "This is Ibrahim Barzani, one of our strike team leaders."

Ibrahim offered me a firm handshake. "Mr. Valentine, it is most excellent to meet you. Your reputation precedes you."

"Nice to meet you."

"This is Hideo Katsumoto," she said. An imposing Japanese man with a shaved head bowed politely, a move which I awkwardly attempted to return. He then shook my hand, and though his hands were thinner than mine, he had a grip like a vice.

"Mr. Valentine," he said curtly.

"Michael, we will be working with Katsumoto during the operation."

"I am happy to have Ling at my side during this operation," Katsumoto said. "She will be my second-in-command."

I wondered how Ling really felt about effectively being

demoted from team leader, but Ling's face was a mask, as always. "You will be with us, Michael, if you're feeling up to it."

"Doing what, exactly?"

"I must be blunt," Katsumoto said. "I do not like the practice of colluding with outsiders. As I'm sure you can understand, they are often security risks and prove to be less than reliable. Ling has vouched for you, however, and we are short on personnel. If you wish, you may come along on the mission and assist however you can."

"You're not an initiated member of our order, so you will not be in the chain of command," Ling clarified. "But an extra hand with as much combat experience as you have would be a great asset to the operation."

It sounded like Ling was talking me up, trying to convince the others that I was worth the trouble they went through to get me. I figured they were just sticking me with her because they didn't know what to do with me. Fair enough. They could have just left me to rot in North Gap, so I didn't feel I had any grounds to complain. I wasn't sure if I was in any shape to fight, but I tried to conceal my misgivings. These people had done a lot for me, risking their lives in the process. I felt obligated to put on a brave face. "I'll do what I can," I said with fake confidence. "But I don't know what we're doing here. I've only been given the briefest of overviews on this entire operation."

Ibrahim and Katsumoto looked at each other, then at Ling. "For operational security reasons, you won't be given a complete overview, I'm afraid," Ibrahim said. "Please, Mr. Valentine, we mean no disrespect. We have procedures . . ."

I waved my hand. "It's fine." I'd spent too long as a mercenary to expect otherwise. "I don't need to know what I don't need to know."

"No, you do not," Katsumoto replied. "Our swords won't be directly involved in the primary assault on Sala Jihan's compound. That will be Ibrahim's responsibility. Our mission is to capture the hydroelectric plant upriver."

"I see." I was honestly intrigued. "Are we going to disable it, cut off their power?"

"In part," Ibrahim answered. "We have acquired detailed plans of the structure. Our engineers have determined the best possible points of attack. We have more than sufficient explosives to structurally compromise the dam forever."

I thought about the huge reservoir upriver from the dam. "You're going to blow the dam and flood the town?"

Ibrahim nodded. "It is for the best."

I looked at the three Exodus warriors in front of me, and didn't know what to say. Flooding the valley would drown thousands of people. The deluge wouldn't discriminate between the deserving and the innocent. The surprise on my face must have been evident.

"It isn't like that at all, Michael," Ling said.

"The dam will not fail immediately. If our engineers are correct, eventually the dam will collapse and flood The Crossroads. They will have time to evacuate. We expect the people who live here will disperse once the power fails. If any are foolish enough to remain in this wicked place, then they do so at their own risk. Regardless of whether or not the mission to kill Sala Jihan succeeds, we shall cleanse this valley and wipe The Crossroads off the face of the earth."

"You must understand." Katsumoto said. "This place was used for horrible things when a lesser man ruled it. Now someone truly evil is in charge and it has only grown worse. Should Ibrahim's attack fail, this is our only hope of ending the human trafficking in this part of the world. Even if Ibrahim succeeds, there is no promise that the cycle will not continue, with Jihan replaced by another, just as he replaced Eduard Montalban before him. It is necessary."

If the people who lived here didn't clue in and evacuate, they would die. Exodus was utterly committed to their mission, to the fundamental belief that they were doing the right thing. I wondered what it was like to have that kind of certainty in life. On the other hand, everything I'd learned about The Crossroads was unsettling. Of all the places in the world that could stand to be wiped off the map, it was pretty close the top of the list.

These people respected me. Despite my misgivings, I was going to stay professional. "Understood," I said simply.

"We will get into the specifics of the operation later," Katsumoto said. "For now, just know that we have discussed this matter at length. If there were not so many tens of thousands of innocent lives in danger, we would not be taking such drastic action."

Ibrahim addressed Ling. "There is another matter we need to bring to your attention. I have met this Lorenzo you spoke of. He is much as you described, driven, yet shortsighted."

"He is a horrible man," Ling said. "But he grows on you."

"So does a fungus." Ibrahim grinned. "Yesterday, Lorenzo went into the fortress and met with Sala Jihan."

Ling's eyes widened. "Face to face?"

"Yes. One of his people, the skinny young man with the long hair and bad complexion, brought me the intelligence they had gathered."

"Reaper?" I asked.

Ibrahim nodded. "They are staying at the Glorious Cloud Hotel. Lorenzo departed that location after he told young Mr. Reaper to see us. He went to the arena, but was involved in an altercation there and disappeared."

I could see the concern on Ling's face. If the damned fool had gotten himself captured it could compromise everything. I was personally, *bitterly* aware of the consequences of getting yourself caught.

"We believe he was taken," Ibrahim said. "Our operative had to leave the scene, as an altercation would have attracted the attention of the Brotherhood, but he was able to take this picture." Ibrahim retrieved a smartphone from his pocket, tapped the screen a few times to bring up the picture, and handed the phone to Ling.

The picture was slightly blurry; the photographer was probably moving when he took it. Lorenzo was being choked out by a large, muscular man with short-cropped, blonde hair. The beard was new, but I recognized him.

My blood ran cold. *"Anders."*

I spent the next half hour filling my Exodus compatriots in on everything I knew about Anders. He had been Gordon Willis' right-hand man for Project Heartbreaker. I hadn't seen Anders since the operation in Yemen, where we recovered a stolen nuclear warhead that was en route to General Al Sabah. I had no idea what happened to him after I killed Gordon.

"He was with Majestic," Ling said. "Is he still?"

"I don't know. I sure hope not. He was in on Gordon Willis' dealings with Eduard Montalban, I know that much. I also know that those dealings were off the reservation, done on the side. After everything was found out, he may have had to get out of the country. Gordon's superiors were mad at him, but I don't know what went on with Anders. Hell, they should have been interrogating his ass instead of me at North Gap. Lord knows the son of a bitch has it coming. I guarantee he knows more about Project Blue than I do."

"What is Project Blue?" Katsumoto asked.

"That is the question isn't it?"

The Exodus man humorlessly raised an eyebrow.

"It's a long story and not relevant right now. But you need to know that cold hearted bastard is one of the most dangerous men I've ever met."

Ling looked thoughtful for a long moment. "Why did he take Mr. Lorenzo? It can't be a coincidence."

LORENZO

Gideon Lorenzo sat on the fallen log, leaned his Model 70 Winchester against the bark, and used a handkerchief to wipe the sweat from his forehead. Dad's bad knee was really bothering him today, and it had been a heck of a hike up the mountain. Bob and I stopped to wait for him in the peach-colored light that came just before dawn in the Texas foothills. Bob took the opportunity to take a long draw from his canteen. Both of us were young, and in excellent shape. It was only a few days after my fifteenth birthday.

"Bob, do me a favor."

"Yeah, Dad?" my older brother said as he twisted the cap back on his old Boy Scout canteen. He was a senior in high school now, and was looking more and more like Dad every day, a veritable giant of a man. Unfortunately, Bob had also inherited the bald genes, and his hair was already thinning.

"Run along to the deer camp, and tell your uncle that we'll be along in a minute. Ammon gets all excited if anybody's late, and he'll probably send out a search party. Hector can stay with me."

"Sure thing," Bob slung his .30-06 over his shoulder and gave me a thumbs up, "Take care of the old man for me, bro."

Dad snorted. "Old man . . . And Bob, remember, if you see something," Dad glanced at his watch. "It isn't legal for another . . . fifteen minutes." As a municipal judge, it really shouldn't have been a surprise that the senior Lorenzo was such a stickler for the rules. There wasn't a hypocritical bone in his body, and even if the rule was dumb, he obeyed it, because he had to sit in judgment of others using the same rules.

"Okay, not like I ever see anything anyway. Hector's the killer. See you guys in a minute." He turned and jogged up the hill.

Dad waited for him to leave, then he patted the log next to him. "Take a seat, Hector. Enjoy the sunrise with me."

I could tell he wanted to talk to me about something. I sat, and waited, my old Savage lever action in my lap. The *forest was quiet. I was uncomfortable in the woods. It was strange, the further I got from pavement, the more twitchy it made me. I liked having noise and people. In the woods, it's just you and what you really are. You can't pretend to be something else when it's so quiet and empty. The woods are about truth.*

But the Lorenzo family loved the annual deer hunt. The younger kids really enjoyed the camping. I didn't mind hunting. Apparently I was really good at killing animals, and they sure did taste great.

"So, how's the leg, Dad? I can take your pack."

He smiled. "Naw, I'm fine." Which was a lie. His leg hadn't been fine since some communist had tried to blow it off. He lived in constant pain, but you would never know it since he never let it change his attitude. "I just wanted to talk to you for a minute."

"That time of year again? I already know. He's not getting out." The parole board had no interest in talking to me. They knew my opinion. If I had one regret in my life, it was that I had not had better aim when I'd stabbed him with that fork, and gotten my real father in the jugular instead of the eye socket.

"No, not that," Dad coughed. "Honestly, we both know he's not going anywhere. This is Texas, thank God. Men serve their time here. No, it is something else."

I waited.

"I'm worried about your future, Hector."

"My grades are better. I'm trying harder in class," I lied. I hated school. Bob was the one with straight A's, and a football scholarship. Dad was probably worried I was going to end up digging ditches. Either that or he was going

to warn me about the dangers of rock and roll music again.

"No, nothing like that. In fact, Mr. Thompson told me the other day that you excel at . . ." he paused, as it was kind of distasteful, "drama. And Coach McClelland says you have a real gift for gymnastics, that you could even take state if you put your mind to it . . . and there's nothing wrong with either of those things," he quickly added. The Lorenzos were manly men, and neither of those things were exactly "manly" endeavors in his view.

"Dad, I promise. I like girls."

He rolled his eyes. "That's not what I meant. It's just that . . . Eh, I don't know how to explain it. I'm concerned about your outlook. You know the kinds of people I've deal with."

"Politicians? Lawyers?"

"No, I was thinking of the people I send to jail, dishonest, thieving, amoral . . . so actually, I suppose most of the politicians and lawyers I deal with would fall into the same category . . . " he chuckled as he thought about it, but then his face darkened, and turned grim. "It's just that sometimes I feel like I get a glimpse of what you're going to be like as you get older. You've got a lot of anger in you still."

I shrugged. Probably true, but all things considered, since I had been taken in by the Lorenzos, I had been a relatively good kid.

"I look at some of those men that I send to jail, and sometimes, I see you, and I worry. Some of them have the same kind of attitude you do. They think that what they are is what they are, and that they can't change. People aren't set in stone."

"I'm not going to do anything stupid, Dad. Don't worry," I assured him. "You guys have been great to me. I won't let you down."

"But I'm not going to be around forever. Just remember, no matter what happens, a man can always repent. They can always change. You know, there're three kinds of people in the world." He ticked them off on his fingers. "Good guys, bad guys, and those that don't care. Now most people, if you ask them, they would say they're one of the good guys, but really, they don't care. They're good as long as it's convenient. Bad guys, well, I'm afraid you know a lot more about them than any young person should ever have to. But you want to be a good guy. Sometimes, life makes it easy to be a bad guy, or for those that don't have the stomach for that, then they fall in that great grey middle ground. But to be one of the good guys, that takes work. It takes honor."

Dad was rambling now. He did that once in awhile. "I'm not going to get in trouble with the law."

He laughed aloud. "Law? Boy, good has nothing to do with the law. You can be the most evil son of a bitch to ever walk the earth . . ." that surprised me, he rarely, if ever used bad language, "and still obey the law. Heck, you can even write the laws. No, good means you do the right thing. Even when it hurts. Bad men can become good. I've seen it happen, and a good man can go bad."

"Okay," I humored him. Sometimes he liked to get philosophical. The Lorenzos were very religious, but Dad had never pushed any of his personal beliefs on his children. He just tried to teach them, and let them choose for themselves. He did make us all go to church every

Sunday, however. I didn't really mind, because there were some really good looking girls at church.

There was a crack of a gunshot from over the hillside. Gideon Lorenzo looked at his watch again. It was a very nice watch, inlaid with silver, with an onyx face, and had been given to him as a present from his father when he had graduated from law school. He sighed. "Looks like Bob jumped the gun by four minutes. That's buck fever right there."

"The scoundrel," I said, imitating Dad's voice perfectly. We both laughed.

He put his arm over my shoulder. "Be good, Hector. That's all that I ask. . . . We better get going."

Then the Sun was up.

It was morning.

LORENZO
Crossroads City
March 15th

It was morning.

My head ached. I cracked open my eyes and scanned the room. I was lying on a bed. I'd been dreaming about my foster father, and the last thing I recalled was him looking at his watch. It was the same watch that would cost him his life the year I turned sixteen. Ruthlessly beaten until his internal organs had ruptured by a gang of worthless hoodlums, because they thought his watch could be hocked for drug money. The law hadn't caught them, but I had.

I'd dropped off the world to find them, and kill them, and I'd never looked back.

The sheets were bright white and smelled like fresh soap. Outside the window, a rooster crowed. The room was empty of decoration. There was only a small table by the bed with a pitcher of water and a cup, and two chairs near the closed door. Both chairs were occupied by men armed with P90 submachine guns.

"Hey." My head was stuffed with a foggy, hung-over feeling. "Bring me that punk-ass bitch, Anders. We've got some unfinished business."

"Good morning, sir," replied the first guard. They both had that eurotrash look that the Montalban retainers seemed to cultivate. Even with Big Eddie dead, his people still tended to look like something from Sprockets. "Your clothes are under the bed. We took the liberty of washing them. Your presence has been requested at breakfast."

At least they were polite. "Where's my coat?"

"The one you stole off the drunk under the arena?" said the second. "It smelled like piss. We burned it. Now hurry up, the boss doesn't like waiting."

Breakfast with the head of the Montalban Exchange? I just hoped that Jill and Reaper had stuck with the plan and bailed when I hadn't come back to the hotel last night. This very well might be my last meal.

The Montalban Exchange building was large, solidly constructed, and sat on a hill overlooking most of the other faction houses. The architecture was vaguely Chinese, with a red roof with upswept corners. The dining room was on the third floor, with a good view surveying the chaotic town, the mountainside, and the mighty gash in the earth that was Jihan's mines. The walls were made of polished local wood and the floor was covered in thick rugs. A giant rectangular table filled most of the room, and it appeared to have been carved from a single epic tree. There was no one else there.

The guards gestured for me to take a seat. They then left me alone, sliding the bamboo door closed behind them.

I could hop out the window. It was a good drop to the ground, but with my acrobatic skill, I had no doubt that I could roll with it and still walk away. Then all I had to do was somehow make it out of town and then cross a whole bunch of wilderness with the Montalbans after me. And that was assuming that they didn't have Jill and Reaper. Anders had clearly known about them. So I sat and waited. Besides, if they wanted me dead, they could easily have done it already.

Drumming my fingers on the table top, I tried to think of what could be going on. Maybe whoever was in charge now was happy that Eddie was gone. Maybe they were going to throw me a big thank-you party. I scanned the room. No balloons. No cake. *Probably not.*

The roof of the Glorious Cloud hotel was visible from here. I had let Jill come along against my better judgment. She wasn't cut out for this kind of mission. I'd given in to her, and now she was in danger because of me. I was such a fool.

"It's been a long time, Lorenzo."

The bamboo door had opened so smoothly behind me that I'd not even heard it. The voice was female and hauntingly familiar. The accent was Swiss.

"Seven years," I said automatically, without turning. "Hello, Katarina."

"Really, that long?" I could sense her walk up behind me. One of her hands landed softly on my shoulder. Her fingernails were painted blood red, and she dragged one up my neck, caressing the edge of my ear. An electric shiver passed through my bruised face. "It seems like yesterday," she purred.

"Still working for the Montalbans, I see."

She kept her fingernails on my neck as she circled my chair. She blocked my view of The Crossroads and stopped directly in front of my knees. Always beautiful, she had aged extremely well. Her lips were full and red, her skin was as smooth as the day I had met her, and her ice blue eyes twinkled with a predatory mischievousness. She was wearing a black silk kimono that was entirely inappropriate for polite company.

"Working for the Montalbans?" She laughed as she lifted one long, perfectly muscled leg, and draped it over my own. Katarina settled down onto my lap, with her fingers intertwined behind my head. I could smell her warmth and her perfume. "Lorenzo, my dear, I *run* the Montalban Exchange now."

"You've moved up in the world," I replied in the most noncommittal way possible. She always had been the ambitious one. It wouldn't have been a surprise for her to grab whatever she could after Eddie's death.

"Indeed," she answered, breathing on my neck. Some of her soft blond hair hit me in the mouth, and I could see down the top of her kimono. "I'm very glad to see you."

"Yeah, I got that impression." This was certainly not

going the way that I had expected. My ex-girlfriend was the capo of a group of hired killers that should want me dead, but apparently she was all about kissing and making up. I tried to remain stoic, but it is difficult to keep a poker face in a situation like this. "So, if you're so glad to see me, why'd you have your thug knock me out?"

"I told him to bring you in. Anders is an efficient employee. Would you rather he have subdued you by force?" She rubbed one hand down my chest. "Mm, you're still doing all those pushups, I see. Maybe I should've told him to be forceful after all. I should have liked to see that fight, I think. Pity."

"Where's my crew?"

"They're fine," she whispered into my bad ear. I could feel her teeth. "Perfectly safe."

I'm only a man, and it was hard to hide my reaction, but I knew Katarina, the human razor blade, far too well to fall for this kind of thing. Besides that, if I was anything, I was loyal. "Kat, I'm glad to see you too, and I'm real glad you didn't have me killed, *but . . .*" I gently grasped her hands in my own, and pushed them away. "Ain't gonna happen. This trip is all business. Nothing personal."

She guided my hands to someplace *really* unexpected. "All business is personal," she said, punctuating it with that sultry laugh of hers.

This was awkward. I don't usually have mob bosses sit on my lap and try to seduce me, but then again, this was the best looking mob boss I'd ever dealt with. "Kat, get off me."

"Very well. I just wanted to see if the fire was still there. I never felt more alive than when I was with you." She leaned in and kissed me, just like the old days, hard enough to almost draw blood. I didn't respond. She broke away. Disappointed? Who could tell with her. "Too bad . . ." Her warm thigh dragged across me as she stood. Katarina stepped back, adjusted her kimono, put her hands on her perfect hips, and smiled. "Besides, our breakfast guests are here. Please, have a seat."

I glanced back at the door. The guards and Anders were flanking the *guests*. Looking past an obviously nervous Reaper, there was Jill. And the look on her face was a mixture of disgust, anger, betrayal, and shock.

We had just moved to a whole different stage of awkward.

I thought back to Malaysia, and the aftermath of the Independence Day Massacre seven years ago.

"Sorry, Kat, it's over."

"Are you talking about our employer . . . or are you talking about us too?" she suddenly looked sad, but I knew that was an act. A year ago I would have believed she was capable of sadness but now I doubted it. Any human emotions Katarina had, had long since been expunged.

"Both."

"I thought you loved me . . ." she said, voice cracking, and this time, I almost could believe her. Almost . . . I turned my back on her and walked away.

I had loved her once, to say otherwise would be a lie, but she was broken inside. There was something wrong with Katarina, deep down, just plain abhorrent. She never talked about her past, and all I really knew about her was what she had chosen to reveal to me, and that wasn't much, and over the last few months I'd decided that she had fabricated most of that too. Not that I was somebody who could say much about that.

"Wait!" *Her voice was plaintive. I paused, just for a moment, weak.* "You can't leave me, Lorenzo. Not like this."

It had been great at first. For the first time in my life I had found someone who was just as conniving and malicious as I was. Ambitious, smart, and for a man like me, who lived his life on the ragged edge of law and probability, she had actually been fun. But that had changed over time.

It was like she was several different people, wrapped into one beautiful, fragile shell. The one that I fell for was a relatively decent human being who had endured a difficult life, a scared girl with a good heart. The next minute she could turn into a cold-blooded murderer, all calculation and ruthlessness, her body a weapon in more ways than one, and when she was off her meds, she turned into a screaming psychopath, flying off in a rage at the slightest provocation. She popped pills like crazy. Not so many at first, but the more jobs we pulled for Big Eddie, the more she had taken. Which Kat you ended up with depended greatly on which personality was running the show that day.

Working for Big Eddie was bad for her. I could see it. No sane person could exist in his world for long without being corrupted, and Kat was now his favorite intermediary. I was never allowed to meet the man. I had tried to get her to leave, but she had refused. Her future was with the Montalbans. That ambition that I had been so infatuated with had required her to turn totally into the cold Kat, with occasional outbursts from the crazy Kat. I was certain that the good Kat was still in there somewhere, but that side of her was weak, so she had locked it away in her cage made of drugs and hate.

Yes, I had loved her, but not anymore.

"Don't walk away from me! Lorenzo!" she shrieked. "Damn you! Don't you leave me! Not like this!" She grabbed onto arm, her nails tearing into my skin. And just like that, she lost it entirely. Kat attacked me, clawing at my eyes, ripping my shirt, her spit hitting me in the face. She was a trained fighter, but when she flew into one of her rages, there was no skill, just savagery. I bore it for a moment, waiting for her to do something stupid like actually start fighting, or to go for a weapon. Finally, I put one hand on her chest and shoved her violently to the ground.

She curled into a ball in the wet Malaysian grass and began to sob. "But . . . But I . . . I need you."

"Goodbye," I said simply and turned back to the house. Carl was watching from the front door. He nodded once and left to get Reaper, Train, and the car. We were out of there. Kat could stay and deal with Eddie all she wanted. A small part of me expected a bullet in the spine, but none came. Apparently she had taken at least some of her medications today.

"You'll pay for this, Lorenzo, I swear to God!" She screamed, cursed, and cried as I walked away. I didn't look back.

"So, what brings you to my neck of the woods?" Katarina asked innocently.

"General thievery. You know how it is. Boring stuff," I answered mechanically.

She and Anders were sitting across from us. Jill was sitting on my right, and Reaper on my left. There was a submachine-toting guard standing at each end of the room. Jill was brooding, her face a mask, barely concealing her emotions. I could understand what she was going through, but thank goodness she was smart enough to let me do the talking. Whatever Katarina was, she was dangerous, and she was also our captor, so Jill was better off holding her rage in for now. I just hoped she would believe me when I had a chance to explain that I was innocent, assuming, of course, that they just didn't drag us all out back and put a bullet in us first.

"How did you know I was here?"

"I was very surprised to hear that a Spanish businesswoman named Maria Consuela Garcia was coming to The Crossroads to do business with Sala Jihan. The coincidence was striking, considering that identity had originally been prepared for my use. I'm such a fan of irony that I felt I needed to meet this person."

"Whoops."

Breakfast had been brought in by servants and sat steaming before us. I had to admit that the bacon smelled really good. A plate was put before Kat first. The boss got a steak so rare it still had feelings. "I had heard you were retired. That was the word on the street."

"This is just a temporary thing I've got to take care of, then back to the old folks home."

"Decent fieldcraft for somebody retired," Anders stated as he helped himself to a heaping pile of pig meat.

"By the way . . ." He paused, pulled something out of his pocket, and tossed it across the table. It was a badly crumpled twenty dollar bill. "I always pay my debts."

"So you're out of the business, and you're no concern of ours, but here you are, in our backyard, with a . . ." Katarina sniffed. "*Crew*. Skyler, it's good to see that you're still alive."

"Uh-huh," Reaper muttered as he chewed, keeping his head down. He had always despised Katarina. "And it's *Reaper*."

"That was such a silly name for a young boy."

"Well, I'm no kid anymore."

"Where are Carl and Train? Oh, wait. That's right. My predecessor here had them both killed. How about that?" Katarina turned to Jill. "And this must be my replacement. Lorenzo always believed in having a pretty young thing on his team. You can get into places that a male thief could only dream of. Oh, but Lorenzo always was *quite* the lady's man back in the day. You have no idea how many times he seduced some poor girl during our scams, whatever it took to finish the job. He could pretend to be anything, for anyone. Quite the heartbreaker, our Lorenzo, but he always came back to his *crew*."

Katarina was baiting Jill, testing her, and sadly, Jill fell for it. The mask fell away, and her temper shined through. "He's my boyfriend, you bitch. We live together."

"Lorenzo settled down? With *you*?" Katarina laughed as she used a knife to cut her breakfast steak. "What are you, twenty?"

"Twenty-*six*," Jill answered defiantly. I had a feeling that if it wasn't for the two guards with P90s, she would have gone across the table and twisted Katarina's head off. "What're you, *fifty*?"

Katarina's eyebrows narrowed. "I'm younger than your *boyfriend.*" I had seen that look before, kind of like how she had looked right before shooting Datuk Keng in the head. She turned her icy blue eyes back toward me. "So, when did you start robbing the cradle?"

I was fourteen years older than Jill. "I make up for it by being immature. It averages out."

"Well, he dumped your skank ass, and he comes home with me. Speaking of which, I would appreciate it if you kept your tentacles off my man," Jill said calmly as she scooped herself some breakfast. "Or we'll have us a problem, *puta.*"

Reaper looked over at me, raised an eyebrow, as if asking if it was okay to watch the catfight. I shook my head in the negative, and then nodded toward the guards. "Jill, machine guns." My ex was not the person to provoke.

Katarina pushed her plate away. "It's Jill, right? Well, listen to me carefully, *Jill.* I have been killing people professionally for the world's most dangerous criminal syndicate since you were wearing a training bra. I clawed my way to the top of this organization by pure ruthlessness. And then, when Big Eddie died, I had to fight every other one of his lieutenants for the scraps. They died. I didn't. So I won." Suddenly she reached across the table, faster than I could react, and stabbed her steak knife into the wood directly in front of Jill. The handle vibrated slightly. I had forgotten how fast Kat was. "So don't think you can come into *my* house and disrespect me in front of my men. Another word, and I *bury* you . . . Now the grownups need to have a conversation."

Jill started to say something, but I reached over and grabbed her hand under the table. She glanced at me, anger flashing in her dark eyes. I shook my head. Jill had no idea what Katarina was capable of, so hopefully the look I gave her conveyed the danger we were in. Anders glanced around, shrugged, and went back to shoveling food in his face.

"Good. Now where was I?" Katarina smiled, and pulled her plate back. Another knife appeared out of her kimono sleeve, one of those fancy, expensive titanium folders. It was razor sharp and zipped through the meat like it was made of air. "Oh, that's right. You were about to tell me why you had the audacity to bring a crew onto my territory to perform a job without my permission."

"Better to ask for forgiveness than permission," I tried to joke. She didn't go for it. There was no laughter when Ruthless Kat was in charge. "If I had known it was you, believe me, I would have asked. I didn't exactly leave the Exchange under the best terms." I was praying that she didn't know that I was the one that had killed Eddie.

"Why are you here?"

"I can't tell you that."

"Very well." Katarina didn't bother to look up from her food. "Diego, kill the girl."

One of the guards lifted his subgun. Jill gasped. "Okay! Okay!" I raised my hands. "Don't shoot. I'll tell you everything." The guard lowered the gun, and waited for further instructions.

Katarina smiled as she popped a piece of ultra rare in her mouth. She chewed with her mouth open, a disgusting habit that had always annoyed me. "Your softness surprises me. You're certainly not the man you used to be. Talk."

"I'm here looking for a man, an American FBI agent. He came to The Crossroads to investigate Sala Jihan. He was kidnapped. If he's alive, then I will rescue him."

"And if he's not?"

"Then I'll kill the people that took him," I stated simply. "Then I'll go home."

"Just like that?" Katarina quipped.

"Just like that."

"Tell me, why on earth would you, of all people, be trying to help an American policeman? Ahh . . . yes. Your brother was FBI, wasn't he? You mentioned that once. Oh, and you were even foolish enough to take on your adopted family's name as your cover." Katarina snapped her fingers, and one of the guards quickly brought her an iPad. He placed it into her waiting hand, then retreated back to his station. She began to read. "Special Agent Robert T. Lorenzo. Disgraced, paranoid, delusional, conspiracy theorist, fired for revealing classified information, disappears from the US, only to arrive in The Crossroads, to immediately stir up trouble by harassing Sala Jihan, which, by the way, is never wise. He's a nosy, self-righteous, goody-two-shoes, law-and-order pig, who meddles in affairs he does not understand, and pays the price."

"So, you've met Bob. Where is he?"

"Sala Jihan has him," Anders spoke up. "By the time I found out, there was nothing I could do."

I turned my attention from Katarina to Anders. "Why would you *do* anything?"

Anders wiped his mouth with the back of his hand. He pushed his chair away from the table and stood. "Because Bob Lorenzo came here to find me."

"I don't understand."

The giant shook his head. "I'm the Fourth Operative."

I opened my mouth, but no words came out. I didn't know what to say. Bob had been right all along. "You're the man that knows about Project Blue?"

Anders dropped his fork on his empty plate. "Take a walk with me, Lorenzo. There are some things you need to know."

Chapter 15: Old Friends

VALENTINE
Crossroads City
March 15th

Our breath smoldered in the frigid air as Ling and I stepped out into daylight. Though the sun only occasionally peeked through the heavy layer of gray clouds, the snow amplified the brightness enough that I put on a pair of tinted goggles. These had the added benefit of helping to conceal my identity. We were dressed in what passed for street clothes in The Crossroads: heavy jackets, knit caps, and thick gloves, most of it either North Chinese or Russian military surplus. All of the high-end cold weather gear I'd been issued might have drawn more attention.

Our armament was limited to what handguns we could conceal. My custom Smith & Wesson .44 Magnum revolver was in its usual place on my left hip, but it was buried beneath several layers of clothing. I could get to it, but it wouldn't be a fast draw by any means. So I'd asked my

Exodus compatriots for something smaller, that I could stash in the pocket of my coat. I was graciously offered several compact handguns. I picked a Taurus Protector Poly, a hideous .357 Magnum snubby with a polymer frame. Ugliness notwithstanding, it fit into the hand-warmer pockets of my jacket perfectly. Being a revolver, it could be fired from the pocket without malfunctioning, and I shoot revolvers better than automatics anyway.

Together, Ling and I made our way across the cluttered, crowded mess that was Crossroads City. Shops and stores of every sort lined the winding street, and where there weren't shops there were ramshackle carts or people selling goods out of the backs of trucks. The air stunk of diesel and burning trash.

At the heart of the town was the literal crossroads from which the settlement had gotten its name. The east-west road from Kazakhstan to Mongolia intersected with a north-south road that ran from Russia into North China. Railroad tracks ran parallel to the north-south road. A bustling train station sat just south of the intersection and seemed to be the center of activity. Scores of people crowded the platform as more boarded and disembarked a stopped train. The station itself had once been very ornate, decorated in old Soviet art-deco style. Much of it had been vandalized, stolen, shot up, or crumbled from decades of neglect.

Twin statues of Joseph Stalin and Mao Zedong flanked the main entrance to the station. Each had their arms uplifted in the air, like something off of an old propaganda poster. Only, Stalin's arm had been missing for many years and Mao had been spray painted with graffiti. His arm was being used to hold up a line of Christmas lights strung up over a noodle stand.

Ling and I had volunteered to go looking for Lorenzo. Even though the picture I'd been shown was blurry, there was no mistaking Anders. I had a score to settle with that son of a bitch and was eager to put a .44 slug through him. I didn't tell Ling this, of course. Revenge might seem unprofessional, and I really didn't want to get left at the safe house. I was sick of being cooped up. I'd been locked in a dingy old building for a long time, and I'd had my fill of it.

We didn't bother going to the Arena. It was public and we knew he'd been carried away. That left us with only one place that was worth checking: the Glorious Cloud Hotel. That was where Lorenzo, Jill, and Reaper were staying under their assumed identities. An Exodus informant worked the desk there and Ling wanted to question her. A pair of Exodus operatives, from a different safe house, were supposed to meet us there.

The Glorious Cloud didn't look glorious from the outside, but given the surroundings it was actually pretty nice. It was very quiet inside, decorated sort of like a P.F. Chang's restaurant. Ling told me to wait by the door and stand watch as she approached the desk clerk, an elderly Chinese woman with a hard gleam in her eye.

People, mostly Westerners, came and went as if The Crossroads was just another tourist destination. Just by looking at the folks inside the Glorious Cloud, one might not get the impression that The Crossroads was as nasty a place as it actually was. I could only wonder what criminal business brought most of the guests to this godforsaken corner of the globe.

"Jill and Reaper were taken from here late last night," Ling said, speaking very softly. "Four armed men, Europeans, came into the hotel, went up to the top floor, where Mr. Lorenzo was staying, and returned a few minutes later, leading them out the door."

"No one said anything?"

"This is The Crossroads, Michael. She also told me that if other Exodus members are here, they didn't identify themselves to her."

"We should check Lorenzo's room."

"Yes. She gave me the key. Come on."

The top floor of the hotel was quiet. There were only a few rooms on the fifth floor, and they were the most expensive ones available. The entire level was designed to minimize noise and dampen sound. Our footsteps barely made any noise on the carpet. An ornate fountain babbled quietly along one wall. The walls were made of red wood and had beautiful tapestries hung on them.

Ling unzipped her jacket. "That's the room up ahead." I nodded and unzipped my own jacket so I could get to my .44. Upon reaching the door, she tried the handle. The room was unlocked. The Exodus operative looked back at me as she pulled an engraved Browning Hi-Power pistol from a holster on her belt and swiped the safety off. I nodded again and drew my .44, holding it close to my chest, muzzle-down.

Ling quietly opened the door. Somebody was talking inside. We entered the suite as quietly as we could. Ling moved like a cat, graceful and silent. Lorenzo had himself a nice setup there, a multi-room suite. The entrance room was a small foyer that led to a central common room. The voices were coming from there.

We swept into the room, guns raised. There were two men in the room. They were armed too, and startled. I had one, a thin man with a brown complexion and dark hair, in my sights. Ling held up her left hand, "Hold on," so I didn't fire. His eyes were big and white as he stared at my revolver. The Glock 19 in his hands was shaking. *He must be new at this.*

"Diamond," Ling said cryptically.

"Sapphire," the other man responded. Ling lowered her pistol, and so did they. I let my .44 linger on my target for just a moment before pulling the big gun back to my chest.

"Michael, this is the other team that was sent to the hotel," Ling said. "They are from Ibrahim's sword."

"Michael?" the other Exodus operative asked. He was a short man, dressed in dark clothes, his face hidden under a watch cap, Oakley sunglasses, and a scarf. His voice sounded familiar. "Val?" *Very* familiar. He pulled down the scarf.

I blinked hard. "Skunky?"

"Hey bro," he said sheepishly, holstering the two-tone Beretta 9mm he carried. "Long time no see."

"Jesus tapdancing Christ," I blasphemed. "What the fuck are you doing here? I haven't seen you since . . ."

He smiled. "Since Mexico? Yeah. I know. Sorry about that." He stepped forward and wrapped his arms around me in an awkward man-hug, slapping me on the back as he did so.

"Friend of yours?" the other Exodus man asked Skunky.

"We were in Vanguard together."

Skunky's real name was Jeff Long. He'd grown up in California, the son of Chinese immigrants. About a year before Vanguard had landed the Mexico contract, he was assigned to my team, Switchblade 4. He had been there on our last mission, acting as our team's designated marksman, when our chopper was shot down. The last I'd heard, Tailor had tried to recruit Skunky, just like he had for me, for Project Heartbreaker. Now I knew why he'd declined. "You're working for Exodus? How? Why?"

"I could ask you the same thing." He grinned.

"I recruited him the same time I tried to recruit you," Ling said. "You were both instrumental in saving Ariel."

Me, Skunky, and Tailor had been the only survivors of Switchblade 4's disastrous operation in Mexico. "Hell, did you try to recruit Tailor too?"

"He wasn't Exodus material." She didn't explain what *Exodus material* meant, but Tailor was a lunatic.

Skunky laughed. "Tailor was one cigarette being put out on his skin as a kid away from being a serial killer."

"He had my back in Zubara."

"Yeah, I heard that went south . . ."

Ling turned her attention back to Skunky. "You two can catch up later. What have you found here?"

"There is some sign of a struggle," he said, indicating for us to follow him into one of the rooms. "The door wasn't kicked in, but there was definitely a struggle."

A laptop sat on the desk in one of the rooms, a screen saver displayed on its monitor. It was connected to a pair of external hard drives. Another cable ran from a USB port to what looked like a modem of some kind. A cable from that ran out onto the balcony, where a compact satellite dish was set up. A pair of headphones was plugged into the machine, still playing heavy metal. The chair was knocked over. Half a dozen empty cans of Monster energy drink were scattered across the room. Reaper struck me as messy. What gave it away was that a half-full can of Monster had spilled on the desk, around the laptop, and hadn't been wiped up. Messy or not, that boy would never let anything like that happen to his equipment.

"This is Reaper's room alright," I told Ling. "So Anders has got Lorenzo, Jill, and Reaper."

Ling cursed in Chinese. "This is not good. They know too much about our operation."

"Do you know the people we're looking for, Val?" Skunky asked.

I nodded. "You have no idea."

LORENZO
The Montalban Exchange
Crossroads City
March 15th

There was a large balcony that circled the top level of the Montalban exchange. The red tile roof was suspended over our heads by giant wooden beams, and the only thing that separated us from a good plunge to the ground was an intricately wrought iron railing, complete with dragons and swans. The breeze carried the rough civilization smells of The Crossroads up to us. Jill and Reaper had been escorted back to the *guest* quarters. Anders and I walked the perimeter while one of the guards shadowed us, far enough back to not hear anything.

"So, who are you? And what is all this Fourth Operative bullshit?"

"Don't get ahead of yourself." Anders picked a spot with a good view of the mountains, and leaned against the railing. It creaked against his weight. As big as he was, Anders was probably a solid two-seventy of muscle. "Let me tell you a story first."

This man had shadowed me for days without being spotted. I already knew he was dangerous. I wasn't in a story mood, but no need to push him. Anders took his time finding words. I got the impression that he wasn't much of a talker. "I assume you know something about my former organization."

I nodded. "Just what Bob said in his notes."

"I doubt he knew much."

"Enough to throw his life away in some vain attempt to stop Majestic for launching Project Blue."

Anders smiled briefly, still staring out over the distance. "Majestic . . . The name started out as a joke. Our organization had lots of names, none of them official, most of those names were just line items on a budget that went into a big black hole. It was the conspiracy theorists that started calling it Majestic. We laughed at them, but it had a nice ring to it, so it stuck. But that was long before I was recruited."

"From where?"

The big man shrugged, not wanting to say any more about himself. "What I was doesn't matter now. Those days are gone. There is only *now*."

"That's very Zen of you, Leif Erikson."

Anders looked over at me, raising one eyebrow, as if internally debating whether he should just kill me on the spot, but he continued. "There's a secret war being fought. It's a cold war, but both sides have spilt a lot of blood."

"Between who?"

Anders looked at me like I was stupid. "Between my guys and the Illuminati."

"Another joke name, I take it."

"Of course. I don't know what they call themselves. It'll do though. You of all people should know all about them. You've served the Illuminati interests most of your life."

"My brother's the conspiracy theorist. I have no idea what you're talking about."

"Just another pawn then." Anders went back to looking at the view, his unkempt beard fluttered in the breeze. "Majestic was founded to fight commies, but they were bound to butt heads with these other assholes. The Illuminati is made up of thirteen powerful families. They're all old, powerful, and rich. They've been pulling the strings for a long time. Their base is mostly European, but they're involved in everything, same as us. Business, crime, politics, currency manipulation, terrorism, you name it, they've got a piece."

"I've never heard of them before Bob's notes, let alone worked for them."

"One of the thirteen families is Montalban. Ring any bells, jackass?"

"Heard of them . . ." I muttered.

"Rafael Montalban was the head of the family. It was supposed to be hands off, but Gordon had him offed in

Zubara. Next in line was his brother Eduard. You killed him. Now their family is in shambles, but the other twelve go about their business, still having their secret war, like nothing ever happened. Whichever side wins steers the destiny of the world."

I could honestly say that I didn't want to root for either side in this one.

"Project Blue was our doomsday contingency plan to destroy the Illuminati once and for all. If the war ever went from cold to hot, my team's job was to cut their heads off in a preemptive strike." Anders cleared his throat and spit over the edge, watching it fall all the way to the bottom. "Majestic is so layered in secrets that nobody ever knows what's going on. The highest levels come up with plans, but they don't want to know how we get the job done. They just want it done. The first operative, his name was Barrington, was given the mission parameters and told to set the contingency plans in place."

"The senator?"

"Former senator. He was the idea man. Gordon Willis was number two, operations, he made it happen. Gordon was my immediate boss in black ops. He picked me and another guy named Hunter to be the boots on the ground."

"Big Boss in Zubara?"

Anders was surprised. "You're better informed than you let on. You met?"

"Nice guy. Had his boys break a couple of my fingers."

"Lucky that's all they did. He was old school, learned his trade fighting Soviets. Me and Hunter did the work for Blue, set everything up, put all the assets in place. It was top secret. So secret that nobody had a fucking clue what they were unleashing. They just gave Barrington a mission and turned him loose."

"So what went wrong?"

"Plan was in place. I never thought we would have to use it. It was too extreme, even for us. When the higher-ups realized just how nuts Barrington was, they freaked. Then Barrington died."

"Killed by the Illuminati?"

"Nah . . ." Anders shook his head. "Somebody above decided he was a liability. Barrington had certain *hobbies* that could lead to blackmail, and that could compromise Majestic. I was ordered to terminate him. He was into some weird, kinky things. Anonymous sick stuff in airport bathrooms, stuff like that. Then one day, when he opened a stall door, it wasn't some messed-up little fag waiting, it was me and I stuck an icepick through his ear hole. We made sure the autopsy said he had a stroke."

"I used that trick once. It doesn't leave much blood."

Anders nodded in appreciation, one professional to another. "Anyway, Blue just sat and waited, kind of forgotten by the higher-ups. Then Hunter died, betrayed to the Zubarans by Gordon. It turned out that my old buddy had cut a deal with Eddie Montalban. Gordon popped Rafael, Eddie got control of his family and deniability, everybody wins."

I'd seen that alliance myself. What Anders was saying jibed with what I'd overheard in Quagmire.

"But then Gordon 'committed suicide.' And then they nab Valentine at the scene? Suicide, my ass. I could read the writing on the wall. Four men knew about Blue, and just like that three were dead, all at the hands of other

Majestic operatives. Somebody had decided to make every one of us who knew about Project Blue go away . . . So that's when I went rogue and bailed."

I had to smirk at that. "One problem with your theory. I know Valentine. He wasn't ordered to kill Gordon by anybody. He did that on his own. Gordon's betrayal got his girlfriend killed. It was as simple as that. But yeah, Majestic is upset all right. Valentine doesn't know shit about Project Blue. They tortured the hell out of him and he didn't know a thing. They were torturing him because they're scared of *you*. Now they're panicking."

Anders raised that one eyebrow again.

"Your bosses didn't drop the hammer on you guys. You fell off the face of the earth for nothing." I laughed. "But since you ran, now they think you're a liability. Hell, dude, you could probably be back in America living it up with your fat government salary."

His massive hand flew around faster than I could react. Anders' fingers clamped around my throat, and he slammed me back into one of the beams. He glared at me, not saying a word, breathing hard through his nose.

"Valentine was working on his *own*, you stupid fuck," I grunted as he threatened to crush my trachea. I could see the turmoil on his face as he realized that I was telling the truth. He had thrown away his life for nothing. His nostrils kept flaring, like the bellows on some giant furnace. I spotted something on his forearm, a little tattoo with a trident and the number four, and made a mental note of it for later. He let go. His fingers left indents in my flesh.

Anders slumped back against the rail with a sigh. The guard approached, seeing if he needed to pump some rounds into me. Anders waved him away, seemingly calm again. "Well, wish I had known that . . ." he muttered. "Too late now."

"All those steroids make you dumb." I rubbed my throat. If he tried that again, we were both going to take a dive off this roof.

"When a Dead Six operative got picked up at Gordon's house I figured they'd ordered the hit." He snap punched the railing hard enough to break most normal men's hands. The metal let out a harsh clang. "I was in F—" He stopped himself. "I was on an operation at the time, when I heard about Gordon. I made it look like I'd been killed by Illuminati and took off. I figured they'd be sending their best after me, that son of a bitch Underhill."

"Buddy of yours?"

"Underhill's the most dangerous man I've ever met," Anders stated flatly. "Old-school operative, came up through the ranks with Hunter. He's killed more people than cancer." Any man that put that kind of unease on a mutant like Anders was nobody I ever wanted to tangle with.

"What's done is done. Tell me the rest of your story."

"Gordon had a good thing going on the side with the Montalbans, so I hooked up with Katarina. We knew each other from a prior . . . business arrangement. I've been here ever since."

"My brother knew to look for you here. Why?"

"My part in Blue required me to make a deal with Sala Jihan. I was the one who had the technical expertise necessary. Bob must have found out something about that. I've got to admit, I was surprised to find out he was here."

"You knew Bob?" I asked, suspicious as always.

"From the FBI." Anders paused, knowing he'd said too much. "Hell with it. He was a field agent when I was HRT, Hostage Rescue Team, before being recruited by Majestic, at least. I'd heard about his meddling in Majestic's business, lots of us had. So I figured why he was here right away. That optimistic bastard probably thought he could flip me. Offer witness protection." Anders gave a bitter laugh. "But his poking around spooked Jihan. The Pale Man's soldiers took him before we could meet."

"And you were going to tell him about Blue? Let him expose Majestic?"

"Why not? I figured they wanted me dead," Anders stated flatly. "Fuck 'em."

"So what is Blue?"

He took forever to respond, weighing his response first. "I was going to tell you, but now things have changed."

So the nature of Blue was to remain a mystery. *Fine*. That was Bob's deal, not mine. "I'm assuming there's a reason I'm here . . ."

"We share a common goal."

"And why should I believe that?"

"Because we have a mutual enemy in Sala Jihan." Katarina's voice echoed across the open space. I didn't hear her join us on the balcony. She still moved like a ninja. Kat had wrapped a giant fur coat around her earlier skimpy outfit. She didn't look particularly happy, which told me that Jill was still alive. Kat smiled. If a cobra could smile, that's what it'd look like, and I wasn't falling for it. "The Montalban brothers are dead, the easternmost Illuminati family is in shambles. The remains of their kingdom picked over by scavengers like me, while the other twelve divide up their international spoils. The only thing that stands in the way of me taking back their old glory is control of this place, which means Sala Jihan must die."

"Not my fight, Kat. I'm done with the whole crime war thing. Congrats on the criminal empire, though. You always were better at this stuff than I was."

"*Au contraire.* This *is* your fight. Jihan has your brother, so by your own admission, you plan on killing him. My spies know all about Exodus. They also want to see Jihan dead, but they would never work with me."

"And I can't rightly say that I blame them."

"You are to be our introduction to Exodus. They will not trust me, but you, they respect for some reason. I want you to act as our intermediary. Alone, he is too strong for any of us to take. Between all of us, Jihan *will* fall. Exodus frees their slaves. You get your brother back. And I control The Crossroads."

"Sounds like a win-win situation," Anders stated.

Kat gave me her most innocent look. "An introduction. That is all I ask."

"The only word I have about who really took Bob is from you and Exodus, and frankly, you're both less trustworthy than the crabs on a five-dollar hooker."

Anders glanced at Katarina. She nodded, giving him the go ahead. He turned toward me. "There's a work crew of slaves here in town. They serve Jihan's garrison and the Brothers. If we were to free them, I know for a fact that one of them would be able to confirm that Bob was present in Jihan's prison cells." Anders pulled something out of his pocket and tossed it to me.

I caught it. It was a large coin, one of those military challenge coins that soldiers carried with their unit insignias and slogans on it. This one had been partially smashed, as if by a hammer. The first side was the Army Special Forces logo, 1st battalion, 19th group, with *De Oppresso Liber*, To Free the Oppressed, underneath. The other side was an ODA number that started with 92, but the last number had been crushed. It didn't matter, I knew it. I had seen that same logo on one of the plaques in Bob's basement, from my brother's old National Guard unit.

"That came from one of the slaves at the garrison. Dumb shit tried to *spend* it at a local shop after the Brothers sent him on an errand. You get one guess where he got it from." Anders said.

I was quiet while the deadly duo studied me. I absently bounced the coin in my palm. This was the first indication that I was on the right path.

"Partners again?" Kat asked.

No way in hell. But unless Ibrahim had an army, I didn't see how were going to get into Jihan's compound. We were going to need every bit of firepower we could muster. However, I needed to find out if they were telling me the truth, because I was mighty sick of being lied to. I spun the coin between my fingers before dropping it in my pocket. "Let's go free us a slave."

LORENZO

"You were *kissing* her!" Jill shouted.

"No." I held up my hands, partially to look innocent, partly to block anything she might throw at me. "She kissed *me*. I was an unwilling participant."

Jill's dark eyes narrowed dangerously. "Yeah, *real* unwilling!"

We were in the Montalbans' guest quarters. The room was actually nicer than our accommodations at the Glorious Cloud, but there were no windows, and the only exit led into a long hallway with guards posted on each end. We were only guests in the loosest interpretation of the word.

"I just sat there," I answered, keeping my voice level. "I told you what happened. Okay, damn it, what should I have done then? And give me an honest answer that doesn't involve her skinning us alive."

Jill folded her arms tightly across her chest and scowled at me. She had a fiery temper, but she also knew that I was right. "I don't know!"

"Well, why are you still yelling at me?" I pleaded.

"Because you suck," she answered.

I clenched my teeth to keep from saying something stupid. I gave it a moment before trying again. "Okay, then, as long as you're being rational about it . . ."

Jill sat on the bed, deflated, or just tired of being mad. "I don't trust her."

"No kidding? Jill, listen to me. There is nothing that Katarina won't do. She's a bona-fide sociopath. Trust her? Of course not. But I'm not seeing much choice. Either we work with them, or they kill us." I put my finger over my lips, and pointed toward the ceiling, to indicate that it was possible our room was bugged. Jill nodded. She knew there were other choices, but nothing that I wanted Kat to know I was pondering on. "I'm going with Anders to grab this slave. If I get confirmation that Bob is, or was, in that brig, then I'll arrange a meeting with Exodus."

Jill stood awkwardly, and hugged me close. "Sorry."

"No, I'm sorry. You shouldn't have come."

"Don't be stupid," she answered, before leaning in, and whispering into my good ear. "Did you love her?"

I paused, uncomfortable, with the love of my life in my arms. *Best to tell the truth.* "Yes . . . once."

"But not anymore?"

"No."

"Why?"

I thought about it for a moment. "Because she brought out the worst in me." And I thought of a nightmare with an old Malaysian woman screaming *murderer* over and over while her crone finger stabbed through my heart. I kissed Jill softly. "You bring out my best." I pushed a note into her hand. It was information for her to sneak to Reaper.

There was a heavy knock at the door. It was time.

Anders was waiting for me in the hall. He handed me a canvas backpack. Inside was my pistol, suppressor, spare magazines, holster, and knives. "Don't get stupid," he suggested. "Your woman and the kid are in our *care.*"

"Me? *Stupid?* Never. Let's go."

"Here, put this on," Anders passed me a surplus Russian army coat. It was heavy and a little bit too big, which worked out well since I was wearing a Spetsnaz armored vest underneath. "There will be a couple of goons. Take them fast."

"Aren't they slaves too? What are the odds of them putting up a fight?" I rocked and locked an orange bakelite magazine into the AKSU-74 he had given me. The weapon was short, stubby, and at the ranges we were going to be at, incredibly effective.

He shook his head. "They'll fight, I promise. Jihan brainwashes them. His soldiers only stop when you put them down." He pulled back the charging handle on his Saiga 12K, chambering a round. "Everybody knows the garrison buys supplies here, and they always pay in gold. We're a couple of toughs looking to make a buck, got it? How's your Russian?"

"Excellent."

"I do okay. Act Russian."

We were going in hard and fast. Anders had led me through a series of alleys and shadowed paths. We were now in the back room of a Montalban Exchange trade house, watching through the dust coated windows. The building we had under surveillance was a two-story, wooden construct, with no ornamentation and very rudimentary signage proclaiming it as a seller of foodstuffs.

I didn't like going in without a plan, but Anders had been doing his homework. He glanced at his watch, one of those giant black things with every kind of dial and display known to man, waterproof down to the *Titanic*. "The house slave usually goes shopping for the garrison around three. He normally has two soldiers with him. If they're buying a lot, then there will be another slave to help carry it back. He's the garrison cook, and they let him pick his own produce. He tried to pass Bob's coin one day while his guards weren't paying attention to get himself a little something."

"What about the Brothers?"

"I've got a distraction in place. When I call it in, some Uyghur separatists are going to firebomb one of the PLA stations south of town. Those guys all hate each other, so that was easy enough to arrange. That's the kind of thing that will draw those hooded bastards right in. We give them a minute to swarm over there, then we hit."

"So, why's everybody so scared of the Brothers?"

He thought about it for a moment. "Because they're badass motherfuckers. The most we've ever seen in town at once is three, so hopefully they'll all head toward the bombing."

"What do we do if one shows up here?" I retracted the bolt on the stubby AK, and let it fly forward, chambering a green lacquered 5.45 round.

"Kill him," he answered like I was stupid. "They're tough, but they're not bulletproof. Then run. They pin us down, we're dead. If I die, Kat will assume you did it. If they catch you, and you say a word about Montalban involvement, you know she'll feed your girl to the hogs. If you're really lucky she'll put a bullet in her head first."

"Kat's a big softie like that," I muttered, watching the street. I was wearing a green knit ski mask, rolled up on my head like a hat. "She's all heart."

"She's the devil's concubine," Anders said. "But she's great in the sack."

I turned away from the street, and studied the former G-man. "You're banging Kat, huh? Tapping the crazy?"

"Yeah. Job perk. Jealous?"

It shouldn't have surprised me. Kat always had liked to

cement her working relationships with a little bit of lust. "Hell no. Been there, *done that*. Literally. Doing it with a sack of angry porcupines would be safer."

Anders scowled.

I grinned viciously, looking up at the big operative. "But hey, who'd have thought we'd be belly buddies? Small world, hey?"

Anders fumed. I could tell he was contemplating just shooting me on the spot. My hands tightened around the stubby Kalashnikov in my hands. I silently dared him to make a move.

Something caught his attention then. He nodded toward the window. "They're here."

A thin man was walking up the front steps of the shop across the street. He was dressed in rough clothes, and flanked by two soldiers wearing snow camo. The soldiers were in their late teens, if that. Both were armed with AK47s. All three men had brutal burn scars across their faces. They disappeared into the building.

Anders pulled a radio out of his pocket, already set to a predetermined channel, and hit the transmit button three times. Then we waited. I could feel the adrenaline begin to flow. I took long, deep breaths. There were several thumps, and in the distance a black cloud rolled up over the horizon. One of the soldiers ran back onto the porch and watched the rising smoke. We gave it a few minutes to sink in, hoping that most of the garrison strength, and especially the Brothers, would head toward the burning PLA station like moths to a flame.

Anders pulled down his mask, hiding his face. I did the same, rolling my eyes when I saw the skull painted on the outside of his mask. "Remember, no English," he said. "Act Russian." He jerked opened the door.

We were moving. I was only a few feet behind Anders' towering form. The street was crowded with armed men, like everywhere in The Crossroads, but now everyone was looking toward the distant explosion. Jihan's soldier was standing at the bottom of the steps, his AK at port arms, watching the commotion like everyone else. Anders threaded his way through the people, remarkably smooth for such a big man. The slave soldier never saw him coming.

Anders' shotgun had a steel folding stock. It impacted the soldier's cranium with a sound like an aluminum bat driving a home run ball over the fence. The man crumpled in a heap, but Anders was already well past. His giant combat boot impacted the door, and the frame exploded in a cloud of splinters.

We had talked about this beforehand. He buttonhooked hard right, I went left. The main room was open, just tables of local and imported vegetables. The foodie in me marveled at the remarkable selection for this time of year. Everything you could possibly want to feed a hungry criminal underworld. "Nobody move!" Anders ordered in Russian. A young man, dressed in the manner of the Triads, started to get indignant, but Anders kicked him brutally hard in the groin and just kept going.

"On the floor!" I shouted at the shoppers. Even if they didn't understand the language, my tone, combined with the rifle muzzle in their faces, got the point across. There were three people in front of me. None of them were who I was looking for. They complied with my orders and laid down. One Chinese man in an apron began to shout angrily about how he had paid his protection money already.

I didn't glance toward Anders. In an operation like this, each shooter had an area to cover. Leave your area uncontrolled to scan your partner's and you were dead in an instant.

Anders' shotgun belched thunder. A table of weird, pointy fruit exploded in yellow pulp. Something moved behind it, crouched low. *The other soldier.* A third blast of buckshot blasted through the wood and food. Jihan's man was still moving. He came up, swinging his AK, already depressing the trigger, and firing wildly around the shop. My Krink was set to semi-auto. I focused on the front sight, already on the soldier's chest, and stroked the trigger three times fast. He jerked as bullets tumbled through his heart and lungs. The top of his head disappeared in a red blur as Anders found him.

"I said, everybody get on the damned floor!" I bellowed, in Russian, over the ringing in my good ear. "Where's the slave?"

"Over here," Anders called. The slave was on the ground covering his head with his hands. Anders bent down, grabbed him by the neck, and dragged him to his knees. "Talk to him quick."

My partner stepped back, scanning the room for further threats. I squatted before the shaking slave. He was confused, his eyes wide, bits of fruit splattered all over his scarred face. "Hey, look at me. *Hey!*" I slapped him once. That got his attention. I pulled the challenge coin out of my pocket and held it in front of his eyes. "Where did you get this?"

"I not know!"

"*Where?*"

"I not seen it," he sputtered, in bad Russian.

I slapped him again, hard enough to sting my hand through my glove. "Liar!"

Believe me, being a jerk to a man that had spent a good chunk of his life in slavery felt just as bad as you can imagine. I despise slavers. But I needed info, and I needed it now, and there was no way we were going to carry him out of here without getting caught. I had told myself that this was for the greater good, because if it helped end Jihan's reign, then it was freedom for thousands, and not just this one.

Anders stomped to the front door, and scanned down the street, obviously impatient. "More coming." He stepped back toward us, glanced around to make sure everyone else's head was still down, then lifted up his face mask. The slave looked startled, like he recognized him. "Clock's ticking."

"Yes, yes! I seen coin. Took from white man. Big white man. American. No hair. No hair." He rubbed his hands over his skull. "Please, no kill me."

"Is the American still alive?"

Now he appeared really scared, his eyes so wide that they appeared ready to pop out, but he looked hopefully toward Anders, almost as if he was asking permission. "Yes, alive, in master's dungeon. In fort. In Pale Man's fort." Once he had gotten past implicating his master, he seemed to decompress, to almost melt down, like he had gotten past the hard part. "Now you let me free? You take me away?" He pleaded toward Anders, tears of relief in his eyes.

BOOM.

I flinched as blood splattered across my face. Anders lowered his smoking shotgun as the slave thudded lifelessly to the floor.

"What the hell!" I leapt up, shocked.

"He saw my face," Anders stated as he rolled his mask back down. He reached down and took the leather bag filled with coins that would have bought supplies for Jihan's garrison. Now it was just a robbery. "Move. Out the back." He gestured toward the rear of the room, then he was gone.

I stared at the body for a moment as I wiped the blood from my eyes with the back of one gloved hand. Then I followed.

Just like the old days.

We dumped the masks, coats, vests, and long guns in the alley behind the vegetable shop, then walked nonchalantly through the rambling streets back toward the Montalban Exchange. Anders had the audacity to be hungry, and stopped at a noodle cart. "You ever try this stuff? It's probably made from cats and dogs, but it's pretty good."

I sullenly waited for him to get his lunch. I had no appetite. "That wasn't the plan."

He paused in his noisy slurping. "What?"

"Killing that guy."

"Your way wasn't working. We didn't have time. I showed him my face because I've got a rep around here. He had to know he was dealing with someone who would just kill him, otherwise he never would have talked in time.

If we let him go, and they caught him, he'd talk, we'd die. And once he told them what we asked about, your brother would die. I'm surprised. Katarina talked you up like you were a mad-dog killer."

"I try to be a little more selective." I shoved my hands in my pockets and watched the passing throng. There was still smoke rising from the PLA compound, but nobody was paying attention now.

"Well, you popped that soldier fast. He was about to shoot me when you got him," Anders said with grudging respect. I had to assume that was his version of "thank you." "Hey man, at least you know your brother's alive." He tossed some coins on the counter as he pulled out his radio.

I had been too preoccupied with Anders' casual murder to think it through, but this meant Bob was here. I still had a mission and a purpose. "I'll set up a meet between Kat and Exodus."

Anders keyed his radio. "It's on," he stated simply, before shoving it back into his pocket. "Your crew will be released and sent back to the Glorious Cloud. We'll be in touch." Anders ordered another batch of noodles to go.

Kat had kept her word, and Jill and Reaper were waiting at the Glorious Cloud by the time I returned. Reaper had even had some time to do some research. He had taken the note that I had slipped Jill at the Montalban Exchange, containing everything I had gleaned earlier, and gone to work.

"Your note said Anders had a SEAL Team 4 tattoo on his arm, and he mentioned being HRT," Reaper said. "So I started there."

"Assuming he's telling the truth." Jill was sitting on the bed next to me, also studying the screen on Reaper's laptop. She hadn't said anything yet about my earlier meeting with Katarina, and I wasn't going to bring it up either.

"Duh." Reaper rolled his eyes. "Do I tell you how to look hot? Do I tell Lorenzo how to steal stuff? No? I used the Majestic files Val took that Bob dropped on the Internet. Then I cross-referenced Bob's conspiracy nut notes. I digitized them while you were screwing around with Exodus, by the way. Then I wrote a—" And as soon as I recognized that he was about to drone on about his anarcho-crypto nerd brilliance I cut him off.

"Get to the point."

"The Project Heartbreaker records had an operative under the name of Anders, attached to Dead Six, and working for Gordon Willis, code-named Drago. But that name was a dead end. He's a ghost. No connection to a real identity."

The way Reaper was talking, I knew he was itching to tell me more. I waited patiently. I had already killed somebody today, so I was feeling kind of mellow. "And with your 'mad skillz,'" I made quote marks with my hands, "I'm sure you got more than that."

"You know it." He started rapidly clicking, bringing up other files. "One of Bob's suspects for the Fourth Operative was a former FBI agent named Simon Andrew Sundgren. Bob said that he had some indication that this guy was a possible because of his prior training, but Bob didn't elaborate what training, but he did mention the guy was HRT. Bob only wrote about the dude for one paragraph, but he was the only one that was former FBI."

He must have noticed that my eyes were starting to glass over.

"Okay, okay." He clicked a wireless mouse and the screen changed. It was a picture of Anders, only younger, clean-shaven, with a sharp buzz cut. He looked like one of those Nazi recruiting posters from World War II, a square-jawed, blue-eyed block of muscle.

"Wow. He looks a lot better without the beard," Jill said. I scowled at her. She raised her hands. "What?"

I turned back to the computer. "So you cracked the FBI database finally?"

"No. I got slapped down hard when I tried that for Bob's file. This is from Google," he explained. "See, just like all the guys working at North Gap had shady pasts, and some of the people that Majestic recruited for Dead Six had legal problems, I figured the rest of their operatives would be similar. Special Agent Sundgren is a bit of an internet celebrity." He brought up the next window. "He apparently shot some people in a standoff in North Dakota. They turned out to be unarmed and were trying to surrender. One of them was a pregnant lady."

"I remember that one. I saw a thing about it on TV once," Jill said. "There was this big standoff with some people that refused to pay taxes. When they teargassed the place, he said that the people came out with guns. The survivors said that they were unarmed and trying to surrender. Gotta love NatGeo."

"So all the intel gathering about our new buddy, Anders, has already been done for us by the internet. Hell, he's even got his own Wikipedia entry. It was really controversial. North Dakota tried to prosecute him. The Feds wouldn't release the official records of what happened, and he claimed immunity. The next thing you know, he just quit the FBI and disappeared. *We* know he was recruited by Majestic."

"Congratulations. You won the Internet." I gently pushed past Reaper and stole his laptop. Anders had quite the resume. Annapolis graduate, US Navy, started out as a nuke tech on a carrier, and then transferred into Naval Special Warfare. Olympic athlete. Won a bronze medal in freestyle swimming. So not only could he fight, he was apparently one hell of a swimmer too. Multiple citations for bravery, left the Navy, joined the FBI, and eventually the elite Hostage Rescue Team. Until he jumped the gun and massacred some people. Then nobody had seen him since. And now former Special Agent Sundgren was kind of an iconic figure for governmental abuses of power.

They had no idea.

"So apparently we're now in business with a jackbooted thug that shoots unarmed pregnant women. Majestic certainly wouldn't want to let a set of skills like this go to waste."

"Friggin' awesome," Jill muttered.

"Okay. Keep looking. None of this tells us what Project Blue is. There's got to be something about Anders that keyed Bob in on him, and when we know what it is, maybe we can figure out what Blue really is."

"I thought you didn't care." Reaper sounded surprised.

It really wasn't my business, I need to take care of my family and get the hell out of here. The world's affairs weren't my problem. That altruistic bullshit was best left for good guys like my brother.

"Well, now I guess I'm curious."

Chapter 16: Dead Leprechauns

VALENTINE
Exodus Safe House
Crossroads City
March 16th

Skunky and I sat and talked for a long time. I hadn't seen him in a couple years, and both of our lives had been irrevocably changed after that ill-fated operation in Mexico. We had much to discuss. He had, of course, heard of the unrest in Zubara, hell, the whole world had. After reading the Project Heartbreaker Commission report, Skunky was sure that I had been killed there.

What was once the Confederated Gulf Emirate of Zubara was now the Zubaran Arab Republic, run by General-turned-President-for-Life Al Sabah and his so-called Arab Socialist Party. He ruled with an iron fist that would have made Saddam Hussein proud. I'd heard you could find videos of Zubaran security forces machine-gunning protesters in the streets on YouTube.

Fat lot of good we'd done there. I was personally responsible, at least in part, for the suffering of the people of Zubara. It took me the better part of an hour to tell him the convoluted tale of how Exodus helped me escape from Zubara, and Sarah's death. I described my encounters with the Lorenzo brothers, the Montalbans, my falling out with Tailor, my capture and rescue, all of it.

When I was done talking, my former teammate closed his eyes and took a deep breath. "Holy crap, dude."

"You're telling me. You know, every morning I get up, I try not to think about it. By rights I've got no business even being alive. Almost everyone I care about is dead. Sarah is dead. The guys I worked with at Vanguard are, except for you and Tailor, and I'm not even sure about Tailor. I can't even contact Hawk because it might put him in danger. Almost everyone that took part in Project Heartbreaker is dead, too. I don't even know what the fuck I'm doing half the time. It's like I'm running on autopilot. I just go along with the flow because I don't have anywhere else to go."

"Is that why you're here?" he asked, a worried expression on his face.

I looked around, to make sure Ling wasn't listening. "At first, that was my reason for coming along. I owe Ling—and I owe Exodus—my life. She pulled me out of hell, risking her own life and killing a bunch of people in the process. I can't just walk away from that."

"Even if you really want to," Skunky interjected.

"Even if I really want to," I repeated. "But honestly, as crazy as it sounds, this feels right to me. I feel like I'm where I'm supposed to be."

"That doesn't sound crazy to me. I was lost when I got home from Mexico."

"That was a bad op," I said.

"Yeah," my friend agreed. "Bad op. I got home, I tried to go work for my parents, do a regular job. I tried really hard at that for almost a year."

"So did I, Jeff."

"What did you do?" he asked.

"Security guard."

"I sold camera equipment." He had always been an avid photographer. He had taken about three quarters of the pictures I had from my Vanguard days. "I did that for a while, but I got . . . I don't know, restless. I couldn't sleep at night and had nightmares when I could. When I thought about some of the shit we did, man . . . I don't know. Someday we're all going to stand before God to be judged. What am I going to tell him? How am I going to explain the shit we did? We got paid really well? It seemed like it was necessary at the time? It was what I was told to do?"

"I think I'd ask him where in the hell he was when all of those horrors we saw were going on."

"It started eating me up, Val, bad," Skunky said.

"Me too, sometimes." In our former profession, we put on a legitimate facade, prettied up what we did by saying we were providing security, ensuring stability, or protecting VIPs. All of that was basically true. We got our hands dirty and fought other people's wars. You can tell yourself that it was just a job, that they were bad guys you killed, but when you're alone on a quiet night, you can't fool yourself with that crap. You know what you did. It ate at me too, sometimes.

"We killed people for *money*." Skunky was more religious than most of my teammates had been. He was the only one on Switchblade 4 that made any effort to attend regular church service. He was a good man, a better human being than a lot of the people I worked with. He didn't really seem cut out for the work we did. He looked right through me. "So now what are you killing for?"

I didn't deny it. What Hawk had said about me was right, whether or not I realized it back then. I'm a *killer*. It's what I do. Everyone is good at something, and God forgive me, that's what I'm good at. I couldn't imagine doing anything else. When I tried to do something else, I was miserable, and that was how I ended up in Zubara. I think that's how I ended up at The Crossroads, too. Maybe it was just my calling.

"I don't know."

"Well I do." Skunky was a more decent human being than I was, but he was a killer too. Deep down, he knew it. "Same reason you're here now, I think. I was falling to pieces back home. The only time I'd find any peace was when I'd go camping up in the mountains alone. Even working for my parents I felt completely alone. They didn't know what I'd been doing overseas. I think my dad sort of knew, but I never talked about it. I couldn't bear to tell them. How do you tell your parents that, yeah, this one time, we mowed down a bunch of protestors in front of a government ministry with automatic weapons?"

I winced as I recalled the incident. That, too, had been a bad op. "Those protestors were shooting at us, Jeff. That's how Roberts and Bigelow bought it, don't you remember?"

"I know, I know. But how many people did we kill that

day? Dozens? How many women and kids? God help me, Val, it was eating me alive. Once I got home, and had peace and quiet, and lived in the normal world, it was eating me alive."

The protestors in that incident had deliberately brought as many women and children as they could with them. Many of the women and children were armed and were shooting at us. Not that that makes you feel any better when you're surveying a mound of corpses.

"I couldn't talk to anyone. I couldn't relate to anyone. I was alone and I was miserable."

"You had PTSD," I said bluntly. "It's okay, I've been told I do too."

"I know. I didn't know it at the time, but I know now. We're both pretty fucked up, you know that? So then I get this email from Ling, asking me to join Exodus."

"I got the same one. I damn near did it, too. If Tailor hadn't approached me, I probably would've taken Ling up."

"I did it. It took me all of a minute to decide."

"So what's it like?"

"I've been on a couple of missions. I can't really talk about what I do. You're not a sworn member of the order, blah blah blah."

I grinned. "No worries, don't get yourself in trouble."

"Anyway, most of what Exodus does isn't violence. I know that's what gets all the press, but that's not what it's about. We help people. We free people from slavery. We bring down warlords. We allow food aid to get to starving people. We bring dictators and warlords down. Exodus helped overthrow Muammar Gaddafi, did you know that? We were in Syria too."

I scoffed. "Look how well *that* mess turned out. I've been in the business of overthrowing nations, man. It never works out the way you think it's going to."

"I know. You can hand people liberty but you can't make them keep it. After that, and what you guys pulled in Zubara, the order got much less enthusiastic about operating in the Middle East."

"That's a smart decision, I think. So I take it you're a true believer? No offense. You just seem into it."

"You have to be, dude. It's given me a purpose. Once you learn about Exodus' history, its founding, and the role it's played in shaping history . . . we are trying to make the world a better place. And we're not trying to do it by social engineering, or telling people how to live, or trying to take control or gain power. We believe in freedom, and that freedom is worth fighting for. Dying for."

"Killing for," I added.

"Yes," he agreed grimly. "And that's why we're so damned good at what we do."

I wasn't sure what to say to that.

VALENTINE
Crossroads City
March 18th

I found myself sitting in the left-hand passenger's seat of a right-hand-drive Toyota Hilux Surf SUV. Ling was at the wheel, beeping the horn at a slow-moving ox cart as we tried to make our way across town.

She swore in Chinese as she stepped on the clutch, shifted gears, and passed the cart. Another horn sounded as we only very narrowly avoided hitting a huge Russian 6x6 truck head-on. Ling cursed again and stepped on the gas. I'd just learned that Ling had a case of road rage, but I still didn't know where we were going. I'd been roused out of bed in the predawn darkness and told to get dressed. I had no idea what was happening.

"Mr. Lorenzo told Ibrahim that he has a proposal for Exodus. Ibrahim is the overall commander of this operation, but he wanted to consult with the leadership before making any decisions. We're going to that meeting."

Exodus spies had told us that Lorenzo and his team had safely returned to the Glorious Cloud. They did not approach him to ask where he'd been, though, for fear of tipping their hand.

"So why am I going?" I asked. I wasn't even a member of Exodus, much less part of the leadership.

"You know Lorenzo better than most of us," Ling said.

I supposed that was true. "Only because we've tried to kill each other."

"That is the best way to truly understand someone." She smiled. "Ibrahim doesn't know him at all, so any of us who have worked with him will be there. We want to get a feel for what he has to say, whether or not he is telling the truth."

"The man is a professional liar and that's a giant understatement. I'm not sure having us there is going to help anyone know that Lorenzo's being sincere. I'm sure he's very, very good at feigning sincerity."

"I'm well aware," Ling insisted. "But you and I also

know more of his background, and we've seen his home. We have leverage over him that he's undoubtedly unused to. It might give us an advantage."

I rubbed my eyes. "All this skullduggery is giving me a headache."

"It won't be so bad. Think of it this way, at least we get to—" Ling cut the wheel hard to the left as a rusted fuel tanker truck pulled out in front of us from a narrow alley. She laid on the horn and what she was saying melted into a swath of Mandarin obscenities. I grasped the "oh shit!" handle and hung on for dear life. Such was rush hour in a place with no traffic laws.

Somehow, we made it to our destination unscathed. We parked behind a deteriorating Soviet-era warehouse and, after having our identities confirmed, were hurried inside by the guards. The warehouse was dimly lit, and full of vehicles, supplies, shelves, and stacks of crates. The air stunk of dust, must, and years of neglect.

There were many Exodus personnel present, going about their daily tasks. Some were working on a truck engine. Others were cleaning weapons. Some were doing push-ups and pull-ups. We were hurried past them, through the warehouse, into a small office in the back. The echoing sounds of the building were muffled as the door was closed.

Lorenzo was there. I barely recognized him since he was dressed in dirty, drab clothing, topped with a surplus Russian military parka. He looked exactly like a resident of The Crossroads. I probably would have missed him completely if he hadn't nodded at me. His eyes gave him away, though. I recognized his eyes. They darted everywhere, trying to scan every angle of the room. I had no doubt he'd arrived at the safe house unnoticed, like some kind of hobo ninja.

Also in the room was Ibrahim, who was quietly speaking with Lorenzo, as well as Katsumoto and a handful of other Exodus people that I didn't recognize. From their demeanor and their presence in the meeting, I gathered that they were the leadership of this operation. Whatever Lorenzo had to say had certainly gotten their attention.

One of the Exodus men put an electronic device on the table and activated it. "The room is secure," he told Ibrahim. It must've been some kind of electronic jammer.

Ibrahim nodded, then turned to address the room. "Gentlemen," he began, then turned to Ling. "My lady," he said formally, grinning. Ling, to my astonishment, blushed and looked away briefly before regaining her composure. Ibrahim was a flirt. "Our ally, Mr. Lorenzo, comes to us with an interesting proposal. He was told to bring it to us, which has some disturbing implications. It seems our operational security has been compromised."

Everyone in the room was taken aback. Ling's eyes went wide, but Ibrahim held up his hands. "Not to fear, my friends. As far as we can tell, our presence here is not known to Sala Jihan or his subordinates. However, a third party has become aware of us."

"Who?" Ling asked. Though considering this town, none of the options were good.

Lorenzo stepped forward. "The Montalban Exchange."

"You gotta be shitting me," I muttered to myself. The Exodus leadership began to murmur to each other.

"As far as I know, it's just a name. It's a remnant of the

criminal organization that Big Eddie, Eduard Montalban, controlled. The Montalban brothers are both dead, as I'm sure you're all aware. Valentine back there killed one of them, and he was there when I shot the other one out of the sky. They're dead and good riddance." Lorenzo's normally calm composure cracked slightly; he hated Eduard Montalban with every fiber of his being. The fact that the man was dead gave him little comfort, it seemed, and he could barely conceal his contempt.

People began to bombard Lorenzo with questions. Before it could get out of hand, Ibrahim raised a hand, silencing the room again. "Mr. Lorenzo, why don't you explain to them what you told me?"

Lorenzo pinched the bridge of his nose, obviously annoyed, but took a deep breath and continued. "A couple days ago I was approached by a representative of the Montalban Exchange."

"Was it Anders?" I asked pointedly, interrupting Lorenzo. Most of the Exodus leadership looked at me with surprised expressions on their faces.

Lorenzo looked grim. "Yes." He must've seen my hackles rising. He very subtly moved his hand, quietly telling me to tone it down. I figured he'd fill me in later. He was right. I didn't need to go airing my grudge with Anders in front of all these people. "So when I say approached, I mean he tailed me, caught me at gunpoint when I made him, and then doped me. I get the impression they're a shadow of what they were under Rafael and Eddie, but they still seem to have a lot of resources, and they have a big problem with Sala Jihan and they want him dead. They want in on your planned operation. They're offering intelligence, personnel, and logistics."

"Intelligence, personnel and logistics?" one of the Exodus leaders asked. "What does that mean?"

"I'm assuming that personnel, means they'll provide personnel," Lorenzo said dryly. "I don't know what they meant by logistics. Maybe supplies, maybe transportation. Intelligence is pretty self-explanatory."

"Who made you this offer?" Ling asked.

Lorenzo paused for a moment, as if lost in a memory. "A woman named Katarina. I used to work with her, a long time ago. She was on my team. I know her well."

"How is it that this woman came to head the Montalban Exchange?" one of the Exodus commanders I hadn't met yet asked.

"She's absolutely ruthless," Lorenzo answered. "That's really all it takes."

"Can we trust her?"

Lorenzo looked surprised by the question. "What? No. No, no. Not even a little bit. She's dangerous and violent."

"Then why should we go along with this?"

"I'm not saying you should," Lorenzo said. "I don't give a damn what you people do. I'm just here to find my brother, and I'm just the messenger. If your raid fails, the chances of me finding my brother go from slim to none. But I can think of some reasons why you might want to consider it."

"What do you mean?" Ling asked.

Lorenzo's mouth split into a mean smile. "I know you guys think you're being all secret squirrel and everything, but you're not. You can't just put this many people into such a small area and not be noticed. I noticed, and I've only been here for a few days. Sala Jihan has been here for a lot longer, and the Montalban Exchange has already compromised you. Also, I haven't seen your battle plan obviously, but how in the hell are you people planning on taking that fortress?"

"We are working on that," said Ibrahim.

"I've been inside that thing. Do you really think you have enough people? How are you going to get them up there? Do you have good intelligence on Jihan's compound? Do you know how many men he has? Do you know where they're all housed, how they're equipped, where their defensive positions are?"

Lorenzo was met with silence.

"Thought so. The Montalbans say they know. They told me to give this to you people." He retrieved a folded piece of paper from his pocket, and laid it on the table. The Exodus leadership crowded around to get a better look.

"This is a map showing the interior defensive positions around the fortress," Ibrahim said. "Including where they house their antiaircraft weapons."

"Katarina says there's plenty more where that came from. She says her spies have infiltrated Jihan's operations. She's ready to make a move, but can't do it without you. You're ready to make a move, and she says you can't do it without her. Look, people, I've been inside Jihan's compound. I've met the man."

The room became uncomfortably silent.

Lorenzo was unfazed. "That's right, I was face to face with Sala Jihan at the bottom of his missile silo. He's not somebody to screw around with. I can give you guys information, but I only saw a little bit, and what I saw told me he's got a lot more armed motherfuckers than you guys have."

"What do you know of our strength?" someone asked indignantly.

Lorenzo scoffed. "Please. You aren't as good at this as you think you are, no offense. I don't know exactly how many people you have here, or what else you might be scheming at, but I know that Sala Jihan has an army in there, a lot more people and weapons than you people could have possibly smuggled into town. So unless you've got an air strike planned or something, you might want to at least hear the Montalbans out."

"And what does she want in return for our assistance?" Katsumoto asked.

"She wants The Crossroads. With Jihan gone, she believes her group can take control of this place and get a share of all of the business that goes on here."

"And trade one monster for another?" one of the Exodus leaders scoffed.

"No," another replied. "We'd be trading an actual monster for a mere criminal."

Katsumoto and Ibrahim looked at each other for a long moment. Lorenzo didn't know about the plan to assault the dam. Neither did the Montalban Exchange, it seemed. The two Exodus commanders nodded at each other.

"I propose," Ibrahim said, "that we at least meet with the Montalban Exchange. They have compromised our OPSEC. If we decline the meeting, they could turn on us, or even expose us to Sala Jihan. We must move carefully, lest we be lured into a trap. You all know the gravity of the situation. Our footing isn't nearly as strong as I would like it to be. We need to be willing to take every advantage offered to us."

The room erupted into loud discussion. Lorenzo stepped away from the limelight and leaned against the wall. He seemed happy to no longer be the center of attention. Ling joined the energetic discussion as the Exodus leadership argued among themselves.

Awkward. I stepped back. The debate reminded me I was an outsider. *What are you doing here?* I asked myself. *This isn't your fight.* I was so lost in my thoughts that Lorenzo was able to sneak up on me. He startled me as he materialized to my side.

"Valentine," he said curtly.

"What the fuck happened to you?" I asked, my voice lowered so the Exodus people couldn't hear. "What is Anders doing here?"

"Come on," Lorenzo said, indicating the door. "I need some air. Let's get away from these crazies." He walked out of the meeting room. We found a dark, quiet corner in the warehouse, away from prying ears, to talk. "You know this Anders guy? He's an asshole."

"You have no idea," I said, not looking at him.

"Then fill me in," Lorenzo said. "The short version. You tend to ramble on when you start telling stories."

I raised an eyebrow at him. "Fine. Anders worked for Gordon Willis. He was, like, his right-hand man or something. Everywhere Gordon went, just about, Anders went with him. He was there in the office the day I was recruited. He was in Zubara. He was there when we raided Rafael Montalban's yacht, too, so I'm guessing he was in on Gordon's schemes."

"How do you know?"

"The yacht raid was not one of our planned operations. It was part of Gordon's plan, part of his deal with Eduard Montalban."

Lorenzo's eyes narrowed. "Makes sense. Go on."

"Anders is an ice-cold motherfucker. I don't know if he feels pain. He kicked the shit out of half my team in Yemen, and he's the only man I've ever met that's a faster draw than me."

"You haven't seen me draw. What were you doing in Yemen?"

I cracked a mean smile. "Oh please, pops, I've got you beat by a tenth of a second, easy. We were there recovering a nuclear warhead that was supposed to go to General Al Sabah."

"We'll settle this on the range someday, kid. So . . . wait, wait a second. Is it my bad ear, or did you just tell me that Anders got his hands on a nuke?"

"You heard me right. An old Russian ICBM warhead. We intercepted the transaction in the middle of nowhere, Yemen. Anders was there for the raid. We lost guys, too. Christ, he let Singer bleed to death. The guy was supposed to be our medic and the cocksucker didn't even open his trauma kit."

Lorenzo thought that over for a second. "Sounds about right. What else?"

"That's all I know. I never saw him after the raid on Rafael Montalban's yacht. I didn't know what happened to him."

"He told me about it. He went underground after Bob leaked all of that information to the press. He fled the country when you killed Gordon Willis. He thought Majestic sent you to clean up loose ends."

I chuckled sardonically. "Yeah, Gordon thought Majestic had sent me to kill him, too. Blew his fucking mind when I told him I was there on my own."

"Were they going to kill him?"

"I think they were going to take him alive, to interrogate him about Project Blue. The guys that were supposed to capture Gordon entered his house while I was confronting him. They captured me right after I shot him."

"Damn. Couldn't have timed that better, could you?"

"I should've just stayed with Hawk. It would've saved me a lot of trouble."

Lorenzo leaned in closer to me, the tone of his voice darkening. "It would've saved us *all* a lot of trouble. You did the worst possible thing: you got *caught*. You *talked*. My brother could be dead because of you."

"You think this is what I wanted? You think I don't regret it every single fucking day I'm alive? You think it doesn't just kill me on the inside knowing that my choices have gotten almost everyone I know killed?"

"I don't give a shit how bad you feel," Lorenzo said. "You got stupid. You let your childish rage compromise you. And you didn't just compromise yourself, you compromised Hawk, my brother, me, Jill, Reaper, everyone!"

"Really? You're going there? Okay, okay, let's talk about your little high-speed chase down a public highway and shooting down a jet. Way to keep it low profile. And using your real last name as your pseudonym? Jesus, Batman, you think they'll ever figure out that you're really Bruce Wayne?"

"First off, that was never *my* last name. Second, that's not even the same fucking thing! I did what needed to be done! And shooting down that jet was awesome and you know it."

I couldn't argue with that, but I felt like arguing anyway. I was sick and tired of Lorenzo jumping my shit. "Whatever. I've had enough of you blaming me for your problems. Enough people have suffered because of me. I'm not going to take responsibility for the people that suffered because of you. I never asked for your help. You didn't have to get involved in any of this. Your brother wouldn't have gotten into this mess if he'd have quit while he was ahead and stopped digging. You're pissed off at him and you're taking it out on me."

Lorenzo stepped back and seemed to deflate a little. I folded my arms across my chest. He thought for a moment, then looked up at me. "I'm trying to help you, goddamn it," he insisted. "I've been where you are. Nothing to lose, nothing to live for, no longer giving a fuck. I lived that way for a long time. Look where it got me. You gave me some advice when were in Las Vegas. Do you remember? You told me to get out of this life, for Jill's sake."

"I remember," I said sullenly.

"I wish like hell you'd have listened to your own advice, kid," Lorenzo said. "It was the first smart thing I ever heard you say."

I sighed heavily, looking around the warehouse. "Yeah, well, it's too late now, isn't it? For both of us. Look at everything that's happened, Lorenzo. Look at all this crazy shit and tell me that it's just a coincidence."

"I don't believe in fate," Lorenzo said stiffly. "Or

destiny, or predetermination, or unicorns, or pots of gold at the ends of rainbows."

"If there were pots of gold at the end of rainbows, I can only assume that you'd have a lot of gold and there'd be a lot of murdered leprechauns buried in Ireland."

Lorenzo actually smiled. "Damn straight."

"Yeah, well, I don't believe in any of that stuff either. But look around you. Can you honestly tell me you feel like you're in control? I don't know, man. There's something wrong with this place, with this whole thing."

"It's a third-world, drug-trafficking, slave-trading, arms-dealing hellhole," Lorenzo said, almost like he was trying to defend the place. "It's going to feel wrong."

"Not like that. I've been to places like that too. I worked in Africa for almost a year, you know. This is different. I can't put my finger on it, but there's something seriously messed up here. We don't belong here. I have a terrible feeling about this whole thing."

"Have you told Ling that? She's pretty into you. She might listen."

I raised an eyebrow at his comment, then shook my head. "Not on this. These guys are dedicated. They're going to go through with it one way or another."

Lorenzo sighed and rolled his eyes. "Bunch of fanatics is what they are. No offense. I can't complain, though. This insanity is the only shot I've got at finding Bob."

"What about your friend Katarina? Is she for real?"

"She's for real," Lorenzo said. "And she's not my friend. The bitch is crazy. Genuinely, legitimately, totally screwed-in-the-head bug-nuts. She's a businesswoman, though. She'll uphold her end of the bargain, especially if she thinks she's got something to gain, but if Exodus knows what's good for them, they won't trust her."

"Exodus doesn't strike me as the trusting sort. I have no doubt they'll have a contingency plan."

Lorenzo gave me a hard look after that comment, but I said nothing more. He didn't know about the raid on the dam, and he didn't need to. This whole thing was already complicated enough.

And for the life of me, I just couldn't shake the bad feeling I had.

Chapter 17: Dance Partners

LORENZO
Somewhere in Kazakhstan
March 20th

There was an awkward silence in the small cabin. Terrorists on one side, gangsters on the other, nobody speaking, kind of like the uncomfortable beginning of a middle-school dance when the music starts and the boys are too intimidated to go talk to the girls. The Montalban Exchange was represented by Katarina and Anders, Exodus by Ibrahim and a tough-looking Czech named Fajkus. Outside the single-room dwelling, several other Exodus members and Montalban goons watched each other with nervous alertness while their bosses talked business.

The meeting place had been agreed upon by both groups. The house stood alone in a mountain pasture forty miles into Kazakhstan. It was a cramped, wooden shack, but since it was alone in a sea of stunted yellow grass poking out of the snow, there was no place for either side to set up snipers or an ambush. It was too open for any of us to have been tailed by Jihan's spies. The lone shepherd who lived here had been given a small sum of money and sent off to watch his goats.

I had introduced the various parties, and was now leaning back in my rickety chair, arms folded across my chest, just an impartial observer at this point. I didn't trust either side, but sadly I needed these people to free Bob.

After sizing each other up, Ibrahim broke the silence. "Lorenzo has told me that you wish to assist us. I'm willing to listen to your proposal. However, you must know that Exodus does not need your help. We are more than capable to accomplishing our mission."

Kat smiled. "No. No, you are not. Otherwise you wouldn't be here today."

"I'm afraid you are mistaken," Ibrahim stated flatly.

"Then why haven't you killed Jihan yet?"

Fajkus scowled. The Czech was probably in his mid-thirties, stocky, with bulldog jowls, and short, spiky, black hair. The Exodus XO wore small, round glasses, and it was rather obvious from his expression that he didn't like this meeting. "The Pale Man will be dead soon enough."

"Oh, but think of all those poor slaves, dying by the score every day, living in squalor and suffering, while their saviors wait in relative comfort." She gestured at the walls of the cabin. The only decorations were antlers off of some animal that I didn't recognize. "That must be infuriating."

"Don't patronize me, Ms. Katarina," Ibrahim said. "We both know that you do not care about the welfare of the slaves."

"Of course not. I care about profit and competition. But for you, every day you wait, every hour, the odds of Jihan learning about you increase. My spies were able to discover you, so you are vulnerable. Should Jihan learn of you, he'll hunt you down like dogs, but still mighty Exodus hesitates." Kat leaned forward and rested her hands on the plank table. "No, you are not ready yet. You lack something."

Ibrahim and Fajkus exchanged glances, conveying information like only two professionals who had worked together for a long time could. Ibrahim nodded. Fajkus turned back toward Kat. "We are waiting for a few more swords, our strike teams, to arrive. Jihan's compound—"

"Is a fortress. Impenetrable walls, every building a concrete bunker, guarded by a legion of disciplined troops, and even if you carpet-bombed the entire place, your target spends most of his time at the bottom of an armored pit designed to survive a near hit from an atomic weapon. To take it will require a huge force."

Ibrahim raised a single bushy Kurd eyebrow in my direction. "Perhaps by stealth then?"

"They're thorough, no discernible gaps," I answered truthfully. "The gates stay closed. Incoming traffic is searched. Walls are too high to scale. Guards everywhere, and there aren't so many of them that they don't all know each other. It would be difficult, but not impossible. I could find a way."

"Trust me. Your usual methods of disguise won't work. I've sent men in before, impersonating slave soldiers, and they were always spotted. Somehow they just know. You can't impersonate a Brother, because nobody on the outside has ever heard them speak. How will you respond when questioned?" Kat shook her head. "You will fail. Jihan cloaks his people in mystery, but that secrecy becomes a formidable defense. You can't get inside the head of something you can't understand."

"Oh, I'll get in," I responded. Kat of all people should have known that. Every defense has a weakness.

"And then what? Assassinate Jihan?" Kat had a cold laugh, more of a cackle. "Many have tried. Yes, that benefits me if you succeed, but if you fail, he'll suspect the Exchange. And even if you manage to kill Jihan, it would be a suicide mission, which isn't your style, and that does not free your brother. No, you need a full assault to assure his death and destroy his organization. It is the only way to be sure."

"So what's your plan then?" Fajkus spat. "Are we supposed to rely on your hired thugs?" He gestured angrily at Anders. "Murderers and trash? You expect me to believe that Montalban scum is going to take those monster walls and watch our back? I say horseshit to that!"

Anders shrugged, seemingly calm, his massive hands resting in his lap. The big man looked bored. He'd been called worse things than hired thug.

Ibrahim raised a hand to calm his subordinate. Fajkus was done, his distrust for the Montalban Exchange having been noted. I liked the Czech. He was angry. He kind of reminded me of a young Carl. Ibrahim nodded toward Katarina. "Please continue."

"Just because your people are suicidal fanatics, do not underestimate what my *hired trash* is capable of. I offer you more than just men with guns, I offer you resources, and I offer you a way into that compound."

Ibrahim kept up his poker face, but I could tell his interest was piqued. "And how exactly do you propose to do that?"

Katarina glanced absently at her absurdly expensive Swiss watch. She raised her head, and an evil grin split her perfect features. "Like this . . ."

The cabin door flew open. It was one of the Exodus operatives that I had met earlier, the Russian woman, Svetlana. She had a big bolt action sniper rifle cradled in her arms. "Ibrahim, we have incoming." Fajkus rose, his hand moving under his sweater to his holstered pistol.

"Don't worry," Katarina said. "They're with me."

A CZ 97B appeared in Fajkus's hand. "Treacherous—" He was cut off as Anders' .45 materialized right under his nose. The big man had moved so fast that I hadn't even seen the draw stroke.

"Calm down," Anders ordered. Svetlana jerked her rifle to her shoulder and pointed it square at Anders' back, then looked to Ibrahim for guidance. The Exodus commander shook his head slightly as he studied Katarina. Fajkus slowly placed his .45 on the table and removed his hand. Ander's pistol didn't move, and it was obvious that the Exodus man was only a few pounds of pressure on a trigger between life and death.

Then there was a noise. Faint at first, but it quickly grew, as the thunder closed on us. The dirty windows began to vibrate, clay pots rattled, and dust fell from the ceiling like fat brown snowflakes. Then it was deafening, as massive engines drove giant rotors, an endless deep scream, like some sort of leviathan descending on us. The room darkened as something blocked the sunlight.

"That's certainly a large helicopter," Ibrahim said.

"It's a Mil-26. The Halo. Biggest in the world, I'm told," Katarina shouted over the noise. "I have two of them." Kat always had liked to make a big entrance. She was such a drama queen. The noise receded as the huge helicopter tore away, demonstration of speed and mass complete. Anders slowly lowered and reholstered his gun. Svetlana dropped the muzzle of her rifle. Fajkus grudgingly returned to his seat.

"An impressive fly-by, but we've already thought of air insertion," Ibrahim said. "They'll see us coming, and shoot us out of the sky."

"I run the finest smuggling operation in Asia. My pilots are better than yours. We can run the mountain passes on night vision at a hundred and eighty kilometers an hour. Radar won't see a thing until we exit the pass. We'll be on top of the compound before Jihan even knows we're there. I can drop all of your strike teams right into his lap. At the same time my men will destroy his garrison in The Crossroads and the Brothers. Once they and their master are dead, the slave soldiers at the mines will collapse."

Fajkus shook his head. "It'll still take a minute to make it from the mouth of the canyon to the target, and our intel indicates there's a Shilka in the compound. That thing will tear your choppers apart."

He was right. I had seen that antiaircraft monstrosity when we had reconned the compound. Flying right into four quick and responsive 23mm cannons with active radar and an alert crew? *Screw that.*

"How do you propose we deal with that?"

Kat examined her nails like this was boring her. She

took her sweet time responding. "You see, this is why Exodus needs me. I've been studying Jihan's weaknesses for quite some time. I have a way to get someone into the compound undetected. I've been laying the groundwork for months. We'll need someone capable of infiltrating when the choppers are in place, then at a predetermined time, that individual will disable the AA. It will be extremely dangerous and require someone skilled."

Every set of eyes in the room turned toward me.

I snorted. "Yeah . . . figures."

LORENZO
Crossroads City
March 24th

The last few days had been spent in preparation. I had gone over my part of the plan repeatedly, and had worked closely with both Exodus and Kat's forces. The choppers were prepped and stashed in Mongolia. Exodus would be riding in style. Kat's choppers could carry a small army, so they wouldn't even be close to full, but if one was disabled, they'd still have a way out. The Montalban foot soldiers were going to assault the garrison in town. The final group consisted of me, Anders, and a handpicked group of Exodus members.

On the other side, Jihan had several hundred fanatical soldiers in his fort. We needed to work fast though, because he and another hundred guarding the dam and around a thousand or so possible reinforcements at the slave mines only a few miles away. We were leaving the dam and mines alone, because it was better to cut off the head and let the body die.

In twenty-four hours the great raid would begin.

Exodus was spread thin. I had not realized at first just how much this operation meant to their organization, but I had pieced together a few facts. Exodus wasn't a huge operation by any means, and the force gathered here was one of the largest they'd ever assembled. Swords had gathered from every corner of the world for this. Ibrahim was their most experienced commander. Exodus literally had all of their eggs in one basket.

The Montalban Exchange was risking just as much. As soon as Kat struck against Jihan, she would either win total control of The Crossroads, or they were done, and they would be lucky to escape with their lives.

I had spent the last four days bouncing back and forth between the Montalban Exchange, the Golden Cloud, and various Exodus meeting places. Today I was once again on the top floor of the Exchange, near a crackling fireplace, sitting around a table with Ibrahim and Fajkus of Exodus, and Katarina, Anders, and a man named Diego from the Exchange. I'd been told Katsumoto was the other hotshot Exodus boss in town, and I was a little suspicious as to why I'd not seen him at any of the meetings with the Montalbans, but Exodus was probably just hedging their bets in case this was an elaborate plot for Kat to sell out their leader.

Reaper and I were at the end of the table. Jill was at the Golden Cloud. I was not comfortable having her near Kat, as I was still waiting for my ex to fly into one of her rages and kill somebody. Though she actually seemed a lot more grounded and *sane* than when I had last been around her. This mafia-don thing seemed really good for her.

In the middle of the table was a scale model of the compound. It was actually rather impressive, with carved foam blocks mimicking each building, the wall, and the surrounding terrain, with a red number painted on each structure to help us keep track. The compound was at the border between the windswept valley and the edge of the mountain. Three sides of the compound were exposed to open ground. The fourth hung over the side of the mountain, and had a near-vertical drop to the rock below. A red arrow was painted on the table, pointing to the northeast, the direction of the canyon mouth, where the helicopters would be coming from.

Katarina reached across the table and moved the toy tank that represented the dreaded ZSU antiaircraft cannon slightly. She turned the turret so it was pointing at me, and grinned. "So, you've had a chance to think it through. Can you do it?"

I stood, so I could have a better bird's eye view of the fort. We had been through this a dozen times, but it never hurt to look again, to try and find that one hidden problem that was just waiting to bite you in the ass. There was approximately two hundred meters from the cliff edge to where the ZSU had last been parked, and most of it would be navigable in the dark without being seen.

"Assuming phase one goes according to plan. Yeah. I can do it. Phase one gets hinky, and I'm probably dead."

"Then we'll abort. Turn around and fly back to Mongolia, and be home in time for cocoa," Kat replied. "If not?"

"Phase one complete. I'll initiate phase two, bring up my team, and when we're ten minutes off the ZSU I'll give the signal," I replied mechanically. I would only be on my own for the initial engagement. After that, in theory at least, I would have some help. I had received some good news from Exodus before the meeting. Shen had arrived, and would meet me at the staging point. I had worked with the man before, and had faith in his abilities.

"At Go, phase three will begin," Ibrahim stood, and moved two plastic helicopters across the board, and into the red path of the red arrow. "We'll move off station, and proceed through the canyon at maximum speed. My chopper will be in the lead position. One minute behind will be the second." Ibrahim had insisted that the chopper he was riding on be in front, that way if I failed and the ZSU blasted something out of the sky, it would be his Halo. That way half of his men could still escape. "That is the point of no return." He slowly sat back down. Once the choppers exited the canyon and were seen, we had to win, or Jihan's forces would expunge our existence from the earth.

Reaper looked up from his laptop. "As soon as I see the radar go down, that's when I'll bring in our eyes. By the way, weather still looks good. Chances of snow the next morning, but we should be clear during the raid." I had been adamant that he and Jill would not be placed in harm's way. Later today they would be leaving town, just in case this all went horribly wrong. Reaper still had a job to do, but it could be done remotely just as easy as it could be done in town. Having my people out from under the gun was going to be one less thing on my mind.

"When you leave the canyon, my men will attack The Crossroads barracks and kill any Brothers present." Diego spoke for the first time. He was relatively young, and had cultivated that Big Eddie Euro-trash vibe, down to the puffy hair and a suspicious amount of eye shadow. Ibrahim's spies had confirmed that when Diego wasn't working for Kat, he was cross dressing at one of the local clubs. Typical Montalban employee, but apparently Kat thought he was pretty sharp. He would be leading the Exchange's forces in town as they surrounded and burned Jihan's barracks to the ground. We still didn't know how many Brothers there actually were, but as of this morning, intel indicated that there were at least two in town.

Fajkus spoke directly to Katarina. "How is your men's morale?" His voice implied what he thought of the mercenaries.

Diego cut in. "The Montalban troops are as good as yours."

I snorted, perhaps a little too impolitely.

Diego's plucked eyebrows narrowed into a dangerous V. He lifted his shirt and exposed a well-worn knife handle. Ibrahim's spies had also confirmed that Diego had participated in a few knife fights in the arena, when he wasn't busy portraying a very convincing Celine Dion. He also had a bit of an attitude around me since I still had the reputation of having been Big Eddie's favorite killer. "You have something to say, Lorenzo?"

I leaned back further in my comfortable chair. "I never met a transvestite I couldn't take in a knife fight."

Diego began to rise, but Kat glared at him. He slowly lowered himself back down, fixing me with a glare that let me know we had unfinished business, or maybe he was going to start singing the theme song from *Titanic*. Hell if I knew.

"My men don't know they're doing this. When we initiate, I will tell them that Jihan has already been killed," she stated simply. "That'll fire them up. What they don't know can't hurt them, and if we fail in the compound . . ." She trailed off. We all knew it wouldn't matter for long. And she meant it when she said *we,* since Kat was going to be on the second chopper. That fact alone helped to demonstrate to Exodus that she was just as committed as they were. "How's your troops' morale?" she asked snidely, already knowing the answer.

"Excellent," Ibrahim said with an honest assurance. He wasn't exaggerating either. I had worked closely with his subordinates in planning this. They were fired up. There were still several other Exodus teams scattered around the world that were supposed to be converging here, but Ibrahim was done waiting. The Kurd had picked a course of action and was committed to seeing it through.

The next phase was the separation of the various teams to take over and control different points of the compound. My group got the brig. Ibrahim was going to personally take the missile silo that Jihan called home. I didn't like that part at all. A commander should be someplace he can have a view of everything, and that's not at the bottom of a giant hole, but Exodus leadership seemed to be very *lead from the front* oriented. We went over secondary plans, who would take over what areas of responsibility should some other team be incapacitated, and finally every contingency plan that we could think of.

It had been a long time since I had worked with this large a group. I grudgingly respected Exodus. Their motives were pure, their training top notch, and their fury justified. They were nuts, but they were devoted nuts. The Exchange was the wild card, but Katarina had been nothing but professional so far. Anders was a brute, but he was also cunning, and by all accounts, very good at what he did. Diego was a weirdo, but in typical Montalban fashion could be counted on to be ruthless and efficient.

We went over a few last bits of business. Ibrahim nodded at me toward the conclusion, his bushy eyebrows scrunching together. I had already agreed to meet with him secretly, to discuss a few other contingency plans that we were going to put into place in case the Montalbans fell through. There was not a lot of trust in this business.

Finally, we were done. We had planned about as much as possible in the time allotted. If we didn't go tomorrow, it would be at least another week before we could do this again. That meant a greater chance that my brother would be dead, Exodus would lose more slaves, and Kat lost more money. None of us wanted to postpone. We were a go.

Ibrahim addressed Katarina, very formally, very solemnly. "On behalf of Exodus, I want to thank you. I know that your reasons for helping us are to your own benefit, but know that the lives and freedom of thousands are in your hands. With almighty God's blessing upon us, tomorrow liberty will shine on the ancient Crossroads again."

Katarina smiled politely. She had a glass of wine in front of her. She picked it up as if she were about to give a toast. "Thank you. I—" There was a knock at the door, and she turned briefly. Anders pulled a cloth over the table, covering the model. "Please excuse me, for a moment." Ibrahim nodded for her to proceed.

The door opened, and two Montalban retainers came in, each one holding the arm of a third, his feet dragging limply behind him. They pulled the semi-conscious man into the center of the room. Kat waved her hand. "Leave him." The retainers dropped the man with a thud, turned and quickly left. The man curled up in a fetal position and moaned. He had obviously been severely beaten.

Katarina pushed her chair away from the table, and strolled toward the man, still holding her glass. The rest of us at the table exchanged confused glances, including Anders and Diego. The injured man seemed incoherent. "Everyone, allow me to introduce you to Dieter, one of my employees." Kat paused, and then threw her wine in his face. He jerked awake as the alcohol burned the deep lacerations on his face. He cringed back from Kat's feet, trying to roll away, his hands raised to cover his head.

"Ms. Katarina! I'm sorry! I'm sorry!" he shrieked.

"Shut up!" she screamed back at him, and then flung the glass into his face. It shattered and he yelped and scurried back further. His back collided with the wall, and he had nowhere else to go. Her voice went immediately back to a normal inflection. "Dieter was working closely with Diego on the plans for the raid. It has been brought to my attention that my *employee* has a big mouth."

"I didn't tell anyone anything!" Dieter insisted, still recoiling. Blood was running down his forehead into his eye, and he instinctively wiped it away with his torn shirt sleeve.

"Only because we caught you in the act before you could open your stupid mouth," she said calmly. "How long have we worked together? We were equals under Big Eddie. So, what, eight years? Eight years I've considered you my friend?" She turned back to address the table. "Ibrahim, if you doubted my sincerity in this operation, don't let your heart be troubled. Allow me to demonstrate the depth of my commitment."

"That isn't necessary," Ibrahim said, stone-faced.

Kat smiled. Her teeth were a sharp white line splitting her face. "Oh, yes. It is." A stainless SIG P232 appeared suddenly in her hand. She spun around, and there were two rapid cracks. Dieter screamed as a bullet exploded through each knee. Reaper was the only one to let out an audible gasp.

Dieter just kept on screaming, a hand on each leg, blood welling up between his clenched fingers. "Shut up! Shut up! You haven't earned the right to scream!" Kat shrieked. The injured man choked back his pain. She walked over to the fireplace, removed an iron poker from the rack, and stuck the tip into the coals to let it heat up. She was again calm as she studied the fire. "This meeting is adjourned. We'll rendezvous at the assigned positions tomorrow. Anders will see you out."

So there she was. I was wondering if that personality had finally been put away. She had been so calm since we had reunited, but apparently not. This was Evil Kat, and from the look in her eyes, and the poker in the coals, I knew the Crazy one wasn't far behind.

I was the last one out. Kat was still watching the poker. I shook my head sadly. If Dieter was lucky he would pass out from blood loss before the metal got red hot.

"She's irrational," Fajkus insisted. "I say we postpone, and find a way to do it without her."

The Exodus members were clustered under an overhang down the street from the Montalban Exchange. Roland, Svetlana, and another young Exodus operative named Phillips met us there. They'd been tailing Ibrahim to make sure their leader was safe. I scanned back and forth, but couldn't spot any eavesdroppers. We hadn't walked very far, so my good ear was still ringing from the sudden pistol shots.

"No," Roland said forcefully. "Every day we wait, more slaves die."

Svetlana spoke up. "Not only that, we're committed to the Montalbans now. If we back off, they could easily sell us out to Jihan. No. To postpone now means that we will have to fight both of them."

Ibrahim folded his arms. Ultimately the decision rested with him. "Lorenzo. You know her best. You were her lover once." He stated that fact without animosity or judgment, I was simply the best source of intelligence. "Will she fail us?"

I probably knew her as well as anyone could. I weighed my answer carefully. "Is she unstable? Yes. Will she fail you? I don't think so. She's as committed as you are, but in a different way."

Fajkus snorted. "Bullshit."

"Katarina is dangerous, but she's focused like a laser

beam. As long as she's targeted on something, she'll see it through to the end. When she's got a goal, nothing else matters and she'll risk anything to achieve it." I hoped I was right, because heaven help us if I was wrong. "She's damaged. By what, I don't know. In a way, she's like some of the slaves you've freed, only she never had someone like Dr. Bundt to help put her back together."

The Exodus members waited for their leader's decision. I had come to like each of these fanatics. Roland was an American, as was Phillips, and they were buddies. How they had ended up here was a mystery, but they were both earnest, smart, and likable young men. Svetlana was a sharp woman and, it turned out, a good friend of Ling. Fajkus was a surly bulldog of a man, but he struck me as honorable and honest.

"This isn't the only way, Ibrahim," Fajkus insisted.

There was a lot Exodus wasn't telling me. They were playing it cool, but I knew they had other plots. First off, the number of men on the choppers was a little smaller than what I estimated they had in The Crossroads, and some of the ones I'd met so far weren't part of the raid. In fact, nobody would tell me where Ling and Valentine were going either. However, you get used to that sort of thing in a business where nobody tells the whole truth.

"Fajkus, old friend. You've seen more combat than the rest of us put together, and I always value your counsel, but today I'm afraid that we must choose to associate ourselves with the lesser of two evils. If we turn back now, then Jihan will find out about our mission, and tens of thousands more will die in servitude. Not on my watch." Ibrahim nodded. "We strike tomorrow."

VALENTINE
Exodus Safe House
Crossroads City
March 24th

"We strike tomorrow," Katsumoto began his briefing. "Our operation will commence simultaneously with the main assault on Sala Jihan's fortress." The Japanese Exodus commander used a laser pointer to indicate the old Soviet fortress on a large Cyrillic topographical map that was years out of date. The map hung on a wooden board propped against the wall. Someone had written all over it in Sharpie, indicating the present-day positions of things.

Next to the map was a large screen, onto which was projected a PowerPoint presentation detailing our assault plan. A laptop sat on a small table at the front of the room, hooked to a projector. I stood off to the side with Ling. Some fifty Exodus operatives, all of whom were taking notes or listening intently, sat in metal folding chairs. Skunky was among them.

Katsumoto continued, using a wireless mouse to advance the PowerPoint presentation as he spoke. "Our first challenge lies here," he said. The laser dot fell on a cluster of buildings on the road that led to the hydroelectric plant. "This is a former Red Army checkpoint that is now being used by Jihan's forces. The road from there to the dam itself is straight, open, and uphill. If we get stalled trying to break through the checkpoint, the enemy will be able to rake us with machine-gun fire and RPGs all the way up to the dam itself. Our strategy will be to smash through this checkpoint as quickly as possible. It's about a kilometer from there to the dam. If we move quickly enough, we will be on top of the dam before its garrison knows what's happening."

Someone raised his hand. "Won't they still be able to hit us with fire on the way up?"

"Yes," Katsumoto said grimly. "Our safety lies in darkness and speed. The raid will commence after dark. To the best of our knowledge, Jihan's forces at the dam are more primitively armed and will likely have limited night-vision capabilities. We will advance up the road without using headlights. This is risky, there is no doubt, but there is no other way. We do not have any personnel to spare to try to infiltrate the checkpoint quietly."

The fifty guys we had were going up against a garrison of over a hundred at the plant itself. They were part of Sala Jihan's slave army, brainwashed conscripts, but what they lacked in training they made up for in fanaticism. If we didn't move quickly enough, the Brotherhood could be called down on us as well, and although we didn't know how many of them there were, apparently they were well trained.

I listened intently as Katsumoto described the rest of the operation. Our initial approach would be made in a small caravan of vehicles, including two old BTR-70 armored personnel carriers that Exodus had acquired in The Crossroads. These vehicles would lead the charge through the checkpoint and up the hill, followed by the unarmored trucks.

The rest of the plan was pretty straightforward. The hydroelectric plant itself wasn't that large, which simplified things. The road that led up from the checkpoint crossed over the top of the dam itself, running from west to east. On the east side, nestled against the mountains on a flat spot, was a cluster of buildings that housed the defensive garrison and part of the dam's operational crew. There was also a group of huge transformers, connected to power lines that led down into The Crossroads. There was only one way in and out of this compound, and that was across the top of the dam.

The reservoir, which was covered in ice that I assumed was thick enough to drive a truck across, was on the north side of the dam. Trying to cross the ice would be too dangerous, as there were no roads that led to the shore, and there was absolutely no cover out there. Also, the water line was about twenty feet below the top of the dam.

The south side was even less accessible. The dam was over a hundred feet tall, with no easy way to scale it. A river flowed from the south side of the dam, but there was no way for personnel to access the interior from down there.

The road across the top of the dam was the only way to access its interior. A large concrete superstructure, centered on top of the dam, contained most of the hydroelectric plant's machinery. You had to go through this building to get inside the dam itself. The actual turbines were buried deep inside, and that is where Katsumoto's team of sappers would be placing their charges. The explosives would have to be expertly placed to permanently disable the dam and compromise its integrity to such an extent that it would collapse, but not right away. That would be quite an accomplishment. Just blowing the thing up right away would have been easier, and I got the distinct impression that that is exactly what Katsumoto had wanted to do.

Our task would not be easy. We were to hold off the garrison, housed in the compound on the east side of the dam, while also holding off reinforcements from the road to the west. We were outnumbered and there was no room to maneuver on top of the narrow concrete structure.

Fortunately for us, Sala Jihan's forces would have their hands full. There would be an attack on his fortress, which would surely draw the brunt of his attention and the bulk of his forces. The Montalban Exchange's mercenaries would attack the garrison in town and create a diversion there. With any luck, the assault on the dam would be low on the enemy's priorities list.

It remained to be seen whether or not we'd have any luck.

Katsumoto surprised me by drawing the group's attention to me. "Mr. Valentine will be joining us on this operation. His reputation, of course, precedes him."

All eyes were on me. I waved sheepishly.

"Mr. Valentine, perhaps you have something to contribute? I have been told that you are a very experienced operator, after all."

Is he putting me on the spot? I looked at Ling briefly. She subtly nodded for me to speak to the group. *Fine.* I didn't know what the hell Katsumoto's problem was, but I wasn't going to be made a fool of. I smiled at the Exodus leader politely and made my way to the front of the group.

"Uh, hello," I began. "My name is Michael Valentine.

I'm not one of those guys that likes to blather on about his credentials, so I'll give you the short version just to assure everyone," I looked directly at Katsumoto, "that I know what I'm talking about.

"I began my career in the United States Air Force before moving to Vanguard Strategic Solutions International. I have seen combat in Afghanistan, Africa, the Chinese DMZ, Bosnia, Central America, and Mexico. Though, being honest, that thing in Central America was pretty uninteresting. I was also involved in the recent mess in Zubara." I left out the shootout in Nevada.

"Who are the team leaders here?" I asked. Several of the Exodus operatives in the audience raised their hands. "Okay, good. Now, how many of you have ever worked with each other before? I mean, actually were involved in a combat operation, or even a training operation, where you worked in concert?"

The team leaders slowly lowered their hands, awkwardly looking around the room.

"I don't know much about how you guys operate in the field," I said. "As was pointed out, I'm not a member of your club. But I get the distinct impression that you primarily operate in small, independent teams, and aren't always involved in direct action. Am I correct?"

Several members of my audience, now interested in what I had to say, nodded their heads.

I nodded back. "Right. Well, boys and girls, that can cause problems. You have multiple teams that will be operating in the same small area. You guys aren't used to working with each other. You may do things different ways. Communication is going to be vital here. This isn't going to be some quick-in, quick-out sneaky secret squirrel shit. We're outnumbered and in hostile territory. It's going to get ugly out there. Things will go wrong. You will take casualties.

"What you need to do, guys, is go over every detail of the plan together. Memorize the terrain as much as you can. Pass that information down to the people under your command. Each person on your team should be able to do the job of another. Everyone should know what the plan is, and what the backup plan is. At no time should anyone out there be wondering what to do. There's always something you can be doing.

"I don't mean for anyone to get discouraged. I've been in combat with Exodus before. You guys are some of the best trained, most disciplined, and most motivated troops I've ever worked with. I wouldn't be coming to this party if I thought it was a suicide mission. Give 'em hell."

With that, I smiled politely at Katsumoto, winked at Ling, and strolled confidently out of the room, even though I didn't really have anywhere to go. I just wanted to make a good exit.

Later on, needing some air to clear my head, I ventured outside into the cold. The sky was overcast, a low blanket of grey clouds blocking out the stars. The world was lit with a dull ambient amber glow from the lights of Crossroads City reflecting off of the snow and the clouds. Snowflakes lazily drifted downward from the sky, and there was no wind. It was almost pleasant. It reminded me of home, of long winters in Northern Michigan as a child.

Behind the crumbling Soviet-era warehouse was a

fenced-off lot where a couple of vehicles were parked. Armed guards quietly kept watch. A couple of barrels had fires lit in them. One had a blazing fire going in it, and was surrounded by half a dozen Exodus operatives, talking and laughing.

The other barrel was deserted, and the fire was dying. I made my way over to it and threw on a couple pieces of wood from the pile stacked neatly next to it. I pulled off my gloves and warmed my hands before shoving them in my pockets. That's when I remembered I was carrying my harmonica.

I removed the instrument from my pocket and examined it by the glow of the firelight. It was an old Hohner Super-Chromatic 12-hole that had belonged to my father. I held it in my hands and remembered him. He died when I was young. After all these years, I couldn't remember what his face looked like.

We'd spend summers at his cousin's hunting camp in the Upper Peninsula, deep in a forest at the end of a dirt road. We'd have a campfire every night, and my dad would play his harmonica and tell stories to us. Sometimes my mom would be there too, but usually she'd go inside and make dinner, since she'd heard all of my dad's stories a million times. But my little cousins and I were always riveted, no matter how many times we'd heard them.

My father would tell us stories about being in the Air Force. He'd been a navigator on a B-52. I remembered laughing as he'd talk about playing his harmonica while in flight, driving the rest of his crew crazy. He told us about the time his BUFF got hit by an Iraqi SA-2 during the First

Gulf War, and no matter how many times I heard the story, it always had me on the edge of my seat.

"I didn't know you played an instrument," Ling said, startling me. Her breath smoldered in the cold air as she stepped close to the burn barrel to warm herself.

I smiled. "I haven't played this thing in a long time. I keep it because it's the only thing I have that belonged to my father. What are you doing out here? Can't sleep either?"

Ling shook her head. "Not yet."

"Something on your mind? Talk to me, you'll feel better. Something about the plan is bothering you, isn't it?"

"The plan is good enough," Ling said. "We're making the most out of the assets we have. It's risky, but Katsumoto and I discussed it at length and I couldn't come up with any viable alternatives."

"But . . . ?"

"This entire operation is bothering me, Michael," Ling said, shoving her hands in her pockets. "Sala Jihan is a blight upon the face of the earth, there's no doubt about it. It's just . . . " she trailed off momentarily, looking around to make sure no-one else was within earshot. "It's just this whole thing seems rushed. We're trying to get more people in place, but Ibrahim won't wait."

"The longer we wait the more likely it is we'll be found out."

"I understand that. My issue is with the timing of this whole operation. We should have waited, gathered our assets more carefully, and moved from a position of strength. Now we're committed to doing this while understrength, having to rely on outsiders for support."

"Hey, *you* asked *me* to come along."

"I didn't mean you, Michael. I meant the Montalban Exchange. I don't like this deal with them. I don't like it at all. That woman, Katarina, is broken. I've seen such things before. In most cases the people were victims of the most horrific kinds of physical, emotional, and sexual abuse. I don't know what happened to that woman, but she's . . . she's . . ."

"She's fucked *up* is what she is." I hadn't met the woman but I'd heard about everything that had transpired with her.

"As you say," Ling agreed. "And there are disagreements on the execution of our own portion of the operation."

"Disagreements? About what?"

"Katsumoto wanted to destroy the dam outright and flood The Crossroads."

I raised an eyebrow. "Thousands would die if you did that. There are people here that are not involved in this. Women and children."

"That is the argument that Ibrahim made. Katsumoto insisted that it was worth the price to destroy the base of Sala Jihan's power for sure."

"Isn't that why they're going to kill Jihan?"

Ling sighed, a puff of steam forming in the air as she did so. "There are no guarantees that he will be successful."

"You guys keep talking about this asshole like he's Sauron in Siberia. Jihan is only a man, Ling. Everyone has gotten spooked by all this hocus-pocus crap he pulls. He's just a warlord with a bunch of crazy, drugged-up followers. I saw the same thing in Africa."

"Perhaps," Ling said, trailing off. "It's just that if Ibrahim fails and The Crossroads remains, then we will have accomplished nothing here."

"What do you think? Should we just blow the dam?"

"I think if Exodus had had such scorched-earth policies when they found me, I wouldn't have survived to join. Yet Sala Jihan is a far greater evil than the human traffickers I knew in China. The plan is the best compromise we could come up with. I just hope it works."

I smiled at her. "I'm glad you're opening up to me a little bit. You're one of the few people I know here. I feel like the outsider I am."

"I admit I can be . . . standoffish . . . at times," she said slowly. "Please don't take it personally. It's just . . ."

"I know how it is. I haven't been super fun to be around lately either. I damn near shot Lorenzo back on the island."

"So I heard."

"Oh, don't worry, it's fine now. I think." I laughed.

Ling smiled. "To be honest, I feel alone too. Shen and Antoine have been assigned to the main assault. They were the only members of my sword that were still with me."

I felt bad for Ling. There's a certain loneliness that comes with command. A lot is required of you to lead men into combat. "What happened to your team?" I asked hesitantly.

"It's nothing dramatic," Ling replied. "We took casualties in Mexico. I wasn't . . . am not . . . the most experienced team leader. I shouldn't have gotten a mission so important, not with Ariel's life hanging in the balance."

It all came back to that girl and her secrets again. "Don't sell yourself short. That was a bad op from the very beginning, but you accomplished your objective in the face of impossible odds. By rights, none of us should've gotten out of that hellhole alive."

"By rights, I shouldn't have been in charge there in the first place," Ling said. "But there was no choice. My team was in Mexico and there simply wasn't anyone else available. We lacked the means to get to her on our own."

"So you hired us. Decker was an ass. How were you able to convince my old boss to go along with it?" Adrian Decker had been the operations manager and CEO of Vanguard Strategic Solutions International. After the fiasco in Mexico, the UN had wanted to put him on trial at the Hague for war crimes. He got out of it, though. Decker always had a way out.

Ling raised her eyebrows. "You don't know? Michael, Adrian Decker had done work for Exodus before. Several times. We don't like to outsource work but we do build working relationships with outsiders. He was certainly receptive to our propositions."

"He was always receptive to money."

"Indeed, but he was discreet and reliable, and his personnel were the best that could be hired for any price. In any case," Ling said, "You know the rest. You were there. It all went to hell. I lost good men."

"So did we."

Ling nodded. "After that, I was given missions that weren't direct action. Support missions of different sorts. Things where a large strike team was not required. Personnel rotated in and out of my sword as necessary. Only Shen and Antoine stayed with me, by their own choice."

"Did Exodus *punish* you for Mexico? Like that was your fault! You did everything humanly possible, and don't you ever let any asshole that wasn't there tell you any different."

"That's very sweet of you, Michael, but it wasn't like that. My confidence had been shaken. *I* had been shaken, to the core. I thought of leaving the order, but Antoine talked me out of it. So I was assigned to what you might call lower stress operations until they . . . and I . . . felt I was ready. The mission to retrieve you was my first serious combat operation since Cancun."

"Well, you pulled it off like a boss," I said encouragingly. "I'm here, ain't I?"

Ling actually laughed. I was glad to make her smile. "As you say. To be honest, I find I do better at the kinds of missions I've been doing. Espionage and intelligence seem to suit me better than door-kicking, as you might put it."

"There were a lot of times, over the years when I wanted to quit," I said. "Vanguard, I mean. After every big deployment I'd swear to myself that I was done, that I was going to go back to the States and get a real job and become a respectable citizen. See how well that worked out for me. I ended up a security guard in Las Vegas. I almost left, though. A few years back I managed to get my pilot's license, and I had an in to transfer to the aviation support division of Vanguard. Flight pay was about the same as the special duty pay I got on the Switchblade teams and there was a whole lot less death."

"Why didn't you transfer, then, and become a pilot?"

I thought for a moment. "Tailor. Skunky. My teammates. Ramirez, my team leader. He was a good guy.

Despite how terrible the work was sometimes, I loved working for him. I didn't want to leave my team. Like you said, they were my family. And also . . ." I trailed off for a moment, looking up into the cloudy sky.

"I don't know how else to live," I said. "This sort of thing is familiar. Comfortable, even, in some crazy way. Standing over this burn barrel in the ass-end of Siberia feels like it makes more sense for me than working in a cubicle somewhere."

Ling put a hand on my arm. "Is that why you came here with me?" She had a worried look on her face. "I'm sorry. I shouldn't have pressured you . . ."

I didn't let her finish apologizing. "No, no, it's not like that. This feels right. I have my misgivings, but . . . I don't know. Ariel said this is where I'm supposed to be. I don't believe in fate, but I really feel like I'm supposed to be here. This sort of thing is what I was born to do. And I might actually get to do some good this time. A lot of the shit we used to do was morally ambiguous, at best. I've done things I'm not proud of. It sounds stupid, but maybe I can make up for it here. Use my skills to help people for once."

"It's why I stay on, you know," Ling said. "What we do is ugly business, but it's necessary. Please don't take this the wrong way, but I'm glad to see that you've stopped running from who you are. I saw this in you in Mexico. And when I saw you risk your life to protect Ariel, I knew that you were also a good man. Don't doubt yourself anymore, Michael."

Ling very subtly moved a little closer to me. I didn't say anything else, not wanting to ruin a perfect, quiet moment of tranquility before the storm.

Chapter 18: Lotus Blossom

LORENZO
2.7 kilometers from Sala Jihan's compound
March 25th

"Spring . . . my ass," I muttered through chattering teeth.

It was damn cold. Mind-numbing, break-your-fingers-off, shatter-your-teeth, fucking-kill-you-dead cold. There was no wind, and the night sky was brilliantly clear, displaying unbelievable billions of stars, but somehow the stillness and clarity made it even colder. All I wanted to do was huddle in my parka and pray to get on with this.

"I got here in January," Phillips replied, with that typical, abnormally-high-morale, Exodus can-do attitude. "This is *nothing*."

"Yeah. Remember when we had that big storm last month? Dude. Now that was cold," Roland radded. "We were way up the mountain trying to survey the compound with telescopes and—"

"And there was like this . . . ice tornado. It was awesome." Phillips made a twirling motion with his hands.

"Well, until Rasheed froze his toe off."

"Yeah, broke it right off."

Both of the young Americans laughed. Even though it was dark inside the ice cave, my eyes were adjusted well enough to see Anders regarding the two like they were dimwits. Shen was squatting at the cave mouth, rubbing his hands together and occasionally blowing on them to keep the circulation up, as enigmatic as ever. He had his gloves off so that he could better operate the thermal camera. Luckily it was plastic, so the odds of him freezing his skin to the machine were relatively low.

Shen had only recently arrived. His usual partner, Antoine, was not exactly built for stealth, and would be on one of the choppers. Shen hadn't fully acclimatized to the altitude yet, but he was in such good shape that it didn't seem to affect him nearly as bad as it had hit me when I had first gotten here.

The five of us were inside a rock indentation, surrounded by fat, shiny icicles. There was a faint touch of wood smoke and yak in the air, drifting up the canyon from the nearby bunch of yurts. The cluster of fur dwellings was far too small to be considered a village, but it was something, and the nomads that made it their home seemed comfortable enough through our thermal and night-vision devices.

All of us were dressed for warmth, in state-of-the-art camouflage parkas and face masks. We looked like a mottled pile of white lumps. Even our weapons had been spray painted or wrapped with white tape. But despite the fancy gear, we were still freezing. The sudden drop in temperature had been unexpected. We probably should've huddled together for warmth, but every one of us was too stubborn or proud to do that.

"Hey, Lorenzo, you know Valentine?" Phillips asked.

"Sadly . . . What about him?"

"Is it true he single-handedly fought off like a hundred soldiers in Mexico?"

Ling had said Valentine had developed a bit of a rep with Exodus. "Hell if I know. Valentine's just another asshole with mental problems and a gun."

"Oh . . ." Phillips sounded disappointed.

"He'll fit in great with Exodus. Anything yet, Shen?" I was ready to get this show on the road. Worst case scenario, the mark would decide that it was too damn cold and just stay in bed. Then we would have to abort the mission and try again next week. Shen shook his head. A mist of ice particles fell from his hood as he did so, and it hung suspended in the small window of light from the thermal cam. "Shit. He's probably not going to come."

"He'll be here," Anders stated.

"It's a little cold for romance," I replied, annoyed, but knowing that overall, Kat's plan was a pretty good one, and she had been laying the groundwork for months.

"You haven't seen this girl . . ."

"Whatever." I still had a hard time picturing one of Jihan's minor business functionaries leaving the comfort of the compound once a week for a clandestine meeting with some nomad's daughter, especially when Jihan had a bunch of slave girls available. Kat had assured me that there was more to it than that, and that the young functionary was actually in love, and had plans of running away with the girl. The functionaries weren't slaves. They were the business people that kept Jihan's finances in order while he was busy being creepy in the bottom of a missile silo.

The young businessman had met the nomad's daughter in town. It was love at first sight, and though Jihan's people were not allowed to leave the compound unescorted, this one had found a way. He had been meeting the girl once a week for the last few months. It was a forbidden love, and if Jihan found out, the young man was toast. However, once a week he risked it anyway. Of course he did. Kat had picked the girl herself, and trained her to be irresistible, a classic Juliet sting.

We were some distance from the compound, but the lights from the walls could be seen reflecting off of the mountain snow above us, giving the place a slight pink glow. The canyon we were watching led directly to the base of the fort. The climb was virtually impossible, but the mark had found a way back and forth, and tonight we intended to exploit it.

Provided he actually showed up.

Roland stirred as something buzzed inside his parka, and he had to struggle through multiple zippers to access his tac vest. There was a flicker of light as he opened the sat phone and studied the message.

"Ibrahim?" Phillips asked.

"No. My girlfriend sent me a text message." He laughed as he read it. "She's back in the States. She thinks I'm doing an internship with Toyota." He pulled off one heavy glove so he could type with his thumb. "Hang on."

Anders reached over and unceremoniously grabbed the phone. The giant pointed a massive finger at Roland's face and wagged it condescendingly, before tossing the phone back to Roland. Anders was a singularly humorless individual. Roland shoved the phone back into his coat and sulked.

Every Exodus team was a little bit different. My experience had been with Ling and her highly formal men. Zack Roland and Nathan Scott Phillips didn't really seem to fit that mold. They were attached to my group tonight because they were both supposed to be very good at this kind of infiltration mission, and they always worked together. Both of the Exodus operatives were in their mid-twenties. Roland was dark haired, and Jill said that he looked like the kid from *High School Musical*, which I hadn't seen, while Phillips was blond, stocky, and perpetually jovial.

"Hey, Shen. I thought you Exodus types were all fanatical and intense. Where'd you find these two?" I wasn't worried about being quiet, since if the mark showed up, he would glow on thermal as soon as he entered the canyon. Plus talking made me not think about the onset of hypothermia. Shen shrugged.

"Brazil," Phillips said.

"We were mission companions," Roland followed.

"Mormon missionaries."

"You know. White shirts. Ties. Name tags."

"Then we ran into some soldiers for a drug cartel. They raided an Amazon village we had been teaching in. And we weren't going to stand for that."

"I thought you guys didn't go for violence," Anders said.

"No, those are Quakers. We're awesome at violence," Phillips said.

"Yeah, we met Ibrahim when Exodus wasted those slavers. After we finished up our two years, we joined up, been on board ever since."

Both of the young men made fists, and knocked their knuckles together, scattering snow. "Heck, yeah!"

I nodded as if this made perfect sense. The Lorenzos were Mormon, and Gideon Lorenzo had been extremely devout. Bob had been a missionary himself, and had gone to Russia, or so I'd been told since that had happened after I'd run off. Exodus seemed to be made up of a bunch of religious types, Christians, Jews, Buddhists, Muslims, and Other. Ling had been wearing an Orthodox cross. I was surrounded by religious nuts. Personally, I didn't know if there was a God, but I was pretty sure there was a Devil. Me and him were old acquaintances. Anders glanced at me and shrugged. Apparently he was also a member of the Church of Moral Ambivalence and Whatever's Convenient.

"Contact." We all perked up at Shen's voice. I was glad to see that the screwing around ceased immediately. Everyone was totally still. "Individual entering the canyon. Heading toward the village."

Unable to make out anyone in the darkness, I slid forward and hunched down behind Shen's view screen. A single blob of white trudged through the hip deep snow. The man positively glowed with heat compared to the frozen black backdrop, a halo of waste heat from exertion escaping his coat and leaving a trail behind him. He was heading toward the nomad's yurts.

Well, I'll be damned. That's true love for you.

"I've got him," I stated as I slid my night vision monocular over one eye and tightened the strap around the top of my head. My head began to freeze as soon as I dropped my hood. The world turned into brilliant green pixels as the lens settled into place. I quickly cinched the hood back up. I studied the other four in the green light. They were intense and ready. "You know the plan. Proceed on my signal. Roland, contact Ibrahim and tell him we're on."

The other four nodded. The great raid had just begun.

It took me longer than expected to traverse the snowfield leading to the yurts. I had hoped to take down the mark outside the village, but the snow was deep, and I kept stepping on hard bits that immediately cracked and plunged me down to my hips. I had to be careful, as noise seemed to travel forever across the stillness. My target was not bothering to conceal his movement, and I could hear him sliding, crashing, and grunting from a hundred meters away.

I could have just shot him from here, but I wanted to talk first. He had an accomplice who lowered a rope so he could secretly reenter the compound. I wanted to find out if there was a code word or something of that nature. *Then* I could shoot him.

There was no pity for this man. He worked for a force of pure evil, and right now that force was my opposition. Even the three good men behind me—and Anders— would have no mercy on him because of who he worked for. In fact, they would have even less pity than Anders. The fact that the functionary was out here because he was being manipulated by Katarina was just too damned bad for him.

It took me too long to catch up. The snow was packed hard closer to the dwellings by constant stamping of the animals and the residents. He was now on more solid footing, and made really good time to the closest yurt. There was a flash of light as the fur door was opened briefly and a shape moved inside. The smell of spices and perfume hit a moment later.

Gliding up outside the entry, I listened, but couldn't hear anything. The fabric walls were surprisingly good at sound dampening. I waited five more minutes for him to get comfortable. There were no sounds from the other yurts, since people who work this hard to survive go to sleep early. I stuffed my night vision set back into my coat. It was handy, but that strap around the back of my head gave me a headache. Luckily there were no dogs barking an alert. Since it had been a long winter, they had probably gotten eaten. Even if the nomads knew I was here, they too were being paid by Kat not to get involved. Montalban money was also the reason they were settled at this particular point, rather than at a lower altitude where life would be a lot less miserable.

The girl didn't know when we would take the mark. Kat told her only what she needed to know, and even then probably half of the information she'd been given was false. So even if she talked too much, nothing would come back to incriminate the Exchange. She just knew that during one of these weekly meetings, somebody was going to pay her boyfriend a visit and she wasn't supposed to do anything about it, other than collect her bonus money.

Finally, tired of freezing, I decided to enter. I figured five minutes was plenty of time for the two of them to start playing Rogue Businessman and the Nomad's Daughter. It assumed that the rules to that would be similar to Heidi and the Storm Trooper. They should be plenty distracted by now. I unslung my Remington ACR, checked the Aimpoint sight, and used the attached sound suppressor to part the airlock-like fur entrance. There was one layer, a small spot of dead air, and then a second layer.

"Going in," I said into my neck microphone.

"Go," said Anders' voice in my ear.

Pausing, listening, no response, I pushed through the thick furs and into the dwelling. Slinking in low, quiet as I could be, it took a moment for my eyes to adjust to the firelight. The interior of the yurt was actually much warmer and comfier than expected. In fact, the heat differential was almost painful. The mark's fur coat was discarded on the floor. The two occupants had their backs to me, and they were speaking quietly, sitting crosslegged on blankets, staring into the fire, which was not exactly the scene I had expected.

He was maybe twenty-five, definitely Han Chinese. Anders had been right about the girl. There was no way he was going to stay away. She was beautiful, probably in her late teens. They were holding hands. Either she was as superb an actor as Katarina, all dopey and moon-eyed, or the two really were in love.

So now I needed to go beat some information out the guy, then kill him.

Some days I hate my job.

The furs absorbed any noise my boots might have made as I stalked closer. With my head tilted slightly to favor my good ear, I could hear them clearly now.

"Come away with me. Please," he said, the tone of his voice was desperate.

"I can't. My people are here, my family. Your home, so far away, as if on the other side of world." Her Cantonese was rough. He must have been tutoring her.

"We must leave soon. The Pale Man is evil. You know what he'll do to me if he finds out about us," he pleaded. I thought of the grinning skull faces propped up on stakes on the railway into The Crossroads. I'm sure the functionary had seen that kind of thing a few times.

"I know . . . He has hurt my people before, taken many of us away. But this is my home. I am afraid."

"I'll protect you. I promise," he vowed with the intensity that only the young and stupid can muster.

Judging by how badly the functionary flinched, the metal end of my Silencero sound suppressor must have been staggeringly cold against the base of his neck. "You're in no position to promise anything, kid. Don't you fucking move." My Cantonese was pretty rough too, but I think I got the point across. And to think that Jill said *I* was bad at communicating.

The girl squealed, leapt to her feet, but tripped on the blankets that she had wrapped around her legs, and fell back down. She rolled over and scrambled on her hands and knees back to the far wall of the dwelling. The functionary didn't move. He knew damn good and well what the cold metal lump resting on his spine was.

"So Jihan knows . . . " he said with resignation, the breath leaving his lungs in one long, painful sigh. Slowly, he turned so he could see me. I kept the gun on him the whole time, until he was staring at my mask. I reached back with my left hand and pulled it down. His eyes widened in surprise. "But you're not one of Jihan's men . . . who are you? Bandit! Leave her be. She has nothing. I'm the one you want. Do what you will with me, but please don't harm the girl. I can—"

I put my left hand back on my gun's vertical foregrip, then stabbed the whole gun forward, ramming him in the face hard enough to chip a couple of teeth. "Will you shut up already?" He stumbled back and raised his hands to his bloody lips. I turned my attention to the girl. She had gotten over her initial shock, and was apparently glad to see that I wasn't a scar-faced slave-soldier. "It's time."

"What?" he mumbled through his hands, glancing between me and his girlfriend. I reached into my coat, pulled out the rubber-banded stack of currency from the Montalban Exchange and tossed it to her.

She caught it in one hand, and immediately used her thumb to fan through the bills to make sure they were all large denominations. "About time," she responded. "Now my family can leave frozen shithole." She stood to leave. "Do what you have to. Tell Mrs. Katarina thanks for money."

"But . . . but . . . *Lotus Blossom*?" The functionary began to cry. "What . . . what are you doing?" He got up and stumbled toward her, pleading.

Now she was angry. "My people taken away to be slaves by your boss. You think I could love you? Stupid. I was paid to love you. You die now. Serve you right." She paused long enough to face him, look him squarely in the eye, and then kick him squarely in the balls. It was damn hard too, like she was kicking a field goal. He doubled over. "Goodbye!"

You can't really slam a fur door, but she somehow managed to. "That sucks," I said cheerfully as I shoved him to the ground. "Now let's talk."

"You're an American?" The functionary responded in English. He moaned for what seemed like forever, then started to cry. "Just kill me. I have no reason to live." His English was better than my Cantonese.

"Man, that's harsh," said the voice in my ear piece. *Phillips.*

"Just shoot him, Lorenzo. That would totally be a mercy killing." *Roland.*

"Guys, stay off the radio," I hissed. I pointed my gun at the sobbing functionary. "The rope to the compound, is there a code word?"

"Lotus Blossom!" he shrieked.

I groaned, and took a seat on the rug. This was going to make for a long evening at this rate, and I had two helicopters full of terrorists and mercenaries waiting on me. "Listen, kid, you're not the first guy to ever get taken advantage of. That's just business. I've been shafted myself a few times. What's your name?"

He took his hands off of his groin long enough to wipe the blood from his lips, and muttered "My name is Wing."

"Okay, Wing. I'm going to break this down for you. I heard what you said earlier. Sala Jihan is evil, we both know it, and as soon as he finds out that you've been sneaking out to meet that hot little nomad and compromising his security, he's going to torture you to death. So you help me out, and I'll go kill him, so you won't have to worry about it."

"You can't kill the Pale Man."

"Oh, I'm pretty sure I can. I'm good at killing stuff."

"You cannot kill what does not die," Wing insisted. "The Pale Man will destroy us all. I was a fool to betray him." Wing started to cry again. He really was afraid of Jihan. "Lotus Blossom! How could she betray me?"

"Wing. Focus. You're not helping me, buddy. If you don't tell me about how to get into the compound, I'm going to hurt you until you do. Do you understand?"

Wing curled up in a really pathetic fetal position, heartbroken and afraid, and probably nauseous from the nut kick. It was actually kind of sad. I could only imagine that if Jill were here she would probably like . . . *comfort* him, or something, and within thirty seconds he would be giving me the keys to the front gate of the compound.

"Hurry up, Lorenzo. Start cutting off his fingers already," Anders said over the radio.

"This is your last chance, Wing. You're pretty much screwed. You either help me, or I kill you. You help me, and I let you go. If I kill Jihan, you're home free. If I fail, at least you've got a head start."

"I don't deserve to live. I've been helping a monster. My Lotus Blossom can't love me because of the evil I've done."

New strategy. "Then this is your chance to atone for you sins." He looked at me, confused. "Atone, make up for, say you're sorry, fix past mistakes. You help me kill Jihan, so we can free the slaves that are her relatives, and then maybe Lotus Blossom will forgive you, and take you back." It was stupid, but from the look on his face, it seemed to work. "You'll be a hero. Come on, Wing. Do the right thing." *You idiot.*

The wheels were spinning. "Yes. I will help you. You will still fail, because I don't think you know what you're dealing with. At least I can go to her and beg forgiveness." He smiled through bloodstained teeth. "Then she'll love me again!"

"Yeah, sure. That's awesome. Code word?"

"The man who lets down the rope, his name is Tausang. He works for me. I just call to him. I pay him as soon as he pulls me up. Don't yell from the bottom, or the guards will hear you. Wave your arms with the flare in the pocket." Wing gestured at his coat. "He'll see the movement, and toss down the rope. When you're close enough to the top to whisper, call him by name. Otherwise, he'll cut the rope, and you will die on the rocks below."

I could tell he was telling the truth, the poor deluded moron.

"Now, I'm going to go and find my love. I'll beg her forgiveness!" Wing stood, a man on a mission. "I know she loves me!"

"Good luck with that."

Wing ran out the exit, not even bothering with his coat, just blundering out into the cold, to go randomly barge into the other yurts. I took off my fancy Goretex, and put on the functionary's grey fur coat. He was bigger than me, but that meant my gear could still fit beneath. My radio crackled in my ear. "You think he told you the truth?" Anders asked.

"Roger that. I'm heading for the canyon now."

"Why didn't you kill him?"

Outside, I could hear someone calling out "Lotus Blossom!" over and over, as well as a few guttural responses in a language I didn't recognize.

"I have a feeling somebody else is about to do that for us." I pulled the stolen coat tight, picked up my rifle, and ducked back into the night.

I stood at the base of the cliff and slowly waved my arms back and forth, road flare burning red in my hand, casting an unearthly glow on the surroundings. The spot I was standing in was basically a tube cut through the black rock by a long-since-disappeared glacial runoff. Now smooth ice covered the walls and hung in bizarre shapes all around, with a single slash of moonlight visible overhead. Through the gash in the ice was the slick wall that seemed to leap up for nearly a hundred feet before terminating at the back of the compound.

My rifle was stashed further down the canyon. It was too large to conceal, and the last thing I wanted was for Wing's accomplice to think something was up and cut the rope while I was halfway up. Anders and the others were coming up behind me, but had to hang back far enough in the darkness to not be spotted.

"Come on . . . Come on . . ." I whispered, ice crystals forming in my goatee as the vapor from my lungs instantly froze. I had to put away my face mask, and Wing's bulky coat was not nearly as warm as my previous garment. There had been a scarf with the coat, and I pulled it up over my face to disguise the fact that I wasn't a twenty-something Chinese man. It still smelled of perfume.

Wing had really loved the girl. This was unbelievably dangerous. All it would take to end his charade was a single slave soldier happening to patrol this area at the right time, and his whole plan would have been toast. He had done this over and over. With my luck, his accomplice, Tausang, had already bailed, and I was waving this stupid flare at some sniper up there with a Dragunov.

Finally, a thick hemp rope flailed out of the darkness and landed with a *thump* against the ice. I tossed the flare and kicked snow over it until I was back in blessed shadow. So either Tausang had seen me, or some slave soldier had a twisted sense of humor. I fashioned a basic harness around my waist, and then gave the rope a tug to indicate readiness.

The rope was pulled taut, cutting into my midsection. I put my boots against the wall, wrapped my extremely expensive neoprene shooting gloves around the rope, and waited. It would have been faster to just climb, but that would have aroused suspicion. I had no idea what Wing weighed, and hadn't even thought of the possibility until now that I would be drastically different enough for his accomplice to notice while he hauled me up. I'd left my equipment below, he was bigger than me, but I had a lot more muscle packed onto my frame, so hopefully it was close enough not to matter.

Now I was up out of the crevasse and dangling in the open moonlight. Somehow the air seemed even colder, or maybe it was just my nerves. The trembling in my hands was either from hypothermia or adrenaline, I wasn't sure. The rope creaked above, and I bounced slightly as Tausang did something with the line. He probably would hoist me up a bit, and then loop it around something so that if he lost me, I wouldn't plummet back into the rocks.

"Looking good, Lorenzo." Anders could see me. The downside was that if the guys below could, anyone looking over the wall above could too. "The choppers are airborne. They'll wait until we're secure before entering the canyon."

The pull continued. I would ascend a few feet, and then pause for about thirty seconds, and then ascend another few feet. At this rate, assuming Tausang had good cardiovascular fitness, I was only minutes from the top, and with that thought, a sudden bolt of dread traveled down my spine and lodged in the pit of my stomach. I rummaged through my vest until I found my radio, and clicked the dial over to another predetermined frequency. I really didn't have time for this, but I needed to hear her voice.

"Jill, come in."

"Lorenzo, I can hear you."

"I'm almost at the top. I'll make this quick."

"Go."

" . . . " I stopped. What was I going to say? That this was dangerous? That my odds of survival were low? That there were a million things that could go wrong up there? That if the raid failed her and Reaper needed to flee the country as fast as possible, and not look back? We had talked about all of that before.

"Lorenzo? Come in."

"I . . ." Honestly, I was selfish, weak, uncharacteristically nervous, and had just wanted to hear her voice. The words didn't come out.

"I know."

The radio was silent. I took a long, deep breath. Cold air filled my lungs and burned.

Jill's voice was authoritarian. "Now get your head back in the game. I need you to come back safe. Got it?"

"Got it. Lorenzo out." I clicked the radio back to my

team's channel. For some stupid reason, I felt better. So I relaxed and enjoyed the view.

The sheer ice wall gave way to black rock laced with fat rivulets of ice, rough enough to actually climb. The lip of the cliff was now just ten feet overhead, and I could hear the grunts of exertion as the rope jerked to another stop and was tied off. A large fur ball, no . . . a head in a hood, appeared over the top, and gazed down at me, as if waiting for something.

"Tausang," I hissed, keeping my face driven as deeply into the scarf as possible.

The shape paused, and the hood tilted slightly to one side. "Password?" he queried softly. *Oh, give me a break.*

"Tausang." I said, louder this time.

The head disappeared back over the lip, and I prepared myself for the final pull to the top.

Then I heard something. A metallic click, like a clasp of a folding knife . . .

Damn it, Wing. Then I heard the sawing. It hadn't been just addressing his accomplice by name. When I had been interrogating Wing, *'The rope to the compound, is there a code word?'* I had asked.

"Lotus blossom. Lotus blossom!" I hissed, but it was too late. The rope was severed.

Panic. The rope made a hissing noise as it shot across the rock lip, pulled by my weight. My hands shot out, scrambling for purchase, for anything. My gloves struck the black rock. My shoulders screamed as I swung like a pendulum and smashed into the mountain.

I opened my eyes. By some miracle, I was dangling by my right hand from a tiny lip of stone. A few more feet down and there would have been nothing at all to grab onto. The glove began to slip. I raised my left hand, bit down hard on the glove, tore it off, and barely had time to put my naked skin on the freezing stone and find another groove before I lost my grip. I spat the glove out and watched it tumble. Then I hurried and repeated that with the other glove, and was able to get both hands grasping tiny bits of stone, legs dangling over the abyss.

I tried to pull, every fiber of my being screaming in pain, fire and electricity scorching through my fingers as the frozen rock cut through my skin, and the outer layer of skin died from the cold. I found a deeper pocket with my left hand, and latched on tight.

The fur shape reappeared above. I was ready. Hanging by one hand, I reached into Wing's coat, and pulled my STI 9mm from the holster, the long suppressor seemingly taking forever to clear. The long tube extended, there was a single match flicker of light from the muzzle and ejection port, and a noise that sounded like closing a fat book hard.

The shape reeled back, and for a brief moment I thought that I had missed, but then he reappeared, and sailed silently over the edge. Tausang's body hurtled past me, close enough to brush the snow off my back, and disappeared into the darkness below. I didn't even hear the impact.

I struggled to shove the long pistol back into the coat, got it roughly secured, and turned my attention back to climbing. Each inch was pure pain, and the rock was jagged and sharp. Blood seeped from my palms and instantly froze into a red crystal pudding. Finally I was high enough to get my boots above the ice layer, and onto a toe hold so I could take some weight off my protesting finger tips.

"Lorenzo's down. He fell off the cliff."

"Son of a bitch. Ibrahim. Abort. Abort."

I paused, keyed my mic, and then realized I was breathing too hard to talk. I forced the words. "No . . . I'm alive. Not me . . . down there."

"What happened?" Anders demanded.

". . . cut rope . . . climbing," I grunted.

"Status?"

". . . little busy . . . right now . . ." I almost added the word asshole, but I was a little distracted.

It took me another five minutes to make it up those last few feet. There was almost nothing to hold onto. I was an experienced climber, but had never done anything like that before. I finally pulled myself up over the lip, and sprawled face first into the packed snow, my legs still hanging over the edge, but not really caring. Hell, if a slave soldier had walked up right at that moment, I would have been too spent to notice until they poked me with a bayonet to make sure I was alive.

Finally, I rolled over. The stars glared back down at me. It took me a moment to catch my breath before I got to my knees, and studied my surroundings. The lip was hidden from the rear of the compound by a few piles of stone and some discarded vehicles, their origin impossible to tell since they were covered in snow. The whole area was cloaked in darkness. The nearest light was sixty meters away in the rear of the compound. I untied the rope from around my waist and tossed it.

"I'm up. Hang on, I'll send down the rope." Tausang

had been securing the rope between two heavy stakes pounded into the ground. My hands burned and ached as I unwound it, made sure one end was still tightly secured, and then threw the remainder over the side.

"Rope is down. I'll secure the perimeter." I studied my palms as I spoke. They looked like cheese graters, practically shredded. Gloveless, my hands were freezing. This was off to a great start. You know how little kids' moms will clip their mittens onto their sleeves to keep them from losing them? Yeah, that didn't seem like such a stupid idea right about now. "And bring up my rifle."

Chapter 19: Joy Ride

✦

VALENTINE
Exodus Safe House
Crossroads City
March 25th

This is it. With all of my weapons and gear, I stepped out of the safe house, into the cold night air. My SIG 716 rifle was slung at my side, and my vest was full of magazines for it. I carried in my hands an AKMS with an under-folding stock, loaded with a seventy-five-round drum. This was to be my dump weapon, something I could lay down some fire with and discard if it got in the way.

The 6x6 trucks that formed the heart of our convoy were in the vehicle yard. They had been hastily fitted with improvised armor. Sandbags lined the beds, and thick metal plating had been affixed to the sides of the trucks. Large-caliber machine guns were bolted to the backs of two of the vehicles, positioned so they could fire over the top of the cab. Heavy 14.5mm KSVs, as near as I could tell, a machine gun nearly twice as powerful as a standard .50-caliber.

I walked up to one of the trucks and yanked open the passenger's side door. The driver, a young Exodus operative who I guessed was from The Philippines, nodded at me as I climbed in next to him. The crew cab was not armored and was vulnerable, but the heaters worked. I chose to be warm over being slightly better protected.

They offered to let me ride in one of the BTR-70s, with Skunky and Ling. These vehicles were in a different yard, being readied at the same time. I politely declined the offer without telling them why. Basically there was no way in *hell* I was going to ride in one of those claustrophobic commie deathtraps. Prudent mercenaries make it a point to avoid old Russian APCs on general principle. More to the point, being the only two armored vehicles we had, they were going to draw fire like a turd attracts flies. They weren't any faster than our trucks and weren't particularly maneuverable. The only way in and out of the troop compartment was through a small hatch on either side, just between the third and fourth wheels. I'm probably five inches taller than the Soviet conscripts those hatches were designed for. If you had to get out while the vehicle was still rolling, there was a good chance you'd get crushed under the wheels. God only knew what condition the internal fire suppression system was in, if there even was one.

So, I said no thanks. I felt better in the truck, where I could see what was going on and could unass the vehicle in a hurry if I had to. Not that that would do me any good if a hail of bullets came through the windshield, but what can you do?

There was no point in worrying about it now. We were about to start our Thunder Run through Crossroads City to the first checkpoint. We'd quickly link up with the other vehicles in town, forming the convoy, and haul balls toward the dam. We were waiting for the signal, the notification that whatever they were doing to infiltrate the compound was happening as planned. If we left too soon we'd tip our hand. If we left too late they might have time to reinforce the dam.

As I adjusted the seat belt around the bulk of my body armor, Exodus troops climbed into the back of the truck and took up positions around the bed. Equipment was loaded into the beds and strapped down. Nobody wanted to get hit in the back of the leg with a crate of grenades that wasn't secured if the truck had to stop in a hurry.

My radio, and that of the Exodus operative in the truck with me, crackled to life at the same time. I turned down the volume on mine as Ibrahim's voice came through. He was transmitting on all of our channels simultaneously, broadcasting from wherever the Montalban Exchange's helicopters were being staged out of. Our radios were encrypted, frequency-hopping types, so there was no chance anyone else could be listening in.

"Attention all elements, this is Sword One Actual. The operation will begin soon. We undertake the greatest, most daring mission Exodus has attempted in any of our lifetimes. The risk is great, the enemy is fanatical and merciless. Offer no quarter, for none will be given to you. Know that our cause is worthy! We go forth into the night, ready to wipe the scourge of Sala Jihan from the face of the Earth. And here, in this place, where the rocks and soil have been stained with

so much blood, where the very mountains have bore witness to so much suffering, we will be remembered for this. This will be our finest hour! The defining moment of our lifetimes! God be with us all." He paused for a moment. *"Commanders, conduct final pre-operation checks. Stand by for orders. Sword One Actual, out."*

While I hadn't done any long operations in the Middle East during my time with Vanguard, we did spend a couple of months training the Iraqi Army before they sent me to Central America. It was an easy gig that paid well. I learned there that Iraqi commanders loved giving big pep talks before operations, and often put more effort into their speeches than they did their actual mission planning. Ibrahim didn't fit that stereotype, of course, but the dramatic speech didn't surprise me. Exodus was an old-school organization that did things the old-school way.

The other Exodus leaders checked in. First was Fajkus. *"Sword Two acknowledges,"* he said tersely.

Next was Katsumoto, his voice imposing and serene at the same time. *"Sword Three copies."* And so it went with the others.

My driver seemed to have taken Ibrahim's words to heart. He was young, couldn't have been more than nineteen. I could see the uncertainty in his face, the fear, which he stoically tried to hide. *My God,* I thought. *Was I ever that young?* I remembered then that I wasn't as old as I felt. Only seven years had passed since I was the baby-faced tyro getting his first taste of war.

"Hey, what's your name?" I asked him.

He seemed almost startled by the question. "Paolo," he said. "Are you Valentine?"

"Call me Val. Where you from?"

"Manila."

"Are you new to Exodus?"

"I am, sir. I have only been on a sword for five months."

"Holy shit, kid," I grinned. "You picked a hell of a first op. Go big or go home, hey?"

"As you say, sir," he stammered.

"How is it you came to work with Exodus? If you don't mind my asking."

"I am an orphan, sir. I was a . . . servant . . . of a drug-trafficking gangster in the Philippines. I was not allowed to leave, until one day Exodus came and killed him. I begged them to take me with them. I didn't want to be left alone. So they accepted me. I am honored to be on this mission, and to be working with someone of your reputation."

Reputation? "What reputation? What have you heard?" I didn't mean to put the kid on the spot. We were getting ready to roll into combat and he was nervous as hell. I figured by talking him up I could get him to relax a little bit. I didn't want a wound-up driver. I was scared too, of course. You're always scared. If you're not, you're a fool. You just get used to the fear, learn to control it.

Young Paolo was new at this, though, and it showed. And he kept calling me 'sir' for some reason. "I was told . . . I mean, I heard that two years ago, in Mexico, you saved Ms. Ling's entire sword."

"Uh-huh. And how did they say I did that?"

"S-sir, I mean no disrespect. I only know . . . I mean, I am only telling you what I heard from my friends."

"Yeah, I know," I said, raising my eyebrows bemusedly. "Please, tell me what you heard." I wanted to keep him talking, keep him focused on something besides our impending mission. The worst part of combat isn't the actual fight. It's before the fight, when you're waiting to go. Even a short wait is agonizingly slow when you're amped up. It drives you crazy, makes you impatient, and causes bad decisions.

Paolo shifted nervously in his seat. "Is it true that you carried Ms. Ling out of the wreckage of a crashed helicopter?"

Hoo boy.

LORENZO
Sala Jihan's Fortress
March 25th

I watched the closest guards through my night vision monocular. Kneeling, I slid around the rear of the derelict truck and tracked the two of them as they rounded the corner. Luckily the back of the compound was where the Soviets had dumped their unrepairable vehicles. There were plenty of places to hide. I was now about fifty meters from the crumbled concrete that had been the rear wall of the fort. There were soldiers positioned on top of the wall, but they were mostly huddled together for warmth on the corners in their machine-gun emplacements. I had seen at least four individuals walking back and forth near the hole in the wall. I knew that we had to make it through that gap to reach the ZSU.

There was a small noise as Anders approached. The

former SEAL moved like a ghost. He was not even breathing hard from scaling the rope, and he was a big dude. He looked like some Viking cyborg with his bristly beard sticking out from under his PVS-15 night vision goggles. He squatted behind me and waited. Shen joined us a moment later. The quiet Exodus operative passed me my rifle. It was so cold it burned my hands as I got the single-point sling over my head and one arm. Phillips and Roland took up a position on each end of a frost-coated APC five meters behind us.

Turning back to the others, I held up my hand, two fingers down in a wagging motion, then four fingers up, then pointed at the gap. *Four infantry patrolling.* Then I made the universal sign for gun, and indicated both machine-gun emplacements that I had spied on the wall, then two fingers, for two men at each position. Then to Roland, I pointed at my eyes, then at the left emplacement, then the right for Phillips. Both men had suppressed Micro Tavors, and if anybody started for those machine guns, they needed to pop them fast. If it came to that, there would be enough noise that the mission was hosed. I looked at Shen and made a throat-cutting motion, then jerked my thumb at the sentries. Shen nodded.

After all of that abbreviated sign language, Anders extended his middle finger to me. And to think that I had said he was humorless.

I took point, leaving bloody handprints in the snow behind me as I crawled to the next truck, axle long since broken and left out here to rot. Anders and Shen were right behind me.

We were all armed with suppressed weapons. Everyone

had one magazine of 5.56 75-grain subsonic loaded, but even then, the action of the weapon could be heard some distance away, especially on a night this quiet, and subsonic 5.56 frankly sucked at putting people down quickly, being basically a glorified .22. My other 30-round magazines were loaded with standard-velocity Hornady TAP, which through the short barrel of my gun and Silencerco suppressor sounded like a regular .22 long rifle, but at 2700 feet per second tended to leave softball sized exit wounds.

My secondary weapon was my STI Tactical 4.15 9mm, also with a can on it. The 147-grain hollowpoint loads were subsonic and relatively quiet, as Tausang had already experienced. Then I had my knives, because though a suppressor was quiet, these were quieter when used correctly. I was traveling relatively light tonight, as my mission depended on stealth rather than slugging it out. That job belonged to the guys in the choppers. All I had was a plate carrier and a battle belt with a few pouches for magazines.

We waited long enough to get a general idea of the guards' patterns, but *pattern* was a misnomer. Tonight it consisted of trying to stay warm. There was a steel drum with fire licking out of it just inside the gap. Two guards would stand next to the drum to warm up, while the other two would patrol outside the compound wall for a few minutes, before trading off. This worked to our advantage, since the fire ruined their night vision.

I positioned my single point sling so that my rifle was slung behind my back, and pulled my fixed-blade Greco. Shen drew a long, thin blade, nodded once, and glided to the side. Anders raised his HK 416 and covered us.

My pulse was beating in my ear, and strangely enough, I was no longer cold. I leaned back into the shadow of the rusted vehicle. I could hear the crunching of snow beneath boots as the guards approached. They stopped only a few feet away, glancing side to side, their scarred faces visible in my night vision. I exhaled slowly through my nose, hoping to not cause a steam cloud. My lacerated hands were leaving a red skin paste in the textured handle of my knife. The two guards, arms folded, weapons slung, hands constantly rubbing together for circulation, took one last look at the graveyard of discarded vehicles. They turned and began to move back to the small circle of firelight and warmth.

Shen and I were on them in a flash. I couldn't watch my teammate as he came around the other side of the truck. I had to concentrate on my own responsibility, and trust in the Exodus operative's skill. I clamped my hand over the guard's mouth and jerked his head to the side. I rammed my knife into the base of his skull, twisted it violently, and yanked it out. Spinal cord severed, he fell, instantly lifeless. I hugged him tightly and dragged him back to the side of the truck. I could feel hot, sticky blood flowing down my arms.

I looked up. Shen and the other guard were gone. There was only a splatter of blood and some disturbed snow. He was good. I wiped my blade on the guard's arm and put it away. I tried not to notice that the slave soldier was probably barely old enough to drive in my home country.

Shen materialized at my side. He patted me on the shoulder, then bent down and gently closed the slave's staring eyes. He whispered something, not to me, but rather to the dead man. I unslung my rifle and raised it to cover our next move.

Anders was now moving forward, through the gap created by us. The last two soldiers were standing around the burning barrel, hands extended, leather gloves hardening just outside the plume of smoke. They were looking right at Anders as he approached, rifle muzzle down in his left hand. The big man's head was lowered, as he slouched forward, appearing shorter than he really was. The guards looked up, their eyes adjusted to the licking flames, just seeing a black mass approaching.

Anders raised the little Ruger MKII and put two rounds into each of the guards' craniums. *Tick-Tick* . . . *Tick-Tick* . . . . The low mass of the action and tiny, low pressure round made it so that the integrally suppressed .22 was literally about as loud as a staple gun, but both soldiers went right down. The big man paused just outside the circle of light. *Tick . . . Tick.* He put one more into each man, just to make sure. Anders shoved the .22 back into his armor, then stepped forward, grabbed one guard by an outflung arm, the other by his boot, and effortlessly dragged them both back into the dark.

Shen and I sprinted through the gap, snow flashing around our ankles as we leapt through the broken slabs of concrete and bent rebar. We slowed to a walk as we approached the burning drum, the knowledge of what we had to do unspoken, born of years of experience. We stopped next to the fire, hands extended for warmth, as if we were the fallen guards. To anyone further inside the compound, watching this area, the two guards had only disappeared for a moment, and now there were two more black blobs clustered around the light, just like before. I scanned across the compound, but saw no other movement. The fire felt good.

There was more motion and a whisper of noise behind us as Phillips and Roland moved through the gap. I nodded my head toward the steel ladder leading to the top of the wall. There were still two machine guns mounted up there. Anders and the young Exodus operatives knew what to do. I made a motion toward the right, and Shen turned that direction, back to the fire, so he could watch that position. I watched the emplacement on the left.

"Psstt . . . Lorenzo," Shen whispered.

"Yeah." My eyes never left the two hunched shapes on the wall. There was an angular black thing mounted on a pintle up there, probably a 12.7mm DhSK heavy machine gun, and if those guards gave any indication that they had seen Anders, Roland, or Phillips, I was going to light them up with my ACR. Something thumped into my shoulder, and sat there, a slightly damp weight. I reached up and grabbed it. They were thin wool gloves.

"You looked like you needed them more than the soldier I removed them from," Shen said simply.

"Thanks." I pulled the gloves on and flexed my fingers. At least they had finally gone numb.

"Target spotted," Shen said, both to my side and in my ear, as he had keyed the radio. "Two hundred meters to the north."

Sure enough, there it was. The antiaircraft vehicle was a brutish, squat thing, sitting on top of a small hill. The only reason Shen had seen it was from the twirling motion of its radar, constantly spinning, seeking targets for its huge guns.

"That's no ZSU." Anders' voice was a whisper on the radio. I could see his shape halfway up the ladder to the top of the wall. *"That's a Tunguska."*

I looked at the shape through my night vision. It looked a lot bigger than it had before. "That's a different one. The one I saw had four guns. This one's taller and has two guns."

"And missiles," Anders said. *"Plan's changed. We've got two antiaircraft systems in the compound."*

The vehicle I had seen when I had toured the compound had been closer to Jihan's silo. This second vehicle was a bad complication. So much for good intel. "We're going to need more time."

Shen fiddled with his radio. "Ibrahim's not responding."

The choppers had already entered the canyon. They would be here in less than twenty minutes. As we spoke, the choppers were tearing along just above the tree tops, navigating a narrow pass. Our radios were not powerful enough to reach them with mountains in the way.

"Take out those machine guns. Fast," I ordered. Then I flipped my radio to Jill and Reaper's channel. "Jill, come in."

"Go."

"Unexpected problem. There are multiple antiair vehicles. We can't reach Ibrahim. Try to reach him. Tell him we need more time. Over."

"On it."

I flipped back to my team. Hopefully Jill could reach

Ibrahim, otherwise those choppers were going to fly right into a stream of giant tracers. I returned my attention to the emplacement. A third shadow was stalking up to the men on the gun, then the shadow went low, below the railing. I bit my lip, ready to open fire. There was some motion, a small bit of noise, and one of the shapes flipped over the wall and plummeted to the ground outside the compound. The second guard started to rise, then appeared to get a whole lot shorter as his head flopped to the side, mostly severed from his neck. A noise like someone chopping firewood hit my ear just a moment later.

I glanced around. There were no other guards close enough to have heard the noise.

"This is Phillips. Southern position secure," he panted.

A moment later, Shen stiffened up as he took aim at the northern point. Then he relaxed and lowered his weapon.

"This is Roland. North secure."

"I was faster," Phillips replied.

"Yeah, but listen to you. I heard you from here."

"Whatever, dude."

"Guys, on my signal, use those machine guns. Kill everything that isn't us. Anders, Shen, on me. We have to reach those tanks. Now."

I checked my watch. We were almost out of time. I made a spinning motion with my finger in the air and gestured toward the Tunguska. Move out.

The next few minutes were a blur. The three of us kept to the shadows under the wall. We would move quickly, sprint to the next piece of cover, scan for threats, and then move again. I spotted guards, but all of them were moving in directions away from us. We had also seen no sign of dogs, which was lucky, as they would have sensed us long ago, but Katarina's intel had indicated that Jihan hated dogs for some reason.

We reached the rear of one of the concrete bunkers, Number Five when it had been a Styrofoam block on Kat's table. There was a ten-foot alley separating the wall of the compound from the back wall of the bunker. There was a single steel door on that back wall, and Shen and I crouched down as we passed it, since there was light coming through a glass slit at eye-level through the door. Anders stayed back, covering the way that we had come from.

I peeked around the corner. We were now only twenty meters from the Tunguska. It was straight up a small snow-covered hill. I could see a few men milling around outside the beast, and could hear the diesel engines running from here. *Good.* The noise would mask our approach.

What the hell, the noise should be enough to mask suppressed gunfire as well. I scanned the Tunguska through my night vision. A thing like that should have at least four people manning it, but I only saw two on the outside. The other two were probably sitting inside, actually running the radar and the guns. I signaled for Shen to approach the tank, and if either of the guards noticed him, I would shoot them.

Shen nodded once, and pulled that same long knife. Hopefully from the Tunguska's vantage point, we could spot the ZSU.

CREAK.

The metal door to the bunker opened slowly. Shen pushed himself back against the wall, knife blade held flat against his chest, the door shielding him from view. A squat figure stepped into the alley, pulling round goggles down over his masked face, an AK47 slung over one shoulder.

A Brother!

He stepped into the snow, goggled head swinging in my direction, the door closing automatically behind him. Shen was up in an instant, the knife a pixilated blur through my goggles.

The Brother sensed him somehow, and impossibly, at the last possible instant moved fast enough that I thought my night vision had malfunctioned. The Brother ducked and sidestepped, Shen's knife flying through the space where his throat had been a second before. At the same time, the Brother's palm struck Shen's chest. The Exodus operative flew back, colliding brutally with the wall.

I turned, my finger already flying to the trigger of my rifle as the Brother stepped toward me, his body uncoiling like a spring, but then the rifle was knocked out of my numb hands, snow from his boot struck me in the face. The son of a bitch had kicked the gun out of my hands. Then he kicked me. *Hard.*

The concrete impacted my back with a great deal of force. My night-vision device went flying into the distance. I went for my pistol, but with the suppressor mounted, I had to carry it in a shoulder holster. Slow to draw, too slow. As I reached across my body, the Brother's leather glove clamped onto my wrist. I jerked my knee into him, but it swept through nothing but empty furs. I locked my left hand onto arm, and tried to leverage him into an arm bar.

He was impossibly strong. Those blank goggles stared into my face and he didn't make a sound.

Shen was back up. I saw him rising behind the Brother's back. Shen latched onto the Brother's slung AK with his hands, pulling back while he kicked his boot into the back of the Brother's knees, a move sure to take the little man down.

The brother grunted at the impact, but didn't drop. He threw a backhand that hit Shen like a sledgehammer. The Exodus operative and the AK went down.

I struck out with my left. He took the blow to the face and barely budged. He swung me back into the wall. I shook loose, the STI coming out of the holster. He smashed me in the elbow, *CHUFF,* and I fired my pistol uselessly into the snow at his side. Now somehow he was holding onto my gun, and bending it back into my stomach.

TickTickTickTickTick.

The Brother turned toward the source of the impacts. Anders was striding forward, the little Hush Puppy extended in one hand. The bolt locked back empty, and Anders dropped the spent magazine. The Brother was still locked onto me, and he spun me, like a discus thrower, and launched me into Anders. We collided, both of us slipping in the snow.

I sprang to my feet. My pistol was in the snow somewhere, so I pulled my knife. The Brother was standing in the center of the alley, in a wide stance like some old-west gunfighter. He put one hand to his side, then slowly raised it, studying his own blood. Anders had hit him several times, but .22s suck. His black mask cocked to the side, incredulously, and then looked back at us. Anders grunted as he got to his feet.

Anders raised his carbine, but the diesel noise died with a cough. They had shut down the Tunguska. There was some yelling from the top of the hill. They probably just ran it long enough to charge up the batteries for the radar. Our opportunity for gunfire had passed.

Shen pulled himself off the ground, the Brother's AK in his hands. He looked at it in frustration, knowing it was too loud. He dropped the mag and racked the charging handle back to eject the chambered round. Shen was prepared to use the rifle as a club. Anders and I were on one side of the alley, the wounded Brother in the middle, Shen between him and the Tunguska crew. I don't know why the Brother didn't shout for help. He had already soaked up several .22 rounds, but he didn't make a sound. Anders stepped past me, a SOG knife held low at his side.

The Brother waited for him, his head swiveling slightly to keep all three of us in view. The goggles were cold and almost insectile. Anders moved first, charging forward, the knife coming up in an eviscerating arc, but the Brother was faster. The knife cut through a layer of wolf pelt and cut the cord of a bear tooth necklace, but no flesh. Then the Brother hit Anders, once, twice, three times, before the big man was sliding through the snow on his face.

Shen clubbed the Brother in the back, and having been clubbed by Shen myself, I knew that the man knew how to put some juice into it. The Brother stumbled, but mule kicked Shen in the ribs. I leapt over Anders, my knife leading the way, and drove my blade into the Brother's side. He jerked away, but I knew that I had scored a hit. Then a black clad fist slammed into my jaw and sent me sprawling.

All four of us were up again, the Brother still in the middle, hands up and open in front of him, his back to the compound wall. He still hadn't made a sound, but now I could hear him breathing, the leather of his mask bulging slightly as he exhaled. My knife was dripping.

Then it was on. All three of us closed on him at the same time. We were all experienced fighters and the Brother had to be losing a lot of blood. It should have been over in an instant.

It wasn't.

It was a flurry of motion and flying frost, yet it was eerily quiet. Shen smashed the AK into the Brother's raised arm. The stock broke off and flipped past my head. Anders and I both waded in, blades singing, but somehow the Brother stayed ahead of them. He danced through the steel, forearms and elbows colliding with ours with bone-jarring force. Shen hit him with the rifle again, hard enough to bend the barrel. The Brother moved like part of the shadows, disregarding the impact, and the next part was confusing because he had kicked me in the side of the head, but somehow Shen was upside down, in the air, then corkscrewed violently into the ground.

Anders finally scored a hit, driving his knife through the Brother's wrist, the blade erupting out the other side, blood spraying everywhere.

Without a tourniquet, that was a fatal hit.

The Brother jerked the knife away, slammed Anders in the throat, sending him sprawling, and pulled the knife out with his other hand. I could hear it grind through the bones of his wrist.

"Shit. Now he's got a knife," I muttered as I got back to my feet. The Brother closed on me. Anders' blade aimed at my heart. I readied myself, but I knew that he was too fast.

THUD.

The Brother stopped, the hilt of another knife sticking out of his back. Shen had apparently found his and hurled it down the alley. The Brother stumbled slightly, then stabbed toward me. I dodged aside, his knife striking sparks off the steel door behind me. I kicked him in the knee, them slashed my knife across his stomach, driving it in deep. He rolled into me, both of us locked together, churning down the wall, the unkillable Brother leaving a trail of fluids.

The clock was ticking.

Not fast enough. The point of the knife was inches from my eye. Somehow I had grabbed his good wrist, and muscles straining, was holding it back. I stabbed my blade into his chest, levering it around his ribs, slicing toward his heart and lungs. But still he fought, the knife descended slowly as he overpowered me. I could see my reflection in his goggles.

CHUFF.

The Brother's head snapped forward violently, colliding with mine in a spray of warmth. His head rolled back limply, and one goggle instantly pooled with blood that then came leaking out the sides. I shoved him back, and he collapsed silently into the powder, his brains leaking out the back of his head into the snow.

Anders was holding my 9mm.

I stumbled back over to the corner and peered around. If the guards had heard that noise, we were screwed. It was dark, but the reflection from the snow was giving the surroundings a faint, almost pink glow. I had no idea where my night vision had landed. There were a few lights around the Tunguska, and I could see shapes moving. Someone was running a hose into the beast. That's why they had shut it down. They were refueling.

There was movement at my side as Shen stumbled forward. He still had his night vision. He scanned back and forth, and gave me a thumbs-up sign. We were okay. I checked my watch again. The choppers would be arriving soon.

"*What's the holdup?*" Roland asked over the radio. "*We've got guards headed our way. I think it's the shift change.*"

I secured my rifle. "We ran into a Brother."

"*Ooohhh,*" he whistled. "*Is everybody alive?*"

"Barely," Shen grunted.

"Guys, pop those guards if you have to. Wait as long as possible though. Anders. Let's go . . ." There was no response. "Anders?" I turned around. The big man was kneeling next to the still twitching Brother and had pulled back his mask and goggles. It was too dark for me to see what he was looking at. The Majestic man stood, dusted the snow off his knees, and joined us. He handed me my pistol.

"What?" I asked as I secured my gun.

"Nothing . . ." He shook his head. "I just had to see if the stories were true."

"What stories?"

"Sala Jihan cuts their tongues out. Okay. Let's do this."

We hit the Tunguska crew hard just as they had finished refueling and turned the engine back on. I took down the man standing at the pump, jerking back his head and plunging my Greco down over his sternum and through his aorta. The other guard looked up in surprise, his mouth forming a perfect O, but he didn't have time to make a sound before Shen's arm encircled his neck. The two of them slunk down on the other side of the Tunguska and disappeared.

Anders bounded past us, clambered on top of the armored vehicle, ducked under the spinning radar dish, and was on top of the turret in a flash. Luckily the hatch wasn't locked. He pulled it back, reached inside, grabbed the man sitting in the commander's seat by the hair and pulled him out. This one did have time to shout, and you would too if a baseball-mitt sized hand suddenly hoisted you out of a tank, but Anders tossed him over to Shen's side, where I heard a hacking noise, and the screaming stopped.

We were past the point of stealth. We had to take these guns out *now*. The choppers were probably already leaving the canyon. I could only pray that Jill had been able to reach Ibrahim. I walked around the front of the Tunguska, to the driver's compartment. He must have seen what happened to his associates, as his head popped down before I could play Whack-a-Mole, and the steel hatch came down, but it landed on the rail system of my rifle. I levered the rear of the gun up, and fired three rounds into the driver's body.

I threw back the hatch, aimed, and fired one more round into the man's face. By this point I was soaked with blood, but didn't have time to care. "Tunguska down," I said into the radio.

"*Guards are almost on us,*" Phillips hissed.

"Shen, Anders, look for that ZSU!" I spat. They both still had night vision, and their odds of seeing it were far better than mine. A light came on in a nearby bunker. Somebody had heard the Tunguska crew's cries. I took cover behind the front of the tank, and braced my rifle.

"Northwest. Four hundred meters," Shen said. I glanced in that direction, but couldn't make it out in the darkness. I would have to take his word for it. "Near the missile silo."

"We'll never make it in time," Anders stated. "We need to get out of here."

The bunker door opened, and a slave soldier stepped into the night air, an SKS in his arms. I shot him three times. The feeble subsonic loads barely made a sound, but they didn't have much hitting power. The soldier looked down at his chest for a long moment, before stumbling back into the bunker. Five seconds later an alarm began to sound.

"Screw that. Anders, can we run this thing?"

"Hell if I know."

"I drove an armored vehicle once," Shen said.

"Let's do it!" I grabbed the dead driver by the shirt and hauled him up and out of the hatch. "Inside!" Shen vaulted into the driver's seat. I crawled on top, and followed Anders into the top hatch.

It was cramped. There were red lights and buttons everywhere. I flopped into a seat. Anders was smashed into a seat behind me. There was a popping noise that I didn't recognize at first, but then I realized that it was small-arms fire bouncing off of the turret.

There were controls in front of me, a darkened screen, flashing LEDs, and a joystick like off of a 1980s-era arcade game. "How do we make it shoot?"

Anders didn't answer. He was scanning across the Cyrillic labels, his mouth moving as he tried to read them. He had pushed his goggles up on his forehead, and it was obvious that reading Russian wasn't one of his primary skills.

I pulled a small flashlight from inside my coat, turned it on, and started going over the controls. "What, they didn't teach you that in Navy SEAL school?"

"It never came up. There!" He did something, and the screens lit up. Behind him was a larger screen, obviously a display for the radar dish. Two bright green blips had just appeared on it. At the same time, Shen must have been playing with the controls, as the giant beast lurched painfully forward, slamming us all into various pointy bits inside before rocking to a stop.

I grabbed the joystick. It was articulated to only move in four directions. Through the screen, I could see the darkened shape of the compounds walls. My best guesstimate was that we were about thirty degrees off of where the ZSU was parked. I pushed on the stick, and the turret rotated, surprisingly smoothly and way too fast. I had to hit the stick the other way to move it back.

"I can't see it!" I shouted, which was totally unnecessary considering we were inside a steel tub together. The small-arms fire had stopped, which meant that the soldiers were now going to do something effective, like set us on fire, or bust out some RPGs. Anders popped out the top of the hatch and started firing his 416.

The screen was mostly dark shapes. This vehicle was pretty advanced, so it probably had some sort of IR floodlight or something, but I had no idea where the controls were. It probably tracked aircraft automatically, as there was no way a human being could track a jet fast enough with this joystick to shoot it down.

There had to be a way. This thing was Russian. Everything they built was made to be run by third world, illiterate goat herders. I cursed under my breath as I read the labels. Too bad Reaper wasn't here. He had probably played a video game where he had driven one of these at some point.

"If you're gonna do something, do it fast!" Anders shouted. Then there was an explosion, and he shouted and fell back down into the hatch. "RPG!" Then he was back out the top, firing wildly.

Then the fates smiled at me. The ZSU must have picked up the incoming choppers, because suddenly there was movement, and headlights, actual headlights, came on, two brilliant white beacons, just on the left side of my monitor. I thumped the stick, so that I was now even with the two lights, then thumped the control down to lower the cannons. There was a illuminated circle on the screen, and I filled it with the black shape that had to be the ZSU. I mashed the trigger.

Nothing happened. *Damn it.* I looked at the stick. There were buttons on the side of it. I pushed one of the buttons, and then mashed the trigger again.

The roar was unbelievable. It sounded kind of like an air wrench removing rusted lug nuts from an old wheel, only magnified a hundred billion times, and reverberating through a steel shell until it vibrated your fillings out of your teeth. The twin 30mm cannons fired explosive shells at a rate that had to be around 4,000 rounds a minute. I had only depressed the trigger for a second, but a line of tracers longer than a football field stretched across the compound. The ZSU exploded in a brilliant cloud of flame and sparks like Thor had gotten pissed off and personally came down from Valhalla and whacked it with his hammer.

"Holy shit!" I shouted. "Drive, Shen! Drive! Back the way we came." There was infantry running around now, and with Phillips and Roland on those machine guns, maybe they could keep them off of our back.

The Tunguska lurched forward with a grinding noise. Anders dropped back down inside, his hands shaking, pulling another magazine from his vest and slamming it into his gun. "When it shoots, it blows fire out the side for like twenty feet!" Then he bounced back up, and kept shooting at random people.

With the sounding of the alarm, every light in the compound was blazing, which helped me see a whole lot better. There were soldiers scurrying everywhere, and I could make out other machine-gun emplacements along the walls. Apparently they hadn't gotten the word yet to rip the Tunguska to shreds. *What the hell?* I had a giant tank, I might as well have some fun.

I jerked the stick, stuck the emplacement in the center of the glowing circle, and mashed the trigger. The jackhammer noise gave me permanent brain damage, but when the thing stopped vibrating, the machine gun, the gunners, and fifteen feet of wall was gone. I glanced back to the radar screen. The two green helicopter blips were right on top of us.

Shen drove the Tunguska like a madman. I was stunned how fast this thing moved under the roar of a twelve-cylinder turbo diesel. I kept sticking various valuable-looking things into the glowing circle and blowing them to bits. Anders popped down and screamed, "Left! Left! LEFT!"

Shen cranked it hard, and the Tunguska spun like only a tracked vehicle can. Something heavy hit us, and sparks flew through the compartment. "Heavy machine gun!" Anders shouted, pulling me by the shoulder, apparently in the direction he wanted me to shoot. There were specks on the view screen, coming from the top of a bunker. *No*. Not sparkles. Muzzle flashes. I mashed the trigger and ripped the concrete roof off the bunker entirely.

"Out!" Anders shouted. He jerked his thumb, and when I twisted to look, I saw fire. We were on fire, lots of fire, and there were missiles sitting on this thing.

"Shen! *Run!*" Anders was already out the hatch and gone by the time I levered myself out after him, and leapt off the top of the still rolling tank. I hit the ground, rolling over as I lost momentum, then sprang to my feet, and sprinted as fast as I could away from the burning hulk. I had no idea where we were and I had no idea if Shen had made it out, but I knew that if I stopped to look, then the damn thing was going to explode.

It did, but thankfully not before I made it around the corner of another bunker. Fire and noise billowed around behind me as the Tunguska's missiles cooked off. Without even thinking about it, I was on my face with my hands covering my head.

Boots stopped in front of my face. I jerked up, raising my rifle. Shen batted it aside. "Let's go."

"You *are* Jet Li," I said in awe. Anders joined us a second later, shoving yet another magazine into his carbine. Heat mirage was rising off of his suppressor. A giant black monster screamed overhead, causing the rising smoke of the burning Tunguska to form pinwheel vortices. The choppers were here, and judging from the volume of tracers flying down from their doors, they were entering a target-rich environment. They tore past, heading for the landing area near the missile silo.

"Roland. Phillips. Report." I shouted.

"*Shooting lots of people!*" One of them shouted over the drum of a heavy machine gun.

"*Bad people!*" said the other.

It took me a moment to get my bearings, but then I tracked in on the noise and the stream of tracers flying from the rear of the compound. A soldier came running around the corner. Shen and Anders dropped him with a volley of quick shots. "Okay, we'll rendezvous at the gap. Don't shoot us."

I could still hear the scream of the choppers' giant engines, and there was a whole lot of gunfire coming from that direction. The compound had devolved into a state of primal chaos. Anders took point, firing as more soldiers appeared ahead of us. Shen had gotten us back nearly to our entrance point, and it only took a few frantic minutes of leapfrogging from wall to wall to near the gap. The alarm was blaring from sirens located on the tops of the bunkers. Random soldiers, slaves, and functionaries were exiting the buildings. We shot anybody that was armed or that looked at us funny.

"Belt-fed's empty! Moving to Roland's position," Phillips warned us. Now only one big gun was blazing at this end of the compound. We had to hurry.

The thrumming beat of the last heavy machine gun was near. We approached the final corner, almost back to the junkyard. A group of half a dozen soldiers were ahead of us, crouched behind a broken concrete pillar. They were trying to sneak up close on Roland's emplacement so they could overwhelm it with rifle fire and grenades. Just beyond the bad guys was a pillar of sparks and flames as Roland worked over anything that moved with absurdly powerful bullets.

"Roland, you've got a bunch of rubble fifteen meters in front of you. You've got soldiers hiding behind it. You might want to do something about that," I suggested.

"On it."

A split second later, the lance of fire shifted to the concrete debris. The giant 12.7 rounds zipped right through the soldiers' cover, blasting shrapnel everywhere, sending up giant gouts of snow, dirt, blood, and meat. There was a secondary explosion as one of the soldiers dropped a live grenade. Anders stepped around the corner and fired a few rounds, just to make sure all of the targets were down.

"Cease fire, cease fire. Get off that wall." The two Exodus men were sitting ducks if they stayed up there any longer. We needed to get the hell out of here and meet up with the rest of Exodus by the choppers. "We're at the corner of building . . . six."

"Okay. Cover us."

The three of us spread out, scanning for threats. I was missing my night vision, but every light in the compound was on now. I took the chance to switch out my pathetic subsonic magazine for something better. There was a veritable storm of gunfire coming from the helicopters' landing spot, and it sounded like a lot more fire than what should have been coming from the expected number of enemy troops. In fact, it sounded like this compound was hell of a lot better manned than we thought.

I flipped my radio to another setting. "Reaper, where are my eyes?"

"Little Bird will be on station in two minutes," he responded hastily. Our little UAV had to stay circling in the canyon until the radar had gone down, only it wasn't nearly as fast as the choppers. *"I'll be feeding to you and Ibrahim."*

"Okay, switching to the command channel." There were so many separate strike teams operating at one time that Exodus was using a bunch of encrypted frequencies to keep from crowding each other. "Come in Ibrahim. This is Lorenzo."

The radio picked up to a live line, but there was a pause as somebody on the other end hammered something with what sounded like short barreled .308. *"This is Sword One Actual. Status?"*

"My team's okay. We're on the rear wall."

"You did well to destroy not only one, but two of those AA guns, my friend."

"Yeah, how about next time we know that there are two first?"

Ibrahim laughed heartily. Even in the middle of a gun battle, the man was chipper. Friggin' Exodus. *"Yes. Your friend, Mr. Reaper, was able to relay to us your message. As soon as he saw the radar go offline, he gave us the signal."*

"How's it going over there?"

"If you would like to come and lend some assistance, it would be much appreciated. There seems to be no end to how many men Jihan has. Once we secure the LZ, we can destroy the Pale Man once and for all." There was more gunfire. *"I must be going now."*

The plan was for Exodus to control that one portion of the compound long enough to take control of the silo. With Jihan dead, it was believed that his troops would collapse. None of us wanted to have to clear every one of these bunkers. Personally I just wanted to get into that prison, find Bob, and get the hell out of here.

Roland and Phillips came sprinting in behind me. Neither one appeared to have any bullet holes in them. "Head for the LZ!" I ordered.

Chapter 20: False Gods

✠

VALENTINE
Crossroads City
March 25th

"You should put your earplugs in," I told Paolo. The Ural truck rattled and crashed down a potholed road at a high rate of speed, bucking and jarring all the while. Everything I saw was illuminated in green through my night vision goggles.

"Why?" he asked. To my eyes he appeared slightly blurry; the focus on my NVGs was set for a longer distance.

I pointed to the roof of the truck's cab. "When that big-assed gun opens up, it's going to be really loud." The Ural 6x6 truck we were riding in had a KPV 14.5mm heavy machine gun mounted in the back, behind an armored gun shield. When the gun was pointed forward, its muzzle was right over the cab. "Seriously," I continued, "It'll be louder than hell and if it gets ugly up there I'm going to be firing right out the window. Either put your ears in now or have tinnitus for the rest of your life."

Paolo shakily nodded his head and, while driving with one hand, put rubber earplugs in one at a time. I had on electronic earphones that protected my hearing and kept my ears warm.

Katsumoto's calm voice broadcast over our radios. *"This is Sword Three Actual. We are about to engage the enemy. Prep for combat."* On cue, the BTRs in front of us sped up. Where we'd been traveling in a column, the rear vehicle pulled up alongside the lead. Both APCs had an armored turret with a 14.5mm KPVT machine gun and a coaxial 7.62mm PTK machine gun. The two surplus Soviet vehicles formed a wall of armor and firepower for the rest of the convoy.

Young Paolo steeled himself and gripped the steering wheel so hard it was a wonder he could still turn it. My own heart sped up as the truck accelerated. Adrenaline hit my system in a pleasant rush. My concerns and distractions faded away as *the Calm* washed over me. My muscles relaxed and I rolled down the window. A rush of cold air blasted my face as I stuck the muzzle out of my AKM out the window. I clicked the safety lever to the full auto position, and checked to make sure that the 75-round drum magazine was locked in. *This is it.*

We caught them completely off guard. All that Jihan's soldiers, sitting idly at the checkpoint, could have seen was several streams of green tracers lancing out at them from the darkness before they died. The checkpoint was just a couple of shacks, a feeble wooden roadblock, and a pair of parked 4x4s. Heavy machine-gun and small-arms fire tore through the shacks and the trucks alike. The noise was terrible. The BTRs blasted through the barricade without hesitation, breaking it off and crushing it beneath their wheels.

We slowed down to make the ninety-degree right turn up the hill to the dam. *Movement in the shack!* The AK roared as I squeezed the trigger, hosing the wooden building with a long burst. Paolo winced at the noise. He looked like he was going to piss himself when the KPV machine gun above us opened up on a vehicle coming down the road to our left. The concussion from each shot was like having a metal bucket on your head while someone banged on it with a hammer.

Just like that, we were around the corner and speeding up the hill. It had taken us less than a minute to shoot our way through the checkpoint, leaving nothing but dead bodies and burning trucks in our wake. We had surprised them so completely that they had only gotten a couple of ineffectual potshots off at us.

The convoy sped up after rounding the corner, beginning the long charge up the hill. The dam loomed over us at the top, brightly illuminated through my NVGs. I couldn't hear anything over the roar of the truck's diesel engine but I had little doubt that alarms were sounding up there. A mix of red and green tracers zipped down the hill at us. There was no cover. The road was straight, two lanes wide, flanked on either side by six-foot snow banks. There was nowhere to go but up.

The two BTRs maintained their armored wall up front, sending bursts of automatic weapons fire forward as we charged. The huge machine gun behind me roared, each burst sounding like a maniac was pounding on the roof with a sledgehammer. I had no targets. There was nothing I could do but sit and wait. The road to the dam was only a kilometer long, but a klick is a long way when you're being shot at.

PING! "Shit!" Paolo cried. He flinched and ducked down in his seat. An incoming round ricocheted off of one of the BTRs and loudly nicked the corner of the cab. Staying close to the armored vehicles didn't help a lot, as our truck was considerably taller than they were, but it was better than nothing.

I involuntarily gasped as an RPG rocket zipped to my right in a flash, barely missing the truck. We'd be at the top of the hill momentarily, but the enemy fire was getting more accurate as we drew closer. Another RPG hit the ground and detonated in front of one of the APCs, causing it to swerve and sending a cloud of dirt and snow into the air.

"Oh God!" Paolo swerved the truck at the last instant to avoid the pothole left by the RPG.

"Just go straight!" I shouted. "Stay on line!" There was a horrible sound of holes being punched in metal and glass. I hunched down in the seat. Holes appeared in the windshield as a burst of machine gun fire tore up the front of the truck. Paolo grunted. He was hit. The Exodus operative slumped over to the right, turning the wheel as he went. I frantically grabbed for it, but it was too late.

I barely had time to brace as the massive Ural truck cut sharply to the right. My stomach lurched as the left-side wheels left the ground. The snow, bright green through my NVGs, flew up at me in what seemed to be slow motion. Every bone in my body was jarred as the truck dumped over on its side. The last thing I remember seeing was a sideways snowbank speeding toward my face.

Everything went black.

Cold.

That was the first thing I consciously thought. I wondered if I was back on the mountaintop at North Gap left out in the elements again. I didn't know where I was, and couldn't remember how I got there. I opened my eyes to pale gray light. Nothing was in focus. I couldn't feel anything. I couldn't hear anything. For what seemed to be a very long time, I was utterly alone.

A long burst of automatic weapons fire echoed in the distance. It was answered by a slow-firing heavy machine gun, and several small explosions. I was able to lift my head slightly. My face was numb. I was on my side, half buried in snow.

Well I'll be damned, I thought whimsically. *I'm still alive.* I lifted my head some more, shaking the snow from my face. My night vision goggles were gone. The sky was clear and the Moon was rising. The snow glowed gray under the white light of the Moon. As I fumbled with my seat-belt latch, I felt something wet and warm dripping on my face. I looked up, to my left. Paolo was still strapped into his seat. His arms dangled lifelessly, as if he was reaching out for me in death. Blood trickled from several wounds on his body and was dripping on my face.

Freeing myself from the seat belt, I searched for my weapons. The truck had slid sideways on the icy road, right into one of the tall snow banks that lined it. The windshield smashed, the cab had half filled with snow, and I had been all but buried alive. I couldn't find the AKM rifle I'd been carrying, but my SIG battle rifle was still slung to my chest. I habitually patted my left side for my revolver. My lucky S&W .44 was still there, and seemed to have saved me once again.

The sounds of battle roared from the top of the hill as I slowly dug my way out through the front window. I had to get up there and rejoin Exodus. I didn't know how long I'd been out, or how the battle was going, but I couldn't stay where I was. Somehow I'd gotten left behind, probably in the mad rush up the hill. There was no way they could stop on the road for very long without getting shot to pieces. Exodus probably saw that I'd been buried and assumed I was dead, like Paolo.

I managed to dig my way to the top of the snow bank, breath smoking in the frigid night air. I looked around briefly, then trudged through the snow away from the road. I took cover under a nearby pine tree with low-hanging boughs. I needed a minute to catch my breath and didn't want to do it out in the open.

The Ural truck had been abandoned, front end shot to pieces. It lay on its right side, blocking half the road. The heavy machine gun mounted in the back hung uselessly, barrel pointing toward the ground. I didn't see any other bodies. Everyone in the back must have survived the crash and probably climbed onto the next vehicle in line to continue the assault.

Looking through the pine boughs, I could see the dam, even without my night vision. It was illuminated by a multitude of amber lights, as well as the moonlight that was now streaming through the dispersing cloud layer. The Moon was low in the sky, barely clearing the mountains. Trees cast long, ominous shadows in the snow, and I began to shiver. I had to keep moving.

It looked like it was about half a klick uphill to the dam. *Shit.* Five hundred meters is a long way uphill, in the open, when the enemy holds the top of the hill. I wore a snow camouflage smock over my clothing, but I was hesitant to bet my life on overwhites. The road was the only option. Trying to plow through hip-deep snow on foot would make the trip take a lot longer and leave me just as exposed.

I reached for my radio. "Sword Three, this is, uh . . ." I didn't have a callsign. Or if I did nobody told me. "This is Valentine," I said. Fuck it, the radios were encrypted. "I'm still alive. I'm at the site of the truck crash. I'm alone, but I'm mobile. I'm going to try to make my way to you."

There was no response. I looked at the radio briefly, then repeated my transmission. Still no response. I swore and changed the setting to unencrypted broadcast, and turned the power up. Somebody had to hear me. "Sword Three, Sword Three, Sword Three," I said, "This is Valentine. I got left behind at the truck crash, but I am still alive, how copy?"

My radio crackled to life. *"Holy shit! It's you!"*

The voice sounded damned familiar. "Who is this?"

"Dude! It's Reaper!"

You have got to be fucking kidding me. "Listen to me. I got left behind. I'm alone, and I'm in trouble. Are you in touch with anybody?"

"Why are you broadcasting on an open channel? Everyone can hear you."

"My crypto shit the bed, or my radio got fucked up. I was in a truck crash. Listen, you need to tell somebody that I'm alive."

"*Where are you? No wait, don't tell me! The enemy could be listening!*"

I sighed heavily. "Look, just tell Sword Three, or someone in that element, that I'm alive and I'm trying to get to them. I'm going radio silent after that, but I'll be listening. Keep me updated, okay?"

"*I don't know where Sword Three is.*" Of course, we'd kept Lorenzo in the dark about the attack on the dam, but Reaper was just glad to help. "*But okay. Good luck! Be careful!*"

Be careful, he says. "Roger, out." I shuffled out from under the pine tree and slid down the snowbank onto the road. Before I could even get going, the road ahead of me was illuminated by bright white headlights coming from behind. *Shit.* I ran back to the wreck of the Ural. There was nowhere else to hide.

Shit, shit, shit! My heart was racing. My breath was ragged in the thin, cold air. I hadn't yet regained my *Calm.* I was alone, scared, and was about to get caught. I huddled by the shattered windshield of the Ural truck, crouching in a dark spot by the snow bank where I had first crawled out. With my winter camouflage, they probably wouldn't see me unless they walked right up on top of me. I readied my rifle, which was wrapped in white gauze, and tried to hold still.

There were two vehicles. I couldn't tell what they were, but they weren't big trucks. Probably 4x4s of some kind. One stopped about fifty yards down the hill, its headlights illuminating the rear end of the truck. The other slowly crept up the road, to the left of the crash.

They're looking for survivors. I huddled even lower,

hoping both trucks would just drive past. Mere seconds ticked by at an agonizingly slow pace. The lights of the approaching truck drew nearer and nearer, then stopped.

Oh hell. I heard two car doors slam shut. Harsh voices in an unfamiliar language. There were two of them. They approached cautiously. I only caught glimpses of their movements as shadows in the truck's headlights, but I knew they were going to find me.

A dark silhouette came into my view, stepping around the bumper of the overturned truck. He had an AK-47. I was out of time.

I snapped off two shots. *Crack! Crack!* Heavy .308 rounds tore through the man's chest. I jumped to my feet, weapon shouldered, and moved forward. The other man came around the truck suddenly and crashed right into me.

Our eyes met for a split second. I was more than a foot taller than him. His face was young. His eyes were black and empty. A strange character was branded into his cheek.

BOOM! Another gunshot rang out, surprising me. The young man's stomach erupted in a horrific wound. My overwhites were splashed with blood. He grabbed his abdomen and crumpled to the ground, writhing in the pink snow.

I realized that my .44 was in my left hand. I'd fired from the hip. My rifle hung across my chest on its sling. I lowered my revolver and fired again, killing the young slave soldier, and holstered the big gun. I had no time. The other truck was still there.

Turning around, I struggled through the deep snow at the front of the wrecked truck. Lit up in the headlights of the second truck, I trudged out of the snow bank next to the truck's bed. The huge KPV machine gun was still on its pintle, muzzle hanging down in the snow.

I squatted down and grabbed the machine gun's heavy barrel. It was still warm. I pushed up, flipping the gun over so it was pointing to the rear. It took all of my strength to hold the heavy beast level. Grasping the gun sideways, I pointed it at the headlights down the road and mashed the trigger.

The gun roared and bucked in my hands. It immediately climbed up to my left, until it wouldn't traverse anymore. I realigned it and fired another burst. Tracers lashed out into the night, each shot producing a blinding muzzle flash. The driver of the truck threw it into reverse and backed down the hill as fast as he could. I had no idea if I hit him or not.

It didn't matter. I had my chance. The gun's heavy barrel swung down and hissed as it contacted the snow. I bounded around the rear of the overturned Ural truck, then back up the hill. The 4x4 the first two soldiers had arrived in was still running. I threw open the driver's door, climbed in, and put the truck in gear. It sputtered and rattled as I sped up the hill toward the dam. I had to rejoin the fight.

It only took me a few minutes to get to the top of the hill. Another guard shack sat on the west side of the dam. It had been shot to pieces, and two dead bodies lay in the snow next to it. Beyond that, I could see the two APCs and the remaining trucks on top of the dam. They'd all stopped near the superstructure. One of the APCs burned brightly in the night, sending thick black smoke curling into the frigid air. The other vehicles continued to fire on the barracks and utility buildings on the east side of the dam.

Exodus was still in the fight. I wasn't going to risk getting my ass shot off approaching in the truck. I put it in park and killed the engine and lights. I left the keys in it, thinking we might need it later.

On foot, I hustled across the road, digging into one of the pouches on my vest as I did so. I found an IR ChemLight, which can only be seen through night-vision goggles, and cracked it. With my left hand on the grip of my rifle, I held the chemlight in my right hand and waved it over my head as I jogged toward the Exodus convoy, wheezing as I went. The cold burned my lungs on every breath. My chest felt tight. I was already out of shape from my exile in North Gap and wasn't close to acclimatized to the altitude. I just hoped to hell Exodus wouldn't shoot me down before I could reach them.

Between the amber lights along the top of the dam and the burning BTR, I could see Exodus personnel scurrying about. A group took cover behind the vehicles and sent fire back across the dam. Others, weapons slung, were hauling supplies from the back of one of the trucks down into the dam itself. In the confusion of battle and the dark of the night, I was able to get pretty close before they noticed me. Multiple weapons were raised at me.

I stopped dead in my tracks and let go of my rifle. "Friendly!" I gasped, struggling to catch my breath. I frantically waved the chem-light over my head, expecting to get shot at any moment. "Friendly!"

"Val?" someone asked. "Val!" It was Skunky. He waved

the others off. "It's Valentine, stand down! Stand down!" He jogged to me, his weapon held at the low ready.

"Holy shit, Val!" he said excitedly. "What the hell happened to you?"

"I got left," I panted. "At the truck crash. Left for dead."

"Damn. Sorry about that. I didn't even know we lost one of the trucks until we were at the top of the hill. I was in one of the BTRs."

"You actually rode in that death trap?" I asked. "Man, Exodus really has got you over a barrel."

My friend cracked a smile. "C'mon, this way. I'm glad you made it."

"How's it going up here?" I crouched slightly and moved toward the vehicles with him. Bullets snapped past high over our heads, but the gunfire was getting more sporadic.

"We caught them completely off guard," Skunky said. We stopped behind the intact APC. "Medic!" he shouted.

"I'm fine," I insisted, but he was having none of it.

"I just want to get you checked out real quick while I fill you in."

I looked down at myself. "Oh, yeah. Listen, this isn't my blood. I'm okay." An Exodus medic, dressed in winter camouflage just like mine, appeared at my side despite my protests.

Skunky kept talking as the medic gave me a quick once-over. "We took the dam pretty easily. The garrison was almost all in the barracks over there to the east. We overran the guards on the dam itself and just poured suppressing fire on those buildings." He pointed. One of the indicated buildings was burning. "Yeah," Skunky continued, "we lit 'em the hell up. Rockets, machine guns, grenades, everything we had. I think we caught most of them in bed. They're still over there, and they've tried to move on our position a couple of times, but we have them caught in a funnel. They're disorganized as hell, too. Like, ten minutes ago a dozen guys just tried to bum rush the convoy. We shot 'em all down before they got within a hundred yards."

"They're fanatics," I said. "Where's Ling?"

"She's downstairs. We've more or less secured the dam. We're placing the explosives now." A long burst of automatic weapons fire, followed by several shouts, then more gunshots, resonated from within the dam. Skunky shrugged. "More or less. Casualties have been light." Before I could say anything else, one of the Exodus operatives up by the intact APC shouted a warning to us. "Shit," Skunky said. "Here they come again. C'mon, get on line!"

I followed my friend around the side of the BTR-70. It was parked perpendicular to the dam so as to form the core of Exodus' improvised road block. The trucks were parked next to it. The burning BTR was farther to the east, blocking the top of the dam even more, and when an APC caught fire, they really *burned*. Any attackers coming from the east side had to run a serpentine of debris and vehicles in order to get to the convoy, while being covered the entire time by Exodus' heavy machine-guns. It was no wonder they hadn't had any success.

But damned if they weren't determined to try. I took cover behind a concrete jersey barrier that looked like it had been sitting on top of that dam for sixty years, leveled my rifle, and steeled myself. Skunky huddled next to me. I'd fire around the left side, and he'd fire around the right. Exodus troops hurriedly took up positions on the line, pointing rifles and machine-guns in the direction of the enemy.

Tortured, malevolent screams echoed from the smoke and darkness. It sounded like dozens of men, or boys. *RAAAAH!* they screamed. *RAAAAH!* again. *RAAAAAAAH!* On the third shout they charged. They fired wildly from the hip, their shots flying high and wide. There were a lot of them, bearing down on us full tilt. I'd never seen such a fanatical mass banzai charge before.

Before I could even get one in my scope the machine guns opened up. The 14.5mm on the BTR roared like the Wrath of God, with a chorus of lesser belt-fed angels backing Him up. I put my crosshair on one of Sala Jihan's soldiers and snapped off a shot. He was ripped apart by machine-gun fire before I could even tell if I'd hit him. I adjusted and kept rocking the trigger. Hot brass belched out of my rifle as I fired, a shot here, two shots there, laying rounds into anything that moved.

The enemy was cut down as they came into view. Their fire was inaccurate and largely ineffective. Few of their rounds even came close to us. There was nothing on top of the dam, except perhaps the burning BTR, that could stop the huge, armor-piercing bullets from the 14.5mm machine-gun. They had no cover. Hell, they didn't *try* to use cover. They just charged, screaming and firing as they ran.

"Reloading!" I shouted to Skunky. I'd gone through a twenty-round magazine just like that. I dropped it out of my rifle and ripped open the velcro on one of my magazine pouches.

"Shit, reloading!" Skunky said. He was out too. *Goddamn*. He had open-topped magazine pouches, so he was a little quicker on the reload than me. We both sent our bolts forward at the same time, leveled our rifles around the concrete barrier, just as a screaming fanatic with a grenade in each hand bore down on us. We shot him down in hail of fire, shouting "Grenaaaade!"

We ducked. The double concussion was skull-rattling. Fragmentation buzzed angrily as it zipped overhead, and pockmarked the far side of our concrete barrier. A few more random shots and it was quiet. Skunky and I made eye contact briefly, then leaned out from behind cover to survey the carnage.

Bodies were strewn across the cracked, snow-dusted pavement. The APC still burned, black smoke blotting out the tepid moonlight, its firelight illuminating the carnage. Most of the enemy had been dressed in a mishmash of Russian and Chinese military gear, leathers, and rags. I estimated that we'd been charged by something like forty soldiers, and we'd killed them all.

"Jesus Christ," I muttered, standing up. My rifle was hot to the touch.

"There can't be many more of them," Skunky hoped, spent brass rolling under his boots as he walked.

"I hope you're right." Something golden glinted briefly in the moonlight. I noticed it as I took a long swig of water. I squinted, straining to make out what it was. A little statue or idol, made of gold (or something that looked like gold from a distance) was lying on the ground. It was on the end of a staff about five feet long. The staff was still clutched, in death, by the slave soldier who had been carrying it. His weapon was slung across his back, unused. The little idol gleamed in the light of the Moon and the burning vehicle as it was slowly enveloped in a pool of blood.

"They're insane," Skunky whispered. "What kind of man inspires that?"

LORENZO
Sala Jihan's Fortress
March 25th

"Damn them! Move Johan's team to the south. Reinforce Nagano," Ibrahim ordered into his mike, one hand pressed against the speaker in his ear so he could still hear over the roar of the nearby machine gun, his other hand dangling with a G3K in it. He saw me coming and nodded. "Do it now! Sword One Actual out. Hello, my friend. How goes it?"

"Not as good as we'd hoped, apparently," I said as I jogged up to him, my team right behind me. It had taken us awhile to make it to the LZ. There were a lot more troops stationed in the compound than we had expected. Anders ran for the second chopper. He needed to check in with his boss.

The two massive Russian helicopters were parked in the snow. One of them was canted at a very awkward angle, its front end broken and smoking, its blades pointing at a drastic downward angle. It had caught an RPG on the way in, and the only reason anyone had walked away from the crash was because of how close it was to the ground when it had been hit. Katarina was probably going to be pissed about the loss of such an expensive thing.

Ibrahim and a handful of Exodus operatives were clustered around the choppers calling the shots, while the remainder had formed a rough semicircle around it. On the far edge of that semicircle was a bunch of really angry fanatics protecting a hole in the ground. On the opposite side was a bunch of other fanatics trying desperately to get to said hole. We were right in the middle. They were unloading explosives and tools from the choppers.

"We have to beat these soldiers back. Many of them protect the silo, and we're having to dig them out like ticks," Ibrahim shouted over the noise. There was an oily explosion in the distance behind us as something else highly flammable detonated. Our plan relied on us to secure that damn silo, because as long as Jihan was alive, we believed his slave soldiers would continue to fight, and fought they had, unexpectedly hard, and with suicidal ferocity.

We were behind schedule. It was only a matter of time before reinforcements arrived from the mines. And if they came before we took the silo, we would have to retreat. Luckily the Halos were so big we could easily fit everybody into one.

"Lorenzo, I need you to help eliminate the guards around that silo," Ibrahim ordered.

I shook my head. "I have to get to the prison."

"Then you will go by yourself," Ibrahim snapped. "Shen, Roland, Phillips, reinforce Solomon at the silo."

"Yes, sir!" shouted the two younger operatives. Shen looked at me, and nodded slightly. He was going to do his duty, no matter what. The three of them ran immediately in the direction of the most gunfire.

"Damn it!" I shouted. "My brother—"

"Your brother is as dead as the rest of us if we cannot kill Jihan!" Ibrahim spat back.

I bit my tongue. He was right, but that didn't make it any easier. I glared at Ibrahim, then took off after the others.

We passed the still-functioning chopper. In the dark, it was difficult for me to ascertain who was standing near its rear door, but as I drew closer, I recognized Anders' massive bulk, and Katarina's slender frame and almost silver hair. She finished telling him something, then slapped the big man on the shoulder. He turned to rejoin us.

"Lorenzo," Kat shouted over the noise. She had a familiar weapon in her hands, and she gestured for me to come toward her. I slowed up, the others quickly leaving me behind.

"What, Kat? I see you've still got Mr. Perkins."

"Yes. He is my favorite." She held up the M79. She had used that same old 40mm grenade launcher on quite a few jobs. It had been a little unnerving when she had given it a name, but she was an artist in its use. "I'm glad to see you made it."

"Thanks, look, I've got to go," I started walking. I didn't have time for her bullshit.

"I just wanted to tell you one thing." She grabbed my arm. I could see her white teeth glowing in the dim light as she smiled. "No matter what happens here tonight—"

Something impacted the sheet metal of the chopper over her head, showering both of us with metal fragments. I flinched down. Kat's smile disappeared, and Mr. Perkins moved to her shoulder as she zeroed in on the muzzle flash from the sniper.

BLOOP

A full three seconds later, there was a small explosion on a bunker's roof and the sniper was permanently silenced. "No matter what happens tonight," she continued talking as she popped open the single-shot weapon to shove another huge shell in, as if nothing had happened. "I just want you to know that I'm really glad you showed up. It was good to see you again."

"Uh, yeah. Me too."

"It has helped me set some things straight, to reexamine my life, if you will." She suddenly leaned in and kissed me gently on the cheek. My face was so frozen that it almost burned. It was strange in that she actually seemed calm and in control. "Goodbye, Lorenzo."

Another bullet impacted near us as somebody opened up from the far wall with an AK. Katarina shrugged and aimed her 40mm. I used the opportunity to run after my team.

The warhead had screamed by so close I could have reached out and touched it.

"Son of a bitch!" I shouted as the RPG exploded fifty feet behind me. Anders rolled around cover and started shooting at the shadows where the rocket had come from. "Reaper!" I hit my mike and shouted. "Come in, Reaper!"

"You've got ten of them moving in a trench ten meters

in front of you, and I saw at least one move into the elevator shaft." Reaper sounded relatively calm, but he should, since he was sitting in a truck miles from here. "*You've got to remember that when they're under a roof, I can't see them on thermal—*"

Yeah, whatever. I tuned out the technical explanation and refocused on the crazy people trying to kill me. I saw a man leap out of the trench and sprint for the elevator. I put the Aimpoint dot on him and started shooting. I must have hit him in the legs, as they flew out from under him and he sprawled in the snow. Somebody nearby with a larger caliber rifle finished him with a shot through his face.

"Phillips!" I shouted over the din. The remaining soldiers must have had a lot of ammo stashed, and they weren't trying to save any of it. The young man looked up from the stock of his rifle. "Cover the elevator door. Somebody's in there."

"Got it!"

There were two full teams of Exodus operatives converged on this spot when we had arrived. We had moved up right between them and hit the soldiers from a third angle. A few feet to my right was an Exodus sniper with a Sako bolt action. It took me a moment to recognize that it was Svetlana under that fur hood and tac gear. A soldier started out of the trench, and she rocked under the recoil as she took the top of his skull off.

I had scrounged up several frags on our trip across the compound. There had been plenty of them just lying around, and the previous owners had been in no shape to argue with me about taking them. They were those nasty little Southeast Asian ones that were wrapped in pre-stressed wire. I yanked a pin and tossed one, waited just a second, then followed it with another. Amazingly enough, even as cold-numbed as my hands were, I managed to land both of them in the trench, but I had gotten a lot of experience chucking grenades back in Africa.

The soldiers in the trench were on the ball, though, because both of the grenades were tossed back out to explode harmlessly in the snow. Sure, I could have pulled the pin and waited a second before throwing them, but I had learned not to trust Third World grenade fuses.

The Exodus team leader to the right must have decided that they were out of time. With a ragged battle cry, the entire group of them popped up and ran toward the trench. It was brave, and maybe suicidal, but no more suicidal than still being inside this compound when the reinforcements arrived from the mines.

The elevator door popped open, and a soldier with an RPG launcher stepped out, but Phillips had been doing exactly what I had asked him to do, and the soldier went down in a spray of arterial blood before he could launch the rocket.

Muzzle flashes erupted from the trench and some of the charging Exodus people went down, screaming as bullets tore through their flesh, spilling their blood into the snow. But some of them made it through, and I could see them silhouetted in the moonlight as they stood on the lip of the trench and fired downward into the remaining soldiers.

Finally, the gunfire stopped. The only sounds were the moans and screams from the wounded.

"Reaper?"

"*They're still warm, but they ain't moving.*"

"Ibrahim. We've got the silo," I said quickly.

"*Understood. Assault element moving in,*" he said breathlessly.

I moved forward, my team right behind me. The young guys looked slightly shocked. These were their comrades that were in front of us bleeding and dying. They each moved to help one of the wounded. I saw Svetlana sitting in the snow at the lip of the trench. Her big Sako was in her lap, and she was staring stupidly at her hand.

I knelt at her side. She had pulled off her glove, and held her delicate left hand up to show me. Her smallest two fingers were missing, just jagged bone stumps sticking out of her palm. "I didn't even feel it . . ." she said.

"Don't worry. You will," I responded as I pulled a roll of bandages out of my pocket and started wrapping it tightly around her hand.

"Ooohh . . ." Her eyes rolled back into her head. "Yes, I believe you're right."

"You're going to be fine," I said reassuringly. The only good thing about the cold was the blood flow to the extremities was slower than normal. "Your friend's charge was stupid. You know that, right?"

She spoke through gritted teeth. "We are Exodus."

"Yeah, now get your ass back to the chopper before you pass out," I ordered. She shook her head, being stubborn. I saw Roland standing nearby. The man that he was trying to help had just stopped breathing. "Roland! Get Svetlana back to the chopper." He quickly complied, helped her to her feet, grabbed her sniper rifle, and half-escorted, half-carried her back in the direction we had come from.

Ibrahim sprinted up to the pit. Behind him was the assault team, each of them carrying climbing rope, tools, and explosives. The doors of the silo itself had been designed to withstand a nuclear war and would take hours to break through, so they were going to go down the same shaft I'd used when I had visited before, but they'd probably still have to cut through multiple blast doors to reach Jihan's quarters.

I noticed for the first time that in addition to his stubby .308, Ibrahim also had a sword on his belt, an actual friggin' scimitar, and it looked like an antique, complete with rubies on the hilt. I had to admit, these guys had *style*. The Exodus commander surveyed his men as they circled the top of the silo. He spoke when he saw me. "Lorenzo, take your team and get your brother. I will be out of contact from here on out. Fajkus is now leading the operation." He was very somber. "Godspeed, my friend."

I nodded once, then went after Bob.

Chapter 21: Poor Life Choice

✠

VALENTINE
The Dam
March 25th

The interior of the dam was dark and smoky. Many of the lights had been shot out in the firefight. I pulled a small flashlight from my vest and used it to help me navigate.

The narrow corridors were filled with the low-pitched hum of the dam's turbines. Above that, voices echoed throughout the structure. Scattered Exodus personnel hurried to and fro, carrying supplies and moving the wounded. An aid station had been set up just inside the doorway. A pair of medics tended to the wounded and covered the dead.

I ran into Ling in the upper level of the dam, almost literally, as she and another Exodus operative were hurrying the other way. "Michael!" She threw her arms around me and embraced me tightly, for just a moment. My slung rifle clattered against the SIG 551 that hung from her shoulder. The air was cold but she was warm.

The other Exodus operative maintained a poker face and said nothing. Ling stepped back, blushing slightly, and cleared her throat. "I was worried when you didn't arrive with us."

"I got left at the truck crash."

"As I feared. And your driver?"

"Yeah, the kid didn't make it," I said. "His name was Paolo."

Ling closed her eyes for just a moment, and took a deep breath. "There is no time to mourn now. We must hurry. The raid on Sala Jihan's main compound is well underway. I just heard Ibrahim on the radio, they're about to breach Jihan's personal quarters. Come with me," she said, and I followed her back outside.

"What kind of nutjob lives at the bottom of a missile silo?" I asked, as we stepped back out into the night air. "And how much longer until the explosives are in place?"

"Not long," Ling replied, before shouting orders to some other personnel in Mandarin.

"How will you be initiating it?"

"Two ways. We're going to have time-fuse as a backup. Our primary means of initiation will be radio. We'll spool a firing wire out to the surface, hooked to a receiver, as we withdraw across the dam. It's redundant."

That was good. If for whatever reason this huge demo shot misfired, it was very unlikely we'd be able to get in, fix the problem, and get back out alive. We only had one shot and Exodus was leaving as little to chance as possible.

Ling changed the subject. "I'm glad that you're well, I truly am. We need every able body we can find now."

That sounded ominous. "What's happening?"

"Reinforcements are coming from the mines."

I closed my eyes tightly and sighed. It wasn't exactly a surprise, but it was far from good news. "How many?"

"Many. Lorenzo's man has a small drone that is tracking them with thermal cameras. They're on their way here now. I don't know what's happening. The Montalban Exchange's mercenaries do not seem to have begun their attack on the garrison in town."

"That's not good. How are things going at the fortress?"

"I have no news of Mr. Lorenzo, if that's what you're asking. Though no one has called me to tell me that he is dead. So far, all seems to be going according to plan there."

"How long do we have?" I asked.

"Maybe ten minutes, fifteen if we're very fortunate. I need you to help me get everything organized up here. Katsumoto is down below with our engineers and demolitions men, supervising the final placement and priming of the explosives. Right where he should be, as that is the primary mission. I have been charged with holding the line up here until we are ready to leave."

"Is there any chance that we can get out of here before they get to the road at the bottom of the hill and cut us off?"

"That is the hope," she said. "But it is not likely."

"We'll hold them, Ling," I promised.

We spent the next few minutes hurriedly trying to reorganize the defense of the dam. The focus was now on the west, where we'd come from, instead of east, even though the east side hadn't been completely cleared and we couldn't ignore it. If we were pushed back across the dam, there probably wouldn't be any escape for us. The terrain on the east side was too rugged for vehicles, and we wouldn't last long hiking around the mountains on foot.

Everybody who could hold a weapon, wounded or not, was put on the line. We were likely outnumbered. If they broke through, none of us would survive. Certainly no one wanted to be captured and taken to Sala Jihan alive.

Our barricade was moved to the very west end of the dam, near where I had parked my stolen truck. The BTR-70 that was still intact rolled into position, once again sideways, blocking off almost the entire road by itself. The other trucks were lined up in such a way that they could leave in a hurry once the explosives were in place, assuming they had anywhere to go.

Sala Jihan's forces would face the same kilometer-long uphill battle that we did. Unlike us, they lacked the element of surprise, they lacked night vision, most of them lacked body armor, and they faced a much more competent foe.

On the other hand, there were less than forty of us that weren't preoccupied setting the charges. Hundreds of Jihan's slave soldiers were on their way from the mines, and more could come from town at any time since the Montalbans had not begun their diversion for some reason.

It wasn't looking good. Skunky joined me on the line, and he seemed to read my mind. "Having second thoughts?"

"Honestly?" I began, as I took up a position behind the armored personnel carrier. "I kind of am. I'm beginning to think this may have been a poor life choice." I cracked a smile, and my friend laughed.

The levity was forced. Beneath it, I was grappling with the growing realization that I was probably going to die in this godforsaken place. Everything I'd managed to survive, from Mexico, to Zubara, to North Gap, and look what I'd gotten myself into: outnumbered with no hope of rescue on the ass-end of the world, fighting somebody else's damned war. I swear to God, it's the story of my life.

I looked over at Ling. She briefly smiled at me, then returned her attention to what she was doing. My bitterness faded. I'd come here for her. I'd had nothing to live for, so I'd gone along to help somebody who did.

The cloud cover had been thinning all night. The Moon was now high in the sky, and pale grey light poured over the land and reflected brightly off the snow. Even without my lost night vision goggles, it was easy to see a long way through the darkness. What I could see wasn't comforting. At the bottom of the hill, turning onto the road that led to the dam, was a long line of vehicles carrying Sala Jihan's soldiers. Their headlights pierced the darkness in front of them as they rounded the corner and started up the hill in a single column.

I zoomed my rifle's scope in to maximum magnification and clicked the elevation knob up to 800 meters. Our best bet was to pour fire on the advancing forces as they climbed the hill. They were vulnerable, and we could make them pay for every inch of ground they covered. I was glad that I'd brought a lot of ammo.

The BTR-70 opened fire first with its turret-mounted 14.5mm machine gun. The weapon's roar would have been deafening if not for my hearing protection, and even so it was loud as hell. Tracers speared out into the night, peppering the convoy from a range of nearly a thousand meters. The machine guns mounted on the trucks opened up next, followed by a few crew-served machine guns manned by Exodus troops. The symphony of automatic weapons fire pulsed in my chest with each shot as the *Calm* enveloped me in its cool, leveling embrace.

If I was to die here, then so be it. I looked over at Skunky, who was holding fire. His SIG 551 was equipped with an Aimpoint, not ideal for long-range shooting. He shook his head slightly at me, smiling in the darkness. "You're kind of scary when you're in the zone like that, you know that, brother?" he said, raising his voice to be heard over the cacophony of gunfire.

Tracers were zipping up at us from the hill now. Sala Jihan's forces were returning fire. *PING! DING!* Incoming fire ricocheted off the armored hull of the BTR-70. *PING! BING!*

I set my scope's reticle on a set of headlights midway through the convoy and squeezed the trigger. My rifle recoiled over and over again as I cracked off an entire magazine. "Reloading!"

"I've got you covered!" Ling said. She leaned around the front of the BTR and fired off several short bursts from her carbine. Bullets buzzed overhead. They were shooting back at us, but inaccurately so far.

"I wish I had my M14!" Skunky said, firing over the rear of the armored personnel carrier. An RPG rocket streaked down from our position, detonating as it impacted a vehicle in the convoy. The truck rolled to a stop and was quickly enveloped in flames. Burning men jumped out of the back and rolled in the snow, trying to extinguish themselves. My active hearing protection allowed me to hear their agonizing screams between bursts of machine gun fire from the BTR. The convoy didn't stop. Not a single vehicle, other than the ones we immobilized, stopped. No one got out to aid the wounded or recover the dead. They hardly even slowed down.

"Keep firing!" Ling shouted. "Kill as many of them on the road as possible!" Sala Jihan's forces continued their relentless push. Several of their vehicles had been disabled or destroyed, but the rest drove around them. Troops dismounted and began to run up the hill at us, screaming like madmen the whole while. The enemy's incoming fire was taking its toll on our defensive position now. One of the trucks with a 14.5mm machine gun mounted on it was shot to pieces. RPGs streaked up and down the hill.

Struggling to overcome the chaos, I fired shot after shot, magazine after magazine, as rapidly as I could accurately manage. My rifle was hot to the touch. The enemy convoy was almost on top of us. Two vehicles, beat-up old cars, swerved out of the line and sped around the others. They accelerated up the hill toward our position. The gunner in the BTR-70 turned his attention to it, pouring fire into the car. Riddled with huge holes and burning, it veered off into the snow bank and exploded. The concussion from the blast rattled us all.

The other car was already on top of us.

"VBIED!" I screamed, pronouncing it "vee-bed," but it was already too late. I barely had time to get down as the little car crashed into the side of the BTR-70 and detonated.

✤ ✤ ✤

The next thing I knew, I was face down on cold pavement. My ears were ringing. Muffled sounds of gunfire and screams swirled all around me, but I just couldn't focus. A bright orange light was behind me, and I felt heat on my back. The BTR-70 was ablaze. The big truck next to it, closest to the four-foot wall that marked the northern edge of the dam, was mangled. The stench of diesel and burning interior filled my nostrils.

I pushed myself up to my elbows and tried to focus. Someone ran past me, coming around the burning APC, then stopped in his tracks. He was dressed in camouflage pants, a tattered brown great coat, and carried a Mosin Nagant carbine with the bayonet locked into place. His eyes were wide as saucers. He leveled the rifle at me and screamed as he charged.

I rolled to my right and pulled my revolver. No time to align the sights, I just shoved it out and rocked the trigger. It bucked in my hand as it roared. The fanatical young soldier's stomach splashed red. His scream turned into a shriek, but he kept coming, stumbling, falling, rusty spike bayonet slicing the air toward my face. I pushed myself out of the way just as the point of the bayonet struck the pavement. The screaming fanatic was carried forward by his momentum, pivoting around his rifle and landing on top of me.

Struggling to sit up, I tried to push the dead weight off of me. Two more soldiers appeared around the side of the burning armored personnel carrier. One had some kind of pump shotgun in his hands and was firing from the hip. The other carried nothing but a satchel full of hand grenades. The shotgunner noticed me just as I acquired him in my sights. The .44 Magnum roared two more times as I ended him. The grenadier had a frag in his hands, pin pulled, when I shot him. He fell over backwards. I barely had time to hide my face behind the dead body on my chest before the grenade exploded.

We were being overrun. There was no time to lie under a corpse in a daze. I managed to sit up and pushed the slave soldier's body off of me. Someone grabbed my arm. Every muscle in my body tensed. I swung my revolver around to fire over my right shoulder. The tritium front sight aligned on Skunky's face.

"Whoa whoa whoa!" he cried, eyes wide. "Holy shit, it's me!"

"I almost shot you in the face!" I snarled, hand suddenly shaking. "Fuck!"

"C'mon, dude," he said, helping me to my feet. "We need to get out of here. We've been— *Get down!*" My friend pushed me back, snapped his carbine to his shoulder, and cranked off half a dozen shots. Hot 5.56 brass bounced off my shoulders and burned the back of my neck. "Damn it, they're everywhere!"

I picked up my rifle and came to my feet. "We need to fall back. We can't hold them here." Everyone else seemed to be engaged in a fighting retreat back to the superstructure of the dam. "Wait, where's Ling?"

"I don't know!" Skunky said, quickly changing magazines. "Come on, we have to go!"

"Ling!" I yelled, trying to make myself heard over the chaos. Bullets snapped past us in both directions. The Exodus operatives were running and gunning their way back across the dam. The extremely motivated, but completely disorganized, slave soldiers were still trying to take advantage of the hole they'd punched in our defensive position. Their own vehicles had piled up, and many seemed to be milling about without direction. They had no leadership and weren't sure what to do. It gave us a brief opportunity to regroup. "Ling! Where are you? *Ling!*"

Skunky shook his head. "Come on, man, she's probably on her way back to the dam. We can't stay here! We gotta go!" The smoke from the burning vehicles was so thick that it was impossible to see very far. Despite the moonlight, we were enveloped in darkness. Ling was out there somewhere, and I couldn't just leave her.

Her voice rang through the hellish scene, clear against the low-pitched roar of battle. She called my name.

"Where are you?" I shouted back. Skunky looked around frantically. We couldn't see but a few feet in any direction now.

"I'm here!" Ling said, stumbling through the smoke. "I'm he—" her words were cut off in a fit of coughing.

"Ling! Oh my God!" I ran to her and grabbed her arm. She'd been injured. Blood trickled from under her wool cap down her pretty face. Her cheeks were smeared with soot. "What happened?"

She was in a daze. "I don't know. I . . . we have to get to the . . . the . . ."

"Come on, we're going back!" Ling only nodded. She was too out of it to argue.

I raised my voice as loud as I could. "Exodus! Fall back! If you're still here, fall back to the east! Move, move, move!" Several shouts of acknowledgment rang through the haze. With Skunky's help, I used the smoke as cover and led Ling back toward the superstructure of the dam.

The chaos caused by the enemy's vehicle-borne improvised explosive device gave us enough of a break in the onslaught to retreat back across the dam. That was the only good news, though. We were now stuck on top of the dam. The only way we had to retreat was east, which would put us on the wrong side of the river and leave us stranded. We had too many wounded to move without vehicles.

I told the remaining Exodus operatives to set up a defensive perimeter around the superstructure of the dam. We'd lost our trucks and our heavy machine guns, but there were still a couple belt-feds on the line. Sala Jihan's forces now had to come from the west, straight across the top of the dam, with no cover. It would cost them dearly. But they were utterly relentless and oblivious to their own casualties. There weren't enough of us left to win a battle of attrition.

Skunky joined the defensive position outside as I led Ling into the dam. I called for a medic and had her sit down against the wall. The Exodus medic, a young woman whom I guessed was from India, knelt next to Ling and began to administer aid.

"You have a gash on your head," the medic told Ling. "It's not very deep. You are very fortunate. Two centimeters closer and this would have killed you."

"She was close to the vee-bed when it detonated," I told her. "The car bomb, I mean. She may have been close to the blast." The blast overpressure is the most destructive component of an explosion. It has a very short lethal radius, depending on the size of the blast, compared to fragmentation. Being caught in it can do instant, horrific damage to the human body, including traumatic brain injury. Having experienced a TBI myself, I was very worried about Ling.

As the medic talked to her, she seemed to come around. "I think it is just a case of shock," the medic said with a slight accent. "She's responsive. Her wound is dressed and I have not found any other injuries. Please stay with her, I need to attend the others."

I nodded and the medic ran off, aid bag in hand. There were many wounded and we were likely running low on medical supplies. Inside the concrete superstructure, the sounds of gunfire outside echoed throughout the corridors. The lights dimmed and flickered with the occasional grenade or RPG detonation.

Ling sat up against the wall and just slowly shook her head. She then buried her face in her hands. I moved closer to her and put my hand on her shoulder. She didn't look at me, but she put her gloved hand on top of mine.

"Michael, I am so sorry," she said.

We didn't have time for her to be sorry. But she needed a moment, she needed help, and I was all she had. "You don't have anything to be sorry about."

"I do," she insisted. "I'm afraid I've led you to your death. I don't think any of us are getting out of here."

"What's going to happen? Will Katsumoto blow the dam even if we're still on it?"

Ling shook her head. "Not if there's any way for us to retreat to safety. I don't think we'll have that chance, though. I think today is the day we die." She squeezed my hand. "I'm sorry, Michael. You've been through so much. You've seen enough of war. I pulled you out of hell and led you right back into it, and I had no right."

I managed a smile for her. "I'm supposed to be here." She actually laughed in that musty, dimly lit corridor. "And I haven't given up yet. Come on now," I said, standing. "Can you walk?" She nodded. "Okay. Your people need you now. They need a leader. If there's any chance at all of us getting out of this alive, it'll be up to you and Katsumoto to make that happen."

Ling nodded again. "You're right, of course. You're right. Thank you."

"They're holding the line up there for the moment. I don't think the enemy has regrouped for their final push yet. Let's go downstairs and see how things are going. Katsumoto needs to be up here leading this fight." I turned down the corridor, but Ling grabbed my sleeve.

I turned around. "What—" Ling stepped forward, closed her eyes, and kissed me. The warmth of her lips, her breath, her body against mine contrasted starkly against the cold, dingy air of the old hydroelectric plant.

She stepped back after a moment, blushing slightly. "I wish we had more time," she said with a sad smile. "There is . . . much I would like to say."

I didn't know what to say, or what to do. I hadn't touched a woman since Sarah died. Before Ling pulled me out of North Gap, I hadn't even *seen* a woman, except for Dr. Silvers, in months. Ling was beautiful, with dark almond eyes and shiny black hair. There was no denying that I was attracted to her. Tailor had teased me about it when we first met Ling, a lifetime ago in Mexico.

You don't have time for high school drama, goddamn it, I scolded myself. I looked into Ling's eyes. "We're not dead yet," I managed, trying to sound reassuring. "Come on, let's get going."

We found Katsumoto and the Exodus engineers in the heart of the dam. Explosive charges had been placed all around the roaring turbines, and daisy-chained together with many strands of red, yellow, and green det cord.

"Katsumoto-sama," Ling said, using a formal honorific. "We are out of time. Our perimeter has collapsed and most of our vehicles have been destroyed. If we wait much longer will we be overrun completely and the mission will fail."

Katsumoto, though small of stature, was a proud man who commanded great respect. His demeanor hinted at a quiet intensity, but he was completely calm and collected. "I know," he said simply. "And I am sorry. The placing of the charges took too long. This is my responsibility. I fear I may have killed us all. This is why I wanted to just destroy the dam. We would not have taken nearly so long to place the charges."

Before Ling could say anything, one of the demolition engineers stood upright. He maintained composure but looked like he was fighting back tears. "Commander! It is I who is responsible. This is my fault!"

Their willingness to assume responsibility for failure was noble, but we didn't have time for finger pointing, even if they were pointing fingers at themselves. "Guys, guys, guys," I said, interrupting. "The question is what the hell do we do now? Your troops are fighting for their lives up there. The enemy is fanatical but disorganized. It's all Jihan's conscripts. We haven't seen any of the Brotherhood yet."

"They must be all at the fortress," Ling suggested.

"That makes sense," I agreed. "And it's the only good news we have. We still have a chance to get clear of this, even if we have to retreat to the east side of the dam and blow it from there."

"We will be stranded," Katsumoto reminded me, "on the wrong side of the river. It shouldn't collapse from the explosion, but once we move off the dam to the east, getting all the way back across it under fire may be impossible."

"I know. But a few people making it out on foot, or at least having the shot, is better than everyone martyring themselves here. Live to fight another day, right? If the dam is disabled, we've accomplished the mission. It's not hopeless yet."

"What do you suggest?" Katsumoto asked.

"They broke through our defensive line but they still have a big choke point there. We're pouring fire on them as they come through, and we can keep that up until the ammo runs out. Then we'll be overrun. So we can't stay here. We have to push."

"The odds are not good."

"No, they're not. But they can only bring so many across the dam at a time, and there's not much cover. Their numbers don't mean much in a fatal funnel like that. We can suppress them with whatever machine guns and grenades we have left. We use smoke and advance under concealment. We only have to push them back west to where the car bomb went off. We can pick up weapons from their dead if we need to."

"Then what?" Ling asked.

"At the western edge of the dam we're at least on the right side of the river. If we have to cut across country on foot, we can link up with the others or get back to town. We can use the stretchers as sleds and drag the wounded across the snow if we have to. The vee-bed wasn't that big. I don't think it disabled all of the trucks. If we break their assault completely, we might be able to get in a vehicle and make it back down the road. Either way, it's better than being stuck on the east side, and it's a hell of a lot better than everyone getting wiped out. It's not much of a chance but it's the best one we've got."

Katsumoto looked thoughtful for a long moment, then nodded his head slightly. "Yes. Yes. Mr. Valentine, you are indeed an asset. We will do as you suggest."

"Your people need you up there on the line," I said. "Are the charges ready?"

"They are," Katsumoto confirmed. "We have only to spool out the wire and initiate the charge. We will have to do it quickly, though. If we delay, if their forces back-fill behind us as we withdraw, they might be able to get down here and disrupt the explosives before they detonate." Katsumoto then looked at the demolition engineer. His winter camouflage smock was stained with dirt. "Prepare the explosives for initiation. Do not begin the time fuze yet. That will be the last thing we do before we make our push to the end of the dam. We have to make sure we can move the wounded before we do that."

"How long will we have?"

"Fifteen minutes. We can initiate sooner if we get off of the dam in time. Everyone needs to be clear in case the dam actually collapses."

"Understood, Commander!" the engineer said. He then gathered his teammates and ran off to complete his task.

"Come," Katsumoto said. He reached behind his back and brought his weapon, a SIG 552 carbine, around. "Let us finish this."

The battle was raging when we returned to the surface. The remaining Exodus defenders were holding the enemy at bay, if only barely. Most of the amber lights across its topside roadway were intact, illuminating the bodies that littered the roadway. Black smoke poured into the air as both BTR-70s continued to burn, one on either side of the dam, giving the scene a hellish glow.

Skunky was among the defenders waiting for us when we emerged. He and several other Exodus operatives came to Katsumoto while the rest held the line. They needed to know what the plan was. Katsumoto took a knee with them, behind cover, and outlined our strategy. The word was passed along to everyone that was still alive. A couple of the 4x4s we'd convoyed up in were still parked by the superstructure and operational. The immobile wounded would be piled into them. The walking wounded would make the final push with us.

I'd done my best to sound confident to the Exodus leadership, but we really didn't have much of a chance. Oh, I thought we could hold them off until the dam blew. I was actually very sure about that, but I was more concerned with getting home alive, and I didn't really think that was looking likely. We had enough firepower to push the enemy back for a while. We didn't have enough to fight the entire column down the road and make our escape. The best we could hope for would be to scatter into the woods, trudging through the snow, hoping to get to friendly forces without being captured, shot, or succumbing to the cold. The wounded almost certainly wouldn't make it.

I made sure my rifle and revolver were both topped off. The hideous plastic Taurus snubby was in my coat pocket if I needed it. The fifth and final round in that gun's cylinder might be for myself, I decided. I had heard enough horror stories about Sala Jihan that I resolved not to be captured alive. Taking a deep breath, I drew my bayonet from its sheath and snapped it onto the end of my rifle. The blade glinted dully in the firelight from the burning vehicles. There were a lot of bad guys out there, and we were going to have to punch through them all.

Skunky saw me fix my bayonet. "It's ugly out there, bro. No matter what happens, I'm glad you're here with me. It's good to fight with you again."

"You too, brother. You too. Now don't get all squishy on me. We've got to shoot some motherfuckers in the face." *The Calm* was overtaking me, and my fears and doubts were falling to the wayside. It's not that I thought I wasn't going to die. It was just that I no longer cared, at least not on the surface.

We that remained were split into several smaller elements. Some would provide suppressive fire while others advanced. This would maximize our chances as opposed to blindly rushing the enemy. Jihan's forces were using that technique and they were dying by the bushel. Ling and I were in the vanguard. Skunky was to remain in Katsumoto's element. I slapped him on the shoulder and joined the troops I was going to be fighting with. We were discouragingly few in number, but that didn't change anything. We had to do what we had to do.

Katsumoto stood up, raising his voice so well that it sounded imposing over the raging fires and the snap and hiss of incoming rounds. "This is it! Our sacrifice will not be in vain! For the Order! For honor! For freedom!"

"For freedom!" the people in my element echoed, Ling's soprano voice standing out from the rest. The passion in their voices was undeniable. These people knew they were going to their deaths, and they wanted to die well. I can respect that, even if it's somewhat antithetical to the mantra of a career mercenary such as myself.

"Suppressing fire!" Katsumoto shouted. His entire element opened up on anything that moved through the remains of our roadblock. He looked over at Ling. "Advance!"

"Let's go!" Ling shouted. "Move, move, move! Advance on me!" Her people formed a tight wedge. They readied their weapons and jogged up the right side of the dam, giving the support element some separation as they fired past us. I lagged behind with the wounded, being out of shape, out of breath, and having had a pretty rough night.

Sala Jihan's army continued to advance around the destroyed roadblock and burning APC to the west like so many ants. The people in the front of my element opened fire as well. Incoming rounds zipped back at us, snapping past my ears and over my head. I just put my head down and ran harder, plodding along in my heavy vest and pack, hoping I wouldn't trip or slip.

A man in front of me screamed. Enemy fire cut

through our little formation, tearing through his leg. He fell. His teammates paused, but they didn't have time to pause. "Keep going!" I screamed, kneeling next to the fallen. "Keep going, goddamn it! I'll take care of him!" I got him to let go of his mangled leg long enough to let me see the wound. The bullet had hit his shin bone and shattered it. He wasn't going to be able to walk. There wasn't much I could do. I pulled a tourniquet from my med pouch and looped it around his leg. A couple of inches above the wound, I cinched it down and twisted the windlass three times. The Exodus operative, who was swearing in German, shrieked at the pain, but it needed to be done.

"Stay here! Hey! Listen to me, damn it! Stay here! Stay down! The truck with the other wounded will pick you up. Do you understand me?"

He jerkily nodded his head, his teeth clenched from the pain.

"I've stopped the bleeding. Hang in there. Good luck!" I slapped him on the shoulder, then was on my feet, running as hard as I could to catch up with the formation. I didn't want to get left behind again.

Ling's element paused about halfway to the wreck of the BTR-70. She had her people firing at the roadblock while Katsumoto advanced his element. As soon as he moved, the time fuse on the explosives was initiated. Ling stopping her element allowed me to catch up and rejoin the formation. I took a knee next to the Exodus operatives, shouldered my carbine, and opened fire at the hoard of slave soldiers descending upon us. Icy wind chilled my neck as hot brass ejected past my face. Bullets snapped past us and over our heads. An RPG rocket screamed by and exploded in the distance somewhere. The pile of bodies at the gap was mounting.

My safety glasses were spattered with blood as the Exodus woman next to me was hit. She didn't even scream; the round went right through her face. I paused only long enough to check her condition. Her pretty face had been obliterated. This horrific sight was burned into my mind, but there was no time to dwell on it. "She's dead!" I said to the man next to her, and resumed firing. *The Calm* kept the emotion at bay. For now.

"On me, move, move, move!" Ling screamed. The other element had caught up with us. It was their turn to provide covering fire while we advanced. We didn't have time to screw around. We were all vulnerable on the top of the dam. Bullets zipped back and forth, finding targets on both ends. Exodus operatives had the benefit of good training and body armor, but they were still dropping. Every second we delayed cost lives.

Another smoke grenade was tossed ahead of us. The white cloud billowed up, concealing us from the enemy and vice versa. Their already poor accuracy only worsened, and we used the opportunity to push ahead.

Another young man in our formation went down in a gurgle of blood. Three of his teammates stopped to help him. "No! Only one of you stop!" I yelled. "Come on you two, keep up! We gotta push! Come on!" Almost losing each other in the smoke, we reached the burning wreck of the BTR-70 at the western edge of the dam. We used the cluster of vehicles as cover and laid into the enemy so the other elements could advance. We had to get clear and survive until the charges. After that? If any of us were alive after that, we'd figure it out then.

There were several ways a person on foot could get through the wreck of the roadblock, and Sala Jihan's slave army streamed through all of them. There were just so many of them! I crouched behind a pockmarked jersey barrier and leveled my carbine at the gaps. *BAM BAM*, two shots here. Swing left, *BAM BAM BAM,* three more shots. *Shit! More of them!* Swing right, *BAM BAM BAM BAM! Change magazines!* It was chaos. We were right on top of them as they crossed through the roadblock. Gunfire rang out in every direction, drowning out the screams of men. The air was filled with heavy smoke that stunk of burning vehicles.

I moved forward. Next to the burning APC was a Ural truck that had been mangled by the explosion. The heavy machine gun mounted in its bed was unusable. There was a small gap between the truck and the north wall of the dam. Jihan's soldiers kept squeezing through one at a time. It was time to close that gap.

I zigzagged around debris and dead bodies in my approach. I rounded an old car that was parked behind the roadblock, its windows shattered, and kept my gun trained on the gap.

BOOM! I flinched as a grenade detonated somewhere to my left. The blast made my ears pop and scared the shit out of me. I snapped my head back to the gap when I heard a blood-curdling scream coming from that direction. I looked back just in time to see one of Jihan's soldiers lunge at me, running at full speed.

His SKS had its folding bayonet locked open. The wind

was knocked out of me as the tip of his bayonet slid in between the magazine pouches on my vest and hit me dead center. I was pushed back, back, nearly falling, until I was slammed against the side of the car. The slave soldier's eyes were wide, and glazed over. His mouth frothed as he screamed at me in a language I couldn't understand. He was trying to nail me right to that damned car.

The ceramic plate in the front of my vest stopped his bayonet. My rifle was hanging uselessly on its sling. My left hand fell to my side and found the grip of my .44 Magnum. I brought it up, pushed it forward, and let it roar. The fanatical soldier's head exploded into mush and the pressure on my chest was gone as he collapsed to the ground.

I raised the gun higher, putting the glowing tritium front sight on the gap, and fired off five more shots in rapid succession as more men tried to squeeze through. At least two of them fell, landing on top of other dead bodies.

I took the second I'd just bought myself to duck behind the car. I opened the revolver's cylinder, held it muzzle-up, and punched the ejector rod with the heel of my left hand. Hot brass tinkled on concrete as I grabbed a speedloader from my vest, rotated the gun muzzle-down, and twisted six fresh rounds into the cylinder. I snapped it closed and reholstered it.

Two Exodus troops took cover next to me behind the old car. The other element had caught up with us. "We need to close that gap!" I shouted, pointing over the hood of the car. They nodded in affirmation as I stood up to move.

I raised my carbine again, approaching the gap

cautiously. My bayonet led the way as I stepped over bodies and vehicle parts. My nostrils were clogged with soot and smoke. The heat of the fire was making me sweat through my parka. I stumbled on a dead man's leg as I approached and nearly fell.

I looked up just in time to see a skinny enemy soldier in a green coat several sizes too big for him lunge through the gap. He charged through so fast, jumping over the bodies of his fallen comrades, that he crashed right into me. I pushed him back and plunged my bayonet deep into his guts. He screamed like a wild animal, dropping the bag of hand grenades he was carrying. I brought a boot up and kicked him off of my rifle, sending him flailing back. He hit the wall at the north edge of the dam, leaving my bayonet smeared with blood. I tried to stab him again, but he was too fast. He grabbed my rifle as I lunged and pulled it past him. Freakishly strong, the wounded fanatic pulled me right into him.

He was screaming at me as we met, face to face. His frothy spittle spattered against my eyepro as he tried to wrap his fingers around my throat. His breath stunk of gruel. He hardly had any teeth.

I slammed my elbows down on top of his forearms, breaking his chokehold on me. Grabbing his coat with my right, I viciously jabbed him in the face with my left fist, over and over again. I knocked out one of his few teeth, then punched him right in the goddamn eye.

Seizing the opportunity, I grabbed his coat with both hands. Grunting, I lifted the skinny fanatic up and shoved him over the edge. I ran to the wall and looked down, just in time to see him crash to the ice of the frozen reservoir, twenty feet below. He landed on his back in a puff of snow and didn't move.

God damn. Out of breath, arms and legs shaking from adrenaline, I picked my rifle back up and looped the sling around me. Coughing and hacking in the smoke, I grabbed the skinny guy's bag of grenades and handed it over to my Exodus comrades. The APC continued to burn, but the sounds of battle began to die down.

Clearing the narrow gap and the pile of enemy dead, I found myself on the west side of the roadblock. Surrounded by dead bodies were more than a dozen cars and trucks parked haphazardly, many still with the doors open.

Jesus Christ, I thought to myself. *Did we kill them all?* That would have been nice, but it wasn't the case. There were dozens, maybe scores of bodies on the ground here and more on the dam, but plenty of Jihan's soldiers were still alive. They were just retreating down the hill. That was odd. We hadn't seen them retreat before.

"Michael!" It was Ling. Her voice cut through the night like a clarion call. She appeared through the destroyed road block, approached, and squeezed my hand. "I'm so glad you're still alive."

"You too," I replied, breathing heavily. "Are you okay?"

"I'm fine. What's happening?"

I pointed down the hill. "We didn't get them all, but they're retreating. See?" In the moonlight, reflecting brightly in the snow, it was possible to see dozens of figures running down the road, away from us.

"I don't understand," Ling said. "They don't retreat. They never retreat. Something is wrong. Where is

Katsumoto?" I shrugged. Ling stepped around me and jogged along the road block, crossing through it at another one of the openings. "Katsumoto?" she shouted. There was no response.

"Ling!" It was Skunky. I was relieved to see him. He held his weapon at the low ready as he made his way to her.

"Where is Katsumoto?" she asked, concern obvious in her voice. "Did he fall?"

Skunky hesitated for a moment. "No, Ling. He stayed behind. At the dam, I mean."

"What? Why? Never mind." She grabbed her radio and hit the transmit button. "Katsumoto, this is Ling," she began, ignoring callsigns and protocol. "Where are you?"

There was no response at first. Ling repeated her query. Then, surrounded by static, Katsumoto's smooth, calming voice crackled over the radio.

"My lady," he said. *"I am afraid I chose to stay behind. You are in command now. I apologize for not telling you. It would have been a distraction."*

Tears welled up at the corners of Ling's eyes. "Why are you doing this? Your place is here, leading your men! Are you injured?"

"I am," he said. *"I can barely walk. But I am at peace. Child, my place is here. I have wounded that cannot be moved. There is nothing we can do for them. It is not right that they die alone. It is not right that I ask my brave warriors to lay down their lives if I am not willing to do the same."*

"This is madness!" Ling insisted. "Come on, there's still time!"

"I'm staying here," Katsumoto replied calmly. *"To*

ensure the demolition goes as planned. I did not ignite the fuse when you left. I wanted to ensure you had enough time to escape, and that the enemy was not able to disarm our explosives."

Tears trickled down Ling's cheeks, almost steaming in the frigid air. "I understand," she said simply, maintaining her steady demeanor despite the tears.

"*I knew you would. Let me know when you are a safe distance from the dam. Go with God, Song Ling. One day, we will meet again.*"

"Until that day," Ling agreed. "Go with God." Ling placed the radio back in its pouch, lowered her head, and took a deep breath.

She wasn't given long to cope. Skunky came running up. "Commander! We have a problem here!" It seemed like it took a second for her to realize he was speaking to her when he began with "Commander." My heart sank into my stomach. I knew it was too good to be true.

Skunky led us back through the roadblock, into the mess of vehicles that Jihan's soldiers had left behind. A kilometer down the hill, through the darkness, a stream of headlights pierced the night as many trucks turned to go up the hill. The enemy hadn't been retreating. They were regrouping and waiting for reinforcements.

I looked back across the carnage. There were few of us left, and we were already cut off. We were out of time.

Chapter 22: The Digging of Graves

LORENZO
Sala Jihan's Fortress
March 26th

"How many of these motherfuckers are there?" Anders shouted as bullets zipped through the air over our heads. The big man waited a moment, then jumped up and fired his stolen AK47 back in the direction of the enemy.

"Apparently lots," I grunted as I leaned around the wall and fired several rounds into the nearest bunker's doorway. The slave soldiers inside hunkered down as my rounds ricocheted harmlessly past them. I wasn't going to hit anyone. I already knew that. I was just trying to keep their heads down for a moment. Roland used that opportunity to cover the distance, get a better angle, and hurl a grenade through the door.

There was a resounding crash as the Russian frag detonated. One of the soldiers inside started screaming.

Phillips limped around the corner, hung his Tavor inside, fired two rounds and the noise stopped.

We had been fighting for what seemed like forever against a neverending stream of men. I would have run out of ammo for my ACR a while ago, except that Anders' 416 had been shot out of his hands and I had taken the rest of his magazines. Shen had a flesh wound across his hip, and Phillips had twisted his ankle, but other than that, my team was surprisingly fine. I couldn't even begin to calculate how many people we had shot to get this far.

"Chief, you're only thirty meters from the prison," Reaper told me. *"There's one more squad of soldiers ahead of you. Maybe a dozen of them."*

"Okay, how's the center holding?" The gunfire from the Exodus perimeter around the choppers was sporadic now. The soldiers had fought with suicidal intensity, but Exodus had held.

"Just pockets of soldiers keep throwing themselves at the silo. Ibrahim's pulled the perimeter around so that most of Exodus is there covering the assault team. There's just one team guarding the chopper and the wounded. I'm feeding info to Fajkus, and he's moving his guys around to intercept any soldiers as they get close. But I think most of them are dead."

News like that made me really glad that I had dropped almost a million dollars into Little Bird. It was like my own personal spy satellite. "How about reinforcements?"

"I was able to jam the radio signals from the compound when the attack began, but somehow the soldiers at the mine knew anyway. There's a column of trucks coming up the road now. Fajkus sent one team to stall them at the front

gates. *Those bastards are going to have a real hard time getting through those big ass gates. But . . ."*

"What?"

It wasn't Reaper that responded, rather it was Jill. *"I've been listening to the local radio chatter while Reaper's been playing flight simulator, and I haven't gotten anything from town."*

"At all?" Kat's mercenaries should have assaulted the Brothers and the garrison in town by now.

"Nothing. Especially nothing about a battle in The Crossroads."

"Shit," I muttered. Diego must have chickened out. Which meant that we had a bunch more bad guys in town coming to help.

"And there's something going down at the dam. There's a big fight going on there that Exodus didn't tell us about. Lots of vehicles went that way from the mine, too."

What? Talk about biting off more than they could chew. What the hell was Exodus thinking? "Okay, be ready for anything."

"Love ya. Bye." It wasn't proper radio etiquette, but I liked Jill's methods better. Jill and Reaper were stationed well out of town, using a vehicle that we had bought on the down low. I didn't trust any of the sides here, and wanted my own ace in the hole. Nobody but me knew where they were parked.

"Anders, we've got maybe a dozen between us and the prison." I flexed my aching hands. The insides of the wool gloves were stained with red, and I figured that quite a bit of it was mine.

"Here's what we do." Anders had, by far, the most

actual combat experience. I'd spent my career avoiding straight-up fights. He signaled toward Shen. "I want you to flank right. We'll cover—" He was cut off by a sudden thunderous chain of explosions. The sky back toward the silo was suddenly bright as yellow flashes reflected off all of the compounds' walls and buildings. Ibrahim had breached the elevator shaft.

Anders' plan went out the window then. The remaining slave soldiers all began screaming. They rose up from behind their positions of cover, and began to run wildly toward the silo, which meant they had to go right through the five of us. It was like the Exodus banzai charge earlier, only it made even less sense.

I opened fire, pumping round after round into the charging fanatics. Red dot moving to one, *tap tap*, then on to the next, repeat. One of them tumbled face down into the snow as my rounds pierced his chest. He continued to claw his way forward for a few more seconds. I watched him in disbelief as I reloaded, but he wouldn't give up until his pulped heart could finally pump no more.

Then it was over. The remaining soldiers were all dead, splayed about in the street, blood slowly staining the snow into pink slush, steam rising from their torn open corpses.

"What was that?" Anders asked in disbelief.

"They were trying to get to Jihan . . . it's like they went crazy," I replied.

"But . . . but . . . they're slaves. Why would they do something like that?" Phillips asked. He was sincerely shaken. Shen shook his head. The quiet man had no answers either.

What kind of man was Sala Jihan, that he could inspire

such psychotic loyalty in people that he had kidnapped from their own homes?

"Screw it. Let's get my brother."

VALENTINE
The Dam

Ling, Skunky, and I stood at the breach, staring down into the darkness. Another line of vehicles was slowly headed up the road toward us. They would be on top of us in minutes. Our only hope now was to spread out and scatter, try to escape on foot through the snow. There was no hope for the wounded who couldn't walk, like the German whose leg I'd put a tourniquet on.

Ling watched in silence. I could see something I'd never seen in her eyes before: *fear.* It was all over Skunky's face as well. And if I was being honest with myself, deep down, hidden beneath *the Calm*, I felt it too. I took the fact that after surviving so much, I was probably going to die in this place, to be a grave injustice. My mind raced for a way out, for some other option besides death and something worse than death, and I was drawing a blank. Ling didn't say anything. She just watched our approaching doom and shook her head slightly. Behind us, the rest of the surviving Exodus personnel were gathering at the burning remains of the roadblock. They were all watching her, waiting for orders, waiting for *something*.

"Jeff," I said, looking at my old friend. "Go back there and make sure the wounded are still being treated. Get everyone together and start figuring out a way to drag the wounded that can't walk across the snow. We don't have a lot of options right now and we have no time. Make litters or something."

"But what about . . ."

I cut him off. "Just do it. I'll take care of her. Go!" He nodded his head and ran off to do as I asked. Ling and I were alone. I put my hands on her shoulders and looked down into her eyes.

"Listen to me," I said. "Your people need you right now. They need their commander. They're counting on you."

"I have already failed them," she said. "Don't you understand? We're all going to die here."

I agreed. "Seems that way. But that doesn't give you the right to just quit on them when they've fought so hard for you. It's not over until the last one of us is dead. You owe it to them to keep fighting until the last. They've earned that."

Ling looked down at the ground for a moment, her face resuming its usual mask. "Yes. Yes, you're right." She looked up into my eyes. "You are a remarkable individual, Mr. Valentine."

"If you say so. No offense, but I just want to go home."

She actually laughed. "As do I. Come, please help me carry the wounded. We don't—" She fell silent as her radio crackled to life.

It was Ibrahim. *"Stand by to breach. Fire in the hole, fire in the hole, fire in the hole."*

"What's going on?" I asked.

"He must be breaching the missile silo. Michael, look,"

Ling said, pointing back down the hill. "They've stopped." Sure enough, the enemy column that had been slowly advancing up the hillside had stopped in place.

"What the hell are they doing?" It didn't take long for me to get my answer. In the most haphazard and erratic fashion imaginable, the enemy column tried to turn around on the narrow road. It was almost comical. Vehicles crashed into each other. The shouts of Jihan's men were carried on the wind to our position. They reversed as fast as they could, seemingly in a panic.

"Holy shit. Is it because of Jihan? Are they going back because they're going after him? Did the fortress call in reinforcements?"

"He's calling to them," Ling said. She spoke into her radio then. "Sword One, this is Sword Three. The enemy from our position is apparently en route to your position. Prepare yourselves for enemy reinforcements."

There was a long delay before Ibrahim answered. *"This is Sword One Actual. Understood. Can you delay them?"*

"Negative, Sword One. We have taken heavy losses. We were about to be overrun when they retreated. Our entire egress plan is going to have to be revised on the fly."

"Understood," Ibrahim repeated. *"Godspeed, my lady. We are about to enter the abyss."*

"God speed to you as well," Ling said solemnly. "Shine a light into the darkness."

I was confused. "What's going on? What's he doing?"

"He's preparing to take his team down into the silo after Sala Jihan," Ling answered, sounding distant.

"It's just a single missile silo, right? It shouldn't take them long to find him."

"There are many places to hide down in that dark hole." Ling paused for a second. "Sala Jihan has proven difficult to kill in the past." Before I could ask her what in the hell *that* meant, she switched channels and spoke into her radio again.

"Sword Three Actual! This is Sword Three X-Ray! Come in!"

Katsumoto took a moment before responding. *"This is Sword Three Actual. Are you clear of the dam?"*

"Negative! Stand by, we're coming to get you! The enemy has retreated. We have time to gather the wounded and commandeer vehicles. No one else has to die here!"

There was a long silence. *"I hope you don't think less of me if I admit to being relieved,"* Katsumoto said wryly.

Ling laughed as her eyes teared up a little. "It can be our secret. Please hold on. We're on our way."

LORENZO
Sala Jihan's Fortress

The steel door to the prison was open. The walls were still painted that sick pea-green that the Russian military painted everything. Starkly naked lightbulbs burned and flickered on the walls. Water dripped from exposed steam pipes. I rushed through first, my muzzle sweeping back and forth, the three Exodus operatives followed me, and Anders brought up the rear.

"Chief, you should turn back to the command channel.

Ibrahim and his guys are roping down the elevator shaft," Reaper informed me. *"Oh, man, they're jumping down. The Pale Man is pwned! Go get that creepy motherfucker!"*

I clicked my radio over. The men behind me did as well. It all came down to this. Even though my mission was to find Bob, what happened in the next few minutes would determine all of our fates. The first floor of the prison was empty. We moved from cell to cell, but the doors were unlocked and nobody was inside any of them.

One of the functionaries was hiding behind some crates. I recognized him from the business meeting with Jill. He was barefoot and wearing flannel pajamas, probably chased out of his nice bunker by Exodus. He started pleading for his life as soon he saw us, but Anders shot him in the heart.

At the end of the floor was a flight of industrial steel steps. We headed up.

The second floor was dark. I turned my Surefire light on and shined it down the hallway. There was a single door made of iron bars that was currently hanging open, a chain and open padlock dangling from it. I stepped through. My light illuminated a long corridor of heavy cell doors. It was musty and claustrophobic.

We all heard Ibrahim's voice come over the radio. *"We're heading down. Be wary."*

"Bob!" I bellowed at the top of my lungs. "Bob Lorenzo!" There was no response except for the echo.

Something moved at the end of the corridor. I lifted my gun. A skinny, shirtless man leapt out of the darkness. He had a Nagant revolver in one bony hand. He screamed at us, his lips spread wide over toothless gums. He started to raise the pistol. I fired a single shot, splattering his brains all over the wall.

The rest of my team turned on their flashlights and started checking rooms. Shen spoke softly. "Lorenzo, it doesn't look good."

I glanced over Shen's shoulder. Inside the first cell was a body. It was a younger Mongol man, but he had a single bullet wound to his head, his body still backed into the corner. The next cell was the same, with another recently murdered prisoner. The man that I had just shot had been systematically executing them rather than letting them be freed.

"We're at the bottom. There is extensive damage from the explosives." I could almost imagine the sounds of his team's ropes rebounding against the wall and the clacking of their weapons. *"Fan out. Wait . . . The blast doors are already open. We won't need to cut through."*

Someone in the background of Ibrahim's radio said something that sounded like *what luck.*

"No. He is waiting for us . . ."

I moved quickly from cell to cell, just long enough to shine my flashlight inside each one. More dead bodies. None of them were Bob. With a great deal of hesitation, I approached the final cell. My light flooded the little room through the bars. There was a large body face down in a pile of dirty straw in the back of the cell.

Ibrahim had left his radio on transmit, as every member of Exodus was eager to hear what happened next. *"Rasheed, cover our exit. We are heading into the center. The launch pad is clear. No sign of life. He's here somewhere. Carmen, check over there . . . Wait . . . What was that?"*

My boot impacted the cell door. I smashed it as hard as I could, over and over, the impacts traveling up through the bones of my feet. "Damn it, damn it, damn it, damn it. Bob!" The lock was too heavy. Shen materialized at my side, having lifted a large ring of keys from the dead jailer. He started trying keys. *Oh, God, my brother is dead.* "Bob! Bob!"

The ancient lock clicked open with an audible snap. I shoved it open and tore toward the body.

Ibrahim's radio was sending the sound of nervous, heavy breathing, in the distance someone else on his team says something that sounded like *there's something in the water.*

I grabbed the arm of the dead man and pulled him over. He was a huge, bald Caucasian. The Exodus operatives raised their lights to help me see. I stared into the dead man's face.

The radio transmitted the sound of splashing, then gunfire.

I stared into the dead man's face. Involuntary tears started to roll down my cheeks.

"*Show yourself, demon!*" Ibrahim bellowed.

It wasn't Bob. It was somebody else.

The radio was a cacophony of chaos. The noise from the silo was indescribable. Something had gone horribly wrong.

I sprang to my feet. "Let's go." I ordered. The three Exodus operatives were standing there, speechless as they listened to their command channel.

There was a sliding, metallic crashing noise from the end of the hall. Somebody had just slammed the main gate.

I shined my light down the hallway. Anders stood on the other side of the now locked gate. "So long, Lorenzo."

"*Anders!*" I raised my rifle, but he moved swiftly around the corner. The muzzle of his AK appeared around the wall as he triggered a burst. I narrowly dodged back into the cell as bullets skipped around me.

"It's nothing personal. We just needed your help, and now we don't."

"You son of a bitch!" I shouted, ignoring the screaming and shooting in my earpiece. It sounded like Ibrahim's team was getting torn apart.

"We needed a way to take Jihan down. Then you showed up. We were afraid something like this would happen, but it was worth a shot."

There was enough space between the walls and the cell doors that a thin man could squeeze in there and have cover. I leapt across the hall and slammed myself into the next doorway.

"You see, it's not just about control of The Crossroads. Sure, that's a plus," Anders explained patiently. He must have realized that I was trying to get closer as he fired a few more rounds down the hallway to pin me down. "But it is bigger than that, way bigger. You have no idea what Project Blue is."

"Why don't you tell me before I kill you, then?"

Anders laughed, that traitorous bastard. "Sala Jihan knew about my part in Blue. Hell, I couldn't have done it without him. He had to go. The Pale Man's a loose end. See, when I figured Majestic fucked me, I decided to fuck them right back. Majestic didn't have the balls to complete Project Blue, but I do."

I jumped across to the next door. I could hear one of the Exodus operatives doing the same behind me. Anders fired another shot, but was answered by a pair of suppressed shots in response that sparked off the bars.

"Seeing your brother here was a surprise. I hadn't seen Bob since he helped get me thrown out of the FBI, that self-righteous asshole. He had finally figured it all out, put all his paranoid conspiracy theories to work, and actually ended up with the truth. That's why I had to grab him."

Jihan never had Bob.

"Oh, just figuring it out now? Yeah. Sucks, don't it? Hell, Bob was locked in the basement of the Exchange while you were there. I'll tell you though, you showing up helped us. It enabled me to get Exodus to do our dirty work for us. That slave we killed back in town? I contacted him beforehand, told him that if he told you a story, I'd sneak him out of the country. We were afraid that the stories about Jihan were true. Personally, I thought they were bullshit, but I've seen stranger stuff. I mean, seriously, Majestic agents get to do some freaky shit, but we needed muscle, and that's where Exodus came in."

"Did you kill my brother?"

"Not yet. He's my Lee Harvey Oswald. When he dies, it'll be on the world news. Not that you'll be around to see it, because it looks like Jihan is going to fuckin' kill all of you. Too bad I couldn't tie up that loose end, but I've got another contingency plan in place for him. Kat loses The Crossroads entirely, but Blue is going to get us something a whole lot better."

I moved again. One more.

"And speaking of loose ends, your hot little woman and

your dipshit sidekick? Yeah, Diego's going to take care of them. We triangulated the radio signals they need to drive your little toy airplane. They'll be dead soon too, just like you."

I took a deep breath and jumped for the next doorway, but there were no more gunshots. I was close enough now that I could get a grenade through the bars and not just bounce it down the hallway back into us. I chucked it through the iron. The explosion came a moment later. It shook dust from the ceiling.

Sprinting the rest of the way, I slammed into the bars, shoving my muzzle through, but Anders was already gone down the stairs.

"Everybody okay?" I shouted. I got three quick yes answers.

The padlock was huge, and shooting it would've just hit us with lots of ricochets. "Breach it," I ordered. Phillips moved up, pulling a block of explosive out of a pouch on his vest.

Ibrahim was on the radio again, except I was having a hard time understanding him. His breath was coming in ragged gasps. He was talking, in short, clipped sentences, apparently in Kurdish, obviously in a great deal of pain. He was tying up the command channel, whispering a prayer. I heard him commend his soul to Allah. There were a few more gun shots, then a loud crack.

A moment later, I could hear something else on the radio, a crunching noise, like bones being snapped. Finally another voice came on. I recognized it, and could picture the pale white flesh and solid black eyes. He had warned me not to come back here.

"*Trespassers . . .*" Sala Jihan muttered. Then the radio went dead.

"Jill. Reaper. Come in."

No answer.

"If you can hear me. Get the hell out of there now. Diego's coming to kill you." I flipped back to the command line as I ran through the snow.

"*Sword Two, on me. Move up on the pit,*" Fajkus ordered over the radio. There was a huge volume of gunfire coming from that direction now. My team was sprinting through the compound, heading toward the choppers. "*What the hell is going on down there? Somebody answer me!*"

"Fajkus! Come in. This is Lorenzo. Anders is a traitor. Watch out." I panted as I ran. I got no response. It was no surprise. The radio net was in complete disarray. Something very bad was happening at the missile silo.

"*Oh God who art in heaven,*" somebody gasped. "*Hallowed be thy name . . .*"

"*Get off the fucking radio!*" Fajkus ordered. "*Somebody give me a sitrep.*"

Then there was screaming. The praying stopped with a series of tearing noises, and that signal died.

"*Fajkus. This is Nagano. Retreat. They're all dead. We've got to—Aarrgghh—*" then that one was gone too.

I flipped back. "Jill! Reaper!" I tripped and sprawled face first into the slush. Rolling over, and bounding back to my feet, I had tripped over the body of an Exodus operative. It was dark, but it was obvious that he had died horribly, his chest torn open, white ribs sticking out.

"*Lorenzo!*" Jill finally responded.

"You've got to get out of there. The Montalbans are coming to kill you."

"*I know. I just shot two of them, I think,*" she replied, sounding rather flustered. "*They showed up, but I had stuck out those claymores just like you showed me. I'm driving now. We're both okay. I don't know where we're going though, I don't think they're following me, but I don't know how they found us.*"

"Tell Reaper that they're triangulating off the radio signal he uses to fly the Little Bird. I'm glad you're okay," I said, still running. "Put Reaper on . . . Reaper? What do you see? What's going on at the silo?"

"*A counterattack. Exodus is getting slaughtered.*" Reaper didn't sound very good. He sounded kind of confused and out of it. "*I . . . I don't know.*"

"What do you see?"

"*Something . . . I don't . . . I don't know . . .*"

"Come on man, focus, I'm going to be there in a second."

"*Don't go there. Run, Lorenzo. Run away. Get out of there. Get on the chopper and fly away. Please.*" His voice was desperate, and . . . afraid? He was miles away staring at a video screen.

"What is it?" It was unlike Reaper to freak out like this. He was young, but he had seen a lot. He had never choked on me before in all the years we had been doing this together. "What's going on?"

"*Quit yelling at me!*" he cried. "*I don't know what it is, okay? Just get away from it!*"

"Damn it! Reaper, listen to me. Take down Little Bird.

The Montalbans found you because of that signal. Take it down now!"

"Okay. Okay. Okay," he stammered. *"Here's Jill."*

"Honey, I'll be in touch. Just keep driving."

"Be careful, Lorenzo." The line clicked off.

Then the choppers were in view. The four of us tore toward them at a full run, our breath leaving clouds of steam hanging behind us. The one working chopper's blades were turning fast, only seconds from lifting off. There were a shockingly small number of people milling around near the choppers, and most of them were spread out in a skirmish line between the Halo and the pit, muzzle flashes indicating that they were firing against the silo.

Suddenly the chopper was airborne, blowing snow everywhere in a giant tornado. As I got closer, I could see a figure standing in the open door of the Halo helicopter. I only recognized that it was Svetlana by the big sniper rifle in her bandaged hands. She turned and shouted angrily back into the chopper's interior, then turned around and gestured for them to go back down to pick up the other survivors.

There was a muzzle flash from inside the chopper, and Svetlana dropped from the back door of the helicopter and plummeted about twenty feet to the ground. She actually landed on her feet, but her legs immediately crumpled, broken beneath her.

"No!" screamed Phillips as we charged onward.

The rear of the chopper swiveled toward us as it continued to rise, tracers strobing from the door gun down into the Exodus wounded as Anders murdered everyone he could. A lone figure stood in the door, braced against a strut, her blond hair billowing in the turbulent wind around her. Katarina waved.

"Kat!" I shouted as I raised my gun and opened fire at the retreating chopper, but it was moving too quick. "Damn it!" That was our way out.

"Where's the chopper going?" Fajkus shouted across the radio. *"Wait, what the hell is tha—"* His radio cut out suddenly.

"Attention, Exodus. This is Katarina. Our business arrangement has, sadly, come to an end."

We're screwed.

My team reached the remaining members of Exodus at the LZ. There were only a handful left, and all of them appeared to be injured. Anders had shredded the skirmish line with the chopper's door gun, and there were screams from the dying. Shen and Phillips tried to help them while Roland attended to Svetlana, who was moaning in the snow, a jagged chunk of bone sticking out the side of her pants.

"Fajkus! This is Lorenzo. Come in." There was only static on the line. I realized that all of the gunfire from the silo had ceased, and with the chopper getting further away, the compound was gradually quieting. After so much commotion, it was rather disconcerting. I glanced around. "Who's in charge?"

The shell-shocked Exodus survivors looked at each other, trying to ascertain who was the senior member still standing.

"I believe that would be me." A deep voice from the direction of the silo. I turned my flashlight on the approaching figures. One large man had a second smaller man over his shoulders in a fireman carry. I recognized them immediately.

"Antoine," I said, glad to see it was somebody I could count on. "What happened?"

"I don't know. Fajkus is unconscious," the tall African grunted as he gently lowered the other man to the ground. Fajkus's parka was covered in blood and torn open in several places. "Everyone else is dead."

"We have to get out of here," I said tersely.

"Agreed," he glanced upward. "Why did the helicopter leave? Why did it fire on us?"

"Long story," I replied, looking over the carnage. Exodus had been exposed. "Fucking Anders. We can grab some vehicles and head for town."

"Negative," Antoine shook his head. "Reinforcements from the mines are blocking the road. They will be here soon." What went unsaid was that whoever had just killed most of Exodus in the last few minutes was still in the compound with us.

I scanned the compound. Flames were billowing upward from a dozen points and the air tasted like burning rubber and diesel. "Okay, we take the back way out, the way my team came in. We rope down to the valley floor, and then hoof it up the canyon."

Antoine glanced around at the many wounded, both of us already knowing that many of them were not going to make it. The Plan C escape route was a worst-case scenario even if you were healthy, let alone carrying a bunch of injured. He raised his voice so that everyone could hear. "Exodus, my brothers. Move quickly. Take ammunition from the dead and the other Halo. Everyone that can walk, help those that cannot. Follow Lorenzo. He will show us the way out."

"Brother," Shen said. I jumped, adrenaline-soaked nerves expecting another one of those silent, hooded freaks to have shown up, but Shen was just talking to Antoine. The two men embraced. "I'm glad to see you made it."

"We must hurry." Ling's former teammates began helping the wounded. There were only a few of us in any shape to fight; me, Shen, Antoine, Phillips, and Roland. There were four others a lot worse off. I couldn't believe it. I didn't know how many men Exodus had brought it, but it had to have been at least sixty or seventy. Svetlana screamed as Phillips shoved the bone back into her leg and wrapped it in gauze.

"Damn you, Katarina," I whispered to myself as I led the way back across the compound, a horde of fanatics only minutes behind us. This was going to be tight.

My radio chirped in my ear. I hit the mike, expecting news from Reaper or Jill. Instead it was Katarina, calling to gloat. I felt an indescribable ball of rage bubble up from inside my stomach. It made me warm.

"*Well, well, well, you're in a predicament now, aren't you, Lorenzo, my dear?*"

"I thought you wanted The Crossroads more than you'd want revenge. I was a fool to believe you."

"*Yes, and I was a fool to trust you all those years ago. Now you know how it feels. You abandoned me when I needed you, and now I'm abandoning you.*"

"So that's what this is about, then?" I spat. I moved quickly through the wreckage of the compound, running forward, and taking up a cover position as the others followed more slowly. "You're willing to let all these good men die just out of spite?"

Kat laughed over the radio, having a good old time. "*No, of course not, silly. That's absurd. I was going to betray them no matter what. That's just sound business. This was a gamble for me to not only utilize Project Blue, but also to become the sole ruler of The Crossroads, like Big Eddie before me. Being able to destroy you along with Exodus was just a happy bonus.*"

I didn't respond. Half of my brain was trying to watch my surroundings, the other half was a calculating how I was going to track Katarina down and kill her. I paused, waiting for Exodus. Something moved in the shadows ahead. I hit the spot with my flashlight, but whatever it was had already moved.

"*Do you know why I'm calling you?*" She didn't bother to wait for my response. "*I just wanted to explain myself, and perhaps, to hurt you a little bit more. I feel I owe you that. After all, I loved you once.*"

"You chose Big Eddie over me."

"*Oh, how stupid you are. You still don't get it, do you?*" she asked as I leapt over more dismembered bodies. An arm dangled from a nearby roof, drizzling blood. "*Of course I was loyal to the Montalbans. I always have been. Back when we worked together, all those jobs that we did, you were Big Eddie's right-hand man, and yet you never met him. I was always the go-between. I was the one that had to prove myself to the Montalbans, not you. I had to earn their respect.*"

"Sounds like a personal problem."

"*Do you remember, once, so long ago, you always*

warned me about how people like us should never reveal our real identities to anyone? I heeded your advice. I never told you my real name. You were weak, and you told me yours, Hector Romasanta. So allow me to return the favor. My real name is Elizabeth . . ."

One of the Exodus operatives slipped in the snow behind me. The injured man he was carrying screamed as damaged nerves struck the ground.

"Katarina . . ."

I kept seeing shapes moving ahead of me, just out of the view of my light, but I couldn't catch them. I kept moving.

". . . Montalban."

I stopped. "You've got to be shitting me."

Her laugh sounded distorted through the radio. The chopper was getting further away, and the reception on my portable was starting to break up. *"No. My older brother was Rafael Montalban. He was father's favorite, as he was the legitimate heir. Eduard, or Big Eddie, as he insisted on being called, was next in line, but Eduard was always a little off, a little crazy, but at least his mother was respected English royalty. Rafael was a prodigy, Eduard liked to burn things and hurt animals. I was the youngest, and least legitimate of all my father's children. My mother was a Swiss whore."*

"Crazy and sleazy runs in the family," I snarled.

"Yes indeed. Eduard hurt me many times, but I thank him for it now, for it made me strong. After Father died, Rafael took care of the legitimate family business. Eddie inherited the dark side. There was nothing left for me. I was unwanted, unloved. So if I could not receive

my family's love, then I would earn it. That is when I went to work with you, to prove my worthiness to my brothers."

"You used me, even back then." This changed nothing. I was still going to get out of here and kill her, but at least it put her damaged nature in perspective.

"Oh, at first, but I really did love you. You were the one that made me choose, choose between happiness and destiny. You never should have done that, Hector."

A thought flashed through my mind, a memory of Thailand, a few years ago, as the Fat Man, Big Eddie's indomitable bodyguard, had arrived to blackmail my team with information about our real families. I had never understood how Big Eddie could have learned so much about me. "You . . . It was you that gave Big Eddie my family. It was you that forced me into the Zubara job."

"Of course. When Eddie told me he needed the best for Zubara, you were the only man for the job. I was glad to give him your real name. I prayed for your death every day. But somehow, impossibly, both of my brothers died instead. Brave Rafael murdered by Majestic, and beautiful Eduard, dead by your hand. The great Montalban dynasty, one of the great Illuminati families for over five hundred years, shattered, and now scorned by the other legitimate families. But fate has smiled upon me. Anders has given me the key to Project Blue, a brilliant plot to put the Illuminati in their place, and with it, I will reclaim my family's glory. The other families will kneel at my feet."

"You're toast. Jihan will destroy you."

"The Pale Man's power ends at the border of The Crossroads. I hoped to use Exodus to end him and regain

this kingdom that Eddie built, but I don't need it anymore. I am on to bigger and better things."

I reached the gap in the back wall. The guards' bodies that we had left in the shadows under the broken rebar were gone. I saw no movement, so I proceeded to secure the rope, my mind still reeling from the information I had just been given. "What about my brother?"

Her voice was breaking up badly now. I could barely hear her through the static. "*Hector, always so loyal to everyone except for me. Your brother is still alive, for now, but only because Anders has a use for him. Blue is coming—d*" Static interrupted the transmission. "*When it—the world—*" The signal was fading.

I smashed the button on my mike. "You know what the last thing I told your darling Eddie was before I blew him to pieces?"

"*What was that?*"

"I'll see you in hell."

The signal was gone.

Chapter 23: Weakness
Leaving the Body

🦅

VALENTINE
The Dam

We'd been given a second lease on life. At least, that's how it felt. The situation was still dire. We'd lost a large chunk of our force, we had many wounded, and our exfil plan had gone to shit, but we were accomplishing the mission, and it looked like we would actually live to talk about it.

Despite the good news, we were in a real hurry. There was no telling when Sala Jihan's forces would return to the dam. We had no idea what was going on at the fortress. No one was answering the radio over there, and the distance and terrain made communications difficult to begin with. Nothing seemed to be happening in town as near as we could tell.

Only one of our original vehicles was still in driving shape, but it didn't matter. We had plenty of trucks to choose from. One had only to pull out the dead driver and not think about sitting in someone else's blood. In this fashion we put together a new convoy and tried to contact the people that were waiting for us at the rendezvous point.

Despite our heavy losses, Ling was actually smiling. Katsumoto, limping badly from a bullet in his leg, was still alive, and we'd beaten back the enemy, at least temporarily. There's a certain rush that comes with completing such a dangerous mission that's hard to explain to anyone who hasn't experienced it. The look on her face gave it away.

It never lasts. Sooner or later reality always catches up with you. It caught up with us when the two of the wounded who had been at the dam with Katsumoto succumbed to their injuries. It was driven home when Katsumoto received a static-filled radio transmission from Antoine.

"Sword Three, Sword Three, this is Sword Four."

Katsumoto and Ling exchanged a knowing look. Ibrahim had been Sword One. Fajkus was his support Element, Sword Two. Sword Four was Lorenzo's team.

"This is Sword One," Katsumoto replied calmly. "What is the situation?"

There was a long pause, filled with static. *"We have failed."*

Katsumoto closed his eyes for a couple of seconds. Ling lowered her head. "Understood. What happened?"

"I do not know. Sword One took his element down into the pit. They are all lost. Sword Two attempted to come to his aid, and they suffered severe losses as well. Sword Two Actual is catatonic. I am in command now."

"Are you egressing on the helicopters?"

"Negative. One helicopter was lost. The other left

without us. The Montalbans have betrayed us. That woman took her remaining men. They fired on us as they left, killing several more men."

"Treacherous whore!" Ling snarled, her hands balling into fists.

"We are cut off by reinforcements from the mines. Our only means of exfiltration is down the cliff, on foot."

"We will come get you, brother. It will take us some time, but we will come get you. You will not be left to die. We will meet you at the emergency rendezvous point with enough vehicles to extract you."

"We will lose radio communications as we go down into the valley. It is a long walk to the rendezvous point, and we are carrying wounded. Our chances of making it are not great. Do not wait for us too long."

Katsumoto's face was a mask of resolve. "The Montalbans have betrayed us, but they will pay dearly for it. Our part of the operation has succeeded. We are preparing to initiate as we speak. This foul place will wither and die."

Antoine actually sounded happy about that. *"That is the best news I've heard all night,"* he said. *"Good luck, my friend."*

"And to you," Katsumoto replied.

"Wait," I said, before the Exodus commander signed off. "Is Lorenzo still alive?" Katsumoto relayed my question to Antoine.

"He is still alive, Mr. Valentine. He is with us. Do you wish to speak to him?"

I took the radio from Katsumoto. "Not really. Did he find his brother though?"

"I'm afraid not. He tells me that that, too was a Montalban ploy. His brother was never here. We've all been deceived." The radio went to static for a moment. *"He also suggests that you go fornicate with yourself."*

"Likewise. Valentine out."

As the last of us cleared the dam, Ling and Katsumoto consulted on a plan. We had too many wounded to all go to Antoine's rescue. Some would not last the night if we had to fight our way to our friends. There was little choice: we'd have to split up.

Katsumoto wanted to lead the element that rescued Antoine, of course. He was the senior Exodus commander on scene now, and saving his people was his duty. His right knee had been shattered by a bullet, though. He could move under his own power only with the aid of an improvised crutch, and he'd lost a lot of blood. He looked tired and pale.

The rescue mission fell to Ling. She'd been through a lot this night, but she only had minor injuries. She accepted her task solemnly and swore to Katsumoto that she'd get Antoine out if there was any possible way. The call then went out for volunteers, those who were still able to fight and wanted to go. As near as I could tell, every single Exodus operative still walking (and some that weren't) raised his or her hand, Skunky included.

Their loyalty to each other was impressive. They were bonded as tightly as any professional army I'd ever worked with. You couldn't help but feel respect for their level of dedication to one another, despite coming from widely different ethnic, national, cultural, and religious backgrounds.

Not everyone could go, and there weren't very many to choose from. Of the original fifty Exodus operatives, only thirty were still alive. Of those, only sixteen were uninjured. Of those, not all could be spared for the rescue.

In the end, six Exodus operatives were to accompany Ling, including Skunky. It was a small element to potentially have to fight across hostile territory. They would have to bring enough vehicles to carry all of Antoine's surviving people. Many were low on ammunition and had to scrounge for what supplies they could get.

For my part, I was leaning on one of our wrecked trucks, drinking a bottle of water from a case that'd been inside. I'd sucked the hydration bladder in my backpack dry and was thirsty as hell. I was leaning because my arms and legs were shaking. Adrenaline dump was hitting me hard. I was exhausted. I just wanted a hot shower and a warm bed to lay in. I think Ling sensed this as she approached, because she seemed to do so cautiously. "How are you doing?"

"I'll be okay," I said. "I just need a moment. What happens now?"

"I will lead my team to the rendezvous point to extract Lorenzo and Antoine's element. I owe Antoine my life several times over. And Lorenzo . . . I asked Lorenzo to come here. Practically coerced him. I owe it to him to not leave him to die without trying to come to his aid. That is not the Exodus way."

"I know," I said. "I just needed a drink before we go."

"Michael, you don't have to go," she said levelly, looking up into my eyes. "I can ask no more of you. I thought I'd brought you to your death, but by the grace of

God we came through. All you need to do is go with Katsumoto. It is as close as you can get to being safe."

"And Jill would never forgive me if I just left his stupid ass there. Besides, you need all the bodies you can get. So stop arguing with me, please. I'm going. I'm in this thing to the end."

Ling looked at me the way Sarah had, very briefly, before putting her mask back on. "Thank you," she managed. "But please, take your water with you. We need to get going."

Damn it, I thought. All of this and I wouldn't even get to see the explosion.

LORENZO
The Cliffs

The last of the injured was tied to the rope and sent spiraling over the edge that I had climbed over just a few hours before. There were only three who couldn't walk now. We had not been able to control the bleeding from a man named Solomon, and his body was behind us in the snow. I would be the last man to leave the compound, which was good, because we'd kicked the hornet's nest.

There was a lot of movement inside the compound. I could see a lot of shadows moving in front of the fires. The gates had been flung open to let the reinforcements inside. I took one last look before going over the edge, and froze. A lone figure was standing silhouetted in front of the burning Tunguska. It was dark at the lip of the chasm. There was no way he could see me, but I felt an involuntary shiver anyway. The black sliver of a man was perfectly still, and somehow I knew he was watching me with deadly, soulless eyes.

Sala Jihan had come up out of his hole.

"You win this one, you son of a bitch."

I went over the edge quickly, a makeshift harness strung around me. My boots would impact the glasslike ice, kick outward, and I would plunge another twenty feet at a time. I hit the ground too fast. The others were already prepared to move out. Exodus was silent, each of them burdened by heavy thoughts and internal pain. Shen was mashing a claymore into the snow just ahead of us. The first soldiers down that rope were going to get a surprise. Hopefully an occasional booby-trap would keep our pursuers cautious and moving slow.

We took turns carrying the wounded, one unburdened man on point and the other at the rear. We passed the nomads' tiny settlement and found it was abandoned. No sign of Lotus Blossom, her family, or their yaks. They apparently had the good sense to get the hell out of the area after I had shown up earlier. Wing's body was probably stuffed into one of the many ice crevasses nearby.

We had memorized terrain maps of this area, not only because it was where my team had inserted, but also because it had been our last-ditch possibility of retreat if everything had gone horribly wrong. The canyon was far too rocky for vehicles to follow, so now we had us a foot race.

My team had been dropped off on the main road, and

we had walked to the nomad village. Now that road was crawling with Jihan's reinforcements from the mines. So our only other options were to hide or to try to walk out the other end of the canyon, which was about ten miles of brutal terrain that finally terminated on a Russian plain just off the Mongolian border. Judging by the ant's nest we had just kicked, the smart money wasn't on hiding.

The going was hard. The footing was treacherous and slick. Only half of the group had managed to retain their night vision, and we took turns wearing it, so that the person on point and the man bringing up the rear could always see. Luckily, the sky was still clear and the snow was so bright and reflective that none of us were totally blind.

Antoine set a brutal pace for the first thirty minutes. We needed to get as much of a lead as possible before the soldiers zeroed in on us. Finally, he called a brief halt. We needed to tend to the injured and better secure their wounds before anyone else ended up like Solomon.

Fajkus was still out. He was badly concussed, with a deep laceration on his scalp and several more cuts on his arms and torso. Nobody knew what had happened to him after he led the counterattack against the silo, but at least we had gotten the bleeding stopped.

The next was an Exodus operative from Korea, named Kim. He had taken a round through the forearm. It had struck him in the wrist, traveled right up the bone, and exited out his elbow. The flesh was totally pulverized. Shen had tied a tourniquet just above the elbow. Kim wasn't looking good. He could scarcely walk, and kept stumbling. He had lost a lot of blood and was barely coherent.

Svetlana was hanging in there. The Russian sniper was in terrible pain, with bones in both of her legs shattered. She had to be carried, and the burden was increased for whoever had her on their back because she refused to put down her heavy sniper rifle. None of us could really disagree with that because all of us knew what the chances of us getting away were, and none of us were the type that would give up without a fight.

Phillips was limping badly now. His ankle was terribly sprained, and the flesh sticking out the top of his boot was black, purple, and swollen to twice its normal size. He grimaced at every step, but would not quit.

There was a muted thump far behind us. Somebody had set off the claymore. Antoine signaled for us to continue. It was my turn in the middle, so I helped Kim to his feet, locked his good arm over my shoulder, and helped drag him up the mountain.

LORENZO
The Mountain

"How many are there?" I asked.

Antoine shook his head grimly and passed me the binoculars. "Too many."

I scanned down the mountain. The glass wasn't night vision, but I could make out the dark shapes moving on the white surface far below us. He was right. There were hundreds of them down there. It was a full-fledged hunting party. Occasionally there would be a flicker of lights as they came across some part of our trail they wanted to examine in the dark.

"They're not having any problem tracking us," I muttered.

"Not much we could do about that, I'm afraid." Which was true, we were leaving a trail that a blind man could follow. "We must go. They're moving much faster than we are."

"Come dawn, they'll be able to track us even faster." I exhaled, leaving a cloud of steam that instantly crystallized in the stubble on my face. If anything, it had only gotten colder as the night had gone on. Stopping briefly to check on our pursuers drove that point home as all the sweat from our exertion froze instantly to our bodies. My hands ached with a throbbing pain that was warning me that something was seriously wrong.

"And dawn will be here soon. It is spring, you know," Antoine said.

"Antoine? Was that a joke? Exodus issued you a sense of humor?"

"Do not tell Ling. She would not approve."

I tried my radio again, but still no signal from Jill. The mountains had to be between us now. Antoine and I ran after the others, following a rocky trail that had to have been created by goats or something else narrower than a person. We knew that it wouldn't take long to catch up. Antoine was breathing hard. He and Shen had only been at this altitude for like a week, and had not had a chance to fully acclimatize before the raid. Both of them were feeling it now.

We caught up to the others a moment later. They had

stopped for some reason, and were clustered together under a rock overhang. "What's going on?" Antoine demanded. "We must continue."

Roland looked up at us as he rubbed his eyes. "Kim . . ."

Antoine nodded once. "Let us say a few words over him. Then booby trap his body. Leave him on the trail." The tall African studied our surroundings for a moment. "There. If we're lucky, it will cause a rockslide and take a few of the hounds with it."

Now there were only seven of us.

Every step was agony. My legs burned and cramped. It would have been a difficult trek even under normal circumstances, but I had Svetlana riding piggyback with her arms encircled around my neck and her legs dragging behind. She was actually taller than me.

"The map said that this canyon was sixteen kilometers long," Svetlana said, "I did not realize that meant an average of thirty up and fourteen down." Her English was good, but her accent was thick.

"It only feels that long because of the painkillers," I responded. "We're on a beautiful mountain walk is all."

We stumbled on for a few more minutes in silence. The snow crunched under my boots. The other surviving members of Exodus were just darker shadows around us.

"So, Lorenzo . . ."

"Yeah?"

"You have a girlfriend, no?"

"Actually," I replied as I struggled over a fallen tree. "I'm in a serious relationship."

"Too bad. You have a nice butt."

"Now I know you're high."

The beautiful Russian laughed weakly. She was not faring well. "If you left me behind, the rest of you could make better time."

"Shut up," I grunted.

At least we were walking generally downhill now, not that that was any easier, as the ground was uneven and I kept tripping and sliding. There was probably another mile of downgrade, but then we faced a difficult uphill battle over the highest point of the pass.

"They're gaining on us," Roland gasped as he sprinted up from behind.

"How far?" Antoine asked.

"They've got an advance party, maybe twenty men. They're about eight hundred yards behind us. The main group was still around the river bend. I don't know how far. I set our last claymore."

That was grim news. An hour ago they had been twice that distance behind us.

"Antoine. Let me slow them down," I suggested. "If we're going to do it, we might as well do it now. We haven't seen any of them equipped with night vision."

"You would be overwhelmed. No. We should stick together."

"You forget something. I don't take orders from you. Sorry, Svetlana," I told her as I stopped and tried to lower her to the ground as gently as possible. She whimpered in pain as her damaged legs touched down. "Antoine, I'm going back there to kill a few of these guys. That'll slow the others down. I'm a way better murderer than pack mule."

Antoine knew better than to try to argue with me. "Very well." Shen raised his hand. Antoine shook his head in resignation. "You too?"

Shen shrugged.

Roland and Phillips started to speak, but I cut them off. "Wrong. Somebody has to be on point, and Antoine isn't going to carry two people by himself."

"Leave me," Svetlana said from the ground. "I'm endangering the rest of you."

"No," Shen said with grave finality. "We will hurt them, then return."

"But—" Svetlana began.

"No. I was there when your brother died on the side of a mountain, and I'll be damned if the same thing happens to you. Phillips, pick her up. Good luck, my brothers. Hurry back." Antoine said as he adjusted the still unconscious form of Fajkus on his back and lumbered on.

I was unbelievably exhausted as I slid in behind the patch of rocks. Shen and I had scrambled up one of the almost-vertical rock faces, tearing our clothing and our skin on the jagged bits, to get above the approaching soldiers. Once we were at the top, I went to one side, Shen to the other. We would try to hit as many of them as possible before retreating. With any luck, the expectation of further ambushes would slow them down from here on.

There we perched, the advance party of slave soldiers now only about a hundred meters and closing. These men were moving quickly. If I had sneezed loud, they probably would have heard it. I tried to take a drink from the Camelbak I'd taken from the crashed helicopter, but the liquid had long since frozen into a block of solid ice. Add dehydration to my list of complaints.

The thief in me told me what I should have been doing. I should have told Exodus to fuck off, and I should have left them. I didn't owe them anything. On my own, I could have already made it to the other side of the canyon or, worst case scenario, I could have hid, and then escaped during the confusion of the soldiers slaughtering the remaining survivors.

Be good, Hector. That's all that I ask . . .

For some reason I kept hearing the voice of Gideon Lorenzo in my head. What I was doing here was suicidal. It was asinine. If I was the man that I had been even a few years ago, I would have ditched Exodus hours ago.

But I wasn't.

I studied the terrain. We were in a good position. We could probably get most of the advance party into the open before we opened fire. The soldiers were moving in the trees, but they had to cross a pretty good-size field of snow with very little cover to get to us. Hopefully we could catch a bunch of them in the open.

Shen signaled me and started passing hand signals. Both of us were wearing night vision. I was wearing Fajkus' pair since he was still unconscious. Shen and I were on the same page: wait until the last possible second and then nail as many of them in the open as possible. I signaled that I would start close and work my way to the rear, he would start at the rear and work his way forward.

The soldiers moved into the kill zone. They were in pairs, and keeping a bit of distance between each pair. Doing the math, the best we could hope for would be to get ten of them in the open at once, and that was pushing it. The others would still be in a copse of trees, and they would probably take cover and start shooting back. Hopefully, without night vision, we would be able to retreat without getting hit.

I had been able to scrounge up one more 5.56 magazine from the crashed chopper, so I had one full thirty-rounder and one other that I estimated was mostly full. By my calculation, I had already fired about two hundred rounds through my ACR since the fighting had started in the compound.

The soldiers were getting closer, spaced pretty far apart, our earlier claymores having taught them a lesson. I signaled to Shen. *It's time.*

It's difficult to be accurate at anything more than short range with a red dot sight through night vision. My ACR had an IR laser invisible to the naked eye, but through my monocular, it was a brilliant beam. I put it on the closest soldier and he was totally oblivious. I flipped the selector to semi and pulled the trigger. The round spat from the muzzle with a muted hiss, a small spark of light the only visible indication I had fired. There was a high pitched sound as the tiny projectile traveled at a rate greater than the speed of sound before the bullet struck the soldier in the top of his chest. He stopped dead in his tracks, then fell flat on his back.

Shen opened up at the furthest visible pair while I quickly shifted my gun to the second soldier and popped him once. Normally I liked to shoot everybody a bunch of times, but I didn't really have a whole lot of ammo left at this point. Besides, if we were lucky, maybe the main body would slow down to tend to their wounded. *Doubtful, but what the hell. Worth a shot.*

I moved from pair to pair as quickly as I could. I was firing on the second group before they realized what was happening. Our suppressed weapons and ability to see in the dark was a huge advantage. Shen and I met in the middle pair as both of us hit the soldier on the right at the same time, and the soldier on the left dove into the snow. It had only taken a few seconds to work across the group.

"Go!" I hissed. We both leapt up and began to scramble back down the rocks. Muzzle flashes erupted from the tree line. Bullets violently struck all around us as the soldiers hosed our general area with automatic fire. I tripped, and tumbled down the last few feet of the slope, sprawling forward, but managing to catch myself with my already-abraded hands. Shen grabbed the back of my coat and pulled me upright. The two of us ran as fast as we could back toward Exodus.

The gunfire behind us didn't let up for almost a minute straight.

And come dawn, they would actually be able to aim.

It was going to be a tough morning.

VALENTINE
The Mountain Road

The dam was crippled, but we weren't out of this yet.

Dawn was fast approaching as our ersatz rescue party wound its way through barely passable mountain roads. I drove a beat-up 4x4 with Ling next to me, and it was slow going. Some effort had been made by someone to keep the roads relatively free of snow, but we continually got bogged down in soft spots. Ling, using a map and her GPS navigated, while trying to stay in contact with Lorenzo's group on the radio. They were constantly fading in and out, as the terrain did a marvelous job of limiting radio range.

We *were* in good contact with Reaper and Jill, who had taken it upon themselves to make a beeline for Lorenzo's location on their own. Reaper was feeding us real-time information from his little drone aircraft, and it was a godsend. Otherwise we'd have had no chance of finding them in time. He said the Montalbans had been tracking his signal somehow, so he would put the plane on standby, where it would just drift in circles on autopilot, they'd move, and then he'd reconnect.

The situation was dire. The survivors of the raid on Sala Jihan's compound were on foot, trudging through deep snow and over rugged terrain. There were only a handful of them left, and half were wounded. They were pursued by a mob of Jihan's fanatical soldiers, numbering well over a hundred by Reaper's best estimate.

Ling was finally able to get someone back on the radio. "What's your status?" she asked.

Antoine answered. *"It is good to hear your voice,"* he said, panting.

"We are on our way. What is your status?"

"Not good, I'm afraid. I hope you have good news."

Ling read off coordinates to Antoine. "This is a place northeast of your position where the canyon reaches the road. If you can get there, we'll be waiting to pick you up.

It's as close as we're going to be able to get without walking. There are no other paths."

"*I understand,*" Antoine said breathlessly. "*Stand by . . .*"

Lorenzo's voice squawked over the radio next. "*Okay, I'm looking at those coordinates you gave us. Shit, that's a long way. Are you sure there's nowhere closer?*"

"*I'm positive, Chief,*" Reaper said, stomping Ling's transmission before she could reply. "*I'm looking at maps and footage from Little Bird. That's the closest place anywhere near your path of travel where you'll even come close to the road. There's another spot up a different canyon from there, but it's even farther away from us, and it looks like it'd be a pretty steep climb to get up to road level. The coordinates Ling gave you are your best bet.*"

"*Acknowledged,*" Lorenzo said. "*Do you still have eyes on us?*"

"*Little Bird's running low on fuel, but I'll be your eyes in the sky for as long as I can. The Exodus guys will probably catch up with us before we get to the rendezvous point. We'll all be there.*"

"*Yes, we will,*" Jill said suddenly, transmitting before Lorenzo could reply. "*You damned well better get there, Lorenzo. I mean it.*"

The radio was silent for a moment. "*It's good to hear your voice, honey,*" he said.

"*Hang on,*" Jill said, sounding like she was trying to keep her fear under control. "*We're on our way!*"

Chapter 24: Pick a Direction and Run

LORENZO
The Mountain

"You're alive. Good," Antoine said as Shen and I caught up.

"We got a few of them, but they're still coming," I bent over, put my hands on my knees, and retched into the snow. Running at this altitude was killer. I stood, wiped my mouth, and noted, "Fajkus is awake?" Ibrahim's second in command was sitting on a rock, his face in his hands.

"Yes, but he is incoherent. He took a severe blow to the head," Antoine nodded toward him. "He awoke screaming, talking about . . . *things* coming out of the silo. Now he is not speaking to anyone."

I watched as Fajkus wrapped his arms around his chest and began to rock back and forth, glancing nervously side to side. I had seen people lose it like that before, especially back in Africa, brains just overloaded with awful shit. "He's

548 *Larry Correia & Mike Kupari*

shell-shocked." In the light of my magnified vision, I could see that the other survivors were deeply disturbed by Fajkus's behavior, their eyes shining bright, wide, and afraid.

"No," Shen shook his head. "He's one of our most experienced men."

Antoine agreed. "Fajkus has seen more battle than any two of us put together. He has been fearless before certain death many times, and his courage has inspired the rest of us. No . . . this is something else."

I felt an uncomfortable shiver, and it wasn't from the cold. "Don't matter what it is, because if we don't keep moving, we're dead." I strode over to Fajkus, grabbed him by the sides of his head, and jerked his face up. He looked confused. "Hey. Listen up." I slapped him, hard. This seemed to startle the others.

And I learned why, really quickly. Fajkus moved, way faster than I thought a stocky fellow could, one hand clamped around my throat as he jerked me forward, and something cold and metallic slammed into the side of my head, a pistol apparently, as I heard him cock the hammer.

"No, you listen, asshole. I'm just fucking fine," Fajkus snarled as he screwed the gun into my ear hole. "As fine as you could be considering that I just met the fucking devil himself. If you had seen whatever the fuck I just saw, then you would need a *moment* too." He sounded calm, rational, but there was something just beneath that, something that indicated that this man was well and truly *freaked out*. "I saw hell open up and take a shit on *my* men, on *my* friends, and now Jihan is going to catch us, and swallow our souls, because apparently we're walking, because *your* girlfriend betrayed us and left us to die, and if I remember right . . . " he shoved the gun in even harder, and the hand around my throat clenched off even more precious air, "*you* were the one who said we could trust her."

"Sir, please, Lorenzo is on our side," Antoine said calmly. "We do not have time for this."

Fajkus's eyes flashed down as he felt my knife press up between his legs. "I'll make time," I growled back as I put enough force to indicate that I was feeling real serious. The pressure released enough from my throat to let me talk. "Get your hands off me."

He let go, and lowered his gun. "Well, I guess you are walking too, so at least you aren't in league with that Montalban Exchange bitch."

"No, I've been taking turns carrying your unconscious ass up a mountain for hours. If I was walking, I would already be out of here." I rubbed my throat, but I didn't put away my knife. "What did you see back there? What happened to Ibrahim?"

He shook his head, mind distant. It took him a long moment to respond. "I don't . . . don't really know. All I know is that Jihan is more dangerous than the Council knew, more than Ariel expected."

I had no idea who that was, but Fajkus was a man whose faith had been shaken.

"And now this is all that remains of Exodus' warriors." He gestured at the survivors, ragged and tired. "We are ruined."

There was random gunfire behind us as the soldiers mistook a menacing tree for one of us. The noise was way too close.

"Keep moving," Antoine ordered, unconsciously taking command. The mystery would have to wait. Dawn was coming fast.

We plodded forward. Roland and Phillips were behind, setting up another ambush. They had demanded a turn. I had turned my borrowed night vision over to Roland and was stumbling along through the shadows beneath the trees, Svetlana again on my back. But it wouldn't matter for too much longer. Dawn was coming fast.

Already we had moved from real darkness to a fuzzy gray reflecting off the snow. Last night, the sky had been brilliantly clear, but now a fat wall of clouds was coming in from the north, the direction we were traveling. We hoped it brought with it fresh snow and the possibility of evading our pursuers. The weather was actually warming up.

According to the map, we had crossed the highest point of the canyon during the night, and it was mostly downhill from here on out. There was one more bulge on the topographical map, but after that we were heading into Mongolia. Jill would be there waiting. As it stood now, we only had one option: forward. That also meant that the bad guys had a pretty simple path to follow in order to catch up.

Gunfire echoed behind us, bouncing wildly off the mountain walls. Roland and Phillips had sprung their ambush. Hopefully they would live through it. Antoine was on point, and he glanced up, listening, trying to ascertain how far away the shooting was. Shen was helping Fajkus, who was stumbling indomitably along, but the head wound had left him dizzy and uncoordinated.

Now that it was quickly brightening, I could see our surroundings better. I had no doubt that Jill would think that it was beautiful, a pristine, virgin-white, winter wonderland. The canyon was only a mile wide at any given point, and we were trekking along the bank of a river choked with ice flows. Sometime during the night we had lost enough altitude to be back in a real forest and the air smelled clean. For a city boy like me that was kind of scary. At one point, I noticed that there were wolves watching us from the trees. Giant, scary dogs, like Reaper had read about on the internet. They looked at us curiously before moving on to eat something without guns.

"—*in. Come in, Lorenzo.*" The chirping of my radio startled me so badly that I almost dropped the sleeping Svetlana in the snow. She snorted loudly in my ear.

"Jill?" I gasped, my throat parched and aching.

"*Oh, thank God. You're alive,*" she said. "*Where are you?*"

"We're most of the way through the canyon, heading into Mongolia. We're close to the coordinates Ling gave us."

"*We're almost there. Reaper's got the Little Bird in the air . . . He's looking at the guys following you right now. He says he can walk you in to us before they catch up.*"

I was too tired to think. "Careful, the Montalbans will find you." My words were slurred.

"*Reaper says he can handle that. He started to talk about trigonometry and the curvature of the Earth or something, I almost drove the truck off a cliff because it put my brain to sleep. Keep going. You're almost there. Reaper can walk you in.*"

"Awesome," I spoke up so the others could hear. "Guys, we're almost to our ride."

"Excellent," Antoine said just before the bullet hit him. *FFOOooooooommmm!*

The shot had come from quite far away. It took the sound a moment to catch up. Antoine fell into the snow, clutching his side.

"Sniper!" Shen shouted as he and Fajkus dove to the ground. Svetlana gasped in pain as I took us down.

"I'm hit!" Antoine shouted, scrambling through the snow and finally coming to rest behind a log.

"Where is he?" Fajkus said. I raised my head and scanned the mountainside. They had to have been paralleling our path on the mountain above us, there was no other way.

The bark on the tree next to my head exploded in a shower of splinters and pulp. "Damn it!" I flinched back down. "I don't see him!"

"Antoine. Status?"

The big man didn't answer.

Shen leapt up, heedless of danger, and dove toward where Antoine was hiding. The two men were like brothers. He was only up for a split second, then back down. A bullet whizzed through the space that he had been occupying, sounding like an angry bee on steroids. The sound of the muzzle blast came a moment after.

Fajkus popped his head up to look, and the snow next to him erupted. That one had been very close. The Exodus leader began to speak into his radio, trying to raise Phillips and Roland to tell them to take cover.

Svetlana was lying on her back, Sako across her chest,

bloody and bandaged left hand hugging the rifle close, as she calmly scanned the mountainside. "Six hundred meters," she stated flatly.

"You see him?" I was scared to lift my head again.

"Not yet," she grimaced as she rolled over and began to low crawl into the trees, dragging her broken legs uselessly behind her. "I could tell by time takes sound to travel."

"What are you doing?"

"What I do best," she said.

"You can't even walk."

"I don't need to," she glared at me.

"Let me do it. You're missing fingers."

She held up her right hand, and then extended her middle finger. "I still have all these. Are you a trained sniper?"

"No."

"Then shut up and spot."

I was kneeling behind a rotted stump, now damp as the temperature, by some miracle, was moving slightly above freezing. Svetlana was on her belly, ten feet ahead of me, covered in pine needles, and scanning the mountainside through her scope. I was amazed how far we had crawled, how fast.

"Reaper, come in."

"Yeah, Chief?"

"Do you have us on thermal yet?"

"I lost you under the trees. It doesn't have X-ray vision."

"I've got a sniper on the mountain approximately six

hundred meters to the northeast. Find him, Reaper. Fajkus?"

"Go." Everybody was switched on to the same channel now.

"Svetlana is going to try to take this guy. As soon as he's distracted, you three need to move. We'll catch up." The main body of soldiers had to be almost on top of us by now. "Where're the Mormons?"

"Almost there," said one of them over the radio. I couldn't tell which because the speaker was breathing really hard. *"The soldiers are right behind us. Roland took a round."*

"Shut up . . . Just a flesh . . . wound . . ." Roland was gasping. *"Jerk."*

This was going to be close.

"Lorenzo," Svetlana hissed. "There are three places I think he could be hiding. I need your help."

"Okay," I answered, scanning the mountainside, waiting for her to tell me which spot to watch.

"When I tell you to . . . stand up."

"Are you nuts?"

"Not for a long time, stupid. Just get up and move to side. When he shoots at you, I kill him."

"That sounds like a good plan," I said sarcastically. But we didn't have much time. "Okay."

Svetlana let out a long breath. "Now."

Despite my brain telling me not to, and every fiber of my being screaming *no*, I stood, ran to the side, and dropped. No shot came.

"Did you see him?" I gasped.

"No. Do it again."

"What? *No.* Screw that."

"Not from same spot. He will blow your brains out from there. Crawl first. Then move when I tell you."

Son of a bitch. I started low-crawling, slush moving up my sleeves and down my shirt.

"Now."

Aw, man. I stood, and it took my brain a split second to process that the burning sensation I felt across my scalp was a hot piece of lead moving at just over 3,000 feet per second. My legs buckled without me even telling them to.

Her big rifle roared.

"Got him," Svetlana said as she worked the bolt. "Lorenzo, are you alive?"

I rubbed my hand across the top of my head. The bastard had creased the top of my skull. My stolen glove came away covered in fresh blood to match the dried blood from earlier. "You sure you got him?"

"Yes. It was one of the Brotherhood. I was a little off center, but with a .338 Lapua, you can be a little off. He won't be shooting back, that's for sure."

I sure hoped she was right. I keyed the radio. "Sniper down. Move. Move." That was two Brothers dead. Through the trees, back the way we came, I could make out Shen and Fajkus, with Antoine hoisted between them. A split second later, two other shapes came running up behind them, Phillips and Roland. "We'll catch up. Jill will walk you in to her position."

"*Moving,*" Shen replied.

"Come on," I said as I stood up, fully expecting to get shot by some yet unknown danger, and ran over to Svetlana. I squatted down next to her, so that she could clamber onto my back. My muscles ached and burned and I hoisted her up. She wasn't light.

"See? And you wanted me to drop my rifle," the Russian insisted.

"You were right, that what you need to hear? Now hold on." Now we had to sprint to the finish. We had to make it through some pretty thick brush, but so did our pursuers. It was a good thing I worked out a lot, because all I wanted to do right about then was curl up in a ball and die. I couldn't ever remember being this tired. Svetlana's bandaged hand was bouncing right in front of my face, and I tried to ignore the missing fingers, and concentrate on my footing, as I half ran, half stumbled forward.

"Lorenzo!" Reaper shouted in my ear. *"Your sniper's back."*

"Impossible!" Svetlana screamed in my good ear. "I shot him in the chest."

"Maybe you missed," I suggested, but from what I knew about the Exodus sniper, I really doubted that.

"No. He must be wearing armor plates," she spat.

From what I had seen earlier in the compound, I could assume that the Brother was probably a dead man walking, and it wouldn't make a lick of difference until his heart finally quit beating, damn fanatical bastards. "Where, Reaper?"

"He's moving downhill. Wait, there's two of them. One's moving fast, and he's got a short gun with some big drum on it, the other's moving slow, like he's injured, and has an old-fashioned rifle."

"Shit!" I hunched forward so I could run faster. We were heading due north, the other survivors were ahead and slightly to the west. The Brothers were to our northeast, and if they could get ahead of the others or get into a position to slow us down, then we would be overtaken by the soldiers.

Svetlana must have realized the same thing that I was thinking. "Get me to higher ground."

LORENZO
The River

"This is good!" Svetlana yelled in my good ear. "Put me down."

I lowered her as gently as possible, which wasn't very gentle considering that I had just sprinted up a rock slope with a hundred-and-fifty-pound woman and her fourteen pound rifle on my back. We had a good view from here, with the river at our back and the forest below us. The Exodus survivors were almost out of the canyon, three quarters of a mile ahead of us. The mass of slave soldiers was even closer, and would be passing below us in the next few minutes. I could already hear snatches of their excited voices on the wind.

Svetlana grimaced as she dragged herself up and braced her Sako across a fallen log. "There. That's where the Brothers will try to intercept." She was aiming at another spot along the riverbank, between us and the others. "They will have to get on top of that hill to get a shot, and then I'll have them."

"Reaper. Status?" I commanded.

"*The Brothers are heading toward the river, a hundred*

and fifty meters north of you. They're blocking your escape. And you've got a shitload of bad guys about to be on top of you. You've got to get out of there now!"

The Sun was coming over the side of the canyon. I could clearly see the path I had to take to reach extraction. My best bet was to head right down the riverbank, right through the Brothers. It was rocky and uneven, and would be treacherous with Svetlana on my back, but it was the only way now.

"Pop these guys, and we've got to go."

"We don't have time to wait for them. Go through the Brothers, and I'll cover you from here," she stated.

I turned back to her. "There's no way I can make it down there and back to get you and still make it."

She gave me a tired smile. "I know."

"Bullshit," I spat. "I didn't carry you this far for nothing."

"Go, Lorenzo. We're out of time."

I started toward her, then hesitated. She was right. We had to take out the Brothers before they pinned down the others. There was no time to argue. I nodded once, hoisted my rifle, and turned to leave. It was suicide. Suddenly my eyes were burning.

"Wait!" she cried out. I spun, expecting her to have come to her senses. Instead, she had pulled her Makarov and set it on the ground next to her. "Let me have your grenade." I pulled the frag that I had found in the Exodus helicopter and passed it back to her. She took it in her uninjured hand. and shoved it in the top of her coat. "I'm not going to let them take me alive. Now hurry, I'll cover you as long as I can. Kill the Brothers."

There was no time for sentiment. I sprinted down the riverbank in the direction of the next high spot, leaping from rock to rock. I kept the stock of my rifle against my shoulder, muzzle swinging wildly back and forth in front of me. I could hear the almost musical noise of the river flowing about twenty feet below. The rocks were slick, and the dirt between them had transformed into clingy mud. There was no way I could have made it with Svetlana in time. That didn't make it any easier.

"The Brothers are almost on top of the hill. Antoine's guys are still vulnerable for at least another minute," Reaper warned. There was a loud *BANG* behind me as Svetlana engaged some of the approaching soldiers. I tried to go faster, but my boot streaked out from under me as it hit a damp stone and I fell painfully to the ground. I shoved myself back up and kept going. The bank was on my left, the hill to my front, and the forest to my right.

I was counting on the Brothers being focused on the others and not watching this direction. I was almost to the hill. It was more of a dirt pile, with one side eroded away by the sluggish river. Raising my rifle, I scanned, looking for movement. Something black passed between the trees, running upward, his back toward me. I snapped the red dot onto him, led the target for just a split second, and fired. The black shape went down into the weeds. I continued running. I had to get to cover.

The other Brother appeared to my right, materializing out of the shadows, a stubby PPSh in his hands, the muzzle already flashing. I flung myself face first into the mud as the bullets zipped overhead, tearing up rock chips and dirt around me. I was a dead man.

Then the shooting stopped. I waited for a moment, then popped up, looking for a target, but the Brother was gone.

"Got him!" Svetlana shouted over the radio.

"They're both still moving! I've got one heading north, one low crawling east." Reaper said. *"Svetlana, you've got about ten soldiers in the open, due south of you."*

"Damn it," I spat through a mouth full of mud, and I rose and headed for the trees. These sons of bitches were hard to kill. The one with the PPSh was wounded nearby in the trees, but I had to take out the one with the rifle right the hell now.

"Lorenzo, you're on your own. I've got company," Svetlana stated calmly, then she started hammering that big rifle.

I was in the trees now. There was blood on the bark of a nearby tree, and a splatter trail leading back into the brush. The Brother with the subgun was hit bad. Maybe he would just do us a favor and crawl off to die. I picked my way through the woods. It was thick, dark, and tangled with underbrush. I kept heading uphill. I knew I was making too much noise, but I was exhausted, in a hurry, and out of my element.

There was a roar of a high-powered rifle ahead of me, and I instinctively ducked. But the Brother wasn't shooting at me. He was shooting at Shen and Antoine. Somebody screamed over the radio. I flipped my selector to full-auto and charged forward. I saw the Brother as he saw me. He turned, still working the bolt of his old M44. I didn't take any chances. I mashed the trigger and hosed the entire rest of the magazine into him. The Brother went down in a spray of fluids and meat, and tumbled over the side into the river below.

I dropped my spent mag, shoved my last one in, and slammed the bolt closed as I approached the edge. I hung over quickly, just to make sure. The Brother lay broken in a spreading cloud of red, half submerged in a shallow slush of ice. I took my time, aimed, and put a final round through the Brother's skull.

"Lorenzo, last one is coming up—" Reaper started to warn me, but I didn't hear the rest. Something small and black came sailing out of the trees and landed in the mud in front of me. *Grenade!* No time to think. I stepped back off the edge and plummeted into the river.

The grenade detonated above with a violent concussion. I braced myself to hit the water, but instead of a splash, there was a crunch as I smashed into an ice sheet. It shattered beneath me, and my legs plunged into unbelievable cold. It was shallow, and I hit the gravel bottom way too fast. It was like an electrical shock traveled up my legs as the ice water hit me. I fell over on my side, and then half my body was submerged in the freezing cold. I pulled myself back onto the ice, and rolled into the mud on the bank.

The final Brother appeared over the top, emotionless goggles studying me for a moment. I had to move, my numb legs clumsy beneath me. The PPSh came over the edge and the Brother ripped a long burst, the ice and water billowing up at my side. I jerked my rifle up and fired wildly at him. He disappeared back over the edge.

I stumbled to my feet and started downstream, wading through the water before he decided to toss another grenade. He must have been out, as he hung the subgun over the side and fired another burst. This one was even closer, striking a string of water plumes right past me. A mist hung in the air. I extended my gun and returned fire, the two of us strobing bullets back and forth. I stumbled, sprawled backward on the ice, and broke through again.

The cold was so intense, so invasive, that I almost blacked out. I exploded out of the water, every nerve on fire, my muscles not wanting to respond, and my hands automatically clenching into fists. I thrashed through the ice and the mud, and flopped face first onto the bank, my body shivering uncontrollably.

I forced myself to breathe and grabbed my rifle. I was shaking so badly that I couldn't even aim. I just raised it toward the brother and jerked the trigger a few times. I wasn't even close. The empty ACR slipped from my quivering fingers and fell into the water as I struggled to draw my pistol.

"*Lorenzo!*" Reaper screamed over the radio. "*Hang on!*"

I fumbled the draw, my pistol shaking badly. The Brother fired and something burned down the inside of my arm. I jerked as the bullets hit me like a sledgehammer. I extended my hand but my STI was gone, torn right out of my grasp. My body was frozen but a flash of heat was spreading on my side.

I was done.

The Brother took his time. His subgun was empty, so he nonchalantly dropped the drum, and pulled another from a pouch on his belt. I knew I was hit, but I was so cold I didn't even know how badly. In the distance there was a huge amount of gunfire coming from where I had left Svetlana. I was so cold and in so much pain that I could barely understand the words over the radio, but somebody had gone back for her. I saw my pistol laying just beneath the crystal surface of the river, but it might as well have been a million miles away.

The Brother shoved the drum in, flipped the lever to lock it in place, and drew the bolt back. He took one final look at his dead comrade floating face down a few feet from me, and shook his head sadly.

"Lorenzo!" Reaper was shouting. *"Hang on, man!"*

There was a strange buzzing sound. At first I thought it was from my bad ear, but the noise was growing. Now it was whistling.

The Brother aimed the Russian subgun at my face.

"Fear the Reaper, motherfucker!"

A black shadow zipped by overhead. The Brother heard the approaching noise, looked up, and then got hit right in the face by Little Bird.

The flying wing smashed into pieces. The UAV didn't weigh much, but it was enough to knock the Brother off balance, and he went over the edge, arms and legs windmilling, until he crashed through the icy crust of the river.

I plunged my hand into the icy water.

The Brother came up thrashing, water droplets flinging in every direction.

My hand closed on my pistol.

Goggled eyes fixed on me, then he scanned around. The Brother had lost his gun. He looked back up at me, then began struggling forward, waist deep in the slush, pushing my way. He reached into his furs and his gloved fist came out clutching a curved blade.

The STI came up, water pouring out of it. My hands were shaking so badly that I couldn't even find the front sight, so I sprayed and prayed, pulling the trigger wildly. Ice cracked. Dirt puckered along the banks. A 9mm round struck the rocks and whined off into the distance. There were splashes all around him. And then I hit him. He staggered a bit. I hit him again, and again, and again. He stumbled, slipping on the slick rocks beneath his boots. He went down in a splash, but then he was right back up, lunging toward me.

I shot him several more times before the slide locked back empty. Blood was spurting from the side of his neck, drizzling down a necklace of sharp teeth.

He was only five feet away as he slowly sank to his knees, the river trailing red around him. It was almost like the Brother drifted off to sleep, as he sank to his side to bleed out onto the rocks of the bank.

"Thanks, Reaper," I gasped, but I didn't know if he heard me.

I wanted nothing more than to follow the Brother's example . . . I'd been shot. I was so cold I couldn't even tell how many times or where. Then I tried to get out of the river, and the pain told me. Blood was running out of my side, just beneath my armor. Crawling, splashing, I made it onto the rocks and lay there for a moment.

This is very bad.

Chapter 25: The Good Guy

VALENTINE
The Mountain Road Rendezvous Point

Distant gunshots echoed off of cliff faces as they drew closer to our position.

We bailed out of the trucks. The Exodus troops with us, few that there were, spread out and took up defensive positions around us. If Jihan's forces were following us down the road, they were sure to catch up with us now. It was a risk we had to take, though. We weren't going to leave anyone else behind.

Ling, Jill, and I waited nervously by the edge of the road. Down to the southwest was a deep, narrow rocky canyon filled with trees. That was the direction they were coming from.

The radio crackled to life. It was Antoine, breathing hard. *"We're here. I have eyes on. We're coming out."*

"I can see them!" one of the Exodus troops said. He and a couple of others ran forward to help their comrades.

566 *Larry Correia & Mike Kupari*

Below us, a handful of haggard-looking people trudged out of the trees. They were all dressed in camouflage, so I couldn't tell who was who except for Antoine. The six-foot-four African was hard to mistake for anyone else. He was weaving badly, and his whole right side was covered in blood.

My heart sank when I saw how few of them remained. The look of shock on Ling's face was difficult for even her to hide. Reaper had warned us that there weren't many left, but it didn't really sink in until we saw it with our own eyes. Jill took off down the embankment, sliding into the snow, and ran forward. Ling and I looked at each other, then followed. They were going to need help getting up to the road.

I followed Ling as she ran to Antoine. Next to him, another Exodus operative whom I didn't know was helping Fajkus, the second in command of the compound raid, along. "My God," Ling asked. "What happened? Is this all that's left?"

"I'm afraid so," He bent over to catch his breath. "Forgive me, I've been shot."

"There's no time to talk now," Fajkus growled. "The bastards are right behind us."

"Where's Lorenzo?" It was Jill. She was running around the clearing almost in a panic, checking every person that had come out of the trees. Someone else came out of the trees, carrying a body over their shoulder. "Lorenzo!" Jill cried, but it was Shen, limping badly, but carrying a blonde woman. "Where is he?"

Ling looked up at Antoine. "He was with you. Was he killed?"

Before he could answer, Jill came running up to us, her breath smoking in the frigid morning air. "Where the hell is Lorenzo?" she barked, her dark eyes flashing with anger. "He was supposed to be with you! You tell me what happened right now!"

"Lorenzo went the wrong way to draw them off."

Jill deflated a little, and covered her mouth with her hands. "Oh no. No, no, no."

He was alive when I saw him last. He intercepted our pursuers. We all would have been overrun had he not done that." Fajkus said.

"But . . . but he's still alive?"

"I don't know."

Jill tried her radio. "Lorenzo! Come in, Lorenzo!"

Shen stumbled up the clearing as the others rushed to help him. He looked exhausted. Two men took the blonde woman between them, and she screamed as they bumped her legs. They were flopping about below the knees, obviously broken.

"Lorenzo was alive a minute ago." She grimaced through the pain. "The enemy was right on top of us though."

"Well, then, what the hell are we waiting for? We're going to go get him!" Jill turned to run away, but I grabbed her arm. "What are you doing, Val? Let me go! We don't have time to waste!"

"I'm going," I said flatly. "You're not."

"Fuck you, I'm going," Jill retorted.

I didn't let go.

Ling stepped in. "Jill, please. Let us go get Lorenzo. It is our responsibility. It is because of us . . . because of me, that he's even in this situation. I owe it to him. Michael and I will go. If he's still there, we'll bring him back."

"He's still there!" Jill shouted, pulling away from me. She turned to walk up the embankment again.

"Jill!" I said. "So help me God, you're staying here if I have to have Exodus tie you the hell up. No one else is going to die here, do you hear me? Enough people have died tonight. What in the hell do you think you're going to do, other than put your own life, and Reaper's life, in jeopardy, huh?"

Jill obviously hadn't thought about that. She wasn't even carrying a rifle. She didn't even have body armor. Letting her go would probably be sending her to her death.

"Jill, please . . . We're leaving right now. We'll find him. We're not going to abandon him."

Tears welled up in Jill's eyes. She was visibly shaking. "Hurry, please," she said quietly.

The door of one of the big Russian vans slid open and Reaper began shouting. "I lost eyes, but Lorenzo's in the river! He's in the river!"

I nodded, then noticed that Shen had a large bolt-action rifle slung across his back. "What's that?"

"It's Svetlana's rifle," he said. "She's a sniper."

It was a *long* way down to the river. "Give it to me," I said, "It might come in handy."

Shen nodded, and unslung the long weapon. It was a Sako TRG-42 wrapped in white webbing for camouflage. I slung my carbine behind my back as he handed me the heavy beast. I worked the bolt to verify that there was a round chambered, and looked through the scope. It was a five-to-twenty power.

"Here," the woman said. She tossed me a single five-round magazine for the rifle. "That's all the ammunition I have left for it."

.338 Lapua. That'll put a hurting on somebody. "Let's move."

Ling turned her attention to Antoine and Fajkus as I began jogging away. "Do not wait for us here. Rendezvous with Katsumoto's group. We will try to stay in contact, but do not linger for our sake. Enough of us have died here already. If we don't make it back, don't come looking for us."

"I understand," Antoine said solemnly. "Go with God, my friend."

VALENTINE
The Mountain Road, above the Canyon

The path was narrow and treacherous as we made our way toward where we thought Lorenzo was. Ling was trying to raise him on the radio, but had no luck so far. Without Reaper to guide us in, there was little we could do but hope. I was on edge, exhausted, and afraid. The woods were swarming with Jihan's men. What I really wanted to do was turn around and head back with the others. I just wanted to get as far away from The Crossroads as I possibly could, and never think about it again.

But as much as I disliked Lorenzo, I was determined not to leave anyone else behind. Not now, not after all this. Twice in my life, I'd been left behind, abandoned by the people I was working for. I know what it feels like and I wasn't about to do that to somebody else.

If Lorenzo was alive, I hoped to God he wasn't bringing a lot of company with him.

"We can get a clear view of the river from there." Ling pointed.

"Keep your head down. We don't know who's down there."

Approaching cautiously, we took stock of the canyon before us. The ground just dropped away in a gap between thin evergreen trees. The grade was steep, all the way to the canyon floor and the river. We had a good view of the river from here. Ling lifted a pair of binoculars and started scanning back and forth.

On the valley floor, in a clearing five hundred yards away was the rusting hulk of a big airplane. I recognized it as an old Soviet Tu-95 bomber. One of its wings could be seen, half covered by a snow, some distance behind it. The other wing was nowhere to be found. A faded red star still adorned its tail. It looked as if it had been there for decades, forgotten. "Looks like they tried to ride it in," I mused. There was no way the bomber was going to do an emergency landing in a place like this, but it was obvious it hadn't just plowed straight down into the ground, either.

We had concealment from the foliage and cover from the boulders, plus a commanding view of the narrow valley ahead of us. It was as good as we were going to get.

I unfolded its bipod and set up the sniper rifle as Ling tried to raise Lorenzo on the radio. "Lorenzo, Lorenzo, this is Sword Three X-Ray. Can you hear me, over?"

Nothing.

"Lorenzo, this is Sword Three X-Ray, please respond. What is your status?"

Ling looked over at me and shook her head.

"Well, we can wait here for a little—"

The radio crackled back to life. *"This is Lorenzo. I'm here, I'm still here."*

"Sword Three X-Ray copies, Lorenzo. Where are you?"

"Fuck if I know. I see lots of fucking trees. I've got a lot of pissed off assholes on my tail. That narrow it down for you?" His breathing was ragged. He sounded horrible. *"I see an . . . airplane?"*

"We're waiting for you at the road past that, Lorenzo. As you come out of the trees, there'll be an open area covered with boulders. Past the wreck, there's a steep, rocky grade up to our position. I don't think it'll be an easy climb. Do you copy?"

"I hear you," Lorenzo replied. *"Fuck. I'm in bad shape here. I've been shot . . . a couple times, and I'm hypothermic and running out of ammo. I hope you got a lot of guys up there."*

Ling and I looked at each other.

"Just make for the plane wreck. We'll cover you as best we can." Ling said. "Get ready. I think he's almost here."

"Take my rifle," I suggested. "It's got a scope on it and more range. It'll be better than your carbine."

I hunkered down behind Svetlana's heavy sniper rifle, scanning the canyon for movement. The tree line we expected Lorenzo to come out of was at least eight hundred yards away, maybe a bit further. The rifle I was using could hit playing cards at that distance, but it had been a long time since I'd done this kind of long-range shooting, and I only had ten rounds. Lorenzo had a lot of open territory to cover past the trees, with only boulders for cover until he got to the wreck of the bomber. And even then, I had no idea how he was going to get up the grade without getting shot to pieces.

Focus, damn it. Can't worry about it now. I slowly pivoted the rifle on its bipod, looking for movement.

"There! I have eyes on."

A lone figure appeared from the trees, slogging through deep snow as fast as he could. Even at twenty power magnification, he was too far off to ID, so I reached for the radio.

"Lorenzo, this is Valentine. I have eyes on one individual that just exited the tree line. Is that you?"

There was a pause before I got a response. *"Valentine? Fuck me. Yeah, yeah, that's me. Where are you guys?"*

"We're up at the top of the grade. We've got you covered."

"Get ready. They're right behind me."

Lorenzo wasn't kidding. Sporadic gunfire erupted from the trees before I could even see anyone else. First, a couple of figures, dressed in brown and green coats, appeared from the trees, hot on Lorenzo's tail. Then a few more, then dozens of them.

"Holy shit."

LORENZO
The plane wreck

I was in very bad shape. The wound in my side was deep. I had my left hand jammed against it, but blood was pouring between my fingers and leaving a trail in the snow behind me. The ice bath had done something to my mind. Everything was foggy and I was having a hard time thinking straight. My heart was pounding in my chest and my mouth tasted like it was filled with pennies.

The soldiers were all around me, moving between the trees. I could hear them shouting. My legs burned as I had to hoist each foot high enough to clear the snow. There were boulders in the clearing. I could use them for cover, then get to the plane, then—

The bullet pierced my left arm. Blood hit the snow in front of me. I let out an incoherent cry, lifted my pistol and cranked off a couple of shots in the direction that it had come from. The snow puckered around me as they fired back.

I made it to the nearest boulder, stumbled, and crashed into it. I slid along it, leaving a smear of blood, then forced myself onward.

The ringing in my ears had gotten worse. I tripped and fell on my face. *Not like this . . .* And I forced myself back up and headed for the crashed bomber.

Valentine and Ling were shooting. I could hear their bullets buzzing by overhead. What sounded like thousands of bullets were immediately launched back at them.

The cockpit of the bomber was mangled, smashed, and rusty. There was a huge gap past that, and I stumbled inside as fresh holes were punched in the aluminum around me. I turned and saw a soldier moving up to my red-stained boulder. The STI's front sight wobbled past and I put a round into his chest. He slid down the rock and collapsed into the snow.

My gun was empty again. I couldn't even remember firing that many shots. I went to reload, but my left arm didn't want to work and my left hand wouldn't close around a fresh mag. "Damn it . . . " So I tucked the 9mm in my armpit, got a mag out with my good hand, and tried to shove it into the mag well. My hand was shaking so badly it took me several tries.

There was movement everywhere. The clearing was swarming with soldiers. There was no getting out of this one.

How'd I end up here? This was what I deserved for putting somebody else ahead of myself. This was all because I'd gone after Bob. I was going to die, and I still hadn't saved him.

I got the slide dropped on another round and shot a soldier who'd run up to the cockpit.

But that wasn't all. I could have left Exodus. I could have dumped them and run for it on my own . . . Yet I hadn't. I could have abandoned them, but I didn't.

The old bomber smelled of animal piss. Bullets were flying through the metal all around me. A scarred face appeared in a decaying window hole and I blew the young slave's brains out.

I could have abandoned them, but I didn't . . .

I'd made my call.

I'd decided to be the good guy.

And then I knew that old Gideon Lorenzo would have been proud of me.

"I'm still getting out of here, damn it. You hear that, Dad?" I fired wildly out the door, driving some soldiers to cover.

Another bullet exploded through the wall and my leg went out from under me. There was a flash of fire and searing pain, and then blood was spilling from my calf.

I rolled over, tried to stand, and fell over. I ended up face-to-face with a grinning skull, probably the remains of one of the bomber's long-forgotten crewmembers. I couldn't walk. The skull sat there, mocking me.

My leg wouldn't respond. I could no longer run.

And just like that, it was over.

VALENTINE

The powerful rifle bucked into my left shoulder as I squeezed off another shot. Two of Jihan's soldiers were taking cover from Lorenzo behind a rock, but I had a clear shot. The heavy slug tore through both of them, and down they went. That's what they got for bunching up. *Fuck you, assholes.*

I worked the bolt with my right hand, angled the rifle down some more, and found another target. *BOOM.* Another dead enemy soldier, I worked the bolt again. The rifle was now empty. I changed out the magazine. "Last five rounds!"

Ling was still using my rifle, firing slow, aimed shots. "How many more magazines do you have for this?" She'd already gone through one magazine and was working her way through another.

I checked the pouches on my vest, retrieving a single twenty-round mag. "Last one."

"I'll make it work," she said. "Keep shooting."

I scanned the snow-covered wreck of the bomber. I could see Lorenzo, holed up in a gaping tear in the fuselage that faced toward us. He was armed only with a pistol, and was only firing when the enemy got close to his hideout.

Two more soldiers were running toward the gap. One had a bag of hand grenades! A moving target, from a few hundred yards away, with a rifle I had no experience with. *C'mon, c'mon . . .* I tracked my target, leading him slightly, and squeezed the trigger.

He crumpled to the snow in a puff of blood. His friend tripped and fell. I worked the bolt and put a round into him, too. A hand grenade went off, throwing up a circle of snow and dust. "Two more down!" I told Ling.

"More are coming," she said flatly, before firing off several more shots.

One of Jihan's soldiers appeared from behind a boulder, carrying a belt-fed. "Machine gun!" They were aware of our position now, but most of the fire they directed at us fell short. I didn't want them peppering us with a belt-fed. I put the crosshair on the machine gunner's chest and squeezed the trigger.

I missed. *Damn it!* I worked the bolt, got control of my breathing, and fired again. *Splat.* Down he went. *Fuck you, too.*

Ling changed magazines again. "Lorenzo has to move now, before we all get pinned down here."

I agreed, and grabbed the radio. "Lorenzo, listen up. This is getting worse every second. They just keep coming. You need to make your move, now. Get your ass up the hill. They're trying to surround the bomber now, and—

shit!" We ducked down as rounds pockmarked the boulders we were using as cover. Splintered rock chips and snow rained down on us from the barrage of gunfire. I keyed the mike again. "They know where we are. We're taking fire. You need to move, *now!*"

There was a long pause before I got a response. My amplified hearing protection enabled me to make out a few pistol shots from Lorenzo's position, over the slow, steady snapping of gunfire from Jihan's forces. They were being smart, moving from cover to cover, and now applying suppressing fire against us.

"*I'm out,*" Lorenzo said. "*I'm out of ammo. Shit.*"

We had to duck back down as more gunfire peppered our position. "Lorenzo, just give me a second, I'll figure this out."

Another pause.

"*I'm not going to make it.*" His voice was flat.

"What? No, goddamn it, you move your ass and get up this hill!"

"*I can't.*" He sounded so tired. His voice wavered as he spoke. "*I don't know if I can even stand. There's no way in hell I'll make it up that hill.*"

Ling and I exchanged a glance.

"What . . . what do you want me to do?"

"*You guys have to go,*" Lorenzo replied bluntly. "*You have to leave me here. Get out of here before they get you too.*"

"I'm not going to leave you there, goddamn it!"

"*Yes, you are. You don't have a choice. There's too many. They're out for blood. If you don't get out of here, you'll die too.*"

Lorenzo was right. Ling placed a hand on my shoulder and nodded her head slightly.

Damn it, damn it, damn it. My mind raced, looking for a way out.

But there was no way. I had one round left for the .338, and Ling was running low too. There were still dozens of enemy troops down there, and they were all heavily armed. It was quiet. They were regrouping. I crept around the edge of the boulder. It only took me a second to find Lorenzo in the scope.

It was like he was looking right at me.

I took a deep breath and keyed the microphone.

"Lorenzo, if they take you alive . . . it won't be good."

Another long pause. *"I know."*

"Do you want me to . . . I mean, I've got a clean shot. I have one round left . . . "

Ling's eyes went wide, but I ignored her and awaited Lorenzo's response. Killing him was probably a hell of a lot more merciful than letting Sala Jihan's fanatics get a hold of him.

Lorenzo let out a raspy, wheezing laugh into the radio. *"That would be funny, wouldn't it? After all this, you're the one who kills me. That'd be precious."* He laughed again, like that was the funniest thing he'd ever heard.

I could see his face behind the crosshairs. I put my finger on the trigger. "Say the word."

He seemed to think about it. The interior of the bomber was splattered with his blood. *"You know what? No. Just get out of here. I'll take my chances."*

"You sure?"

"*I am. Is Jill safe?*"

"She is. She's with the others. Reaper too."

"*Good. Do me a favor. Get her out of here. Get her far away from this place. Please.*"

"I . . . I will, Lorenzo. I swear."

"*Don't tell her what happened to me. If she thinks there's any chance I'm alive she'll try to come back for me. They'll get her too. Make something up, but don't let her come after me.*"

Ling took the radio from me. "Lorenzo, I'll tell Jill that you died a hero, so that others could live."

"*That's a little dramatic, don't you think?*"

Ling smiled sadly. "It's mostly true."

"*Heh . . . How about that?*" His voice had grown very quiet. "*I'm the hero. Never figured that's how I'd die.*"

Ling looked like she was going to cry.

"*One more thing, Valentine,*" Lorenzo managed. "*Find my brother.*"

"I'll try."

"*Okay,*" he hesitated. "*Now get the hell out of here. I'm turning off my radio.*"

"I'll see you around someday, Lorenzo."

"*So long, Valentine.*"

We left the heavy Sako rifle as we scrambled back up to road level. A few stray shots hit the rocks around us, but none of them were close. As we headed for the road, I could see the wreck through the trees. It was hard to tell, but it looked like Sala Jihan's soldiers were about to drag Lorenzo away.

"Michael, we have to go!" Ling insisted. I turned and left without looking back.

LORENZO

I dropped the radio on the bloody floor. It lay there in a pile of spent shell casings.

The soldiers were approaching cautiously. They could see that I was done.

Poor Jill . . . but she deserved a better man than me anyway.

My eyelids were too heavy. The world was getting very dark.

I could hear angry shouting, but I couldn't understand what they were saying. My chest was rising and falling. Rising and falling.

There was movement inside the plane. They were approaching cautiously. Someone squatted next to me. He was wearing a heavy coat and a fur-lined hood. Beneath the hood was skin as white as a corpse and two pitch black eyes.

"Greetings, son of murder. I warned you not to return." The devil turned back to his minions. "Take him."

A rifle butt smashed me in the face. Boots stomped on my ribs. Rough hands grabbed me and pulled me through the rust. I was lifted up and carried into the cold.

Gideon Lorenzo was standing in front of me, big, strong, and kind. Nothing like the broken, battered, dying shell I'd last seen on his death bed.

I felt him put his arm over my shoulder.

"You were good, Hector. That's all that anyone could ever ask. We better get going."

Then the Sun was up.

It was morning.

VALENTINE
The Rendezvous Point

Ariel had told me that Lorenzo had been trying so hard to live a peaceful life, and Ling and I dragged him into this mess and got him killed. I didn't say it out loud, but we were both thinking it. I could see the pain on Ling's face.

We caught up to the other survivors at a predetermined rally point.

"I can't tell her, Michael." Ling rubbed her face with both hands. "I just can't."

Jill came running up as we got out of the truck. There was a flicker of hope as the doors opened. It was painful to watch it die. "Where . . . where's Lorenzo?" she asked. There was fear in her voice. Reaper stood a few feet behind her, not saying anything. "Val, where is Lorenzo? You said you were going to go get him!"

I steeled myself. "Jill . . . "

"No. No. Please." Tears welled up in her eyes. What little color there was on Reaper's pale face drained out.

I gently placed my hands on Jill's shoulders. "He's gone, honey. There wasn't anything we could do."

"Damn it, Val," Jill sobbed. She buried her face in my shoulder and cried, while hitting me with her fist. "Damn it. You said you'd bring him back. You *said*."

Reaper just sat down in the snow, not saying anything.

Ling spoke up, softly. "Lorenzo's action is what allowed everyone else to get away. These people owe him their lives, and we all owe him a debt of gratitude. His sacrifice was noble. I'm sorry for your loss."

Jill continued sobbing. I held her in my arms and wished like hell there was something I could say that would help.

"We need to get going," someone said. "The longer we stay here, the more likely it is none of us get out of here alive."

He was right. We had to go. But Jill needed a moment, and I was going to give her that moment.

"I'm sorry," I told her. The words sounded hollow and pathetic. "I'm sorry this happened. I wish there was something I could have done. But listen to me. We need to go."

Jill didn't move.

"Jill, Lorenzo made me promise that I'd get you out of here, you and Reaper both. So we need to get going right now. Don't make a liar out of me."

"He told you that? He thought about me?"

"Of course he did, honey. He loved you."

"Did he say that?"

"Yes he did," I lied. "Now come on, please, let's get out of here."

Jill collected herself, and shakily nodded her head. A cold wind blew through the mountains, and she shivered.

Epilogue: Finest Hour

🦅

VALENTINE
Exodus Safe House
Olgii, Western Mongolia
March 26th

The town of Olgii was less than a hundred miles, in a straight line, from The Crossroads. Even still, it had taken us hours and hours to get there on narrow passes and around mountains.

There wasn't much to the Exodus safe house. It was one of the bigger buildings in the remote Mongolian village; an old warehouse with snow drifted up against one side of it. Exodus personnel were, as Ling suggested, waiting for us. We pulled the vehicles around back. Medics rushed out with stretchers to carry the wounded. A few guards nervously kept their eyes open, afraid that Jihan's forces would appear out of the blowing snow. I couldn't shake the unnerving feeling that we weren't nearly far enough away from The Crossroads.

584 *Larry Correia & Mike Kupari*

The inside was dimly lit, but plenty warm. One side of the main floor was set up as a small medical facility. The other had cots and blankets. They told us they were preparing a hot meal, which sounded good. I was starving. I felt disgusting, too, covered in sweat and blood, and wanted to take a hot shower if one was available. Both of those things could wait, though. I was completely exhausted. I had been running on adrenaline for far too many hours now, and I just could not go on. I found a cot in a dark corner of the warehouse, stripped off my boots and socks, and flopped down on it. I was asleep within minutes.

I awoke some time later. The howling wind outside rattled the old building. No light came in from small, high windows. It was dark out now. I'd slept through the entire day. Someone had been thoughtful enough to leave a big bottle of water next to my cot. A small crowd of Exodus personnel had gathered at the other end of the warehouse, like they were having some kind of meeting. I grabbed it and took a sip as I left my bunk to figure out what was going on.

A rough semicircle had formed around Ling, who had a printout in her hands. The Exodus members looked to her expectantly, even though she wasn't technically their leader. I didn't know where Fajkus was, or what had happened to Katsumoto. No one paid me any mind as I moved through the group, bare feet on the cold concrete floor, to hear what Ling had to say.

". . . have fully briefed the Council on everything that happened. In case anyone here hasn't heard the full story of what happened . . . we failed." The demeanor of the crowd darkened slightly, but Ling continued. "Sala Jihan lives. We few here are all that remain. Of those not with us, we don't know how many are missing and how many have died. It's . . . probably better to assume the worst."

Just like with Lorenzo, I thought bitterly.

"We have, however, arranged transport out of here. It will take them about twenty-four hours to get here, but they're sending an aircraft to Olgii to pick us up. This safe house will be abandoned, and no one else will be left behind here. We've left enough behind as it is."

The small crowd solemnly nodded in agreement.

Ling paused for a moment, trying to decide what to say. "I want . . . I want you all to hold your heads high. You all fought well. Be proud of that. For every one of us that fell, it cost the enemy twenty of his own. But I will be blunt, for you all deserve nothing but the truth, ugly as it may be. This is the worst defeat Exodus has experienced in any of our lifetimes. But such is war. In war, sometimes you win, and sometimes you lose. We have been bloodied, and we have been set back, but we are *not* broken!"

There were a couple voices of agreement in the crowd. Others nodded.

"Even in our darkest hour, do not give up hope. Do not give in to despair! Mourn the dead, but honor their sacrifice by finding the strength to carry on. For six hundred years, Exodus has stood alone against the darkness. For six hundred years, we have known victory and defeat, success and failure. Our order, our brotherhood, our fight continues, because our cause is just. We will recover from this setback. We will recover and carry on, learning from our mistakes and coming away better prepared than ever."

Ling had the crowd transfixed. Even as an outsider, I found her appeal to be moving. She was a much better leader than she gave herself credit for.

"The road ahead will be hard," Ling said, lowering her gaze slightly. Her dark eyes shimmered, as if she was fighting back tears. "We have all lost . . . so very much. But even on such a terrible day, let us not forget where we came from. Let us not forget why we do this, what we fight for. If we give up, if we say it's too hard, if we don't continue on, who will? Who will stand for the weak against the strong? Who will fight for the oppressed and the enslaved?"

There was no answer from the crowd.

Passion filled Ling's voice, giving it clarity and purpose. "Our work is just, and noble. Our work is necessary. We cannot turn our backs on it, even now. For if we give up, if we do not continue on . . . no one will. The cycles of suffering that we struggle to break will continue, and the world will grow that much darker."

Ling paused, taking a deep breath. Her voice was lower when she spoke. "You all fought magnificently. You are the finest men and women I have ever had the honor to serve with." A tear trickled down her cheek. "I am proud of you. I am proud to count myself as one of you. So please, hold your heads high." She fell silent, and quickly made her way out of the room.

A man stepped in where Ling had been standing, taking over from her. "Yes, thank you, Ling. Let us all take a moment to say a prayer for the fallen."

As the group bowed its head in prayer, I headed back to my cot to put my boots back on and find Ling. I wanted to make sure she was okay.

✢ ✢ ✢

I found Ling outside, alone.

Mercifully, the howling wind had died down. The sky was overcast low, and the lights of the town gave the clouds an amber glow. Ling's breath steamed in the cold air as she stood, arms folded across her chest, staring into the distance. As I approached, I could tell she was crying.

I surprised her when I gently placed my hand on her shoulder. She turned to face me, with tears in her eyes. Ling then surprised me by wrapping her arms around me. She pulled me close to her, buried her face in my shoulder, and quietly wept.

Reciprocating her embrace, I held her tightly, and rubbed my hand up and down on her back. She squeezed me even tighter as she cried, struggling to regain her composure. I didn't ruin the moment by opening my stupid mouth.

After a little while, Ling looked up into my eyes, but didn't let go of me.

"Hey, you," I managed.

She sniffled. "I'm so glad you're okay. I just . . . I just couldn't bear it if I lost someone else I care about. I couldn't bear it. I'm barely holding on, Michael."

Looking down into her eyes, I agreed with her. "I know. It's been—"

My eyes went wide as Ling leaned up and kissed me, deeply, passionately. Her soft skin was hot against mine in the cold air. She pulled me tightly against her.

I didn't know what I was doing. I didn't think I was ready for this. I didn't know what 'this' even was. We were in shock, exhausted, both badly needed a shower, and had barely escaped with our lives. It was the worst time for something like this.

But God help me, it felt right. I held her tightly, reciprocating her embrace and her kiss. After a moment, we pulled apart. Ling's eyes were locked onto mine, studying my face for approval. I smiled at her, and she kissed me again. I held her close to me, closed my eyes, and for a wonderful moment, forgot all the horrors I'd seen.

The next morning found the Exodus safe house bustling with activity. It was only a matter of hours before the plane that was taking us away was to arrive, and Exodus was busy preparing to leave. Everything they couldn't take, they intended to destroy, leaving behind as little evidence as possible.

I barely saw Ling that morning. At first I was worried, wondering if she was avoiding me. Had we jumped the gun? Was she regretting kissing me? Did I take advantage of her? Did it get weird?

I saw her for the first time that morning when she came out of one of the back offices with Fajkus. At first she didn't acknowledge me, and I was concerned. But when her compatriot had his back turned, she looked over at me, dropped her professional demeanor for just a moment, and smiled at me. Then she winked at me, and a stupid grin split my face. As soon as Fajkus turned to face her again, the mask was back on, and she was as solemn as ever. I couldn't help but laugh at the rapid transition.

"How are you holding up, man?" It was Skunky. I was

outside the safe house, getting some fresh air for just a moment. The air was cold and still. It wasn't snowing, but was still overcast, and thankfully the wind had quit. It was so cold out it froze your boogers right in your nose, though.

I turned my attention to my friend. "All things considered?" I asked, but just left it at that.

Skunky nodded knowingly. "What about your friends?"

"I don't know. They're both still in shock. Jill is . . . was . . . Lorenzo's girlfriend. Reaper's been with him for years. I guess another member of their team died in Zubara. You know how it is, man."

"Will they be okay? Do they have a place to go?"

"Are you kidding? Lorenzo practically owned an island in the Caribbean. He was loaded. They'll be fine, but money doesn't replace the man."

Skunky looked around the snow-covered valley that Olgii sat in. "What about you? Where are you going after this?"

I hadn't actually thought much about it. Now that it had been brought up, I didn't have a good answer. I just shook my head. "I don't know, man. I guess it depends on where Exodus drops me off. I don't know where I could go. It's not safe for me to go home. They're looking for me. The government, I mean. For all I know they have every federal agency looking for me. Anyway the only place I could go in the States is Hawk's, and all I'd do is put him in danger. He already stuck his neck out too far getting involved in this."

"Have you . . . I mean, I don't want to sound like I'm pressuring you, or giving you the sales pitch, but have you thought about becoming a member of Exodus? You already know more about the organization than most of us do. You've been on our biggest op in living memory. There are plenty of us that would sponsor you in. You'd just have to, you know, take the oath and commit. We'd take care of you, though." Skunky lowered his eyes just a bit. "And we could really use new people right about now."

My friend had a look in his eyes that I hadn't seen since the debacle in Mexico, our last operation as employees of Vanguard. There was uncertainty in his eyes, even fear. I could see it on the faces of all the Exodus operatives. It was plain in how they carried themselves now, and in how they spoke. There was precious little laughter or joking. Their ridiculously high morale had been shattered. Those missing or dead would likely never be found, and never be giving a proper burial. It was heartbreaking to watch such a proud organization, one that I owed my life to, smashed like that.

As much as I liked them, though, and as much as I didn't want to disappoint Ling, I didn't feel that joining Exodus was the way I should go. They asked for my help, and I gave it. "I don't know. Let's wait until we get out of this godforsaken place before we start talking about my future. I need a vacation. I can't go back to Hawk's, but there's got to be somewhere I can go."

Skunky looked thoughtful for a moment. "Speaking of Hawk, have you contacted him at all? You just dropped off the map last year. He probably thinks you're dead."

I suddenly felt very guilty. "I wanted to call him when I was on Lorenzo's island," I said, "to tell him I was okay. But it would've put him in danger. They might be watching him, monitoring his phone. Hell, they might've picked him up. They fucked with my mind when they had me, man, drilled into my head. I don't know what all I told them. For all I know I betrayed Hawk and he's dead already." A pit formed in my stomach as I thought about it. *Oh God, what did I do?*

Skunky read the look on my face. "Listen, we have encrypted satellite phones. You can call him. The odds of them tracing the call are pretty slim, and even if they do, we'll be out of here in a few hours, and I'm pretty sure we ain't coming back."

"It's still risky. I'm sure your boss won't approve."

"I don't plan on asking my boss, bro." He retrieved from his pocket a Benchmade *Infidel* automatic knife. Each member of a Switchblade unit was issued one. "I was Switchblade 4 first. Knife check!"

Allowing myself to smile, I retrieved my own Benchmade and snapped the blade out. "Check!" We both chuckled.

"No time like the present," Skunky said. "Let me go get the phone." It turned out that Skunky's satellite phone was much nicer than any I'd ever used. I had to have him show me how to use it. "Do you remember Hawk's number?" he asked.

I thought about it for a second. "I think so. Hang on." I dialed the long sequence of numbers necessary to connect with a US phone number, pressed send, and waited. It rang several times, then stopped, beeping at me.

I showed Skunky the screen. "What's it doing?"

He squinted and looked at it. "They're requesting a video chat."

"This thing can do video chat? I bet that's expensive."

"Yeah. There'll be lag, too. Just 'press accept' and hold it a couple feet from your face."

I told Skunky to keep quiet while I was talking, and rotated the phone so that the only thing visible behind me was the wall of the warehouse. I suddenly had a bad feeling, and wanted to give as few visual clues to my location as possible. I took a deep breath, and pressed accept.

After a short pause, Hawk's face appeared on the screen. He looked like hell.

Oh no. "Hawk? Are you—?"

"Val?" he asked, sounding hoarse and raspy. "Goddamn it boy, you're dumb as a stump! Why the hell did you—" Hawk grunted in pain as someone punched him in the head. My heart dropped into my stomach. The phone on the other end was pulled back so I could see him, bound and handcuffed. A man in a suit pushed him onto the floor and kicked him in the stomach.

Somebody has Hawk! I mouthed to Skunky. His eyes went wide.

A new face appeared on the screen. I'll never forget it for as long as I live. He was an old man, with gray hair and hard lines in his face. His eyes were pale and piercing.

"Mr. Valentine," the man said. "We've been waiting for you to call."

"Who . . . ?"

He interrupted me. "Now you listen to me, boy. You have no idea the world of shit you're in. My name is Underhill. You know who I work for. I was retired up until about two weeks ago. They called me out of retirement and gave me every resource at their disposal for the sole purpose of finding you."

My eyes narrowed. "What do you want?"

"If you want Mr. Hawkins to live, you'll do exactly as I say. You will tell me where you are, and you will wait for me there, for however long it takes me to arrive. Then you'll come in with me, and we'll sort this whole thing out. If you refuse, I will kill this man, and I'll still find you. That part is inevitable, nonnegotiable. One way or another, I'm bringing you in. You only get to decide how much you, and Mr. Hawkins here, suffer before it's done."

Before I could answer, Hawk shouted to me. "Val! Don't listen to him, boy! I'm already dead! You run! You—" I couldn't make anything out for the next few seconds. The phone was tossed around so fast, with the lag, I couldn't tell what was going on. There was commotion, yelling, a fight. Somebody shouted at Hawk again.

"Fuck you!" was the old gunslinger's reply. Then a pair of gunshots, then silence.

I felt the color drain out of my face. I looked up at Skunky. His eyes were wide, and he covered his mouth with his hands, but he said nothing. My knees went weak. I wanted to throw up. I struggled to maintain my composure as my heart raced and my head spun.

After a moment, Underhill's face returned to the screen. He looked as ice cold as ever. "Mr. Hawkins is dead," he said flatly. "His choice, not mine. Now you have a choice, son. No one else has to die. Tell me where you are, and this all ends. If you don't tell me where you are, I will kill however many people it takes to get to you. Either way, I'll find you. So what's it going to be?"

My heart rate slowed. My senses were heightened. Everything slowed down just a bit as *The Calm* washed over me. My blood ran as cold as the arctic wind blowing against my face.

"I'll tell you how it's going to be, old man," I said slowly. "You people have taken everything from me. I have nothing left to lose. You won't have to find me, because I'm going to find *you*. I'm going to find you, Mr. Underhill, and I'm going to kill you. I'm going to kill *all* of you. That is a promise."

There was a pause from the lag of the satellite connection, before an unpleasant, predatory smile split Underhill's face. "We'll see about that."

I pressed the end button, hanging up before anything else could be said. Skunky stared at me wide-eyed as I slowly lowered the phone. My hands started to shake. My teeth ground together. An icy rage bubbled up from deep inside me.

This isn't over.

MORE...
ERIC FLINT

Time Spike (with Marilyn Kosmatka)   978-1-4391-3328-6 $7.99

Boundary (with Ryk E. Spoor)   978-1-4165-5525-4 ◆ $7.99

Threshold (with Ryk E. Spoor)   HC: 978-1-4391-3360-6 ◆ $25.00
PB: 978-1-4516-3777-9 ◆ $7.99

The Crucible of Empire   978-1-4516-3804-2 ◆ $7.99
(with K.D. Wentworth)

The Warmasters   0-7434-7185-7 ◆ $7.99
(with David Weber & David Drake)

Crown of Slaves   978-0-7434-9899-9 ◆ $7.99
(with David Weber)

Torch of Freedom   HC: 978-1-4391-3305-7 ◆ $26.00
(with David Weber)   PB: 978-1-4391-3408-5 ◆ $8.99

THE JOE'S WORLD SERIES

The Philosophical Strangler   978-0-7434-3541-3 ◆ $7.99

Forward the Mage   978-0-7434-7146-6 ◆ $7.99
(with Richard Roach)

THE HEIRS OF ALEXANDRIA SERIES

The Shadow of the Lion   978-0-7434-7147-3 ◆ $7.99
(with Mercedes Lackey & Dave Freer)

This Rough Magic   978-0-7434-9909-5 ◆ $7.99
(with Mercedes Lackey & Dave Freer)

Much Fall of Blood   HC: 978-1-4391-3351-4 ◆ $27.00
(with Mercedes Lackey & Dave Freer)   PB: 978-1-4391-3416-0 ◆ $7.99

Burdens of the Dead   HC: 978-1-4516-3874-5 ◆ $25.00
(with Mercedes Lackey & Dave Freer)